© Niall Kerrigan

About the Author

London-reared of Irish parents, Kate Kerrigan worked in London before moving to Ireland in 1990. She is the author of two books published in the UK, *Recipes for a Perfect Marriag*e and *The Miracle of Grace*. She is now a full-time writer and lives in County Mayo, Ireland, with her husband and sons.

www.katekerrigan.ie

Ellis Island

Ellis Island

Kate Kerrigan

HARPER

NEW YORK · LONDON · TORONTO · SYDNEY

HARPER

This book was originally published in 2009 by Pan Macmillan UK.

FIRST HARPER PAPERBACK PUBLISHED 2011.

Library of Congress Cataloging-in-Publication Data is available upon request.

ISBN 978-0-06207153-8

11 12 13 14 15   ID/RRD   10 9 8 7 6 5 4 3 2 1

For Niall

Ellis Island

Prologue

It was snowing on the Jersey Shore. My mistress had wrapped herself in fur. A gray mink coat trailed behind her on the ground like a wedding train, her snug cloche hat forcing her glossy bobbed hair into neat curls under her cheekbones. Standing in the grand entrance of her country home, Isobel Adams snapped open her purse and quickly applied a slice of scarlet lipstick, puckering her perfect lips together a few times to secure the stain. "How do I look, Ellie?" She seemed nervous.

"Very well, Ma'am."

Isobel was beautiful, like a photograph. She shrugged with delight, plunged her hands into a mink muff and called, "Wish me luck . . ." as she ran out the door.

Alone in the house, I walked up the grand sweeping staircase that divided and curved out on either side toward the bedrooms. Bedrooms that would soon be filled with strangers with whom I would be obliged to share the intimacy of my servitude as I prepared hot bed-jars, emptied chamber pots, washed out socks and undergarments. Chores that had once been acts of love for my husband had become a job for which I was being paid.

Once, picking up some socialite guest's clothes from the floor, I had noticed a lost button, and a hemline torn by a sharp heel—snagged while dancing the Charleston, no doubt. When I pointed out the flaw to the lady and offered to repair it, she said, "You're a darling!" and gave me a dollar tip just for offering, and another dollar later when the job was done. I was delighted, but then that night as I slid the bills into an envelope to send home to John, I felt cheapened. I was being paid to perform these small acts of domestic love for strangers while my husband set his own fires and cooked his own dinners. John needed the dollars, but he needed me home more.

I lit a fire in the mistress's bedroom and picked out an outfit for her to change into when she came back from her walk. A black satin robe embroidered with brightly colored peonies, a red silk nightdress, fresh stockings and her favorite pointed slippers, which earlier I had packed in tissue paper. I laid them across the bed, wiping a layer of dust from the black lacquered bed-end with the hem of my apron, then went to the window and stood for a moment to look at the day. The crisp, sunny morning had turned gray and watery. Snow fell in heavy, sloppy clumps from the trees. The white blanket that had descended in the night and made the world glistening and magical was slowly disintegrating. There was a car outside, crystals of snow still sitting on its roof. There was no driver, but as I looked farther down the empty street, I saw my mistress walking with a man. He was much taller than her, and her head leaned into his shoulder, her arms tucked under one of his, clutching him as if she were cold—despite all the fur. Their backs were to me and they were walking toward the promenade. Knowing she would be gone a while, I decided I had time for a cigarette. Turning away from the window, I put my hand into my apron pocket and it fell upon John's last letter. In the mere touching of the envelope a wave of sadness pushed me down onto the bed.

Would I ever again walk with him on a cold day, feel the breeze of his breath on my face or look into his tender eyes?

I always had more life in me than I knew what to do with—but it was John who had taught me how to love.

PART ONE

IRELAND
1908–20

Chapter One

The first time I fell in love with John, I was eight and he was ten.

One day, Maidy Hogan called down to the house with a basket of duck eggs and asked my mother if I could play with her nephew. His parents had both died of TB and he was sad and lonely, she said. But for his aunt coming to ask for me in the way she did, my mother would never have let me out to play with him. My mother didn't approve of boys, or playing, or of very much at all outside of cleaning the house and protecting our privacy. "We like to keep ourselves to ourselves," was what she always said. She didn't like us to mix with the neighbors, and yet she was concerned that our house was always spotless for their benefit. Perhaps the fact that she made an exception for John Hogan made him special to me from the first.

John called for me later that day. He was tall for his age, with bright blue eyes and hair that curled around his ears. He didn't look lonely to me. He seemed confident and looked me square in the eye, smiling. We went off together, walking and not talking at all, until we reached the oak tree behind Mutty Munnelly's field. Before I could get the words out to challenge him, John was a quarter of the way up the oak, sitting astride its thick, outstretched arm. I was impressed, but angry that he had

7

left me standing there. I was about to turn and walk off when he called, "Wait—look." He ducked suddenly as a fat blue tit swooped past his face, then took a white cotton handkerchief out of his trouser pocket and inserted his hand into a small hole in the trunk. He carried the fledgling down to me, descending the tree awkwardly with his one free hand. "It's hungry," he said, carefully parting the white cotton to reveal the frantic baby blue tit. "We could feed it a louse—there should be some under that stone."

I hated insects, but I wanted to feed the blue tit, and I wanted to impress him. So I kicked back the rock, picked up a woodlouse between my thumb and forefinger and carefully placed it into the bird's open, hungry beak. As it swallowed back, I touched the top of its little head with my finger and felt how small and soft and precious it was. I looked at John and my heart flooded through. It was the first time I remember sharing love with somebody.

"I'll put her home," he said, and climbed back up the tree.

My parents were never loving—that is, not toward me.

My mother was from a shopkeeper's family who were largely deceased. Her grandparents had survived the famine years through holding on to what they had while their neighbors starved. They were hated in the locality, and her father had lost the business because of his own father's sins. My mother bore the scars of her family history in her acute privacy and unwillingness to mix with anybody, not even her own child.

My father at least loved the Church. He had failed the priesthood and been sent home from Maynooth College. Nobody ever knew why, but it was certainly not that he had disgraced himself in any particular way. It seemed he was just not considered devout enough. He had made the mistake of thinking that

God had been calling him, when in fact He hadn't. My father was fond of saying that it was his decision. That he had chosen a life in the civil service over life as a priest, yet he went to Mass every day—twice on holy days of obligation—and took as many meals in Father Mac's house discussing parish business as he did in his own. Whenever he was asked, my father would say that it had been a difficult decision to make, but that marriage and children were his vocation. Yet he and my mother slept separately and had only one child. My father's room was as austere as a monk's, with a huge crucifix over the bed. My mother and I shared a bed in another room, and yet I could never say that I felt close to my mother or knew her especially well. We slept with dignified respect for each other's privacy, arranging ourselves back to back, silently, never touching.

Maidy and Paud Hogan were in their late sixties when John came to live with them. They had never had any children of their own and treated this young orphan as if he were their son. Maidy was a generously built and warmhearted woman, well known in our townland as she had delivered half of the children in the area. Even though she wasn't trained, Doctor Bourke recognized her as a midwife and nurse and consulted her on matters of childbirth and nutrition. Paud Hogan was a quiet man, a hardworking small farmer. He was not schooled, but he knew by its Latin name every plant and flower you could point out—facts learned from the *Encyclopaedia of Nature*, which he kept high on the mantel over the fireplace. John's father had been Paud's beloved younger brother Andrew. When Andrew died and his wife, Niamh, was tragically taken six months later, Paud closed up his brother's house and took John in straightaway.

John knew how to do everything. The Hogans were old, and

they wanted to be certain he would be able to fend for himself after they were gone. So they taught their charge how to grow vegetables, cook a decent meal, and one end of a cow from the other. John was an easy child to love. Andrew and Niamh Hogan had showered their only son with affection, before turning him serious and dutiful with their early, tragic deaths. I knew John's story before I met him. Everyone knew everything about everyone in our townland. Aughnamallagh numbered less than one hundred people scattered in houses across miles and miles of identical fields bordered with scrappy hedgerows. The monotony of our flat landscape was broken in places by shallow hills and lakes, which were little more than large puddles.

My parents' house was on the edge of the village, just three miles from the town of Kilmoy. My father was an important man, a civil servant working for the British government. And we should have been living in a grand stone house in the town itself, where he would not have to walk for an hour each way and my mother could get turf delivered directly to the back door, and not have to muddy her boots walking to the stack herself. However, the house they had given us was outside the town, and as my father was apt to say on the rare occasions my mother questioned him, "Who are we to argue with the Great British Government? It is our duty as citizens to be governed by them as we are by God." Even though my parents kept us deliberately apart from our neighbors, news of one another was unavoidable. It carried across the church grounds in hushed tones and sideways glances after Mass, across the still air of the grocery shop, in the sucking of teeth and clicking of tongues when someone's name was mentioned. My mother's ear was sharply attuned to second-hand scandal, for the very reason that she was too distant from our neighbors to receive it firsthand. So I had heard my parents talk about John as a pitiful orphan—although, as I got to know him, John's life seemed anything but pitiful to me.

That first summer, my mother was taken up nursing an elderly aunt in the village and so it suited her for me to spend my days with the Hogans and their nephew. My mother told me I had to be kind to John because the Lord had taken both his parents from him. She saw that she was doing the Hogans a favor by allowing me to keep their orphan nephew company.

John called for me each morning and we went exploring. Through his eyes, the ordinary fields between our houses became a wild, exciting playground. John turned grass into Arabian Desert sand, and ordinary muddy ditches into raging rivers we had to conquer.

"Slip at your peril," he would say, as my small feet walked comfortably across a narrow fallen tree. "These waters are infested with sharks!"

He knew every animal, noticed their presence in shaking leaves. "Rabbit!" he called on our second or third day out together, and I chased after him into the boundary bushes. John foraged around and pulled aside clumps of leaves to reveal the smooth, dark burrow entrance. I sat firmly down on a large stone and insisted that we wait there for a fluffy ball to come out. "It won't come. It's afraid of us," said John, peering down into the tunnel. "There are probably hundreds, *thousands* of them down there—but they won't come out."

I imagined the ground beneath us alive with busy, burrowing rabbits, frantically hopping over one another, panicking about John and me. The idea of the two of us sitting quietly in the still day with all this mad activity going on underground made me laugh. It was as if there were two worlds—their world and ours—and I liked that. "If it came out now, I'd only want to kiss and cuddle it," I said.

John looked embarrassed; he picked up a stick and sliced the air with it. "I'd chop its head off and skin it and cook it into a stew." I started to cry. Once I started, I couldn't stop—not because of the rabbit any more, but because I was embarrassed to be crying in front of John and I was afraid that he wouldn't like me; that I would ruin everything. "I'm joking," he said, "I wouldn't ever do that to a rabbit, Ellie, sure I wouldn't, stop crying now, Ellie, don't cry." I did stop, but I remember thinking how boys were different from us, and that I should be more careful how I carried on if I wanted us to stay friends.

When the sun was directly above us in the sky, we ran over to his house, where Maidy had our dinner waiting for us.

I loved eating in that house. My own mother was frugal with food, not for lack of money, but because she had no fondness for it. My father ate in the presbytery in town in the middle of the day and she felt there was no need to go to trouble for me alone. Her meals were meager, modest portions organized in shallow piles that never touched one another and made the plates look huge. In contrast, Maidy Hogan shoveled piping hot, sloppy stews onto our plates until thick, brown gravy spilled over the edges of them onto the table. There was never any room left for the potatoes, so they went straight onto the scrubbed wooden tabletop where we piled them with butter, often still watery with milk from the churn, then tore them apart and ate them with our hands. Afterward we'd have apple tart, or soda cake with butter and honey.

Maidy was as round as her cooking was good, and Paud was wiry and still strong at sixty. He worked hard to provide food for her, and she made sure that the meal she prepared with it was worth the work. I ate like a savage at that long, wooden table. I ate until I thought I would burst inside out, until I could barely move and would have to sit teasing ants with a stick on the front step, waiting for my stomach to settle. The first time I ate with them, Maidy asked, "Does your mother not feed you at all?" I stopped eating, blushing at my greed, my spoon still poised. She patted my head as apology, encouraged me to continue and never said anything again.

John always cleared the table and cleaned up after dinner; that was his job, wiping the grease and crumbs from the table and sweeping the floor beneath it, then washing the four plates in a bucket of water warmed on the fire and polishing them dry before placing them carefully back in the cupboard. I was never allowed to help. The Hogans made me a part of their family, yet they treated me like a treasured guest always. They loved me like a daughter, but they never overstepped the mark and made me into one. They had a talent for knowing the right way to be with people.

Late in the afternoon, John would bring me back to my own house. Although I was still full of Maidy's food, I ate a silent meal with my parents. In the gray twilight then we would kneel and say the rosary. The coldness of my father's praying voice settled on me as a vague fear. An ache for life burned in my stomach.

Chapter Two

In September, John and I started back at school and I was afraid I was going to lose him.

There were fifty or so children with ages ranging from six to thirteen, and we were crammed into two small rooms with two teachers. We sat in lines of four at long, wooden desks. Our uniforms divided us. Along with about one-third of the girls in our school, I wore a long navy wool shift—ordered up from Galway by Moran's, the outfitters in Kilmoy—and a long white cotton pinafore, laundered and starched twice weekly by my mother. I had boots that I wore every day and, when they wore out or pinched too hard, my parents replaced them. Other girls wore slips of dresses, torn cardigans and no shoes. Their lack of status was further announced by the dirt on their faces and under their nails, and by their matted, untidy hair. Although we mixed in the yard during break, in the classroom the teachers saw to it that the clean girls sat together near the fire, while the dirtier ones sat nearer the door, to minimize the stench of poverty. The boys seemed more similar to one another, as they all wore shorts and even those who could afford shoes chose not to wear them, apart from on the coldest days. As the boys got older, their legs crammed awkwardly flesh to flesh under the shallow desks, naked to the thigh in outgrown shorts, scabby bloodstained knees quivering with the cold, making the metal legs of the desks rattle against the stone floor until the teacher would come over and bring their fist down on a desktop. Some of us lived near the school—John and I included—but many had to walk up to five miles every morning to get there, and five miles home again.

When we got back from our summer holiday that year, many of the boys were missing. Their fathers had noticed strength in their sons during the summer and put them to work farming full time. That was what John would have liked, I feared. He never listened to the teacher Mrs. Grealy, but was always looking out the window—not dreaming, like some of us, but studying the apple tree outside the school gates, as its colors changed with the season.

"There's nothing happening out there, John," I said one day as we left to make our way home. "It's just a tree."

He smiled. "There's more happened in that tree today, Ellie, than will happen in this classroom in a lifetime."

I raised my eyes to heaven, imitating Maidy, and he laughed. I loved making John laugh. When he laughed, I felt like he belonged to me.

As we passed the gate, he reached up casually into the tree and picked off an apple, handing it to me and saying, "See?" As if he had grown it himself for my benefit, just by looking out during lessons.

It was tiny and hard and as bitter as Satan's tears. "Yuk!" I said, spitting and making him laugh again. "You're a stupid eejit," I said, and he chased me home.

When winter came the school became bitterly cold. We all moved into the same classroom for warmth, and each child was asked to bring in a piece of fuel with them to put in the small, open fireplace. However, many of the children were from families too poor to keep their own fires burning, or were too stunted and weak to carry even a sod of turf five miles or more. By lunchtime we could barely see the pages we were writing on beneath the fog of our own breath, or hear the teachers above the clatter of chattering teeth. John complained to Paud Hogan about this one afternoon. "It's school business," Paud said, but John insisted, "There's enough turf in the county, Pa, to warm a small school, surely." We were sitting on the edge of his fireplace, roasting ourselves, and Maidy had to poke us out of the way to get to her cooking. John pushed and pushed until Paud agreed. The two of them loaded the cart with their own bail of turf, then called on every farmer in the area for contributions until they had the cart piled with enough fuel to keep the school cozy all through the winter.

Everyone loved John, and I felt honored that he was my friend. Even though ten-year-old boys didn't like to be seen playing with eight-year-old girls, John was happy to walk me home from school, openly waiting at the gates for me if I dawdled. But at break time, John played with boys his age and I was stuck standing with Kathleen Condon, who had thick glasses and was as disliked by me as much as by the other girls. I didn't know why I got stuck with her. I wasn't ugly or annoying like Kathleen—in fact, I was smaller and prettier than many of the popular girls. I decided that was probably why the others hated me: they were jealous of my looks, and the fact that my family was better off than theirs. It hurt, not being invited to play with the others, but I pretended not to mind. In any case, I didn't like the way they carried on, bragging about their devotion to the Blessed Virgin and gossiping about the neighbors like old women. My mother didn't gossip, so I never had any news. And I had always been taught that it was unseemly to talk about one's private prayers and devotions. I had voiced this opinion once and imagined that was another reason for their rejection of me.

Nobody liked Kathleen because her glasses made her eyeballs swim around her face like big, frightening fish, but she was just the same as them—always trying to get in with the others—talking nonstop about this one and that one, telling me that if the communion wafer touched your teeth, you'd be sucked down into the ground by Satan when you were sleeping. One day, when I refused to act out a tableau where she was the Blessed Virgin and I was a Sinning Advocate prostrate at her feet, she finally told me the real reason nobody liked me. "Your grandpa killed baby children when their mas came looking for food and he wouldn't give them any, and your father loves the bastard British."

I didn't cry. I just told her she looked a fright—which she knew anyway—and pretended she hadn't said anything, but my stomach was turned inside out on itself all afternoon.

I was quiet on the way home and John asked if there was something wrong. "You don't have to tell me if you don't want to," he said.

"Kathleen Condon was awful to me because I wouldn't play her stupid game." I didn't tell him what she had said. I didn't want him despising me as well because of my family. "I hate her and I'm never going to play with her again."

John stopped to break off a long stalk of blackberries, pulling his sleeves over his hands and freeing the bramble from the mangled hysteria of the hedgerow with a ferocious twist. He served me the ripe berries as we walked on, passing them to me in soppy handfuls, his stained palm a platter. "Don't do that, Ellie," he said. "Poor Kathleen has nobody, only you."

My mother's aunt was still ailing in the spring. By now, I had a comfortable routine: John always walked me home after school, but, three days out of the five, I would carry on with him to the

Hogans' and spend the afternoon there. They would feed me, then allow me to follow John around the farm as he did his chores. I was scant help to him. Mesmerized the first, second, third time I saw him milk a cow, after that it was my mission to distract him. I'd call and challenge him from some hiding place, clamber up a tree and squeal for his help; one time, I lay down under his favorite cow and urged him to squirt the milk directly into my open mouth. He failed and I got soaked in milk and muck. It wasn't hard for me to untether John from his duties. It seemed that all that mattered was our happiness. I discovered freedom and joy, and I grabbed it with both my small hands and didn't let it go until I got back to my parents' house.

For all the freedom she gave us, Maidy was a tidy woman and hated to send me home to my mother with muck on my uniform.

"Pssht, child. Your mother will think I have no respect for her if I send you home in that state!"

Tired of nagging and scrubbing stains off my skirt, one day she put me into a pair of John's working trousers—the ones he changed into after school to keep his shorts clean and his legs protected from all the cow muck and dirt on the farm. They looked comical on me, but Maidy insisted on rolling them up to my knees and leaving on only my woollen undershirt, which she then covered with one of her aprons, binding me up in its voluminous, flowery print until I looked like a package.

I ran and ran that afternoon. With my legs protected, I fled down a hill of nettles and climbed up the spindly silver birch tree by the road before John reached me, panting comically as if he couldn't keep up. He was afraid of that tree because the branches were too small to hold him. I was light enough that I knew they would hold my weight. I had always wanted to climb that tree, but John had never let me up it on my own, in case I fell.

"Come down, Ellie—the branch will break and you'll fall."

"You're just jealous because I can see the world from here and you're stuck there on the ground."

"It's dangerous, Ellie—I mean it, come down."

I was a little anxious, because I realized John knew better than me. Yet at the same time I felt in charge of the world, protected by my distance from the ground. I could say and do anything I pleased; nobody could reach me. In any case, his fear made me more defiant. "Won't never come down, John Hogan—won't never, ever . . . You'll have to come up and get me!" I felt dizzy from the running and my high position.

Miss Kennedy, the priest's housekeeper, came down the road on her bicycle. She was quite pretty and younger than my mother, but I didn't like her. She sat near the front in Mass and acted very holy. But once, when I was bored, I studied her face after communion and saw her watch every person coming back up the aisle as if she were measuring them for a coffin. She was creepy and I was a little scared of her. But from my vantage point in the sky, she looked like a small beetle.

"Hey—Miss Kennedy!" I shouted.

She pretended she didn't hear me, so I shouted again.

"Hey—Kennedy!"

John looked up at me, daggers. I knew I was in trouble, but I didn't care. "Good afternoon, Miss Kennedy," he said like an altar boy, touching a nonexistent cap as she passed the tree. Then: "You've done it now—come down from that tree at once, Ellie Flaherty, or I'll whip you!"

I was laughing so hard he had to come up and get me in the end. The tree bent, but it stayed with us and didn't break.

Chapter Three

When John dropped me home that evening, my father opened the door to us and I knew there was something wrong. He gave John a cursory greeting and closed the door in his face.

My father was a vague figure in my life. I knew the map of my mother's dour face, the sour smell of her breath in the mornings, her apologetic way of moving about the house, the cold, dry touch of her skin as I accidentally brushed against her in the night. But I was not so familiar with my father. He slept in our house, but I viewed him as everybody else did—an important man to be feared. As known, and yet as strange, to me as our local priest.

He walked into the dining room and I followed him. The good mahogany table was set for tea, yet there was the smell of polish in the air. The teapot and milk jug looked awkward with each other; this was not our usual time to eat. My father was never here at this time. Everything was wrong. Through the kitchen door I could see my mother keeping herself busy laying out bread and ham, which we would not eat. My mother's face was set, too determined on her duties.

"Were you wearing a pair of . . ." My father's long face looked particularly stern, his jaw set, the words sputtering out of him as if each was a poison pellet and he was unable to spit out the final one. "Were you wearing a pair of . . ."

I didn't finish the sentence for him. I knew enough not to do that. And I was puzzled.

"What were you wearing this afternoon?"

I felt relieved. Perhaps I wasn't in trouble after all. "Maidy put me in a pair of John's trousers so I wouldn't dirty my uniform." He closed his eyes and his features contorted as if he were in pain. It was as much emotion as I had ever seen on my father's face. My stomach tumbled although I wasn't sure why. I said, "*Sir.*"

Father went out into the hallway and opened the tall cupboard where he kept his umbrella, and took out a wooden cane. It had been there all along, waiting for its day. Waiting for me to sin. "Do you understand why I have to punish you?"

"Yes," I lied. I had never been punished before; I had always been a good girl and done as I was told. That counted for nothing now, though. I had given cheek to Miss Kennedy and I had to be punished. Perhaps my real crime had been climbing trees, and laughing and feeling free and full of excitement and laughter. Perhaps it was a sin to feel as happy as I did with John, and if that was the case I didn't care. If I was a sinner, then so was John—and Maidy, and even Paud. If Satan sucked me down into the bowels of hell, then I would have them with me and it wouldn't be so bad.

I took six strokes on each hand. Each one stung more than the last. I flinched, but I didn't cry out. Each time the cane struck, it burned my skin and an ember of defiance glowed inside me. *I will do as I please.* I kept saying it to myself over and over again. *I will do as I please.*

My father then said ten decades of the rosary with me. Not rushing, as he usually did, but lingering on each word, relishing each as a jewel. "*Hail Holy Queen . . . We beseech Thee . . . Oh clement, Oh loving, Oh sweet Virgin Mary . . .*" Infusing the words with adoration, and with another emotion that I recognized in my father only when he was praying—love. And all the time I was thinking how stupid it was that all these words were tumbling out of him and yet he had been unable to say the word "trousers" earlier.

My parents stayed up late that night, talking urgently. I knew they were discussing me. They rarely talked, and it was strangely comforting falling asleep to the sound of their muffled voices coming up through the floorboards.

I lay on my side of the bed and thought of what John would say when I told him I had been caned for wearing his trousers. He would be sure to say something good that would make the bad feelings go away.

The following day my mother was waiting for me outside the school. I had thought that my punishment the night before had been the end of it.

"That's the end of it now." My father had actually said that. "We won't talk of this again."

Yet there she was, all buttoned up like she was going to Mass; gloves, hat, boots and bag, all tightly packaged; her long skirt raised precisely so that it neither touched the ground nor revealed her ankles. John and I were the first out, as usual.

"Good afternoon, Mrs. Flaherty," John said, as we reached the road. She looked through him as if he wasn't there and suddenly I realized why everyone hated my mother. In that moment, I hated her too.

She walked quickly and silently, all the time gripping my still-burning hand in her bony fingers, pulling me. The journey that seemed so short with John took forever. The magical hedgerows, usually teaming with life, were thick and dead. My mother's silence threw a blanket over nature.

When we got home, my father had left lessons for me to do, mathematics and catechism. If I finished my study before tea, he had said I was to help my mother with her chores. My mother never let me help with the chores. She liked doing everything herself. She had paused over the words, "Your father said you are to . . . to help me in the house," letting me know that it was his idea and not hers. I made sure I lingered over my study, so as not to be hanging around her apron.

The dining room where I sat was like a tomb. There was no air. We had heavy mahogany furniture and the walls were padded with shelves, packed with my father's religious tomes. The chubby, cross face of Pope Pius X judged us from the mantelpiece over the tiled fireplace, and when the kitchen door was open and the light came in, you could see the image of Christ's Sacred Heart on the opposite wall reflected in the pope's face— scarlet and bleeding and very, very sad. Maidy had a portrait of the Sacred Heart on her mantelpiece, but there was always a box of tea in front of it, and sometimes a jar with flowers covered the bloody heart, so Christ didn't seem as gory or unhappy as he appeared in our house.

My father came straight home from work that evening and we ate together. Boiled bacon with cabbage and potatoes. We had linen napkins and a starched cloth and silver cutlery. When my father was not with us we ate in the kitchen, but my father expected better.

"He is used to fine things," my mother once explained to me. "He was nearly a priest." She always made a fuss when my father ate with us. Polished the knives, and moved the salt and pepper this way and that. It was as if she was afraid of him. Not in a bad way, only in the way you'd be afraid of a priest—or God.

"This is very nice, dear," he said to my mother. She moved

her lips slightly to indicate a smile. "How did you get on with your lessons, Eileen?" He always called me by my birth name.

"Very good, Sir."

He closed his eyes, smiled and when he opened them again said, "You know you can call me 'Father,' Eileen."

I wanted to tell him that he could call me Ellie—except that I didn't want him to. I did not want to be there with either of them. I wanted to be with John, in his house, eating bacon served up in wet, salty hunks, washed down with fresh milk drunk straight from the jug. Not these dry slices that got caught in my throat, and lukewarm water from glasses with spindly stems.

That night I lay in bed next to my mother and imagined that John was going to come and rescue me. I waited until my mother fell asleep, then I sat up and stared at the window, willing him to come climbing through it to carry me off to live in his house with Maidy and Paud. I was sure they would have me. I didn't know that I could put the word "love" on it because they weren't my real family, but they weren't John's immediate family either and they loved him. My parents didn't love me, I was sure of that, and perhaps if I could just get to the Hogans' myself, Maidy might persuade them to let me stay. I sat and waited until my eyes began to close. I fell to sleep imagining my body was suspended on the branches of my silver birch. Like a princess on a bed of leaves, waiting to be rescued.

Chapter Four

Life went back to how it had been before I met John. Dull, dead days; the boredom barely broken by meals and Masses. My mother collected me from school and I spent my afternoons in the house studying and praying and being "good." On Saturdays, my mother dressed me up in my woollen coat and bonnet and sent me to town to visit the parish priest's house with my father. Miss Kennedy, recovered from the shock of seeing me wearing John's trousers, always made a great show of giving me her special biscuits.

"Look at that now, Eileen—your favorite currant biscuits. Aren't you a lucky girl?" my father would exclaim. He glowed when Miss Kennedy was in the room.

"Thank you," I would answer, nibbling discreetly. *They are not my favorite. They are dry, the currants look like dead flies, and Maidy Hogan makes the best buns and biscuits in the world.* That was what I wanted to say, but I just ate the biscuits and felt sad. Everything made me feel sad; everything I saw reminded me of where I wanted to be. Mysterious wildflowers lost their magic now that Paud could not name them for me. Even biscuits didn't interest me because Maidy hadn't made them. Sometimes, when I thought of John and me climbing trees and chasing sheep and laughing all the time, my heart hurt so badly it felt like I had been punched.

I saw John every day in school. He came and spoke to me in break time, but he was popular and always got called away again by the other boys. In any case we were never alone, because Kathleen was always stuck to me. I'd stand at the wall looking over at him laughing and wrestling with his friends and I'd think: *He's forgotten about me, he's not my friend any more.* I didn't cry when my father caned my hand, but I wanted to cry when I thought John didn't love me.

One day he sent one of the boys over to distract Kathleen. "Show me them glasses, Condon, till I can see through them." Paddy Molloy was no charmer, but it did the trick. Poor Kathleen was grateful for any attention she got.

John took me aside. "My ma wants to know if you can come over this Saturday?" Maidy wasn't his ma, but he called her that anyway.

"I can't, my ma won't let me." I never called my mother "Ma"—only when I was talking to other people.

"Is it because of what you said to Miss Kennedy? I said you shouldn't have climbed that tree, I told you . . ."

I was raging—it was as if he was saying this was all my fault. "It was not! It was because I was wearing *your* trousers!" John blushed and looked away. Immediately I was sorry I had said about the trousers, but I couldn't take it back. Anyway, it was true.

"I'd better get back to Paddy," he said, and he turned and went back to the boys.

My heart was broken. I had ruined everything. John would never speak to me again, I was certain of it. I went to the toilet and sobbed into the sleeve of my sweater until break was over.

*

That night I felt sick and could not eat. I moved food around my plate, but did not put it in my mouth. My mother said nothing about it.

The following day was Saturday. My father was out and my mother was getting us ready to walk into town for groceries when Maidy Hogan called to the door.

My heart leapt.

"I've come to see if Eileen would like to come around to us this afternoon?"

Even the sound of her voice warmed me.

"I'm afraid that won't be possible. We are just leaving to run some errands."

"I'll send Paud down with the cart to save you walking."

I flinched. My mother would never be seen traveling in a horse and cart, or even riding a bicycle. When we had to go any distance, my father ordered a horse and trap and a driver to take us. As I got older, we were one of the few families in the area who could afford to hire a motorcar. Otherwise we walked. Heads high, shoes shining, that was how we went about—my father called it "maintaining dignity and decorum."

"There's no need, we're fine," my mother said, tartly.

I was hiding in the drawing room, peering through the door into the hall. My mother's profile was sharp: chin set, mouth tight. I wished I could shrink down to an inch high, rush out the door between my mother's legs and jump into Maidy's pocket. Then she could take me home to live with her without upsetting my parents, and I could be happy again.

"But thank you for offering," my mother added. Her hand gripped the side of the front door.

Before she could close it, Maidy said, "Is everything all right, Attracta?" My mother flinched at the sound of her Christian name. Maidy went on, "Only we haven't seen Ellie in a while and we . . . well, we just hope there isn't anything wrong?"

"Wrong? What could be wrong?" In my parents' world nothing was ever "wrong." Yet everything felt wrong to me.

"Oh no, I just mean . . . well, John and Ellie are such good friends, and as we haven't seen her for a while I was worried that, well—might we have done something to offend you?"

I looked intently at my mother and thought I saw her face soften slightly. I thought she might explain about the trousers, and then Maidy would laugh and say "sorry" and they would agree "no harm done," and everything would be back to normal. But I also knew in my heart that wouldn't happen. My father had not even been able to say the word "trousers," so my mother would certainly not be able to explain the upset. She paused, then said, "No, Maidy."

"Well then." But Maidy wouldn't let me go that easily. "Perhaps she'll be free to come down another day soon?"

"Perhaps," my mother said. It was a lie, and I knew it. "Good-bye now."

She closed the door before Maidy had even finished saying "Good-bye."

I knew then that I was trapped. Trapped in this house, praying and sitting still and being "good." Trapped in my own body, never allowed to skip or run, or climb trees or laugh out loud, or say and do anything I pleased, ever again.

They were going to keep me inside forever.

A week passed. John smiled at me across the playground and came over a few times and tried to talk to me, but he kept getting called away. I didn't mind that, because the fullness of our friendship wasn't for other people to see. I was just glad that he didn't hate me, especially after the way my parents had behaved.

The following Saturday, early—just after breakfast and our

single morning decade of the rosary—there was a knock on the door. My father had shaved and was getting dressed, so my mother took off her apron, settled her hair in the hallstand mirror and opened it nervously. Who could be calling at this time? I quickly took up my position at the drawing-room door.

"Good morning, Mrs. Flaherty." It was John. "These are for you."

He was holding an enormous bouquet of flowers, mostly roses and lilac. The Hogans had wild roses scrabbling abundantly up the side of their house, almost covering their doorway—and a huge lilac tree that smelt so sweet on a warm day, you could get giddy just standing next to it. He thrust the bouquet into my mother's hand before she could object. I could smell summer off them.

"And I've these for you as well," he said, holding out a wooden box of duck eggs. I was sure I saw a smile strain on my mother's lips. He had charmed her. It was working!

"Thank you, John. Maidy must have sent you down . . ."

"Oh no, Mrs. Flaherty. I came down myself to see if Ellie would like to—"

"We have no need of flowers, thank you, John, nor eggs." My father had leaned over my mother and was going to close the door.

"But they are from the best of our laying ducks, Sir . . ."

"No matter," said my father, removing the box of eggs from the crook of my mother's arm and handing them back to John. My mother clung to her flowers. "And I suggest you consult your guardians before purloining their goods to give away to the neighbors. Good day." He shut the door in John's face. John immediately banged on it again, and my father raised his eyes to heaven. "A tearaway—and small wonder, with no parents to guide him."

"The eggs were mine to give away, Sir," shouted John through the door. His strong voice sounded distant, muffled by the thickness of the wood.

I rushed out of the drawing room and faced my father. "The ducks are his—Paud gave them to him, and John reared them himself. The eggs are his to give away!" My father glared at me, but I didn't care—I stood firm. "You can cane me if you like, Sir, but those eggs are John's to give away."

His eyebrows rose and his mouth tightened. I suppose he was thinking that perhaps he would cane me, but then he seemed to think better of it and, looking out of the window, said only, "Whatever the case, he's gone now." He took the flowers from my mother. "I'll give these to Miss Kennedy for the church. They'll come to some use there." Then he opened the door and left for the day, leaving us standing—my mother's arms still crooked where the beautiful flowers should have been, and me friendless.

Chapter Five

My plan was simple. I would not eat until my parents let me see John again, or until I died. Whichever came first.

After John came round to the house that day, I realized that he had done his best, and his best had not been good enough for my parents. I had dreamed that he might climb up to my bedroom window and carry me off in the horse and cart to the Hogans' to live happily ever after. But even if he did, I knew now that my parents would come and get me, and that was no good either. I needed my parents' permission to see him so that everything could be back the way it had been before.

My mother didn't notice at all. That was my fault. I always ate breakfast alone, and she picked up the bowl of porridge and scooped the leftover mush away into the bin without even looking. At dinner I was frightened of offending her, so I swirled the food around and made it look as if I had eaten some of it. My mother was as thin as a rake and not interested in eating herself, so she didn't pay attention to any food I left behind. By the end of the second day, I was feeling very weak. Not wanting to cheat, I had even given my school bun and milk to Kathleen. On the third day I was late for school because I had to sit down on the road to rest. I realized this was going to be much, much harder than I had thought, and I hadn't even got my message across.

On the fourth day I felt floaty and light-headed. After my mother threw away my breakfast again, I murmured five decades of the rosary and prayed that my father would have his tea with us that evening. If we could eat formally at the dining-room table, I could sit throughout with my hands on my lap and he would notice my protest. But he didn't. My fifth day of not eating was a Saturday, and I was too weak to get out of bed. My mother called me from the bottom of the stairs for my breakfast, but I could not move. She came up to see what was the matter. She stood at end of the bed. "Are you sick?" she said.

I whispered, "I have a tummy pain."

"I'll bring your breakfast up."

At last, I thought, she'll notice.

Ten minutes later, she came back up. She helped me sit up in bed and placed a tray across my lap. The tray had a cloth on it that was embroidered with flowers and swallows. I wondered if she had embroidered it herself or if someone had given it to her, but I didn't ask. On the tray was a bowl of porridge and a cup of tea in a china cup and saucer.

"I'm not hungry."

My father came into the room. He was dressed and ready to go out for the day. He was in a hurry to get away, and seemed even more distracted and cross than usual. "What's the matter with her?"

"She doesn't feel well."

"Is she not eating her breakfast?"

"It's probably best she doesn't eat if she feels sick."

He picked the spoon up and let some porridge slop back into the bowl. "Perhaps you should give the child something she might want to eat."

My mother's lips clamped into a tight line. She picked up the tray and went downstairs.

He followed her, saying, "If she's not better later, I'll call Doctor Bourke out to her. I'll be back by six."

I lay down and drifted quickly off to sleep.

I woke up to the sound of Doctor Bourke's gentle voice. He was leaning over me, saying, "Wake up, Ellie, now, there's a good girl." It was dark outside and the faces of my parents, who stood behind him, glowed orange in the lamplight. They looked warm and worried. For a moment I felt happy, as the doctor checked my pulse and felt my forehead. "Her temperature is normal, but her blood pressure is very low. She's pale—you say she wouldn't eat earlier and she's been asleep like this all day? Has she been vomiting?"

"She's been perfect all week," my mother said.

"Eating all right?"

"Well, yes."

I knew I had to say something, otherwise this could go on forever and I might die. "I haven't eaten for five days." It burst out in a sudden shout, which surprised me—and them. My mother took a sharp breath and put her hands up to her mouth. Her eyes went wide and frantic as if I had let out a terrible secret. Perhaps she had known all along and wanted me to die? My father looked at my mother. She looked back at my father, shaking her head.

Only Doctor Bourke looked at me. "Have you been feeling this sick for five whole days, Ellie?"

Would my father and mother be mortified if I told the doctor how I deliberately hadn't eaten? Perhaps this had been a terrible idea after all. But then I had a good thought—my father wouldn't punish me in front of Doctor Bourke. In any case, he *couldn't* punish me now that I really was genuinely sick. Doctor Bourke's face was soft and kind, and I decided to spill out everything in front of him. It felt safe. "I didn't eat because I'm not allowed

33

over to play with John Hogan any more, because Maidy put me in his trousers so my uniform wouldn't get dirty, then I climbed a tree and gave cheek to Miss Kennedy." His eyes widened. I didn't look at my parents. I was too afraid, so I just kept my eyes on Doctor Bourke.

He didn't turn away from me. He said, "I see," with a straight, serious face. Then: "Well now, Ellie, that sounds like a dreadful business altogether. Now tell me—are you sorry for what you did?"

I could see where he was going. "Yes, Doctor, I am very sorry."

"And did you say sorry to your parents for the trouble you caused them?"

I realized I hadn't. But then, it hadn't been presented to me as an option before then. "No, Doctor Bourke, I didn't."

"Well, perhaps if you apologize to your parents, then they will let you over to the Hogans' house again and we can forget all of this starving yourself nonsense."

I looked up at my parents. They were like statues. I did not know whether they were frozen with shock because I had starved myself for five straight days without them noticing, or because of the way Doctor Bourke had spoken to me. I guessed it was a mixture of both. My father wore an expression I had never seen before. He looked a little afraid.

"I'm sorry," I said.

Doctor Bourke stood up and went over to my parents. "There now, no need to worry any more," he said touching my father on the shoulder. "I expect this young lady will be ready for her dinner shortly, and maybe we'll persuade John to bring down one of Maidy's famous apple tarts before too long. Doctor's orders!"

My father let out a cough, but there was nothing he could

say. There were only two people more important than my father that I knew of—Father Mac and Doctor Bourke. He had to do as he was told. Doctor's orders! I was a genius for waiting until now to say anything; my plan had worked.

Before they left the room, my mother came over and touched me on the head. Her hand faltered before she laid it gently on my hair. It felt so wonderful that I closed my eyes and smiled. Then it was gone, and she followed my father and the doctor downstairs.

Chapter Six

John and I were barely parted after that until it was time for us to leave national school. Most children finished their education at twelve because secondary education was too expensive for the majority, but my parents had arranged for me to go on and board at a convent school. John had missed a year of schooling when his parents were sick, so he had been held back a year. Although he had already been offered an apprenticeship with a cabinetmaker in Dublin, Paud—who had left school at nine himself—believed that fourteen was time enough to start work. So he and Maidy arranged for John to stay in school for an additional year.

I was there when they broke the news to him.

"Now you can stay with all your friends for another year, John. Isn't that grand?"

I got a thrill, because it meant we would be leaving national school at the same time, and I wouldn't be left behind there on my own. But it disappeared when I looked at John's shocked face. He was devastated. I knew he was longing to get out into the real world. When Paud had originally told him about the apprenticeship, John had come running over to me at break time and nearly exploded with excitement. "I'll be in Dublin, Ellie, working like a man. The cabinetmaker is an important person, making chairs and drawers for all the big nobs in the city. I've started on a box already, and a leather belt for my tools!"

John had talked of nothing else for months, only his toolbox and belt, and had made me study each of them a dozen times. That was my penance. His was this—being told he had another year of school to get through. I had never seen John lose his temper, but surely by the look of him he would lose it now.

Maidy and Paud hadn't a clue what they had done. They thought they were doing the right thing, and that John would be happy. When my parents did the "right" thing, they didn't care whether I was happy or not. Sometimes I was happy with what they decided—like deciding to send me to board in the convent school when I was twelve. But sometimes I wasn't happy—like the time they wouldn't let me see John. With the Hogans it was different. Everything they decided was to make John happy. But this time they had got it very, very wrong.

"Thanks, Ma; thanks, Pa. That's great." He smiled—a forced, halfhearted smile, but at least a smile—then shot out of the house calling over his shoulder, "Come on, Ellie, we'll go and see if that poor bird has flown us." He ran and ran to the bottom of the field, me chasing after him, and I thought that maybe everything was all right after all. But when we got to the stick shelter we had built to hide an unfortunate fluttering blackbird we had found the day before, he threw himself down on the grass and put his head in his hands. "No! No! I can't stick another year of school, Ellie! How—*how*—could they have done this to me?"

I was shocked, and a little hurt. It seemed he was desperate to leave me after all. "Then why didn't you say anything?"

"There would be no point."

"But Maidy and Paud would do anything for you. You'd easily be able to get them to change their minds." I peeped into the shelter, but the bird had gone—recovered and flown, I innocently hoped.

"That's not what they want, Ellie—you wouldn't understand."

I hated it when he said that. "I *am* eleven years old."

John smiled at me, but it was a poor excuse for a smile. He was sad in a way that frightened me. John was my protector and my sunshine. I didn't like it when he was worried or when his face was darkened by shadow. "They need me," he said. "That's what it is. Maidy and Paud need me at home for another year."

"But that's terrible," I said stoutly. "That's selfish of them."

"No." He started to pull the delicate, but now empty, birdcage of sticks apart with his hands. "I'll be gone from them long enough." He said it wistfully, as an old woman might say it. As if it was a fact of life, just one of those things. But it struck me like an iron rod. John would enter the adult world before me, and I was being sent off to school. In a year's time we would be separated. I too needed him for another year, to get used to the idea of his leaving. Dublin seemed so final. Maybe he would never come back. I felt like crying, but I didn't want John to think I was a crybaby. So I stood up and went behind him, put my arms round his neck and buried my face in his shoulders, and tucked my knees in around his waist as a signal for him to carry me. With me draped round his shoulders like a cloak, John stood up and carried me on his back until we reached the silver birch. I couldn't climb it anymore; I was too big.

"Carry me all the way home," I said. I knew I was heavy for him, but he kept walking. I didn't want to get down because I was still feeling sad, and I thought perhaps he was feeling sad too because he didn't run or throw me about like he usually did when we played piggyback. He just walked on steadily, like the donkey carrying Mary through Bethlehem. Just before we reached the house I leaned down and whispered: "Don't let me go."

I wondered briefly why I had said it when we were so near home already, but then John said, "I won't," and the sad feeling became something else. Something warm and comforting, like one of Maidy's special teas.

Chapter Seven

We said our good-byes at the beginning of the next summer. I went to the train station with Maidy and Paud to wave him off.

"Don't cry." He said it to Maidy, although she was crying already, so I knew he was really saying it to me. "I'll be back before you know it." But the train was already moving away from us, and he was moving with it, toward his new life, waving and delighted to be leaving us behind. As his eager hand disappeared into a fog of smoke, I had a sudden fear that I might never see him again.

It was the longest summer, the summer he left.

My parents let me loose, but most of the time I had nothing to do, nowhere to go. I went up to Maidy and Paud a few times, but it felt like a betrayal of my own parents, being with them while John wasn't around. So I wandered through the fields, made chains out of daisies, held thick blades of grass between my two thumbs and tried to make a single flat note, as John had shown me. I found a hedgehog one day, a frog another—but both of them meant nothing without somebody to share them with. I was lonely; but worse than the loneliness was the boredom. I thought that summer would never end.

My father took me about with him a little. Dressed up in my good coat, sitting in presbytery parlors nibbling dry biscuits and listening to him talk "parish business." Sometimes the priest would ask my father about English politics. On account of his being a civil servant, my father was something of an expert on Home Rule and the possibility of Ireland separating from England and governing itself. "I have said it before and I will say it again . . ." My father always sounded so certain, so authoritative when he spoke about politics. ". . . the House of *Lords* will never pass Home Rule for Ireland." His accent altered slightly when he said the word "Lords." Delineating it from the religious "Our Lord" with an English inflection, yet infusing it, somehow, with equal respect.

When any subject came up that was remotely interesting to me—a snippet of gossip about a morally unsound woman, or a neighbor who drank too much—I would be sent outside to "play." Standing listlessly, pointlessly, in the center of a manicured garden imagining what would happen if I climbed a tree . . . How many people would gather to talk me down? How long could I stay up there before I got cold and hungry enough to face the mob, to take my punishment? I hadn't climbed a tree since John had gone. There was no point in climbing trees without an audience. John was my audience.

One Saturday, my father took me to visit the Monsignor. "He is a very important man," he reminded me as we approached the lane up to his house, "so mind your manners." I could tell he was regretting having brought me.

The house was huge, like a palace, and the housekeeper laid out a table with more food than I had ever seen in one place at any one time. My eyes nearly popped out of my head when she brought in the first few plates and laid them down on the starched tablecloth. Currant scones, a cream sponge stuffed with raspberries, two apple tarts; a tiered cake rack piled with tiny sandwiches, made with slices of bread so thin they were almost transparent. And still the food kept coming: slices of turkey, ham and beef; a whole cooked chicken; soda cake spread with butter and glazed with honey. "Is there a party?" I wasn't allowed to speak without being spoken to first, most especially to clergy, but I just couldn't help myself. My father glared at me, but the Monsignor laughed. He was from the North, so he had a funny, swingy voice and a pleasant face. He was friendly, but also fat—small wonder, I thought.

"No, my pretty wee girl—it's all for us. We call it 'high tea.'"

My father seemed to calm down. When we sat, he took my plate and served me a piece of ham, a slice of turkey and some soda cake. When I had finished it, carefully chewing with my mouth closed, I crossed my knife and fork on my plate and waited. I was longing, longing for more. There was so much of it—and all for us. The housekeeper, who was pouring the tea, said, "What lovely manners" and gave me a plate with a slice of tart dolloped with thick, whipped cream. The cream was sweet and cold and the tart still slightly warm. I wanted to tell the housekeeper that, in my opinion, this was the best tart I had ever tasted, and that I knew a thing or two about apple tarts on account of having eaten in Maidy Hogan's house. But I didn't dare.

When I had scraped every morsel from my plate, the Monsignor smiled broadly at me and said, "You're a great wee girl altogether—have a piece of cake," and he held me out a slab of the sugary, fruit-laden sponge.

"No," my father said. "She has had enough—haven't you, Eileen? We don't want to indulge the child."

The Monsignor's face fell further than I would have expected. "No," he said, "I suppose not."

The girls in national school said that boarding in a convent school was like going to prison. Kathleen Condon said the nuns beat the bad girls at the beginning of the first term, so that by the time their parents came to take them home for holidays, the bruising had gone down. She said we'd be eating nothing but porridge and bread and water day in and day out, and that we wouldn't be allowed to speak outside of mealtimes. She said we'd have to say the rosary at least five times a day and would be made to do the stations over sharp stones in our bare feet until they bled.

Despite their warnings, by the end of that summer, I was desperate to go.

Chapter Eight

The Jesus and Mary Convent was ten miles away from our village.

I had never been so far away from home before. The night before we left, my mother packed my father's navy suitcase with my things. There was a heavy Foxford blanket in Madonna blue with a wide, silk ribbon trim. A soft feather pillow with a spare linen case, a brand-new dressing gown, along with two nightgowns, pressed and starched. Pants and vests were folded discreetly in a corner. There was a new, leather-bound prayer book that my father had bought me, along with a box containing mother-of-pearl rosary beads. I opened the box to check the beads, and my heart fluttered with excitement at the sight of them. Without thinking, I lifted the glittering string and laid it across my wrist like a piece of jewelry.

My mother took the beads from me, saying sharply, "Remember what they're for, Ellie." She snapped the beads back into their box and packed them away. "You are a big girl now, you must remember your rosary every day, now that your father won't be there to guide you."

The convent building was like a white palace, square at the front with steps up to an ornate door and two long wings at either side. My father asked my mother to stay in the car with the driver; he knew the Reverend Mother and would take me in himself. She kissed me, a cold dry peck, but I felt it as a fond good-bye. When I looked back, her face was set and staring straight ahead and, for the first time, I understood my mother's sadness and discomfort toward me as a kind of love.

It was early in the morning, before nine, but it had been a hot summer and the air was wet and heavy with the stench of manure from the carriage horses, snorting discreetly and biding their time before the long journey home. I could feel my skin prickling beneath the heavy wool shift and my hair frizzing under the navy bonnet. There were girls, all dressed like me, everywhere—hundreds of them, kissing and hugging their parents, talking to one another, flattening their starched pinafores, straightening their bonnets, giggling, gesticulating, clattering into the still morning air like a huge flock of squawking birds. Suddenly I was terrified. This was going to be like school, only a million times worse because there was no John and there was no escape—not even to my parents' house. I didn't want to go to prison after all. I reached for my father's hand and he took it with no verbal acknowledgment, but a firm squeeze. I wanted to cry.

He walked me up the steps toward the door. It was made of very dark wood and had scenes from the crucifixion carved into it: violent, bloody images. "It's always good to remind us of Christ's suffering," my father said, although I knew he meant to comfort me. As we reached the top of the steps the enormous door opened and out stepped the tallest nun, the tallest *person*, I had ever seen. She was a full foot taller than my father and he looked up at her and said, "Reverend Mother, what a pleasure to see you again."

"Aloysius Flaherty? God bless you! How is the Monsignor?"

"Very well, Reverend Mother. This is my daughter, Eileen."

I wished he hadn't drawn her attention to me right at that moment, because I was struggling not to laugh. I could feel the stream of giggles bubbling up inside my chest. She was so tall that she made my father look small and silly. She wasn't a bit frightening, as one might imagine a very tall nun would be. Her head, with the wimple and everything, seemed as big as my own body, and yet her face was sweet. She looked as amused as I was by her gargantuan size. "Eileen, I am so pleased to meet you." She smiled (her teeth were the size of duck eggs!) and I felt she meant it. Then she leaned down and looked me in the eyes. "You're a good holy child, Ellie, I can see that." Now I was sure I would laugh, but then to my surprise I found that I didn't want to anymore. She said to my father, "We'll take very good care of her, Aloysius."

"Thank you, Reverend Mother." My father gave my hand to the nun, and as my fingers disappeared entirely into her enormous fist, he patted me briefly on the head and went back to the car without turning round.

Standing on the top steps, the Reverend Mother called the crowd to order. The parents said their last good-byes in a matter of seconds, and the girls were ordered into a silent line. All this time she was holding my hand, and I was mortified, having to stand there beside her with every girl in the school looking up at me. I think she had forgotten I was there. As the last of the girls filed into the building, she absentmindedly let go of me and prodded me gently into the line.

The girl in front of me had a bold face and a shock of unruly, curly red hair on which her bonnet was obviously straining to keep itself from falling off. Just before we got to the refectory, she turned round to me and said in a thick Mayo accent, "I'm sticking with you—you're in with the Mother."

*

Silence was a feature of life in the convent school, but it wasn't the cloying, dead silence of my home. It was the silence of reverence and respect, and it sat like a light veil over the joyful, excited babbling of busy girlhood.

My first friend was Sheila, the redhead from Mayo. That first day, she stayed with me all the way into the main hall, where we were instructed to gather for assembly. In the time it took us to shuffle in line through the gray, unfamiliar corridors, and despite the calls for "Silence in the corridor! Silence in line!," she told me her name, that she was a "townie," that her father was a "prominent tailor" in Westport, that she had three older brothers and that her mother suffered from "nerves," which is why she had been sent away to school.

"I don't mind," she whispered, as we sat down together in the hall. "It gets me out from under my brothers' stinking feet in the bed. You're a townie too—I can tell by the cut of you. We'll stick together, you and me, against all the dirty aul culchies."

"Poor people live in towns because they've no land," interrupted another girl, leaning across me to admonish my new friend. "All hunched together like hens in a box. My father has five hundred acres of fine farmland—we don't *need* to live in the town."

"And dirt under his nails like a savage!" Sheila retorted, shockingly.

For a moment I was frightened of being in the middle of these two scrappers. Frightened mostly that all the other girls would find me out—realize that I was the one no one liked. Perhaps Sheila, with her daft hair and her frank manner, was Kathleen Condon, and I'd be stuck with her in a corner with the whole school hating us, day-into-night, for the next five years.

"I'm Maeve. What's your name?" The farmer's daughter poked me.

"Ellie."

"And where are you from?"

"Kilmoy." I added quickly: "It's only a small town—and my father's a big man in the government office."

The girls looked at me and then at each other. I wasn't sure if they were impressed or appalled, neither culchie nor townie. Then Sheila pinched me in the arm—"Clever girl you are!"—and I laughed out loud as a young nun called, "Silence for the Reverend Mother!"

My life had changed completely and I embraced it. Each day began with Mass, and even though the church was cold, and the prayers no different from the ones we said at home, there was a feeling of holiness that I liked. Our priest, Father Matthew, was softly spoken, so that the ceremony became a seamless stream of words and actions, spilling off the altar like the morning mist rolling across the fields outside.

Breakfast was simple, but it was the best meal of the day because you felt hungry and deserving. Warm porridge with honey and creamy milk, brown bread with plenty of butter, and hot tea—sweetened with sugar on a Sunday. The nuns kept a small farm and they grew all their own fruit and vegetables; there were plenty of them and they weren't afraid to work, so we enjoyed the fruits of their labor. Sugar was limited generally, but the nuns could afford it and they were passionate bakers. They fed us like princesses with a different dessert after each meal: apple sponge; bread-and-butter pudding; soda cake dripping with raspberry jam. And in case their food turned us hungry girls into hogs, they drummed etiquette into us at every turn. In our first household-management class, Sister Agnes called the girls around to watch me set a place for dinner. "Very good, Eileen." I glowed with pride as my knowledge of correct cutlery placement, taught to me by my mother, finally came into its own.

A lot of things fell into place for me that first year. The etiquette and good manners that had made me feel stilted and punished as a child now stood me in good stead. A devotion to the Virgin Mary deepened inside me with the nightly rosary, in a way it had never done before, despite my father's daily efforts. The twenty girls in my dormitory all knelt by their beds, knees softened by the blankets that we were allowed to put under them, our bellies warmed with hot milk as we chanted by the light of Sister Agnes's lamp.

Chapter Nine

The first school year flew by and, before I knew it, I was facing three long months with my parents again. This time I was armed with books to help me against the boredom. Knowing I was an only child, Sister Stephanie had packed me a box from the school library, including *Little Women* and the adventure stories of H. Rider Haggard. She also packed some religious works, as a consolation to my father, who disapproved of fiction.

I had not seen my mother in nine months and, when the carriage driver left us at the gate, I saw she was standing, waiting for us at the door. Her hair was pinned back, but escaped tendrils were flickering about her face. As the car pulled up, she brushed her hands down her front to straighten her dress and I realized she was still wearing her apron. She began frantically to untie it, and I felt a clip of love. I held on to the feeling so that when she greeted me with her cheek, I embraced her with my two arms and put a warm kiss on her dry skin. She did not respond, but she did not pull away.

My father took the car straight back into town and, after unpacking my things, I joined my mother in the kitchen. She was at the fire boiling some linens—the kitchen smelled of carbolic from the soap.

"Can I help you, Mam?" I asked. There were some eggs and butter on the table. "I could make a soda cake—I know how."

My mother raised her eyebrow, almost imperceptibly, and nodded at the table. I could not believe how easily she let me help her, and realized, shamefully, that I had never offered directly before. As I walked round the kitchen, gathering ingredients—a mixing bowl, a jug—I kept waiting for her to tell me to stop, that she did not need my help, but she didn't. Just before I began measuring out my ingredients, she came over to me and carefully put an apron over my head, tying it at the back. When she had finished she patted me gently to indicate she was done, and I felt her touch as tenderly as if it had been a kiss.

That evening she presented the bread, spread with butter, to my father.

"This is excellent bread, Attracta," he said. "Sweet—like a cake."

My mother and I exchanged a smile. It felt like a reward. "Ellie made it," my mother said.

"Well! Did she really?" He looked over at me and I flushed with pleasure at his approval.

I called up to the Hogans'. Maidy looked older and Paud smaller than I had remembered. It had been less than a year since I had seen them, but so much had happened.

"Look at you now, you're a young lady," Maidy said. "All tidied and smart." She put a mug of milky tea down in front of me and a slice of apple tart directly onto the table. When I hesitated slightly, she asked, "Would you prefer a plate, Ellie? Of course you would . . . Where are my manners?"

"No, no!" I felt terrible. "No, Maidy, don't be silly, it's fine." As I bit into the tart, its acid sweetness made me remember how much I had missed being here. "When is John home?" I had not realized how much I had been wanting to see him until I asked it.

"John won't be home for a while yet again," said Maidy.

I nodded and smiled. Then, quite unexpectedly, I began to cry. I had hardly spared him a thought that past year, and yet now that I was faced with the prospect of not seeing him, I was all upset.

"Whist now, Ellie—poor, poor love . . ." Maidy said it under her breath, then came and put her arm round me.

"I'm sorry." I made myself stop crying. "How is he getting on in Dublin?"

Maidy sat down at the table with me, something she rarely did, and cut herself an enormous slice of pie and started to talk. She told me how the boss in Dublin was working John very hard, every day of the week barring Sunday. He had nice digs, cheap, and the landlady was kind and a decent enough cook— but not so decent as to be better than Maidy. He had made friends, a lot of friends from all walks of life, she said.

"I thought he might have written to me," I said.

"Sure, he doesn't know where you are, love." Then her face saddened and she said, "Although he writes to us seldom enough now."

"Why is that?"

She got up from the table and started to busy herself. Her tart was left, untouched on the tabletop. "Oh, he's busy, you know. With his new friends."

Paud, who had been quietly plucking a bird in the corner, suddenly called out, "He's joined the Volunteers, Maidy—say it out, why don't you?"

"Quiet, Paud—she's only a child!"

I knew who Paud was talking about. They were the rebels

who wanted the English out of Ireland and for us to run the country ourselves. My father didn't approve. "They say they are seeking justice, Father," I often heard him argue with the priest after Mass, "but in truth they are vagabonds, intent on destruction and anarchy."

I liked the idea of John being a vagabond—it sounded exciting, like Robin Hood. Then I felt upset again, because he was living a wonderful new life without me. So I started chatting and boasting to Maidy and Paud about my own life—how delighted I was with the convent, how I loved my new friends, how kind the nuns were, how we ate like princesses and each had a bed to ourselves. As I was leaving, I said, "So, I do hope John is happy in Dublin." I didn't mean it as I said it, but as soon as the words were out of my mouth I knew it was important for me to wish him happiness. My year at the convent had turned me into a good person. Being good worked. It had paid off with my parents, and now somehow it would pay off around my feelings about John. My childhood friend had moved on, and so had I. However hard my summers would be without him, it was essential to wish him well with all my heart, and let him go. More than anything, I had to keep proving to myself that I could be happy without him.

Chapter Ten

I called up to Maidy and Paud a few times over that summer, and the next three summers, but John was never there and, by and large, I really did end up forgetting about him. I got caught up in the drama of convent life: the sharing and betrayal of each other's small secrets, girls sending flirtatious messages out to the working boys who came to dig the gardens, others trying to win favor with the nuns. Only the brightest girls were accepted for vocations, and only the truly wicked allowed themselves to get caught up with romance and boys. Between the bad girls committing—or threatening to commit—sins of the flesh, and the rest of us speculating as to which of us were going to enter the convent, we had plenty to keep us entertained.

As for the holidays, I found they passed more quickly and easily if I conformed to my parents' way of doing things—cooking and housekeeping with my mother, and saying the rosary each night with my father. They allowed me, then, to spend the rest of my time reading. Books were my escape. I was able to leave my own cravings behind while I absorbed myself in the lives of my heroines. *Anne of Green Gables, Little Women, Wuthering Heights, Jane Eyre*—I read each of them over and over again, stepping into the hearts and loves of the women, feeling their passions and their grief.

The summer of my seventeenth birthday, my father took my mother and me to the shrine at Knock to see where the Blessed Virgin had appeared in 1879. My father had been a child himself when it happened, and he said it had been the news of that miraculous event that had inspired his great devotion. We stood by the church wall where the miracle had occurred and tried to count the number of crutches that cured invalids had left there over the years. There were too many to count. "The Lord's mercy knows no end!" my father declared, merrily. Inside, we said ten full decades of the rosary kneeling on the stone floor before the altar.

I was freezing cold and bored throughout the day. I kept remembering how I had celebrated my birthday with my school friends before the term broke up. The girls had gathered round my bed after lights out, and Sheila had got in beside me, her cold feet warming themselves on my calves, gripping my hands under her arms and releasing them only to kiss them and tell me she loved me. We talked by the light of our single "birthday" candle and nibbled at Maeve's secret stash of biscuits. They presented me with gifts they had made themselves: a napkin embroidered with my birth date; a crocheted cap; a knitted bobble to sew onto a scarf; a pretty cozy for a boiled egg. It was pure joy.

The journey home from Knock was long and we stopped for a "birthday picnic" on the way. The rain slashed loudly on the roof of our hackney carriage, and the windows steamed up while we ate our sandwiches in the awkward company of our driver. "I think I might like to join the convent," I said. I don't know why I said it, except that I had been thinking how much nicer it was at school than it was at home. How wonderful it would have been to stay there for the whole summer. After the chatter at school, I had become unused to the terrible silence in our family and sometimes felt compelled to break it. Saying I wanted to be a nun seemed an appropriate silence breaker after a day in Knock. We talked about becoming nuns in school all the time. It didn't mean anything. We were just speculating— making conversation.

As soon as the words were out of my mouth, I realized I had made a terrible mistake.

My mother did not look at me at all, but studied the back of the driver's neck, and chewed cautiously on her sandwich as if she feared it was going to choke her. My father paused from eating, then held my eye for a moment, smiled gently and said, "We will have to talk to Mother Superior and see if she thinks you are suitable, Eileen."

"Probably she will not," I said, looking away. But it was too late. I could tell by his face he was bursting with joy.

The following day was a Sunday and, unusually, we slept through early Mass at eight and went to the busier service at eleven. I wore my navy school uniform and cap, as I always did on a Sunday. Some of the village girls that I knew from national school wore brightly colored cardigans and adorned themselves with brooches and lace gloves and the like. None of the local girls spoke to me, not even Kathleen Condon. I wondered if Sheila and Maeve had friends in their parishes or dressed prettily for their Sunday Masses. We never talked about our lives outside the convent.

Father Mac had a low, slow, droning voice that would put you to sleep—and, with some of the older parishioners, actually did. The day was warm, so the wool of my uniform was making me itch and I found it was a struggle to sit still.

When Mass was ended, I separated from my parents and hurried out by the side door of the church so that I could disappear for a few moments and scratch myself. I stood by the back wall of the church and shoved my hand as far down the back of my tunic as I could stretch. Then, to my horror, I realized that I wasn't alone. There was a group of young men standing over by the cemetery wall, some fifty feet away from me. There were three of them, huddled together, talking quietly and smoking. The tallest of them looked over. I noticed that he smiled at me as I walked quickly back around to the front of the church to find my parents. They were standing with Father Mac and the pig farmer, Frank Collins, a broad man with big whiskers and strong opinions. "They were *not* our leaders, Frank," my father was arguing with his usual authority. "As British citizens, it is our duty to obey the law of whatever land we live in. As Christians, we must answer to a higher force than Mr. Padraig Pearse—isn't that right, Father?" Neither man answered him.

It was all anyone ever talked about these days: the Uprising. "Please be upstanding for 'the Uprising!'" Sheila used to call in the refectory. Then she would leap up on a chair, raising her hand to her forehead in a mock salute, and we'd all follow. We knew what was going on, but our interest was vague because the war never touched our lives. If any of the girls had brothers who were involved, they were never told. They were sent to convent school where they'd be safe. It was fashionable among us older girls to mock the rebellion as men's foolish obsession with war. Nobody we knew had died; it was just something that seemed to be happening far, far away. Like the World War. Terrible—but nothing to do with us.

I stood there politely, my eyes wandering across the dispersing crowd. I had just noticed Maidy and Paud when one of the young men I had seen around the back—the tall one who had smiled at me—walked up to them. He had sideburn whiskers trimmed to the top of his mouth, and he wore a shirt and tie. His hands were tucked into his trouser pockets and, beneath the side of his tweed jacket, I could see the suggestion of braces. He was broad and mannish, and the world stood still when I looked at him.

It was John.

He smiled at me, and it was the same smile from the same face I had always loved, but the love felt different. It shot through my skin in a wave of heat until my hands were trembling and my cheeks burning. As he moved toward me I became over-whelmed with a feeling I did not recognize, so I turned my back and began to walk away from the church, my mother following me. As we reached the road, I suddenly felt foolish. John was my old friend. My brother. When I turned to go back to him, I saw that he was surrounded by people. Or, more specifically, girls in brightly colored cardigans and hair combs. A volcanic anger rose up in me. If he wanted to talk to them before me, then that was that. He was welcome to them!

I practically ran home from the church, my mother trailing after me. But when I got back to the house I could not settle. I tried to help my mother, but I was nervous and kept dropping things. I was too anxious to read, too distracted to pray. I lay awake all night thinking about John with the stupid girls from national school, John smoking with his friends, John smiling at me. When I tried to think of John and me playing together as children—the John I knew and loved—the years of soft images in my memory kept getting wiped by the brief, bright pictures from that day. His chin was broader, his cheeks harder, his eyes narrowed with experience; the shadows of a man made his face so compelling to me that, when I closed my eyes, I could think of nothing else but looking at him again.

I felt sad and angry and wanting.

Chapter Eleven

If I was going to see John again, as I was aching to, I needed to do something with myself that would make him see that I was better than those other girls. More sophisticated, worthier of his attention. But I was too plain. I had no pretty things, no frivolities that would attract the attention of a man.

I looked through the wardrobe, but even as I opened the door I knew it was hopeless. I had just my uniform and drab work-clothes. My mother had made me a yellow dress with white daisies on it a few years before, but I had long since grown out of it—it barely reached my knees and stretched tight across my chest. Embarrassed to draw attention to my curves, even from my mother, I had never asked her for another.

My mother and father were leaving the house to go into town for the day. My father had hired a hackney for them, and the gesture had put my mother in good form. She was wearing her Sunday hat and tailored navy coat as she opened the lid of the small box on our hallstand, taking out her lipstick and face powder. My father's coat was still hanging on the stand, and she pushed the sleeve of it aside to reveal the mirror under-neath, before applying the makeup carefully. I had seen her do this often, but watched her now with special care.

"Are you sure you won't come with us, Eileen?" she said. The powder softened her skin to a creamy white and the lipstick brought her face to life.

"No thank you, Mam," I said. "I shall study for the day. I might call up to the Hogans' later." Just saying it set my nerves quivering. I felt that by saying it to my mother, I would have to make it real and go, even though I was terrified.

"Good girl," my mother said, smiling, but her approval was lost on me because as she turned to go, I caught the smell of roses trailing behind her as she closed the door.

When she had gone I ran upstairs to the chest of drawers, took my mother's bottle of rosewater and pressed it to my wrist. It slipped and spilled onto my shoes, but I bent down and soaked up the excess with my sleeve so that it wouldn't be wasted. I found a hair comb on the dressing table and used it to secure the dark curls back from my ears, but it made my face appear large and my jaw wide—so I quickly took it out.

I could not allow myself to despair, so I continued my search in my mother's drawers for some trinket to brighten me up. I found her locket, but it was too valuable—and what if I lost it? She was wearing her pearl necklace. Suddenly I came across my old yellow dress and I had an idea. I ripped through the hem with my mother's dressmaking scissors and folded it into a kerchief, which I tied around my neck. Then I ran downstairs and opened the hallstand box. I quickly puffed over my face with the powder and applied the lipstick. The top was pointed where my mother had been rolling it for years into a sharp tip. Her lips were a thin line, but I had inherited my father's full, broad mouth; I struggled to get the color on without damaging the delicate red pencil. I checked in the mirror. My eyes looked dark and worried beneath the heavy eyebrows and the black curls of my long hair. I smiled at myself, an unconvincing smile—then threw myself out the door. I knew if I looked too long at the reflection, my face would persuade me not to go. Then John would go back to Dublin with the taste of another girl on his lips and my life would be over. I took a deep breath and told myself that the yellow of my scarf and the red of my lips made me appear bright and cheerful, even if that was not how I felt inside.

When I got to the house, John was not there.

"He went out walking," Maidy said. "Wait for him. He was sorry to have missed you on Sunday."

I waited for an hour, drinking tea and anxiously wiping crumbs from the corner of my painted mouth. Maidy went about her work, telling me bits of news, her gossip ebbing more and more often into an awkward silence, the longer her son stayed away.

When the hour was gone, I stood up to leave.

"I'll see him another time," I said. Maidy smiled at me, and it nearly broke my heart.

As I was leaving, I saw John walking along the road toward the house. He was with one of the men I had seen him with outside the church, and two girls. I knew the girls. They were from the year above me in national school. Silly, pretty girls. One of them was sitting on a bicycle and John was pulling her along. I wanted to cry.

"Here he comes," said Maidy brightly.

"I've got to go, I'm late," I said, moving forward. I didn't want Maidy to see me upset.

"Stay." She put her hand firmly on my shoulder. "Stay and see your old friend."

I remembered that Maidy loved me too. So I went back into the house, dried my eyes, pinched my cheeks and got ready to face the competition.

Five minutes later, John walked into the house alone. "Ellie Flaherty," he said, grinning with broad teeth and blue-eyed mischief, "you were very shy, running off from me after Mass the other day."

My anxiety flew from me like a fairy and I felt immediately happy. His voice sounded deeper than I had remembered it. "It seemed to me that you had enough company to be getting along with."

"You'd need a bit of idle chatter in your head after listening to Father Mac droning on like that."

"John!" Maidy shouted, but she was smiling. "I declare you've become godless since you went up to Dublin!"

"Maybe I have," he said looking directly at me as he said it. I tried to stop myself from smiling so widely, but I couldn't. "Will we go for a walk, Ellie—what do you think?" It felt like a threat more than a question. In some part of me I knew what it meant and my knees buckled. "We'll walk down to the silver birch, Ellie, and see if you can still climb up it?"

Maidy took a tea towel and flicked it to the back of his legs. "You'll do no such thing, John Hogan. You're not too old for me to take the stick to you. Ellie is a young lady now, and don't you forget it."

"I might do it all the same, Maidy," I said, joining in. "Would you have a pair of old britches about the place that I could put on to save my skirts?"

"Go on!" she said, chasing the two of us round the kitchen with the wet tea towel. "Get out of my house before I flatten the pair of you!"

We could barely stand up for laughing when we got outside and we chased down to the bottom field. As the silver birch came into sight, the jokes subsided and our pace grew slower. We walked in comfortable silence listening to the birds and feeling the summer breeze in the space between us. When we came to the rocks by a boundary ditch, we sat down. John said, "Do you remember how you used to make me wait for the rabbits to come out?"

"Until you said you'd kill one of them and cook them in a stew."

"You cried . . ."

"I don't cry as easily these days." I balked inwardly at the lie. I had been close to tears all day at the mere thought of him.

"You were sweet," he said, looking me in the eyes. Then he looked away. "There's something you should know about me, Ellie." I held my breath as he paused, waiting for whatever more he was going to reveal of his feelings. His eyes still downcast and serious, he said, "There is a war in our country, Ellie. I don't know how much of it you know about, but I need you to know I'm involved."

"Yes, I know, you're a rebel," I pushed in. I was annoyed that he had broken our moment by talking about war. I could see he wanted to talk more about it, but I wouldn't be distracted. "Who were those girls I saw you with earlier? Were you going with one of them?" I blurted it out. I needed him to stop and take notice of me.

John looked up and I met his gaze with a deliberately arched brow. He smiled and said, "Maybe both . . ."

Hurt, I turned my face away from him.

"I'm joking, Ellie—come on."

It was a cruel joke, but then, how could he possibly have known the terror that was in my heart.

He took my chin in his palm and turned me to face him again. Gently, he reached his fingers up to my neck and untied my yellow scarf, throwing it over to the bushes, where it caught on a branch and hung.

"What did you do that for?" I asked.

"You don't need it—you don't need any of that stuff at all."

I was going to retrieve the scarf, but he put his hand on my shoulder and held me back.

"Don't you know, Ellie? There could never be anyone but you."

Then he pulled me across to him and kissed me for the first time.

Afterward we lay on the grass and looked at the sky. I was bristling with excitement, my toes curled in my boots, waiting for him to kiss me again. "Tell me about your adventures, John," I said, placing my hand across his chest. "Tell me about all your vagabonding with the rebels . . ."

John sat up, moving my hand away. "It's not like that, Ellie," he said. "It's not a game."

I was embarrassed he thought me so flippant. "I want to know, John—really." Except that I didn't. I just wanted to hear him talking so that I could adore him and could silence him presently with another kiss.

"I watched a man die," he said.

His words shocked me so much, I immediately wanted him to stop talking. "John . . ."

"There was blood everywhere. I tried to stem it with my hands. His eyes were still open . . ."

I saw I had lost my courting John in this sturdy, serious profile of a man talking about war. I barely listened to what he was saying as the fear grew deeper and settled inside me. A vague, unspoken notion gathered in my heart. It was inevitable that John would get caught up in this mess. It was who he was. Finding turf for the school, attempting to rescue me from my parents, fighting for the freedom of his country. Things outside of himself called to John all the time. Despite my father's arguments, this was a call to justice, and John would be powerless to resist. But I did not need John to fight this war for me, and I did not want him to risk his love fighting it for anyone else. This wretched war that I had mocked with my school friends might be a just war, but the only injustice I knew was that the man I had barely been given the chance to love had witnessed death, and so might die himself. My heart went cold and I shivered myself back into his words.

"He was only a year older than me. I felt the life ebb out of him. It changed me, Ellie."

I did not know what I could say to comfort him. This was his moment of love—a soldier confessing the horrors of war. I knew I was supposed to admire his bravery and self-sacrifice, but all I felt in my heart was the terror of losing him. I wanted *my* moment back, with my red lips and my yellow scarf and the drama of love—the simplicity of kissing under a clear blue sky—the clarity of new love, fresh happiness, unsullied by the past and unworried by the future. If John wouldn't give me my moment back, then I was going to take it for myself.

"I love you, John Hogan," I said, and I leaned over and kissed him for the second time.

Chapter Twelve

Everything changed that year. Sheila and her family had emigrated to America, so she didn't come back to school. We were all shocked and bewildered at her loss, as none of us had had the chance to say good-bye.

"I heard her oldest brother was in the Republican Brotherhood," said Ger Conway, who lived in the next town along. "Her father wanted to get him out of the country, but the stupid eejit never turned up at the boat and they ended up leaving him behind anyway."

Many of the girls came back to school that September with revolution in their hearts. A fifth-year from Sligo changed her name to Constance, after the revolutionary Countess Markovitz, and boasted about spying through the gates of Lissadell, the Markovitz stately home, and seeing that renowned aristocrat walk the grounds with a gun. Another told of how her young uncle had lost a finger when his gun misfired during an ambush. But even though I had the most exciting story of all from that summer, I didn't tell anyone about falling in love and I didn't boast about my lover's war adventures. I kept John close to me by keeping our world a secret—as I had always done.

Falling in love with him had turned my world on its head.

The convent that I had enjoyed so much up till now suddenly

became a prison. The comfort of my friends was cloying and intrusive; the serenity of the nuns irritated me; the silence made me want to shout. I felt at one point I was going to burst, and so I wrote to Sheila and told her about John and my fears for him. Sheila was wild and feisty and I knew she'd understand. I missed her, and trusted her partly because she was on the other side of the world. I was afraid if I told anyone else, they would try and take it away. Maeve would have been initially thrilled, but I knew that she had a vocation and that she assumed I was going to join her. "We'll have to look after each other now that Sheila's gone," she'd said.

All the girls, and Sister Stephanie, the Reverend Mother and my parents were expecting me to enter the convent. I was bright. I would do my matriculation and move into the provincial house as a postulant—a formality before I was received as a novice. Over the following two and a half years I would train to teach, before taking my final vows at the age of twenty. I would then stay in the Jesus and Mary Convent, living and working for the rest of my life. It was a plan I probably would have fallen in with, had I not met John again that summer. Falling in love had swept away my flimsy vocation like a butterfly in a storm, flailing and fluttering with doubt, then dashed on the hard rocks of certainty. At times I wished things were as simple as they had been before—that my future was assured, with my teachers and my parents satisfied, and I myself content enough. The craving for John's company, for his affection, was so great that part of me wished I had not gone up to the Hogans' that day and learned how he and I were meant to be together forever. But I had. And there was no going back.

We wrote each other short, urgent letters. I told my friends the correspondence was with a maiden aunt who had grown attached to me during the summer. John told me little of his life, only that he missed me and loved me. He said he was cutting his apprenticeship short to come home. He was worried about Maidy and Paud; there were troubled times ahead and he wanted to be close to them, and to me. I wrote to him once and begged him to come and get me. I wanted to run away from school and get married. John would not entertain the idea. He wrote: "I need money to do well by you, Eileen. I'll not marry you poor. Two years will be time enough to set things right."

John came home the following summer from Dublin. He moved in with Maidy and Paud, and we were inseparable. He didn't talk about the war and I did not ask. It seemed to me as if it was over. I made myself believe the fighting was something that had happened in Dublin and could surely not touch the simple, quiet life we enjoyed in the country. In any case, that summer it was as if we were children again, walking the fields, laughing and talking, our friendship stronger than ever. Maidy and Paud were so happy to have their John back from Dublin that they would not hear of him helping on the farm for the first few weeks he was home, and my parents trusted me to spend the days as I pleased. The sun shone, the hedgerows were heavy with fruit and we were beyond happy. We experienced the freedom of touching each other and enjoyed long kisses hiding in the soft grass, but we always held ourselves back from what we really wanted.

One day, toward the end of the summer, my father came into my bedroom. It was early evening and I was getting ready to go out. John had been in Ballymorris looking for work and I had spent the day helping my mother in the garden, cleaning out the henhouse and tearing back the weeds from the edges of her rhubarb patch. It had been a balmy day, and the room was filled with an orange light. I checked myself in the mirror and wished

John was there to see me looking as warm and rosy as I did.

"I've made preparations for us to travel to Galway to collect what you need for the convent. They have asked that you start back a week before school opens, so you can settle in before the new students arrive."

My stomach tumbled over on itself. I thought I was going to be sick, but I kept my voice steady and said, "Yes, Father."

Later that day, as we lay on a mattress of heather in his father's bog, John kissed me harder than he had done before. I could feel the savage drive in him and instead of pulling back as I usually did, protecting us both from mortal sin, I pushed my hips toward him and ground myself into him. John pulled himself away, but I could feel his frustration.

It was an opportunity and I took it. I reached over and stroked his face, down across his chin and neck, then reached down and moved his hand into a caress across my breast. "Will we marry now, John? Then we can do as we please."

He reached up with his free hand and firmly stopped me by the wrist, but I knew that I had won.

The day before my father was due to take me back to the convent to start as a novice teacher, six weeks after my eighteenth birthday, John and I ran away and got married. He collected me at dawn and carried me on the back of his bicycle to Ballymorris, where we caught the morning train to Dublin. I was shivering with the cold and with the enormity of what we were doing. On the train, John tucked me inside his greatcoat and I clung to his chest. I didn't speak in case I might say something that would make him change his mind. So I listened for the thud of his heart and felt the hardness of his bones, the warmth of his blood and told myself that he would look after me.

We walked to St. Dominic's on Dorset Street. It was a Franciscan church and John knew the friar. A small, chubby man, he shook John's hand and greeted me so warmly that I felt we were doing nothing wrong. When John told him we had no certificates with us, he asked us to swear an oath that we were both baptized and free to marry. The chapel was cold and dark, and the familiar scent of incense reminded me that my father should be there. The friar called out the sacristan, a small man with a face like a ferret. "Mr. O'Neill will be your witness," he said. "I will count as the second." It was clear that they had done this a hundred times or more.

The ceremony was short and somber, but we both said our vows willingly. When we were finished, the friar stood with us outside for a few minutes and John talked politely with him. He asked John about men whom I had never met, and I tugged at John's hand to indicate that I wanted to move on. I was excited, anxious to enjoy my new husband. Before we left, the friar put a hand on both our foreheads and blessed us, "Be kind and gentle to each other always."

The sun was shining and it was so hot that I removed my coat and carried it across my arm. We walked down Dorset Street and turned left toward the heart of the city. I remembered Sheila telling us all how she had come to Dublin and drunk tea in a cafe in the city center. Looking around me, I was enthralled, tripping over my feet as I stared in shop windows, mesmerized by the glossy carriages and the women in feather hats with pale faces and scarlet lips. I saw five or more motorcars trundle past, their noisy engines belching out smoke—smart men at the wheels with hats and suits and big, delighted heads on them. I remembered the place Sheila had talked about—Bewley's Cafe. I would get John to take me there.

Suddenly, from about halfway down Sackville Street, the landscape changed. To our left the tall, elegant buildings gave way into a no-man's-land of rubble. Stones and dust and bricks in a disintegrated heap stood next to half a building with ornate windows and fancy coving that must have been a grand shop. Its side torn off, it looked like a once-lovely woman now destroyed. John stopped and his arm went limp where I was holding it. He was staring at a huge building to our right—like a palace, with tall, white pillars at the front. I was reminded of illustrations I had seen of ancient Rome. "It's beautiful!" I said.

He looked at me as if I were mad; he was as white as a sheet. I looked again. Behind the beautiful facade, there was just sky. The fifty or more windows echoed despair and defeat like the cavernous eyes of a skeleton. Burned out, gutted.

"Is it the GPO?" I felt so stupid for asking.

Now John was gazing at me strangely—it was as if he wanted to say something and had then decided to hold back. My blood ran cold. Was this where the boy had lain dying? If so, I didn't want him to name it. I didn't want to think about death on our wedding day. Searching my new husband's face for reassurance, I saw that he was gone from me. His shining eyes reflected the rubble that lay all around us, piles of concrete and dust. A cloud passed overhead; the rubble disappeared from his eyes, but the war was still alive in them. There was no love here for me, only for his country and for the boy whom he had held during his dying moments. I felt ghosts were calling to him in a language I didn't understand.

I grabbed his arm again, bending it into a crook, letting him know that I needed him too, and started to walk, all but dragging him alongside me. So we marched through the debris of my husband's war: scraggy waifs building castles out of broken bricks; half-naked workmen hanging from the side of buildings; fancy city people—all of them blind to the destruction, as I might have been had I lived here. As I *wanted* to be.

John stopped again at a pile of dust and crumbled stone in the center of the road. A small breeze caught up a puff of gray smoke, some of which settled on the bottom of my skirt. "Bastard Nelson." It was the only thing he had said since we had left the steps of the church, and he didn't sound like himself, but a triumphant yet embittered stranger.

I'd had enough. I wanted my day back, my John back. I tugged at his arm and said, "Come on, you silly man, and take me into Bewley's for our wedding breakfast." Defiant in the face of his war reverence, I added, "Or am I not enough of a lady for you?" I held his eye firmly and did not waver. Not for one moment did I betray my fear—that I had pushed him into marriage, and so God was going to punish me by sending him back to war. I stood and cocked my head to one side, expectantly, until I drew a smile out of him. The smile that made him belong to me again.

"You are too much of a lady, Ellie Hogan," he said, grabbing my face and kissing me firmly on the lips in front of his hated, disintegrated Nelson. "That's the problem."

Chapter Thirteen

We telegrammed our parents from Dublin, and went home to Maidy and Paud's house to take the softest blow first. We passed Paud in the field on our way in. He shook John's hand, but did not follow us up to the house. Maidy did not greet us properly at the door. She was tight-lipped and continued about her housework, deliberately ignoring us. I was distraught. I had never seen Maidy like this before. John was not worried. "She'll forget soon enough," he said, when she left the room.

"Indeed and I will not!" she shouted back. Then, unable to hold on to her anger, she came back in and pleaded, "Why did you do it, John?"

Would he tell her I had put pressure on him? "We're well beyond the age of consent, both of us. We waited until Ellie was finished school . . ."

"You did *not*," she retorted. "Ellie was to join the convent then and teach. Arrangements had already been made, John."

"Ellie is eighteen, a woman. She can make up her own mind."

I realized that Maidy must have been speaking with my father. "What did my father say?"

"He said . . ." She paused, as if she did not want to tell me, and instead looked over toward the fireplace. I followed her eyes. Poking out of a grain sack slumped beside the hearth was the blue feather pillow from my bed at home. Maidy found a flint of anger—her lips tightened and she burst it out of her: "He said to tell you he has already paid out your dowry—to the nuns." Then her face collapsed with regret and her voice softened to the mild Maidy I loved. "He left your belongings. I didn't open them out, but the bag was damp, so I just kept them by the fire."

A sob rose in my throat. My dowry. I had not thought consciously about it till that moment, but now I realized I had been depending on it. I knew I could live without my parents' love, but in that moment I did not know if I could live without their money. I ran over to the bag and emptied it out across the floor. My blanket, my pillow and all of my clothes. But not my Jesus and Mary uniform, or my valuable rosary beads, or the precious prayer book. "Damn those pigs!" Anger and despair came howling out of me. I grabbed at the shabby pile and began to tear into everything, ripping the fabric, shredding everything I owned into rags.

John came over, gently pulled me back and put his arms around me. "They'll come round, Ellie," he said, adding, "I'm your family now."

We stayed with Maidy and Paud for a few days. I slept on the settle in their kitchen and John on the floor. We met in the fields during the day to make love—and for those first few weeks our new marriage was just an extension of the friendship it had always been. John went into town and made contacts in the pub—Maidy disapproved, but reluctantly conceded that John needed to keep "in" with the men of the town if he was to get work. I helped Maisie a bit with the farm, cleaning out the henhouse and trying to milk the cows, but I was not born to farming and she found it easier to wait on me than instruct me. I was comfortable with the old couple looking after us, but on the third day John broke the news to them that we were moving on. "We're going to live in my parents' cottage. It's time we had our own place."

Maidy's face collapsed. "But it's in the middle of nowhere, John—miles from the village."

"I'll get work. There's plenty of work for a good carpenter."

Paud left the room. He wouldn't be driven to speech if he was angry. Maidy's eyes followed her husband out of the room, but she kept talking to John. I had never seen her so worried. She pleaded with him: "Work's not that easily got, John, you've got none up to now—and the cottage hasn't been lived in for years, it will be in a desperate state. And it's five miles or more away from here."

"It's a fine cottage and it belongs to me." John had a certain look about him that made me know he wasn't going to change his mind. "Don't worry, I'll tidy it before moving my new wife in." He put his arms round my waist. "I'll make it perfect for you, I promise."

John went to the cottage on foot and I stayed behind with the old couple gathering up our things for our new life. I was excited about sharing a home with my new husband. Our own fire, our own roof to sleep beneath—he would build us a bed and a cabinet, which, in time, we would fill with crockery, and life would be perfect. Maidy and I sewed up the things I had torn in temper, and I turned the remains of my old yellow dress into two pretty cushions, which I embroidered with some wool I had unfurled from an old sweater of John's. We stuffed the cushions with soft, shredded hay and dried lavender. Maidy gave me two cups, two plates, two spoons, a knife and a mixing bowl. Paud gave us their old pot oven, which they had replaced some years before, but first he had to take it to the blacksmith to be mended. He had only eggs and a chicken to offer as payment, so I gave up one of my new yellow cushions instead. "I need an oven more than I need decoration," I said, when Maidy objected. When Paud returned with the shining pot mended as good as new, he said, "Theo blushed like a woman when I gave him your pretty cushion. He'll look after you again."

John came back after five days and we loaded the cart with our new belongings. It seemed like a lot. The bedding and household bits were added to with a sack of grain, vegetables for both planting and eating and other food to get us started—a tin of tea, baking soda, some butter and eggs, a bag of apples and a cooked chicken. Paud tied a cow to the back of the cart and stuffed three live chickens into a wooden box, where they clucked and squealed until we were afraid they'd kill one another. The horse started to pull off slowly, irritated by the cow at its rear: "Come on, Ellie—hop on."

"Are you sure you can spare it all?" I said to Maidy.

"It will start you off in any case," she said and kissed me warmly. "You know where we are if you need us."

It was almost dark when we arrived, and raining. John jumped off the back of the cart to open the gate and then ran ahead in front of us, shouting, "Welcome to John Hogan's house, which he shares with his good wife, Eileen!" But my heart sank as Paud drove the cart after him through the gate.

The house was mottled with moss, its ancient whitewash gray and hanging off in wide, peeling scabs. The grass around the front of it had been scythed back and there was a pile of wet mud at the door, where John had obviously dug the earth to plant vegetables. Inside was not much better: dark and cold, with one broken chair, and a table that John had upside down on the floor with his tools scattered around to fix it. At the fireplace were a few half-cleaned tin pots and caddies, and in the corner a large pile of fresh turf. The fireplace itself and the wall all around it were black with soot. John must have seen the expression on my face, because he said nervously, "Don't worry—the chimney was broken, but it's fixed now. We'll be warm anyway," then hopped from foot to foot like he had as a young boy. "Well, Ellie? Is it good enough for you, Ellie? Will we be happy here?"

I wanted to shout at him for being so foolish. I wanted to cry and scream out, and run from the room. How could he expect me to live in a filthy hovel like this? I looked from the damp patch on the floor crawling with woodlice, to the bare walls streaked with brown water and, finally, I looked again at John. The eager brightness in his face was fading.

Paud was holding his hat and staring down at the ground. "I'll be heading off so," he said.

"No," I said, and I held the eye of my sweetheart, my husband. I gathered all the love I had in my heart for him and I placed it on the sooty, dank dirt of our new hearth. "You'll stay and have supper in *our* house tonight, Paud. John will take you back in the morning."

Chapter Fourteen

Despite my fears, the first few weeks in the cottage were wonderful. Our new home was tucked well back from the road at the end of an all but invisible lane, and we had trees all around us. I cleaned and scrubbed the filthy little house until it turned into a palace. Together, we whitewashed it inside and out, and polished the flagstones; John fixed the table and two chairs, and made a footstool for himself that doubled as a milking stool. The apple trees were heavy with fruit, and I made cakes and tarts and bread in my new oven. Maidy and Paud had given us a sack of potatoes—some for seed, and some for eating. I made potato cakes and spread them with butter and, in the mornings, fried an egg alongside them. Our three hens were laying well, and our cow was lazy and happy and full of milk. We had no meat for the winter, but John was confident that he would get money from his carpentry soon enough and would be able to invest in a few more animals by the following spring.

John was a hard worker, a good farmer and a fine carpenter. He fixed the half door of the cottage and made us a pretty dresser, although we had little for it to hold. Life was sweet. We rose early, worked hard until noon and made love every afternoon before tending to our chores again. John had made us a bed, and I had stuffed a mattress with horsehair, sheep's wool and hay. Each night we fell into it exhausted from our labors, still bristling with love for each other. The sound of our breathing shadowed by the rustling trees, our warm bodies drawing out the sweet scent of the animal hides, it was as if we were the only people in the world. We had everything we needed and I felt as if nothing could touch us, we were so happy.

We were barely in the house a month when the first of the men arrived. John collected him from the road. He was wearing a brown greatcoat and a cap pulled down over his face. When he removed it, he had a bruise the size of a fist on his face. He looked unkempt and dirty, but his accent was educated enough. I offered him a basin of warm water to wash himself, and when he went into our bedroom, I asked John what had happened to him.

"He took a savage beating from the police in Belmullet six days ago and he's been on the run ever since."

"The poor man!" I said. "Who is he?"

John looked at me as if he was surprised I didn't already know, and then as if he was wondering how much to say. "He's a man I met in Dublin." He added quickly, "He's not a criminal, Ellie. He's fighting the cause."

When the man came out, I sat him in a chair by the fire and dressed his face with iodine, then passed him a bowl of hot soup. He laid it down on the stool beside him and wiped the palms of his hands against his eyes. I could tell he was crying and went about my business until he had stopped. "Thank you, Ma'am." They were all the words he spoke to me before he left the following day.

After that, not a week went by when we did not have unexpected visitors. John greeted each one as if he were a long-lost brother. We fed every man who came into our house. At times, they would stay overnight. John never put anyone out in the shed, but laid a good turf fire for them and put down hay matting in the kitchen. I would retire to bed, while the men stayed up drinking. It was the only time John ever drank, when he had his Brotherhood friends about him. They were good men, by and large, and often as I lay in bed I overheard them talking about me.

"He's the lucky man, with a woman like that to look after him."

"You're well out of it, John—stay at home and mind your pretty wife."

"He's doing his bit . . ."

"And she too—this bread is delicious."

I was happy to "do my bit." As well as supporting my husband, I was carving out an identity for myself, proving that I was a generous, warmhearted woman of the people and a Fenian—the complete opposite of my parents. These strange men filled our house with life, and gave me a sense of purpose. I liked having them about, knowing that they were impressed by me and all of them thinking how lucky John was to have me. I knew we were running a safe house for fugitives, a serious offense and one for which we could be shot, but I trusted that John would keep us safe, and in some part of me I relished the adventure of it.

It was only after a few weeks, when I began to see that our supplies of food and turf were running low, that I started to worry. We had become too caught up in feeding other people, and barely had enough left to feed ourselves.

I tackled John over it one morning after a frugal breakfast of oatmeal and water sweetened with the last scrapings from our honey pot. I washed it out with a teaspoon of water from the kettle so as to extract every morsel: it would be the last sweet thing we would taste for a long time. "We're running very low on food, John. We need to start cutting back on visitors and looking after ourselves."

"We can't turn them away, Ellie. We have to do our bit." He took a mouthful of tea and looked away from me out of the window, pretending to check the sky for rain, when he was only in the door. Suddenly I realized that John had made promises that were nothing to do with me. This was why he had been so keen for us to move back into his parents' house—not because he had wanted to live out our dream of rural bliss, but so that he could continue to "do his bit," looking after his fighting friends in our hidden-away cottage. It was no accident that these men had started "turning up," looking for our help. It had been arranged, in secret, behind my back. I felt betrayed and angry.

"I'll go into town today and look for work," he said, resting his mug on the table and standing up to leave.

"I won't starve, John, not for Ireland—not for anyone." It came out sharply, more sharply than I had intended, yet I was glad it was out.

"What do you mean?"

I straightened my apron and drew in my breath. "I hate the British as much as the next person, but not at the price of our own livelihood. We've done our bit, but we can't afford to go on feeding your rebel friends, John. They are going to have to find some other house to hide in." There. I had said it. Put my foot down as maybe I ought to have done before.

John's face darkened and he said quietly, "I left my war because I loved you more than I loved my country."

John went into town that day and he came back alone. The men stopped calling to our house after that. I don't know if it was

John who stopped them or if they had just left the area, and I never asked.

He got no work that day, and we had no money and no food left to see us through the winter. Poverty was the war we fought from then on.

Luck kept escaping out of our house: one of our hens got killed by a fox and the other two stopped laying; our cow fell sick and died. It rained, and rained, and rained so hard that winter that nothing grew and water came down our chimney and made our small fire hiss and smoke. We went to bed early and rose late, clinging to each other's body under the blankets, our skin sticky with lovemaking, glued together and afraid of what might happen if we let go. Afraid that one might be blaming the other, afraid to make plans for the next meal, the next fire. Afraid of the future because of what it might hold. Each day we became more and more tainted by our failure; I stopped cleaning the house, John stopped walking into town to look for work. We hardly spoke for fear one of us might name the truth.

Early each Sunday morning we walked the pitch-black roads to Maidy and Paud's house. When they came home from Mass, we were there, waiting at their door. I was afraid to go to Mass myself for fear of meeting my parents. I did not want them to see me looking down-at-heel—I had become prideful, as well as godless and poor. Maidy and Paud fed us and for a while pretended they saw nothing wrong. But one Sunday, Maidy let out a small cry as John, gaunt as he was becoming, buried himself into the leg of a chicken as if it were his first. "Dear God, John—won't you move, the two of you, back in here? At least until the spring?"

John wouldn't hear of it. Maidy and Paud had little enough of their own without the strain of looking after us. "Nonsense, Mam—we're managing fine. Aren't we, Ellie?"

I nodded demurely and moved my legs closer to the fire in the hope that I could carry some of the heat home with me. I would have moved in with them in an instant, but I didn't have anything left to fight John with. I felt I had failed him, making him marry me as I had. If we were poor now, it was my fault. We should have waited. In darker moments, on a Saturday night, when the frugal supplies Maidy had sneaked into my bag the week before had long gone, and my stomach yawned raw with hunger, I thought perhaps I should have left John to his fighting and stayed in the convent. We were hungry and cold and tired, and I was running out of hope. Yet at night, wrapping my arms round John's chest until our ribs locked, I would know that no matter what hardships we had to suffer, we were meant to suffer them together.

In the end, Maidy persuaded John that we should at least stay with her and Paud for the whole week of Christmas. After the festive dinner, we gathered, full bellied and laughing about the fire. I sat opening Christmas letters from my old school friends. My father had forwarded them to the Hogans'—a sign that my parents were softening toward me, perhaps. There were special cards from Maeve and Sister Stephanie. Maeve's missive was dramatic and hysterical with love; Sister Stephanie's disappointed, but warm. Then there was a letter on strange, tissuey paper I did not recognize. I unfolded it, and gasped in surprised delight as four bright cerise feathers fluttered out into my lap. They were as vibrantly colored as I imagined fairy wings to be. The address at the top of the letter was in New York. Sheila!

My darling Ellie,
    New York is the most beautiful place—you can't imagine. I am working for a rich woman as a lady's maid and

life is good excepting for that I miss my family. Things
didn't work out as good when we arrived in America. My
father's job fell through and my brothers started boxing. My
father was threatening to send me home to Ireland to marry
old Padraig Rooney, so I ran away. Mrs. Adams gave me
a job when I answered an advertisement in the paper and
she said she liked my face. She is decent and kind and pays
me $10 a week. When I told her what had happened to me,
she was scandalized and said as she needed another maid,
she would send a ticket home to any girl I knew who might
have the same plight. I told her your name. I know it was
wrong and that you might be married to John by now, but
in any case you could come for a year and earn a fortune to
send home. You can send a telegram to the address above,
and I will gather all of the information you need to get
here. I miss you and am longing to see you and hear news
from home and of Jesus and Mary Convent.

All my love, Sheila

PS: I thought you might sew these feathers to a hat. They
fell from the hem of one of Isobel's dresses—she has so
many you couldn't count!

With a cry of delight, I pushed the letter into John's hands.
"It's from Sheila in New York! We could both go! Maybe this is
the answer to all our worries!"

I hoped he would be as excited as I was, but as he read, his
mouth grew tight and he handed the letter back to me without
saying anything. I remembered then, too late, how John had answered me when I told him about Sheila's father taking his family
to America to keep his son from the struggle. "They should have
stayed and stood their ground," he said. "They should have been

proud of their son wanting to stay and fight." In John's mind, people leaving Ireland for a better life elsewhere were unpatriotic.

I was furious with myself for having pushed Sheila's letter on him so suddenly, when I ought to have held back and introduced the idea to him with more finesse, more subtlety—biding my time.

"What's that about?" Maidy asked, curious.

"I've been offered a job in America, in New York, as housemaid to a wealthy woman." I smiled and shrugged, as if it was of no importance.

"Oh no," said Maidy, shaking her head. "There's no need for anyone to go chasing off to America. You'll manage grand here." Her voice was trembling now. "We'll all help each other—won't we, Paud? What would they want to go to America for?"

Paud said nothing, only picked up the fire poker and stabbed at the turf until a puff of smoke and sparks got sucked up the vast chimney. The answer was one word, unspoken and yet always there. "Money": a short, ugly word that emptied itself all over the question.

John got up and went outside. I followed him. He was at the gable end of the house with his back to the wind, lighting a cigarette.

"What's the matter? Why are you angry?" I said. "It's worth us considering, surely?"

He exhaled, and the wind snatched the smoke sideways. "I've done this to you," he said. "I've not made the good life that you deserve here. That's why you want to go to America."

I hated to hear him talk in such a way. My strong, spirited John—poverty had made him doubt himself. This was what I wanted us to get away from. "I don't want to go to America, John. I just think we should consider it. Give ourselves the chance to build a better life. We could make some money and—"

He cut me off. "It's all about money with you."

I was hurt that he was accusing me of such heartlessness, but also angry that he couldn't see that, right there and then, there was nothing more important to our lives than money—or, rather, our lack of it. "We have to survive."

"There is more to life than money, Ellie."

"Like loyalty, John—and love? Have I ever denied you either? Go on—say it out loud—do you think I care more for money than I do for you?"

He threw his cigarette onto the ground and crushed it under his boot. "No, Ellie, I don't."

I sensed he had wanted to fight, but had suddenly lost the will. I threw my arms round his neck and said, "I love you, John—more than anything else—more than all the money in the world." His arms were weak around my waist, his hold loose. I kissed him, with the reassuring affection of a mother more than the longing of a wife. "Let's go back inside—I'm frozen."

"Go on," he said, "I'll follow you." As I turned, he bent and rescued the half-smoked cigarette butt from the ground, studying the shreds of tobacco in his palm before dropping them into his pocket.

Chapter Fifteen

In the January following that Christmas, our lives changed forever.

The British government opened its prisons and sent over troops of violent thugs to quash our revolution. We called them the Black and Tans, because of the color of their uniforms.

I was in town the day they arrived. I had cycled in to do my messages. Maidy and Paud had given us five more laying hens for Christmas, and I had two dozen eggs in a basket to barter with or sell. Dear Maidy had also given me an old coat of her own; I had nipped it in at the waist, shortened it to my calf and sewn on a green tweed collar and cuffs torn from an old coat of John's. I thought I was all style, and was looking forward to showing myself off.

The hill down to the main-street shops was steep, and I got off my bicycle at the top and started to walk, carefully holding a cloth over the eggs to protect them from the bounce of the rough road. The low whitewashed cottages on the outskirts of the town gave way to the two-story buildings of the merchant class, with the grand spire of the Protestant church presiding over them. I was just thinking how I would wrap the eggs up better next time, when a group of men, about eight of them, came out of the police barracks—a gray, imposing building a few doors down from the church. They were not policemen, and they were wearing uniforms that were not of the British army. They had jaunty little caps with bobbles on them that made them appear almost local, and they were carrying rifles. It crossed my mind that our own lads might have got themselves uniforms. They stopped outside Doherty's pub, then two of them went in, leaving the others standing around outside. Almost immediately four town lads come out with their hands above their heads. They were Tommy Condon—Kathleen's older brother, who was something of a simpleton; Padraig Phelan, a pleasant schoolteacher and a friend to John; the new curate, a nervous-looking man who had on a scarf covering his collar; and Cahill Murphy, a freckle-faced, cheeky lad whom I remembered as a small boy in school, and who couldn't have been more than fifteen. A uniformed man was prodding Cahill Murphy with his rifle and screaming in a Scottish accent, "Move—you fucking Irish scum!"

The sound of his shouts made my insides tumble, and yet I was drawn closer to them. I propped my bicycle against a wall. There had obviously been some kind of mistake. As I approached, several other women of the town joined me, among them Mary Murphy, Cahill's mother—a fierce, substantial woman who would tan his hide surely for getting caught in the pub at his age. She walked straight over to the group, and said, "I'll handle this."

As she pushed through them, one of the men turned and knocked her, hard, to the ground. I thought maybe it had been an accident, and ran forward to help her up. Yet another man held Mary down with his foot on her chest, and said, "The whore probably has a gun on her. Take her inside and search her." As Mary struggled to escape like a trapped dog, the young soldier ground his foot into her abdomen until she stopped. I had not thought it would be possible to silence Mary Murphy, and her humiliation was terrible to witness. A crowd was beginning to gather, and she carefully curled her body into a ball and held her hands up to her face. Cahill's insolent expression had crumbled into confusion. Tommy Condon was crying.

"Let her up!" a man shouted from the back of the crowd.

Another called, "Let her go, man!"

Nobody moved forward because the men had their guns trained on us. The anger and fear emanating from them were palpable; the air around them fizzed with danger. It felt as if there was no reason in them, or sense. I was terrified, not just for myself, but for what they might do to Mary when they got her inside, so I spoke out. "I'll come in with you, Mary," I said.

The one in charge, a short, thickset man of no more than forty, nodded at the young soldier to release the poor woman. As I helped Mary up, she clutched her stomach and yelped in pain. Cahill cried out, "Mammy!" but the soldier behind him whacked him across the head with the butt of his rifle and sent him tumbling to his knees. By this time, the whole village had gathered. We all called out "No!" in unison, and some of the crowd pushed forward.

"Get back, get back, you Irish fuckers!" the soldiers shouted, as if they were being attacked. Then, clearly thinking better of conducting their business in the street, they marched the four young lads across into the barracks, training their guns on the boys' backs and also at the crowd, as they shouted at everyone to back off. "It's all right now, everyone," the new curate called back to us, his voice high-pitched in terror. "Just a misunderstanding, e-everyone go on home and about your business now . . ."

In the confusion, the soldiers left Mary behind. I persuaded her not to follow her son over to the barracks. "There's no sense making it worse, Mary. He'll be out in an hour when they realize he's only a young lad."

"He was in the pub," she said, "and he's only fifteen. I've told him a thousand times he's not to go near the pub. He'll get us all in trouble . . ." Mary's two brothers came to take her from me. I handed the elder one her shawl and they wrapped it gently around their shattered sister's head, guiding her hands up to her chin that she might hold it in place. As I watched the two men take her off down the road, I still was not sure exactly what I had witnessed.

The following day it was Maidy who came to tell me that Cahill Murphy had been beaten to death in the police barracks. "He'll be out in an hour," I had said to his mother. Standing in my kitchen, dry-eyed with disbelief at that innocent boy's death—that was the moment my war began.

That night, Padraig Phelan came to our house and asked John to captain a unit. "We need you," Padraig said. He reached under his long coat and pulled out a rifle. John took it and, across the safety of our hearth, he looked for my permission. He was tall and broad, his waistcoat stretched across his ribs, his white shirtsleeves rolled to the elbow. The gun sat across his chest as natural as a woman cradling a baby. He was born to fight. I didn't want my husband in danger, but a child had been murdered. I took the gun from John, kissed the cold gray steel of its barrel and handed it back to him. "You'll stay for dinner, Padraig," I said.

Later that evening, I sent John outside to fetch some turf and while he was gone I turned to Padraig. "I'm happy to do my part as well, Padraig, but feeding you all before left us nothing for the winter." John came back into the room before Padraig could answer me, but I held Padraig's eye as he rubbed his mouth and chin with his long, gentleman schoolteacher fingers, then finally gave me a small, serious nod. I knew John would be angry if he ever discovered I had put a proviso on our loyalty, but we'd be no use to anyone if we were hungry.

In bed that night, I could not sleep. The moon glared through the window, casting a gray pallor over my sleeping husband's face—it was a cold light, the color of death. I reached across and touched the broad softness of his mouth with my fingertips, then held the back of my hand to his cheek. His skin was warm and the fact of his aliveness leapt through me, and I had to take my hand away and bring it to my mouth to suppress a sob.

Padraig helped us out. He lent us a few cows and sent his nephew—a skinny, pasty boy called Liam—to help me care for them, allowing John to captain his unit full time. For the next three months my husband left the house early in the morning and came back late at night. I did not ask where he was going when he left, or what he had done when he came home. I spent my days working in the house with only young Liam for company. Mid-morning I would call the boy in for a breakfast of bread and milk, and as the days passed his embarrassed silence gave way to easy chat. All Liam wanted to talk about was war—who had got shot, who was in what unit, what the Black and Tans had done to this one and that one. Shootings, death, injury: every day I was subjected to the bravado of a teenage boy anxious to brandish a gun, until I banned all talk of war in my house.

Every night I fed the men whom John brought back to shelter, and treated their cuts and bound any ankle swollen after a fall. His unit was training out in the rough bogs—crawling on the sodden ground like animals, if their boots and coats were anything to go by. Each man left his boots at the door for Liam to clean, then washed his hands in a tin bucket before coming into the house. Each had with him his own tin plate, which I piled with hearty stews full of old, rich meat and earthy vegetables. I never saw a gun again after that first night. John had the men leave their weapons in the sheds, and they followed his lead by never discussing matters of war in front of me. I was proud that these men respected John, and deferred to him. Some of the younger boys called him "Captain." On one occasion, when I was out of the room, I heard John talk down a young hothead keen on revenge. "It's as important to know when to lay down a weapon as when to pick it up" was all he said. I hoped it ran true to him, because despite the pride of being married to such a big man, I was afraid for John every moment of every day. I held on to the thought that the Irish Parliament, Dáil Éireann, and the British would come to an arrangement before too long, and life would return to the way it had always been.

John tried to keep my fears away—always saying, as we kissed in the mornings, "See you later—the usual time," to reassure me that he would be home safe. But in my heart, I knew that one day soon the training of his unit would end and the fighting would start.

There were so many coming through the house by now—thirty laid out on our kitchen floor one night—that our neighbors started calling in with food and turf to help us out. "I'm too old to fight," said one old man as he handed me an enormous ham, "but there's hair on that pig will help keep them English bastards at bay surely."

One fine Thursday not long after, I was sitting plucking a chicken by the back door. John had killed and bled it from the neck before he left that morning, so its skin was still warm enough to pluck easily. The sun was moving across the wet grass, causing spangles of light to shoot up from it so that I had to shade my eyes. It was a pure, clear day, and the land spread out in front of me, sloping out and down toward the horizon. The sky was blue and the clouds white and the world looked perfect, like a picture postcard.

I had sent Liam into town on the bicycle with some eggs not an hour beforehand and was enjoying the peace of being on my own. Even though the day was fine, there was a slight breeze, and as I plucked the feathers started to scatter all over the place. They flew all about my face, sticking to my lips and hair, and I became annoyed with myself for not having had the sense to hang the chicken until it was cold, then immerse it in warm water before plucking, as was my usual method. With the feathers damp, it gave a much tidier finish. As I made this mental note, Liam came running suddenly round from the front of the house, causing me to jump up and drop the cursed chicken, with all its feathers flying in a messy cloud.

I was raging. The stupid child had clearly run my bicycle into a ditch and broken a week's worth of fine eggs. "Where's my bicycle? Where are my eggs?" The ludaramaun—and I was the worse eejit, to have trusted such an important mission to him.

Liam had collapsed in a heap of panic and exhaustion, breathing so hard he could barely speak. Between gasps, he pushed out, "Captain's been shot, Ma'am. Captain's been shot . . ."

The world changed. My head was full of terrible noise, and yet somewhere at the center of me was that calm, cold place where I had known all along this was going to happen. From the moment John had told me about the dying boy, on the first day we had kissed, I had feared losing him. The waiting was over—the worst had happened. It was almost a relief. "Where is he, Liam?"

Liam was panting and pawing the air with exhaustion.

"Where is he?" I grabbed the stupid boy by his collar.

"Up beyond Pat Sweeney's bog . . ."

"Show me!" I pulled him up on his feet and thrust him, stumbling, along in front of me. At the road, he pointed across Sweeney's fields. "Go for the doctor!" I screamed at him, then lifted my skirts and scrambled across the ditch, into the open field, and ran faster than I had ever run in my life. I ran through two fields and would have run a dozen more when I saw two men coming rapidly toward me down the slope. It was Padraig and three other lads, and they were carrying a body with them.

As soon as he saw me, Padraig started shouting, "Go back, Ellie, get back to the house! Get a bed ready! Go back, go back!"

But I flew on, tripping over my petticoats. "John! John!" I ran beside the men screaming his name. He was unconscious, silent, swinging limply between them. From the waist down his body glistened black in the bright sun, dripping blood. Then I knew Padraig was right—there was nothing I could do here. I had to make things ready in the house. I raced back home ahead of their procession.

I covered the bed with our cleanest, crispest sheet, and when they brought him in I had them lay him down. The cotton turned red in an instant. They all stood around, caps in their hands, shocked, white faced, like around a coffin. I wanted to howl at Padraig, "This is all your fault!" Instead, I ordered them from the room to lay a fire, to boil water, to watch for the doctor. The wound in my husband's side was a mess of pumping blood. I ripped the skirts from my one good dress, which was hanging on the back of the bedroom door; I thrust the material into the wound and pressed tight. "John, John—wake up!" Maybe he was better unconscious, out of pain, but I feared he was falling into the sleep that comes before death.

Suddenly Doctor Bourke was beside me. "Here's a nasty

business, Ellie." The familiar understatement of our family doctor's voice sucked relief out of me, and despite my best efforts to restrain myself, tears started pouring down my cheeks. As the doctor removed the wadding I had made with my skirt and checked the wound, John's eyes flashed open with the shock of pain. Doctor Bourke said to me, "This won't be nice, Ellie. I have to get that shot out. You can go into the kitchen, I can manage this."

"No. I'll stay and help." I put my arm round the back of John's head and held him as firmly as I could. As the doctor prepared his instruments, I talked and talked to my husband— whatever came into my head poured out of my mouth in a stream of stupid, cheery words. "Do you remember the day I wore the trousers and climbed that tree?"

"You were the talk of the village, Ellie," Doctor Bourke joined in. "A living disgrace." But his voice was detached as he concentrated on the job in hand. "Mind yourself now, John . . . get yourself ready . . . here, Ellie . . ." He handed me an ether-soaked pad. When he parted the wound, John jerked bolt upright in the bed and shouted out in pain. I pushed him back down gently and held the ether to his face, and carried on talking, talking. I mimicked the nonsense of the local gossips.

"I saw Peggy Geraghty in town yesterday in a new blue coat and carrying a brace of pheasant—that husband of hers is surely a poacher . . ."

"Oh, for the love of God," John cried out and shook his head and grimaced a kind of smile at me, so that I didn't know if he was cursing the pain or the inanity of my chatter—so I kissed his face and stroked his hair, and kept talking on until Doctor Bourke had strapped and bandaged his hip and leg and waist, and John had sunk back into a haze of etherized sleep.

"Now, Ellie," said the doctor, wiping his face on his sleeve.

"I think we both deserve a cup of tea." I ran out to the kitchen to make it for him. Padraig and the others clamored for news of their captain, but Doctor Bourke came to the doorway of the bedroom and dismissed them. "I'm sure Ellie will be happy for you to call again tomorrow," he said. As soon as they were gone, he said to me, "Never mind the tea." I poured him a whisky instead. He knocked it back, but shook his head when I raised the bottle to offer him another. "I've done my best to set him up, Ellie. But the hip is shattered and only time will tell if it heals. I'm no expert, but I've done all I can."

Maidy and Paud wanted us to move back in with them at once, but for the first few weeks it was impossible to move John without causing him pain. As my husband lay in bed, slowly healing, I struggled to manage the farm and the house chores on my own. Young Liam was gone, signed up full time to the IRA. Padraig called to the house with offers of financial help, but John would not take anything from him. He would not take anything from anyone, now that he could not fight. He even made Padraig take back his cows.

His injury changed him. He was irritable and irrational. He hated that his fight had been cut short. He felt abandoned by his unit and mollycoddled by his wife. After the first month, he kept trying to get out of bed and walk. He became angry when he fell, and angrier still when I admonished him for trying. Once he shouted back at me, "This is my house, woman—leave me alone!"

I was helpless to make things better. Every time I reached for him, he moved farther away, until I found myself working alone in spirit as well as body. At night I would lie beside his broken body and watch the last glowing embers from the fire, knowing that a bedroom fire was an extravagance we could not afford, but building it anyway to try and restore some warmth into our marriage.

After six weeks I had cooked the best of our hens to keep up my husband's strength, and the foxes had taken the one remaining. Our grain and turf and hope had all run out. Ignoring John's angry objections, I locked up the house and Paud came to collect us.

Chapter Sixteen

Maidy set John up on the settle-bed in the kitchen and he lay all day by the fire. She gave him potatoes to peel in a bowl and peas to shell. She was able to boss my husband about and placate him in a way I could not, and being closer to the town meant that he had more visitors. Padraig called often and kept him up to date with news of politics and ambushes. So John's mood improved, but his body did not. His flesh had healed, and the pain was almost gone, but even after six weeks he still could not walk. He tried every day, but whenever he went to stand up he fell back.

Doctor Bourke examined him and his expression was serious as he took Maidy and me aside. "John's hip is not set right," he said, his eyes on the floor.

"What does that mean?" I asked.

He looked back up at me and said, "I can't be sure, but there's a possibility that he won't be able to use that leg again."

Maidy took it in her stride. "Sure, we'll say nothing to him yet, but wait and see."

I was reeling. "Do you mean he might never walk again?"

"It's hard for me to tell, Ellie," he said, "I'm not a specialist in this type of injury."

"Is that a 'yes'? Do you know?"

"Ellie!" Maidy said.

"No, no—you're all right," he said, gently patting Maidy aside. "It's a specialist he needs. There's a consultant I know of in Dublin, Ellie, but . . ." He stopped and sucked his teeth.

"He costs money," I said.

"Yes," he replied.

It always came down to money.

"How much?" I asked.

Maidy began fussing and clattering about the place. She was furious with me for speaking out of turn. Talking about money, under virtually any circumstances, was considered the height of rudeness—especially in front of those few people who had it, like doctors and priests. In our lives, transactions were agreed in a series of coded nods and winks. In the market, men passed their money to and fro in closed fists. Acts of charity were dressed as trade-offs. If a local big shot wanted to help a poor neighbor, he would call to the house and ask for some favor: a daughter to come and clean or mind the children. Then the neighbor's problem—be it paying a landlord or acquiring a few bags of grain to get them through the winter—would be duly sorted without money, or even talk of it, being exchanged. Doctor Bourke was notoriously charitable, and Maidy feared he might think I was begging for help.

But all Doctor Bourke said was: "These people are not ordinary doctors, Ellie. To get an operation like that in Dublin would cost in the region of one hundred pounds."

Maidy dropped a cup—and made a tremendous fuss about it.

Over supper that evening I tried to force the three of them—Maidy, Paud and John—to discuss how we might raise the money. They would not even talk about it. Paud left the house on some imagined mission; Maidy stood up from the table and began her furious tidying again. I knew them well enough: they felt guilty they did not have the money saved. John was so furious when I suggested approaching Padraig for "compensation" that I gave up trying to reason with any of them.

Late that night I took Sheila's letter out of the dresser drawer and reread it. Ten dollars a week. I could earn enough money to pay for John's operation in just ten weeks in America—twenty at the most, given paying back my fare and whatever small expenses I might incur while I was living there. If I sacrificed a year of my life, there would be more besides, to set us up here for life with a bigger farm and the house all neat and perfect for us to start a family, so that neither of us would ever be in this position again.

I did not sleep that night, rolling the possibility of it over and over in my mind. The more I thought about it, the more it seemed that going to America was the right thing, the only thing, to do. People did it all the time. John had Maidy and Paud here to look after him, and I could be back before he was up walking again, and even go to Dublin for the operation with him.

I knew there was no point in discussing it. John would fight me every step of the way and persuade Maidy to talking me round into staying. So while they were all still asleep I got up again, hurriedly wrote a letter to Sheila accepting her offer and cycled into the post office at first light to post it.

Two weeks later I got a letter back.

I am beyond happy that you are coming. You will love it here, Ellie, we will have such adventures and gather such treasures, my darling, darling friend.

With the letter was another envelope, bearing the White Star Line logo, a red flag and star. I recognized the design from newspaper reports on the sinking of the *Titanic*. I stood up from the kitchen table and walked over to the settle, and I handed the letter and ticket to John. At first he was shocked and disbelieving. "What's this?" he said. "Who is it for?"

"It's for me," I said. "I'm going to work with Sheila in America. It's the only way we can raise the money for your operation."

He threw the ticket at the fire, missing by inches, then tried to get up from the bed and finish the job. He threatened and cursed, but presently wept and pleaded with me. "Don't go, Ellie, don't do this."

"I am doing this for you," I said.

"Don't say that, Ellie," he said. "Don't try to tell me you're not just running away."

I stared, shocked, for a moment made speechless by his accusation. "I have never," I said at last, and as the words started to come out, anger rose up through me, "run away from *anything* in my life. Not when you moved us into that cursed hovel of a house, and not when you joined the stupid IRA, John Hogan . . ." Furious now, John tried to get to his feet. "Go on then!" I screamed. "Get up! You see? You can't! That's why I am going to America!"

"Hey, hey, hey . . ." Maidy walked in on us. "What's all this?" Seeing John flailing to rise, she helped him from the bed to a chair at the table, then sat down beside him herself.

"America," I said quickly, sitting down on her other side, anxious to win her over. "I'm going there to earn money for John's operation."

"She's not going," John said, tight-lipped and shaking his head, "and that's final."

"Is this true?" Maidy asked, looking directly into my face. She seemed neither disapproving nor approving.

"Sheila has sent the ticket," I said, clutching it safely to my apron. "It's all organized."

"She's my wife. She can't go to America without my permission. She's making a cripple out of me . . ."

"You made a cripple out of yourself!"

"Hush now, the pair of you."

Afraid to look at each other, John and I both looked at Maidy. She studied both our faces, and after a few moments she said, "John, you'd be well advised never to cross a woman as stubborn as this one when she has her mind made up. And, Ellie, you should have told us before now but . . . well, what's done is done." And she patted us both on the legs and got up to go about her business.

Before I could move, John reached across her empty chair for my hand. "Don't go," he said. "Please don't go. It doesn't matter about the money, Ellie—I'll get back on my feet again soon, I promise. I can feel it. Please. We'll manage."

I folded both of my hands around his one. I remembered the boy who came to my mother's door, with his eggs and his flowers. Tears came to my eyes. I said, "You tried to rescue me once, John. Now you have to let me do the same for you."

With the ticket Sheila had enclosed all of the information that I needed to get my paperwork in order, including instructions on procuring my passport in Queenstown and a money order for forty dollars, the minimum amount needed to get into the country, with firm instructions to bring it back to her intact.

Maidy contacted my parents and told them I was going. Part of her hoped, I know, that they would make their peace and send us money. But my father simply had a car sent round with my case and the last of my possessions—my rosary beads, prayer book and good Sunday coat. I did not know whether the gesture was intended as a good-riddance rebuttal or a generous act of grace, but I was too desperate for it to matter anymore.

The night before I left, the warmth that had been missing from our marriage since John's injury surged back in an urgent flood of words and affection. We talked about our future and what John would do while I was away. It would be a year, no more than that, no more than twelve short months. We were agreed. John would have the operation and get back on his feet. Then he'd get proper, paid work and I would come back from America with a big bag of money. We said everything we had not said in the weeks before, quickly inventing hopes and dreams to distract us from the terror of saying good-bye. We painted a picture of how our home would be—whitewashed with curtains and bedcovers, decorated with dainty crockery and full of food. John would slate the roof and buy the furniture that he did not have the skill to make, and a mattress and an iron bed frame, and a shiny new kettle. We would get a horse, and a plow, and a cart while we were at it. There were great times ahead, we agreed—mighty times. We talked about building a corn store, a henhouse. Then he let me make love to him. We lay for the longest time, my head resting on his chest, his warm hands covering my head as I held my cheek to his heart and listened to him breathing, knowing this would be our last night together for a long, long time.

"One year, Ellie Hogan," he said. "Just one year is all." They were his last words before we fell asleep and again, the following morning, when we said our final good-byes. "One year, Ellie Hogan—just one year is all you'll be gone." I leaned and sank my face into the shoulder of John's woollen sweater, and swallowed my tears so hard that the lump felt like a stone dropping down into my chest.

I asked to be taken to the train by Paud alone. I could not bear the drawn-out pain of saying good-bye, and Paud's quiet nature suited me. As the train pulled out of the station, I gazed out of the window and watched the world turn into snippets, fields and rivers and rocks giving themselves over to hills and cattle in an instant. Only the sky remained constant.

I arrived at Queenstown station in the mid-afternoon. It was buzzing with people. There were cases and trunks piled up everywhere. The ornate iron brackets of the station roof were painted a dark bottle-green, the glass ceiling splattered with the debris of seagulls. I stared at the tiny red bricks of the wall, and the stone flags worn with the soles of a million passengers. A flash of colored feathers through the window of the first-class waiting room caused a flicker of excitement in my chest, as I remembered the feathers Sheila had sent me and where I was going.

Outside the station a group of men were playing cards using a trunk as a makeshift table; a small band of musicians had started playing and a gang of children danced around them. A drunkard tried to drown them out with his own song, and others stood around laughing as an old woman berated him. I became aware that I was not merely an observer, a visitor to this scene, but a part of it. The *Celtic* ocean liner would dock here from Liverpool tomorrow and I would be leaving on it for New York with all of these people. The color and music and bustle were the beginning of my adventure. I was doing this for John, but the journey would be mine alone.

I stopped at a booth where they were selling day trips to Youghal for three shillings and asked the attendant to direct me to the American Consulate, where I lined up for three hours to present my papers and get my passport. Then I walked along the quay to the Commodore Hotel, where Doctor Bourke had secured me a room overnight.

The Commodore was grander than anywhere I had ever been, with dark red carpets that my boots sank into like soft bog. I was grateful to be wearing my Sunday coat. I handed in the letter the doctor had given me to the uniformed lady behind the reception desk. She handed me a key with a heavy brass key ring, and as I took it I thought with shame that I had not thanked Doctor Bourke sufficiently for all he had done for us, and for his kind friendship. He had never presented us with a bill for the attention he had given John, and this hotel stay was a parting gift from him. In the room, I drew across the heavy silk curtains and lay in silence on the bed. My skin felt cold and nervous of the starched linen sheets. I tried to sleep for a while, but kept flinching awake as if I were afraid to dream.

Early that evening, I walked up a steep hill with houses lined along one side like a deck of cards. At the top was a cathedral and I went inside to light a candle. The candle box was empty and every candelabra lit, flames burning already for the hundreds heading off the next day. Outside I stood against some railings and looked down at the harbor and across the bay. The buildings of Spike Island prison made a sharp outline against the gray water, which stretched as far as the eye could see in endless, endless ocean. My breath caught in my throat, as I realized that I was going out there in the morning. "I'm a little afraid." I said it out loud, as if John were there.

"You'll be all right," I thought I heard him answer—but it was only the wind from the sea.

I did not check my bag through, but carried it onto the boat with me. I had so little. I stood in line and had my clothes inspected for cleanliness and waited while they shone an electrical light into my eyes to check it for cataracts. I presented my papers and answered their questions: Was I married? What was my last address? The man asked: Could I read and write, and had I good mental health?

Then I boarded the *Killarney*, a small tender boat that took us out to the ship. As we pulled up alongside RMS *Celtic*, the side of it rose up in front of us like a monstrous wall, seeming so high and so broad that one could imagine it was holding the entire ocean at bay.

One hour later, I was on the third-class boat deck facing out to sea as the vast ship pushed through the water. Surrounded by strangers, I felt as I had on that first day at the Jesus and Mary Convent, facing the unknown—alone, but with no desire for company. The wind whipped tendrils of hair around my face, slashing them against my skin where they stuck, salty with sea spray. Most of the passengers had crowded to the stern of the boat, waving good-bye, peering at the diminishing port, searching for their loved ones in the shrinking crowd—all the wailing wives, the distraught children. I looked ahead and wondered what kind of a place I would be coming to. The ocean seemed too vast, as big as the world itself, and yet here I was, riding across it to another land. The adventure of it struck me as a swell that rose up from my feet and through the pit of my stomach. The waves were watery hills. I looked again to the back of the boat. As the sea sucked us forward, the land grew smaller and smaller. I realized that soon Ireland would be not where I lived, but a memory.

I was on my way to America.

PART TWO

AMERICA
1920–24

Chapter Seventeen

The boat reminded me of school, in that I was sharing a cabin with three other girls—two sisters, Joan and Anne, from Cork, and a girl from London, called Ethel. The sisters had brothers working in Boston and they were going over to work with them there, in a food-tinning factory where one of them had risen to the position of floor manager.

"We're going to send for the others as soon as we can," said Anne, the elder of the two. She told us each one by name and age, babbling excitedly, her hands waving about her face, all friendly freckles and rotten teeth. Joan sat stuck to her sister's side, looking doleful. Her eyes were cloudy and worn like an old woman's, occasionally burning bright with flashes of fear. There were thirteen of them altogether, nine back at home with the parents and an aging grandmother, surviving on posted dollars. "Soon we'll be all together again—in America!" Anne said.

"That ain't never going to 'appen," Ethel said. "Thirteen of you? You're 'aving a laugh—don't you Irish never give it a rest?" Ethel spoke like a cockney Black and Tan. I had heard John mimic them, mocking their harsh accents and saying words like "ain'tcha." He would complain, "They can't even speak their own language properly and they won't let us speak ours."

How Now Brown Cow. We had had elocution lessons in the convent to teach us how to enunciate our vowels properly and speak English like young ladies. Ethel was not a young lady, but I didn't mind. She looked like fun. She had a chubby figure and her fat feet were squeezed into tiny, high-heeled shoes. She wore a fitted maroon coat and stockings that she tugged at as if they were too tight. Her lips were painted with a slash of red and her cheeks were garishly rouged. I guessed that she would be full of stories and anticipated the entertainment of hearing them, in just looking at her exotic getup. I was hungry for distraction and could tell from the Cork sisters' shabby clothes that their story was the same as mine. Desolate rural Ireland. Rain. Hunger. Hardship. Sadness. War. I felt sorry for them, but had also had my fill of poverty. I hoped the RMS *Celtic* might give me a taste of putting it behind me.

Our cabin was tiny, but it was clean and there was an air of luxury about the dark wood presses and paneling. There was a washbasin at the center of it, and a small cabinet above that with a mirror as a door. On either side of that were four beds, called "bunks," one piled on top of the other and made from what looked like large pipes. Each had a new cotton sheet stretched across a soft mattress, a down pillow and a blanket with "RMS Celtic" embroidered onto it.

"Toilets is da-an the hall, I seen them on the way in. There's a baarf in there an' all. I'm gonna 'ave a right soakin' later, so you lot can get to the end of the queue."

The Cork sisters laughed. They did not have the faintest idea what Ethel was saying. I laughed with them and briefly longed to share the joke with John, but when I called his face to mind, I became paralyzed. I tricked myself into thinking of Paud instead.

Paud had taken my traveling to America particularly badly.

His brother had died on an emigrant ship to America as a young man, and he was sure I would be traveling in terrible conditions. Ireland's history of famine coffin ships and horror stories of below-deck steerage class had kept many of his generation at home. Maidy had made thorough investigations and learned that the RMS *Celtic* had been newly reconditioned after it was torpedoed in the Irish Sea by the Germans in 1918. In January of that year she had resumed the Liverpool to New York service and was considered one of the grandest ships in the world. Maidy had told Paud, "One thousand third-class passengers it can carry, and Fionoulla Nolan's sister Nuala traveled to New York in five days and said it was like a luxury hotel." "How would she know?" Paud had asked angrily. "It was far from luxury she was reared." And nothing Maidy said could persuade him things had changed. I wished he was there at this moment to see that Nuala Nolan had been telling the truth.

"I'm bloody starvin'—let's go and find some food," said Ethel. "Hang on . . ."

She took a lipstick from a tiny bag decorated with pearl buttons and sliced it across her lips without even looking in a mirror, puckering them together and spreading the red stain in an angry blur. Then she unbuttoned the top two buttons of her coat, pulled up each breast with a pronounced guff, before lighting a cigarette, which she let hang from her lips. As she marched out of our cabin and down the corridor, we three Irish paupers scuttled after her like Pied Piper children.

The third-class dining room was enormous—rows of long tables were dressed with spotless linen and set with cutlery. At the back of the room, counters were set against the wall with lines of shiny soup terrines, piles of bowls and plates and long metal dishes with lids. Some people were sitting and eating, others standing at the counters, as young, uniformed men opened and closed the lids of the metal serving trays. I thought the whole setup very elegant. I felt for my coat buttons, wishing that I were better dressed beneath it, then I turned and saw the look on the Cork sisters' faces: openmouthed, overawed by it all. Joan looked at her older sister as if she wanted to turn and run. Anne seemed at a loss, as if she might cry. For all the poverty I had tasted, I realized, I was from a middle-class home. I understood refinement. I had read books, and learned manners and eaten with Monsignors at tables set better than these. I could fold a napkin and I knew which spoon to use for dessert cake and which to use for soup. These girls had, by the cut of them, rarely stepped outside their farm. There was every possibility they had never been to school. If I was nervous of the adventure ahead of me, these waifs were completely unprepared.

Ethel was already at the counter flirting with a handsome young waiter, who was piling her plate with food. I stood between Joan and Anne and took the arm of each. I walked them across the soft linoleum floor and sat them down at a table near the food counter. I could feel the legs collapse from under each of them as they sat down, and I realized that they were probably half starved. I fetched them both a dish of soup and a bread roll; placing the food in front of them, I guided their hands to the correct spoon and showed them which plate to use to butter their bread. They had the soup demolished before I sat down with mine, so I collected their dishes and went up for more. Ethel was still standing flirting with the soup boy. I interrupted her firmly to ask the boy for a refill.

"Seconds already? Blimey—the starving Irish, eh?" she said, winking at her new boyfriend.

"There's worse things in life to be ashamed of than being

hungry," I said in my very best elocution accent, looking right at her as if I knew what she was.

Her jaw dropped open and I felt guilty, but it had needed saying. The soup boy grinned and I could feel him watching me as I walked back to the table with my two bowls of soup.

Chapter Eighteen

There were all kinds of distractions on board; the RMS *Celtic* was like a city in itself. There was a games room, where the children could play table tennis, and the adults play cards. A shop sold sundries such as sweets, magazines, newspapers and postcards. It also contained a post office. There was a hair-dressing salon, which had a permanent-wave machine; I noticed several women who had begun the voyage with long hair, tied up to their heads in buns and plaits, emerge down to supper with it short and curled; it was all the fashion. There was a "lounge" where people gathered in the evening to listen to the radio. Others met and sat around talking in the smoking room.

Ethel and I went into the smoking room on our third day, right after breakfast, as Ethel wanted to teach me how to smoke. It made me cough, but Ethel said I should persist as women needed to know how to smoke—it showed you were sophisticated and independent. I knew she was right. There was a yellowing American newspaper left out on a table, and the headline read: 19TH AMENDMENT PROMISES WOMEN VOTING RIGHTS. I pointed it out to Ethel, but she just shrugged. I felt like telling her that sophisticated and independent women should be able to read as well as smoke.

Ethel's bawdiness had started to offend me. She got drunk in the bar every night, then woke us up to tell us about the latest man who had fallen in love with her, blowing smoke all over our windowless, airless cabin. My charitable feelings toward the Cork sisters were also wearing thin. Joan would sob herself to sleep, then howl out in her dreams for her mother. After my third night of broken sleep, my pity ran out and I just wanted to throw the whole lot of them overboard. I longed to be in the company of people who knew and loved me. I was starting to forget who I was, and I needed John to remind me. Sometimes I felt as if the part of me that mattered most was still wandering the fields behind my husband's house, while only the husk of me was here, smoking and eating my fill in the company of strangers. I wanted to be on solid ground again, to be somewhere I might settle. I was counting down the hours to seeing my darling Sheila and starting work, so that I could begin saving for my return.

On the last day, I bought a postcard with the words "Hands Across the Sea" emblazoned above a picture of two hands shaking, with the Irish and American flags in the background. I had not written to John at all since coming on board. Every time I sat down with my pen, the tears came and I was afraid of where they might lead me. I was afraid I might start crying out for him in the night like Joan for her mammy. I agonized for a moment and then wrote quickly:

> *The* Celtic *is pure luxury, like Nuala said. Not to worry, I have made friends and am managing fine. I am not seasick but missing you.*
>
> *All my love, Ellie*

It was the best I could manage.

Ethel followed me into the shop and bought a fresh pair of

stockings and a fancy bottle of perfume. It cost her all the money she had. "I don't need money no more," she said. "Frank'll look after me."

I hoped this Frank, Ethel's great benefactor, whom she had met just once in a London pub and who had sent her a ticket and an invitation to join him in America, was everything she hoped he would be. Mostly I just hoped that he would turn up and that I would not be stuck with her. But while she annoyed me, in my heart I felt sorry for Ethel. She had no family, and seemingly few friends to advise her not to chase off to America after a man she barely knew. The sisters, poor as they were, had reliable brothers to meet them.

Late that afternoon, Joan came chasing into our cabin where I was resting. "Wake up, wake up, Ellie! We're there—we're in America!"

I followed her, running up toward the deck. Others were running too, thumping along the narrow corridors in a steady sprint, one after the other, like rats in a pipe, pushing up the steep, iron stairs, our excited chattering and clattering picking up volume, echoing off all the metal.

As we came out into the open air, there was virtual silence. Single voices were snatched and muffled by the wind of the boat moving steadily forward. We were united in amazement at the Statue of Liberty—a beautiful white goddess, she seemed to welcome and warn us with her spiked crown and her impervious expression, and we stared in amazement at the upstretched arm and its gold cone. As we came in closer, even standing on the deck of our vast ship we came barely as high as the hemline of her folded robes. She reminded me of our enormous Mother Superior, and for a second I flickered with excitement that I would soon be able to share that observation with Sheila, in person.

Beyond Lady Liberty was the city itself. It was a dull day and the tall buildings emerged from the gray horizon like ghosts. We stood, a small and shivering crowd of newcomers, silenced by the skyline. It was as if it had emerged from under the sea itself, grown out of the vast nothingness of the ocean we had come to know over the past week.

We anchored within view of the city. The *Celtic* had docked late, so we third-class passengers had to stay on board before being processed at Ellis Island in the morning. We watched from the deck as the first- and second-class passengers were ferried across to land in fancy boats. One had a striped awning as a roof that flickered precariously in the breeze, and there was a band on it playing music for the fine people in first class. Some of the men on our deck were drunk and called obscenities across to a well-dressed lady negotiating the steps down to her fancy ferry. Shocked by their language, she put her hand over her mouth, taking it away from her head, where it had been holding her hat. The feathered confection flew into the sea, darkening into a floating stain on its surface. The men laughed and I felt a tug of anger at their cowardice. I was concerned for the woman, privileged as she was, and wondered about the lady I would be working for with Sheila—would she be as grand as the lady with the flown hat?

"Quick, Paddy, quick! There's a party in first class!"

It was late that night when Ethel ran into the cabin, feverish with excitement and slightly drunk. She had a red feather stole wrapped round her neck and was carrying a yellow feathered fan. She looked more like a fat hen than the glamorous moll she clearly intended. "Getta move on—we're missin' it!" She dragged us out of our beds, pushing us into our clothes and pulling us after her.

We ran through the dimly lit corridors, then through the empty dining room, which had been our home for the past week. She dragged us through the kitchen, all closed up now that its last meal was served, and up a set of steep winding stairs—swearing as her heels caught in the metal grating. We came out in another empty kitchen and followed her through a set of double doors straight into the first-class dining room.

The walls were paneled, lined with ornate patterned paper, the ceilings and pillars decorated in gold. Tables had been pushed to one side, apart from those that were being used as makeshift stages. The carpets were too soft to dance on, but were ideal for sleeping, as one or two of the drunker gentlemen were proving. There was an Irish music session in full swing, with two squeezeboxes, three fiddle players and a bodhrán. Ethel immediately ran over to the bodhrán player and hitched up her skirt to dance on a table while he frantically drummed. As she started, another lad joined him with his own bodhrán— positioning himself to gaze up Ethel's skirt. The last night on board, and she will surely be the popular one, I thought cruelly. To my surprise the Cork sisters joined her, leaping up on the next table and showing her how it was done. Everyone was singing and dancing, and drinking and laughing, as if there were no tomorrow. A wave of unexpected sadness washed over me. I felt alone, as if I were the only person who knew about tomorrow. I didn't feel in the mood. It didn't seem right to join in the fun without John.

"The Irish, eh? They sure know how to party." It was an American accent. A man had suddenly appeared at my side. He was tall with sandy blond hair, longish and swept back from his forehead. He was wearing the garb of a rich American, a laundered dress shirt with a silk tie casually draped beneath its collar as if it might drop to the ground. If it did, no matter—

doubtless he had several others to replace it. He was obviously a first-class passenger, somehow still aboard, not a third-class trespasser like the rest of us. Panic rose up through my face and I felt my cheeks burn. Then Ethel looked across and waved flirtatiously. I decided that if this man's presence didn't bother her, there was no reason for it to bother me. So I ignored him and took a few steps to the side.

"Say—have I offended you?"

"How would you have offended me?" I knew it was a mistake to have spoken at all. I had no desire to provide even five minutes' amusement for this rich Yankee. That was Ethel's domain. Yet I was curious as to who he was and, if he were a first-class passenger as he looked, why he was still on board. I took another furtive look at him and he grinned, holding out his hand. "I'm Charles Irvington. My father has shares in this ship." My face must have betrayed fear, because he said quickly, "I like to hang back sometimes after a dull trip and party with the paddies. This," and he spread his opened palm across the scene of drink and debauchery in front of us as if it belonged to him (which in a way it did), "happens quite often. But it seems you're not the partying kind?"

"No," I said. Although relieved at not being in trouble, I was now annoyed that lonely thoughts of my husband had been interrupted by the presence of another man. That I couldn't help but notice this man was handsome was another, enforced disloyalty. Still, I bided my time before I walked away. I didn't want to be too obviously rude, just in case. Then, as he smiled down at me, I noticed his teeth. They seemed unnaturally perfect to me— completely straight and very white, like a row of large expensive pearls, gleaming in the light from the chandeliers.

"How on earth do you get your teeth that color?" I blurted out. "They're pure white!"

He flung his head back and roared with laughter. I threw my hands up to my eyes and pretended to be dazzled by the brightness of the teeth. Then I started laughing too—at my own joke, mind.

He said, "I had too many teeth when I was a kid, so my parents had an orthodontist fit me with a brace to make them straight. I wore it for years, so I was a pretty ugly kid, but then I guess it worked out in the end, huh?"

I hadn't a clue what he was talking about, but I nodded and went to walk away to indicate that the conversation was finished.

"Also I stay away from candy—though I have a weakness for Tootsie Rolls."

I kept my back to him and continued walking, but he was making me smile.

"I have a tub of White Bright toothpaste back in my cabin if you'd care to come up and take a look?"

I laughed a little, but didn't turn round.

Chapter Nineteen

Long barges took us into Ellis Island early in the morning. Now that we had abandoned the monstrous, solid safety of our ocean liner, the barge felt flimsy, even more so on the first floor. Beneath us was our baggage, and it almost seemed as if we were characters from a children's nursery rhyme floating across the ocean atop a large suitcase. We sat facing one another on wooden benches, our bodies tipping from side to side—adrift, uncertain, many of us silently wondering if our future in America would be secure.

Talk among the Irish over dinner each night had often included horror stories of our ancestors being left to die on coffin ships. One man, Michael O'Beirne from Strokestown, took to always sitting near us and talking of little else, much to his wife Mary's embarrassment. "1847, ladies, the *Naomi* and the *Virginius*. Major Denis Mahon of Roscommon—the dirty black Protestant bastard—chartered them to get rid of his tenants, and my family among them."

"Oh quiet, Michael, we've heard it all before," his wife chided him, but to no avail.

"Strokestown, a ravaged district, ladies, and so he threw those of us that couldn't fit in the poorhouse on a boat and shipped us off to America."

"Canada, Michael."

"And half of us died. *Half.* How do you like that?"

"Stop being morbid, Michael, it's impolite," she'd say, looking across at me apologetically. "Besides, times have changed."

"You say that, Mary, but look around you . . ." Michael was a nice man, but all his talk of the famine made me uncomfortable. There was still shame in my family as to how we had survived the famine and, like his wife, I had been reared to believe it was uncouth to talk about such things as poverty and illness. However, that was not the case for Mr. O'Beirne, it seemed. "And you and I both know that your own cousin was sent home with TB not two years ago . . ."

"It was nothing more than a chest cold," Mary said, looking over at me, mortified.

"Worse again," the husband interjected, "to be sent back for no good reason, on the whim of some official."

"And she was a distant cousin, hardly related at all," she added, pleadingly.

Michael and Mary O'Beirne now sat across from me on the barge and were uncharacteristically silent, the reality of our journey finally hitting home. I caught the sharp stench of sea, which had become so familiar to me, and felt suddenly tired. I was tired of eating with people I didn't know, of sleeping badly in a room with strangers, of missing my husband, my home. I was exhausted, yet I had spent my first week away from home just sleeping and eating; the working part of my emigrant journey had not even begun.

Across the harbor, large ships were offloading onto vessels like ours. As we came closer to the island, what had seemed to be a small scattering revealed itself as dozens and dozens of packed barges, hundreds of people pouring off them onto the jetties as others hung back to wait.

On land, the walkways were packed with people, pushing past one another to get inside the long, redbrick building. The two Cork sisters clung to the back of my coat as I pushed my way through the front door and into the baggage hall. Bags, trunks and cases were everywhere. Enormous carpets rolled into huge colorful pipes, exotic cushions, sacking packages bound with rope, wooden stools tied with blankets—all piled up on top of one another. Everyone's life was hidden in these dense mountains of belongings—people pulling and poking at them, trying to get their things back, their carried remnants of home. Strong men wheeled boxes as big as themselves on enormous trolleys, stronger women pulling trunks five times heavier than themselves. I felt relieved, suddenly, that I had been able to fit my life into one small bag. I looked around to ask somebody where we needed to go next. There was a woman in a long black dress with a sharp nose who looked as if she might know. "Excuse me," I said, "do you know where we are supposed to go?" She threw up her hands and shouted at me in a foreign language. I pretended not to be shocked, said a pointless "sorry" and looked around.

People were lining up a long, wide staircase to my right, so I went toward it, hoping this was the next stage along. The two sisters were still clinging to my coat. "Where's Ethel?" I asked, but they both shrugged, wide eyed and overwhelmed. I was looking forward to passing them into the care of their brothers, but at the same time felt that perhaps it was good that I had somebody else to look after, otherwise I might fall apart myself. I noticed that most of the people on the stairs were from our ship, but, as on the barge, few of us were in the mood for talking. Some of them had already fetched their luggage and were hauling trunks and large cases up with them, step by step. I did not know what we were lining up for and was glad when Mr. O'Beirne came up behind me. "Ladies," he said, "here we are queuing for the good doctors of America—hope we're all feeling bright-eyed and bushy-tailed?"

"We're to be tested again?" I asked. We had already been examined in Queenstown.

"Indeed," he said, anxious to share his expertise with us. "Six-second medical exam, they call it—just a quick once-over. They pull the eyelid back with a hook . . ."

"Wh-at?!" his wife Mary shouted.

". . . it's just a formality. You fine, healthy young girls have nothing to worry about."

The sisters' hands tightened on my coat, and a bad feeling rose through me. I had felt the truth when I first saw Joan's cloudy eyes, but had buried that knowledge like a bad memory. I reached back and took a hand from each girl and gave them a squeeze. I didn't look round because I didn't want to draw attention to Joan. In my mind's eye, I could see again that almost imperceptible veil of fine cotton which shadowed that frail child's view of the world.

I held their hands and chatted nicely to the O'Beirnes until we reached the top of the line, then stood in front of the three doctors who were performing the inspection. They had peaked caps—like police or army. I went first, standing with my back against a pillar to steady myself as the man gently pulled back the lid of my eye with a small hook. It didn't hurt—just stung as the cold air hit my eye and made it roll from left to right. When he was finished, he looked me up and down coldly for a few seconds. His look was not offensive, but studious, like the way a man might look at a cow on market day, checking it for health and vigor. When he gave me his approval and asked me to move along, I stood aside and nodded across to Joan, who was watching me anxiously. Anne had to push her forward into my place. She stood in front of the doctor and began to cry.

I said a silent prayer that her tears would clear the clouds away like rain, then went back up to the doctor and said to him, "Excuse me, Sir—my friend had something in her eye yesterday and, in trying to clear it out, I used perfume instead of water and . . ."

He was surprised I was still there, but said nothing. He had barely touched Joan's eye with the hook when he shook his head and took a piece of chalk from his pocket and wrote "CT" on the arm of her coat. I looked round and saw Michael O'Beirne whisper something into Anne's ear. Anne called out, "No!" and rushed forward to Joan and, in fairness to him, Michael O'Beirne came with her. The doctor looked at me and said, "I'm sorry, your friend has trachoma and needs to be sent to the infirmary."

"It was just an accident," I persisted. "There's nothing really wrong with her!" We all of us—Anne, myself and Michael— converged on Joan. "It's all right," I said. "They'll have a hospital here to make you better."

"I'm afraid not," the doctor said, "she'll have to be sent home." Two uniformed men moved from the side of the room when they saw us gathering around the doctor. "It's all right," the doctor said, waving them aside. His kindness was not reassuring, but rather an indication that our situation was tragic and not uncommon. "Are you related to this girl?" he asked me.

"No," said Mr. O'Beirne, firm and paternal, his arm round Anne's shoulder. "This girl is her sister and I am their uncle. They are in my charge." The doctor was happy to be talking with a man, and Michael said to me softly, "You go on ahead there, girleen, I'll deal with this. Don't fret, I'll look after them."

I looked back one more time and saw Mary O'Beirne next in line, looking scared as her husband was taken through another door with the sisters.

*

I was now in a room that was as wide and as big as a town. It was packed with people sitting on row after row of long wooden benches. At the top of the room were little cubicles with desks in front of them, where officials were calling people up to answer questions—about what, I didn't know. There were two wide pillars and a massive banner of the Stars and Stripes hung between them, supported by a balcony that went round the whole of the room. One or two people were up there looking down on us. We were some sight, surely. A thousand, maybe two thousand people? I didn't even know what a thousand people looked like, to help me guess. The noise was deafening. Above the base sound of people chattering in a dozen languages, and the pierce of crying children, men were walking through the crowd calling names. Red with the effort of shouting, and the frustration of not being heard, they belted out: "Mary Murphy!" "Antonio Balducci!" "Ludmila Kuchar!"

I looked round for somewhere to sit. There were children asleep on boxes, their fathers' greatcoats thrown over them. Mothers wearing scarves wrapped round their heads like nuns, and blankets slung round their shoulders, cradling nursing children to their breasts. Small, dark-skinned people with slanting eyes and straight hair cut into severe shapes, swathed in fur that looked as if it was still warm from the animal. There were Africans—I recognized them from textbooks on the missions I had learned about from the Jesus and Mary sisters. There were groups of men with beards down to their waists and curls at each ear, wearing long coats and strangely formal hats. There were impossibly beautiful women with jet-black hair and skin the color of cooked honey, gesticulating wildly with equally beautiful young men. There were old women in long skirts patterned with garish flowers, their heads swathed in brightly colored fabric, their skin like old leather, their expressions blank—beyond sadness, beyond confusion—following some stubborn son.

I saw a group of Irish people, unmistakable among all this exoticism, white skinned and grubby, so I went and sat with them. I can't remember who they were or how long I sat there or what small talk we made, but I stayed with them until my name was called. My stomach was churning with an unnamed fear. That I would get in, or not get in, to America was not it. Rather, it was just the realization that I was here. That I had made the journey and was now in a room, on the other side of the world, with all these people from every corner of the world. I felt invisible until I heard a man shout behind me, "Mrs. Eileen Hogan!"

I went up to the desk and a man checked my particulars against the ship's manifest. Within a few minutes I was walking down a staircase. The bottom of it was clogged with people kissing and hugging one another. I saw two young men standing together and knew at once from the look of them that they must be the Cork brothers. I went over and introduced myself, and explained about Anne and Joan. They were distraught, but thanked me. They were healthy-looking, strong men—they would know what to do. "Where are you going?" they asked.

"Manhattan," I said, showing them Sheila's address.

The shorter, older of the brothers nodded toward a crowd of people at a desk marked Money Exchange. "Do you have money to change?"

I had the money order that Sheila had sent me as evidence for the authorities that I would not be arriving in America empty-handed. But I had to return it to her untouched. "No," I said.

He walked me out of the hall and onto the Manhattan ferry, giving me instructions on how to get to Fifth Avenue. Before he rushed back to his younger brother, he pressed two dollar bills and some coins into my hands, saying, "Thank you for taking care of my sisters." I took the money, my hands closing around it too eagerly. Fear had made me forget my manners.

The final leg of my journey took less than ten minutes. As the barge drew into my final port, Manhattan, my eyes strained into the sun as it glittered off a million windows, buildings that stretched up to the sky—yearning toward God Himself. This was a new world, a new life, a new beginning, and for the first time since leaving Ireland I felt intoxicated. My fear turned, finally, to excitement. I wished John was with me, but this was an adventure I would have to experience alone.

I stepped off the boat onto the jetty at Pier A and then onto solid ground at last.

Ireland was in my heart, but under my feet was America.

Chapter Twenty

The crowd fanned out from the quayside, bustling past me as if they had been here before. My insides were swaying, so I just started to walk. I stopped at the mouth of a wide road and pulled Sheila's letter out of my pocket, even though I had memorized the directions.

"The address is 820 Fifth Avenue. Walk up Broadway as far as Madison Square Park, then take Fifth."

I took the wide road and at the first junction looked up to where the street names were placed. "Broadway," said a small, neatly placed plaque on the side of a building. It seemed strange, such a small sign on such a wide, important street.

The buildings stretched upward forever, and I had to strain my head back farther than it would go to see the top of them. In places it seemed as if they had closed in and made the sky disappear. As I passed a horse carriage plodding nervously at the edge of the road, the smell of its dung crawled up my nostrils—sharp and pungent. My ears rang with motorcars' horns and streetcar bells, as the various vehicles crudely negotiated one another on the wide road. Only the streetcars seemed to move at any speed, belching out black smoke, clogging up the atmosphere even more; the car drivers called to one another, their voices like angry sirens.

The air closed in on me, hot and wet—there were so many buildings and so many people that it seemed as if there was not enough air to go round us all. The pavement was so crowded, I kept crashing into people. "Look where you're going!" one woman said, pushing her sharp elbow into the top of my arm, glowering at me with protruding, angry eyes. She was my mother's age, but was covered in rouge and wearing shabby high-heeled shoes and no coat.

I kept wanting to stop and stare: at a man in a full-length black-and-white fur coat and a wide-brimmed hat; at a woman being pulled along by two huge gray dogs as big as donkeys on leather leads; at a couple arguing outside a bar; at a shop window filled with flowers in buckets—flowers for sale, in a place with no air and no sky. I walked past drugstores selling electrical appliances that could toast bread; billboard advertisements advertising everything from evaporated milk to ladies' hosiery; barber shops with men having their chins shaved, the barber standing over them as if to slit their throats in full view of the passing public. After one, maybe two miles, I began to doubt my sense of direction. Was I going round in circles? How could any place be so relentlessly . . . *occupied?* Surely, after almost an hour of steady walking, I must be near the end of the city itself, and yet Broadway seemed endless, far longer than any street had a right to be—even in America. My bag was getting heavy, my feet were pinching in my boots. Perhaps I had missed the turning for Fifth Avenue. I decided to cross the street to check another sign up high on the side of a building.

I negotiated the road carefully, squeezing myself between the tight line of cars, but just as I nearly reached the other side, one of them started up and nudged me, no more than that. I tripped and fell onto the pavement, my bag spilling its contents out in front of me. For a moment I lay there, shocked at what had happened. I expected somebody to stop and help me, but as dozens of shoes—clacky high heels, smart black leather, dusty-brown boots—passed by my face, I realized it wasn't going to happen. Mortified more by my lack of composure than actual pain, I stood up and dusted down my coat. My petticoat had torn and a foamy strip of it was dipped in the muddy gutter. As I picked it up to tear it off, I caught the eyes of a passing Negro man—there was a soft pity in his face, and a reluctance. Neatly dressed, his skin and hair as glossy as his shoes, he came over and, pointing up the street on whose corner we were standing, said, "If you need to sit down, lady, Washington Square Park is just at the end of Fourth Street. There's benches there where you can rest."

"Thank you," I replied. I was too embarrassed to ask him if we were still on Broadway or where Fifth Avenue was. I just wanted to get away from where I was standing and get my dignity back.

"I was new here once," he said, holding me back briefly with his words. Then, as he walked away from me, he pushed his hands out either side from his waist, his pink palms in a theatrical spread, and said, "We all was."

I walked up Fourth Street until I reached the park. It was a short walk, and the man was right, it was a good place to wait and rest. I sat down on a bench and looked around me. The grassy areas were parched and patchy—hardly green at all and scattered with crunchy leaves, the messy debris of the giant trees that rose up from the dead earth like ancient buildings. Over to one side there was a woman feeding pigeons. She stood in the center of the gray mass of birds pecking frantically at her feet, their wings flicking their black undercoats, making dust of her coat. There were squirrels too. As one sped up a tree, another identical one rushed up after it—tricky twins, unbothered by the humans who were occupying their space. A young woman lay on the grass next to my bench, her elbows resting on a pretty woollen rug and a day bag of intricate tapestry gaping open at her feet, as a young man tried to distract her from her reading. There were numerous people talking and eating together and alone; several lay snoozing in the warm, muggy air. I thought what an extraordinary place this was, when people could perform such intimate acts as sleeping and eating in full public view. At home, even the old men of the road who tramped homeless around Ireland didn't eat in public. There was one who called to our house and my mother always gave him a cooked potato. He was too dirty to let in, but she wouldn't have him dine alone and always stood with him as he ate it at the door.

The animals seemed more relaxed here too, quite content to mix with us humans. The rabbits and pheasants at home hid away from us in case we'd catch and eat them. Here the people were feeding the wild animals, and dressing their dogs up in fancy collars and being dragged down the street by them! I wanted to share my revelation with John and felt the customary shock of grief that he wasn't there at my side—a feeling that had become familiar to me in the past days. It seemed so pointless, seeing all these interesting things, having all these adventures, without him to tell them to. I steadied myself. I would write, I told myself.

But then I caught the smell of cigarette smoke—that familiar smell of Paud and Maidy's kitchen, in mid-afternoon after the dinner was done. And suddenly John was there . . . and not there. The full cruelty of our parting hit me for the first time: not the usual sharp stab, but a heavy body blow to my chest. The absoluteness of grief. Winded with the reality of what I had done, I collapsed into a wretched mound of shuddering tears right there on the park bench. I was in full view of the world, but it wasn't my world.

> *"A garden that never knew sunshine,*
> *once sheltered a beautiful rose,*
> *in the shadows it grew, without sunlight or dew,*
> *as a child of the city grows.*
> *A butterfly flew to the garden,*
> *from out of the blue sky above,*
> *the heart of the rose set a flutter,*
> *with a wonderful tale of love."*

The young man who had been on the grass next to me was standing in front of me singing. He was wearing a straw boater hat and a white shirt rolled up to reveal bony, hairless forearms, which he stretched forward in a comical, pleading pose, before sitting down next to me, grabbing both my hands and, still without introduction, belting out his chorus in a surprisingly low and confident baritone, given his skinny stature.

> *"They call me Rose of Washington Square.*
> *I'm withering there, in basement air I'm fading.*
> *Pose in plain or fancy clothes?*
> *They say my turned up nose*
> *It seems to please artistic people.*
> *Foes, I've plenty of those . . ."*

"Oh, shut up, Bradley—can't you see the poor girl doesn't need singing, she needs food?" The girl had been lying on the grass listening to him sing, but now he was sitting down next to me. She stood up and came over. "Here," she said, pointing a large round cake at me with sugar crystals stuck to its top. I blushed with a mixture of shame and anger at the implication that I looked as if I needed charity.

"No, thank you," I said. "I'm not hungry." I was starving of course, and the proximity of the cake was making me hungrier still.

"Oh, take it," she said crossly, thrusting it into my hands. "I've two more in my bag."

"She's Jewish," the boy said. "They always carry food around."

"Don't be so bloody rude, Bradley—in any case, there's no shame in being hungry."

"Only in being a lady . . ."

"I'm not a lady, I'm a woman!"

"Ruth's a suffragette," he said to me, by way of explanation. "They think they're men, actually."

"I wish I *was* a man, then I'd punch you to the ground."

"No, you wouldn't, because you're in love with me!"

"Of course, Bradley, because *everyone's* in love with—"

"Ugh—it's salt!" I suddenly cried out. The cake had become irresistible with their bantering, but it wasn't sweet as I had imagined it would be. The crystals on the top of it were lumps of salt!

"What's the matter?" Ruth said.

Bradley started laughing. "She thought your pretzel was a sweet cake."

"Oh my goodness, what a shock." Ruth was full of concerned panic, as if I were a child who had burned myself. "Make yourself useful, Bradley, and get the lemonade out of my bag—here, spit it out." And she thrust a white cotton handkerchief at me.

"No," I said, "it's good." And it was. Once I got used to the flavor, the dry cake-bread tasted wonderful and, washed down with the lemonade, it revived me and I felt completely cheered. Ruth sat and watched my face as I ate, checking my approval and delighting in my pleasure. As soon as I was finished, she offered me another. "Bradley can go without," she said. "His *maid* is probably cooking a meal for him as we speak."

I looked at him, trying not to appear hungry as I was.

"Truly—I insist," he said, sweeping his hand dramatically in front of him.

So I took it, willingly and gratefully. "Thank you. You're a real gentleman," I said, teasing.

"And you," he said, resting his hand on his concave chest and sweeping the other out in a dramatic bow, "are a *lady*." Then we both looked pointedly at Ruth and laughed.

We passed an hour or so in the park, the three of us talking and teasing one another like old friends. I told them about my journey and, in the telling of it, it turned from the ordeal of leaving Ireland from harsh necessity into an exciting adventure that had led me to enjoy their amusing company and their lemonade. I did not tell them I was married or talk about the war or the tragic circumstances that had led me here—and in the not telling of it, the pain of my reality melted away.

"Are you poor?" Ruth asked. "Is that why you came to America?"

I bristled briefly, then thought of explaining how my parents were rich, and how I was educated—but in the end, I realized, it didn't matter. These people were happy to talk to me in any case. So I swallowed my pride and said, "Yes, I'm poor. That's why I'm here. I have a job working for a lady on Fifth Avenue."

"My parents were poor," Ruth said. "That's why we came here. Bradley's a blue-blooded boy, never done a day's work in his silly little life—hardly a man at all."

"Nonsense. I work for a living!"

"Oh yes, that's right—writing poems. *Very* hard work . . ."

*

Bradley and Ruth walked with me part of the way up Fifth Avenue, amusing me with anecdotes, pointing out landmarks—their benefits and pitfalls. They distinguished hotels from brothels, theaters from music halls, private gardens from public parks and tenements from apartment blocks. They layered sites with their stories, making the city seem dense with all that had happened within it. As its newest inhabitant, I felt eager with the promise of what might happen yet.

I barely noticed the time pass until we stopped under a gold statue of a man on a horse and a beautiful winged woman leading him along.

"Who is he?" I asked.

"Some savage general who plundered the South in our Civil War," Ruth said. "Men are such *fools* for fighting."

"We'd better say good-bye here," Bradley said. "We've a long walk back."

We said good-bye fondly, but made no plans to meet again. It was enough that the lighthearted kindness of these two strangers had made this huge and frightening city seem more like home, and had given me enough faith to believe I could continue on. As they waved and headed back downtown, I found myself feeling excited at the prospect of seeing Sheila again.

I ran so fast toward her, I almost missed 820 Fifth Avenue.

Chapter Twenty-One

Shelia had told me her employer lived in an "apartment block," but I had never seen a building like it before. There was a carpet on the pavement outside, and an awning to protect residents from the rain. There were two magnolia trees standing sentry, and the black door to the building itself was inlaid with brass filigree flowers. As I stepped onto the carpet, a man came out of the building. He was dressed like an army general in a long, dark red coat, with shiny brass buttons and a peaked cap. He walked smartly toward me—evidently too polite to run—and headed me off at the door.

"Around the side," he said. He had a Cork accent.

"I'm Ellie," I said. "I've come to—"

"Around the side," he repeated firmly, nodding to his left, "and down the first set of steps. That's the servants' entrance—go!"

I was blushing with shame and walked as fast as I could in the direction he had pointed. The building seemed never ending, and when I reached the next street along I looked back and was relieved to see the uniformed man was still standing there, watching after me. He waved a gloved hand at me, to turn the corner. I was halfway down the next street before I found some steps leading to a basement. They were treacherously steep and at the bottom of them was a small courtyard, as swept and clean as if it were an inside room. I knocked on the large heavy door and heard an unmistakable voice from inside call out: "It's her, at last, it's surely Ellie!"

"Hurry, hurry," I said in my head, my hands wanting to paw at the wood as I realized how anxious I was to see a friendly face from home. I barely recognized Sheila when she opened the door. The curly red hair had been replaced with a short, straight bob and she was thinner, and flat-chested.

"I thought you'd never get here, I've been up and down waiting for you all day—I had Grumpy Flannery at the door warned to look out for you!"

We embraced and kissed and I clutched at her as we entered the building. "Oh, I've so much to tell you." I squeezed her arm with excitement. "I don't know where to start, I've had such adventures—"

But she cut me off, saying, "There'll be time enough to talk later, Ellie—we'd better get you upstairs, or there'll be no job for either of us." She started almost running down a corridor that was so long I could not see the end of it. We were in the basement of the huge building. The walls were striped with thick pipes and painted a dark red, and there were narrow alleys running off at either side, each one exactly the same as the next—it was as if we were lost in the bloody bowels of some vast animal. All the time Sheila was talking, "Mrs. Flannery, she's the boss and a tyrant, she has us all killed-out. She's married to Grumpy—only we don't call him that to his face, we call him Mr. Flannery—or His Lordship, if we're feeling cheeky. Precious, she's the scullery maid. She's a colored, but she's nice. She's in love with David, he works in maintenance, and nobody knows about them because . . ." I could barely keep up with the speed of her feet or her words, as she grabbed my hand and hurried me alongside her.

Suddenly, she stopped outside what looked like a cage. She pulled back some black crisscross bars revealing a tiny box of a room, then indicated for me to get in. I felt a little frightened, but I couldn't object. I stepped inside and she followed, then closed over the bars. I was petrified, but looked at my friend's face and she smiled at me as if nothing was untoward. There was a black metal panel on the wall with buttons, which Sheila pressed. After a few seconds the cage began to move upward. My stomach lurched with shock, and I thought I was going to be sick.

"Twelfth floor," Sheila said, looking up at a strip of numbers that were lighting up as we rose. "Here we are!" And we juddered to a halt. She pulled back the cage doors and we came out on another corridor, except that this one was full of daylight. There was a glass wall directly in front of us, behind which was a busy kitchen, like something you would find in a big, grand house. On the far side of the kitchen were large windows, through which I could see only sky. My legs gave way slightly as I realized how high up we must be. "This is the service area— kitchens, laundry—our bedrooms are down the hall." Sheila dragged the "a" out slightly in "ha-all." "Though I spend most of my time upstairs, in the apartment."

I stared at her.

She laughed. "Isobel lives on the next floor up, we live down here—it's kinda confusing. I'll show you around later—you hungry?" *Kinda* . . . Sheila looked and sounded so different now, it was making me a little nervous. I followed her into the kitchen. "Ellie, this is Mrs. Flannery." Sheila's voice suddenly lost its American twang, as she introduced a woman who was about the same age and build as my beloved Maidy, but with a face as pink and fierce as a cross sow. She was standing at a long wooden table, as big as our whole kitchen at home maybe, her wide hands kneading a lump of bread the size of a small child. She wiped her hands on her apron and stood back from the table to look me up and down, as if appraising cattle. I bobbed slightly on one knee, afraid to look her in the eye in case it be construed as cheek, and mumbled, "Pleased to meet you, Ma'am."

"Don't genuflect, child, I am *not* the Blessed Virgin." The accent was pure Cork—like the husband's. "And don't call me Ma'am—I'm not the Queen of England, either."

The girl washing dishes behind her giggled and, without turning, Mrs. Flannery swiftly slapped the back of her knees with the damp towel. The girl stopped laughing, but turned and smiled at me. The whites of her eyes and her teeth shone like pearls against her glossy, coal-black skin. Small wonder they called her Precious.

"Are you hungry?" Mrs. Flannery was asking.

"A little, but . . ."

"Sit down there and I'll give you something. Precious, bring me some bread and cheese—quickly, child! Sheila, where in God's good name have you been all day? That one upstairs has been in and out, driving me half-demented all day. Oh, never mind, here . . ." A lump of yellow, crumbling cheese appeared in front of me on a large plate, alongside the softest, whitest bread, the like of which I had never before tasted in my life. I ate the food greedily, drinking at the glass of milk that had been put down beside it, and the very second I was finished Mrs. Flannery prodded me in the back and said to Sheila, "Right—get the new girl settled and get back to work."

As Sheila marched out of the kitchen with me behind her, the old woman called after her, "And no sitting idle around like a lady. Remember who you are!"

"That aul bitch should have no authority over me anyhow." Sheila was flushed with annoyance. "I'm Isobel's personal maid and answer to her directly. I don't do the dirty jobs—only minding my lady's pretty things and dressing her hair for parties. This is our room, Ellie . . ."

We had entered a small windowless room with a low ceiling and a single bed. It was smaller than the ship's cabin I had traveled in to get here. There was a line of coat hooks on the wall, hung with Sheila's clothes, and a small dressing table to one side, the top of it strewn with makeup, baubles and perfume bottles. Suddenly I felt tired and sat down on the bed. Sheila read my expression as disappointment. "I know it's small, and Mrs. Flannery said I should put Precious out of her room, but I didn't want her sleeping in the kitchen, and—"

"No, no," I said, horrified. "I'm just tired after the journey."

"We can sleep top-to-toe, it'll be fun."

"It's perfect," I said. I could not quite believe where I was. The cage, Sheila's strange hair—it all felt unreal, like a dream. The paper on the wall beside me was peeling and a troupe of faded ballerinas danced along. The last in the row had her arm torn off at the elbow, but she smiled on regardless. For a moment I closed my eyes and wondered, if I imagined hard enough, that I might be returned home.

When I opened my eyes again, Sheila was beaming at me and holding both my hands in hers. "I am *so* happy you're here, Ellie. You are going to *love* New York."

Sheila left me alone in the room, while she ran back to work. I lay down on the bed and closed my eyes. When I woke it was dark and my dress was stuck to me with the heat. I regretted not having undressed before I settled. The room was airless and its blackness bore down on me. I felt sick with the realization of where I was. A heavy, immovable dread sat like a rock in the bottom of my stomach. Every inch of me craved home, craved

John. I had been stupid to come, heartless to leave him behind.
What was I doing here?

The electric light flashed on. "Up! Get up, Ellie, quick!"
Sheila threw some clothes at me. "It's your uniform, it's an old
one of mine, but it should fit. Isobel wants to meet you now, so
we'd better hurry."

Yawning, I dragged on the uniform, a black dress shockingly
short—it barely reached my calves. Sheila jerked my hair back
from my face into a tight knot at the nape of my neck and placed
a white cap over it, then unfolded a starched apron and pulled it
over my head. "There," she said, turning me toward the mirror
of the small dressing table. "You look like a proper servant."
She took a small packet out of her apron pocket and handed me
a flat silver-wrapped stick, which I at first assumed was a cigarette. "Here, have some gum—it'll freshen you up."

I peeled back the silver paper and, as I put the stick into my
mouth, the taste of mint exploded, flooding my mouth with
water. In summer, John used to scythe back the mint outside
our front door and fill the house with its clean, powerful scent.

"And don't swallow it, it's not candy!"

We came out of the bedroom and walked past the kitchen,
which was dark and empty of life, aside from a small lamp.
Its windows glowed a faint yellow from the lights outside. It
was obviously the middle of the night. With everyone in bed, it
seemed odd that Sheila was taking me to meet the mistress at
this time, but she was so anxious, and taken up with us getting
where we were going as quickly as possible, that I didn't challenge her.

I followed her through a door and up a dimly lit flight of
stairs. At the top of them was a wide door leading to another,
long corridor. It occurred to me that this was how I had imagined the rabbits lived—constantly running along long tunnels,

leading this way and that. Sheila fled ahead of me along the corridor. It seemed as if we ran for miles, past two or three doors
until finally she stopped outside one of them.

"Are you ready?" she said. I had seen and heard so much
on my journey that I thought I was ready for anything. But it
was Sheila who seemed hesitant now, saying, "I hope she likes
you, Ellie—I'm sure she will." I was about to ask why she was
worried, when she said, "Oh God!" and spat her gum into her
hand, then held out her palm for me.

"Oh—I've swallowed it!" I said.

"I told you not to!"

"What'll happen to me?"

She clapped her hand up to her mouth, as if too shocked to
say.

"Sheila?" Suddenly, I was a little frightened.

Then she winked at me and laughed. "Nothing, stupid." I
walloped her, and the two of us giggled as if we were outside
the Mother Superior's office waiting for a telling-off. "Come
on," she said, taking my hand. "Let's get this over and done
with."

Chapter Twenty-Two

The room beyond the door was vast, as big as a church. The very walls shimmered and seemed lined in gold. Across the room, facing us, was a long black cabinet, glossy as if it was wet and marbled with veins the color of flesh. Above it, a mirror reached up toward a ceiling that was twice the height of any of the others I had seen in this building; its beveled edges glittered with a thousand prisms, catching light from the dazzling crystal chandelier at the room's center. Against another wall stood a four-poster bed. The sides of it were hung with yard upon yard of pink silk, and the headboard was made of what seemed to be mother-of-pearl. At the center of the bed reclined a slim woman with short blond hair and delicate features. She was lying on her stomach, propped up on her elbows as she smoked a cigarette. An ornate black robe was barely draped over her naked shoulders. She was surely not yet thirty years old. She waved the cigarette lavishly in our direction—"Sheila, my darling! And this must be the new maid!"—then dropped it onto the silk coverlet.

Sheila ran across the room and rescued it, placing it carefully into an ashtray on the bedside table. She straightened up a bottle next to it and the mistress said, in a nasty tone, without turning her head, "I had a little nightcap, Sheila, as you can see." Then she looked at me and gave me a wobbly smile. Her eyes were dead and sleepy, her voice mossy and uncertain. "How do you like our little home, erm . . . ?"

"It's Eileen, Ma'am."

She threw her head back and laughed, for no reason I could fathom, then fell sideways across the bed and rolled toward the ashtray, where she fumbled around for her smoldering cigarette before eventually knocking it, and the ashtray, to the floor. I thought perhaps she was stone mad, until Sheila picked up the drink bottle and waved it at me to indicate it was empty. I felt a little stupid then. I had never seen a proper lady drunk before. In truth, I had never thought such a thing could happen.

"Come on, Isobel," Sheila said soothingly as her mistress's head lolled to one side, near unconscious. "Let's heave that skinny, drunken ass of yours into bed." She pulled back the silky covers and reached under the pillow for a nightgown. "These are kept in the dressing room, I'll show you in a minute, Ellie, but I always hide a spare one under the pillow when the master's away, so we can get her undressed quicker when she gets like this. Get the gown off . . ." Sheila was running around the room emptying ashtrays and gathering up bottles. She seemed to know where to look, and conjured up three from various hiding places. "Come on, Ellie—for God's sake, get her undressed and into bed!"

I undid the lady's belt and peeled the black robe down her arms, exposing the flesh. My hands were shaking with nerves. Supposing this rich, unstable creature woke up and caught me undressing her? Her skin was so white and translucent that her veins and bones were almost visible. I balked at her nakedness—her hip bones stuck out like spoons under the skin, a glossy triangle of shockingly lustrous hair between them. Her breasts were strapped to her chest with a wide bandage. Panic and revulsion pounded in my chest. This was not what I had imagined my job would be. I wanted to go home.

"Don't forget to unstrap her . . ." Sheila said firmly.

Almost weeping with a mixture of fear and embarrassment, I found the edge of the bandage tucked beneath her armpit and carefully eased it out. Sitting her up and supporting her back with one hand, I unfurled the gauzy strip with the other until I had released the two tiny breasts, the nipples tightening as they hit the cold air.

Sheila, having finished gathering up rubbish, came and helped me put the nightgown on, then between us we lifted Mrs. Adams into the bed, tucking the covers around her. I picked up the black robe and draped it across a purple velvet chair next to the bed. It was intricately embroidered with peony roses—the most beautiful item of clothing I had ever seen.

"Better hang that in the dressing room," said Sheila, "so Isobel can pretend she didn't pass out again."

16th July 1920
Dear Ellie,

You are only gone two days, but I don't know how long this letter will take to get to you, so I said I would write in any case. I had a surprise the day after you left when Doctor Bourke arrived up with a wheelchair, and Padraig with him, to take me up to Dublin for a meeting with some of the generals. The men at the top had heard I was shot and sent for me to go up and get a medal. There was no grand ceremony, Ellie, so not to be worrying you missed out! The war goes on, so there is not too much cause for celebration yet. It was just a few men gathered in a safe house in the north of the city. Like all our business, sadly, a secretive affair, but it was good to be acknowledged. I have been feeling so useless of late at my not being fit and able to fight, but they assured me I had done my bit. Padraig talked of you to them too, Ellie, and all those you had helped—and there was several of them there that had tasted your bread and enjoyed your cooking and your company and they attested to your generosity and kindness. I was more proud of that, in truth, than the trinket they presented me with.

The journey home was an adventure again. The train guard guessed by the cut of me in the chair that I was a soldier, and smuggled us both into the parcel carriage. The stationmaster saw him, but let me through without the price of a ticket—so we have made some money already. It was quite some adventure, as a gang of Tans got on in Athlone and the two of us looking for all the world like we were fugitives, even though it was not altogether true, on this occasion in any case!

Paud could not pick us up from the station, so Padraig had to walk me back in the chair. The wheels were rough on the road and it was backbreaking work for the two of us, after traversing the smooth pavements of the city in such comfort. I would have crawled the last three miles had I been even able for that. It's surely only half-a-man you left behind, Ellie—although still I cannot think of you as gone.

I know you are set in what you did in going to America, but I would happily never walk again for to have you back here beside me.

The house is quiet now without you. Maidy has a stew on for the dinner. I can't think of much more to say, but will write again tomorrow in all likelihood.

I hope your journey was quiet and that you met with Sheila all right. Please write and let me know you are safe.

> I love you and I always have,
> Your husband John

*

The following day I woke with a start. Sheila was gone from the bed, although her side was still warm. Again, I was immediately aware of the strangeness of where I was and the enormity of the mistake I had made in coming here. John's letter had arrived yesterday while I was asleep, and Sheila had finally produced it from her apron after we had got her employer safely to bed.

Now, I found pen and paper in my bag and wrote:

Dear John,
   I am coming home as soon as I can raise enough money
for the fare. I hate it here. The job is terrible. The woman of
the house is a grotesque drunkard, made of skin and bone,
and I'm expected to strip her and put her to bed. I miss you,
John, and Maidy and Paud and my home, and I wished I
had been to Dublin with you that day. I realize I made a ter-
rible mistake in coming here. I feel so miserable . . .

I stopped and looked over what I had written, but as I was about to continue, Sheila ran into the room, so I quickly screwed the paper up and threw it under the bed.

"Ellie! Why aren't you dressed? We're going to be fitted with new uniforms!" She was beside herself with the adventure of it. "Mademoiselle Dupont *herself* will be measuring us up! And Isobel will oversee the fitting!" she squealed.

We were under orders to wait in Isobel's dressing room—a vast anteroom off her bedchamber, furnished with a delicate gold-framed chaise longue and walls lined with rails and racks of clothes, stacks of shoes and hat boxes—more than I had ever imagined might be in the biggest shop in Dublin. I was terri-fied by the idea of meeting the drunken woman I had stripped the night before. At the same time, my eyes strained to accommodate the bright colors and the glittering textures. There were fuchsia-pinks and hot oranges brighter and more beautiful than any sunset; peacock-blue marabou features puffing out from the cuffs of an evening coat; a long collar stiffened with thousands of tiny pearls; a faceless head sitting on a clear glass table, wearing a fringed skullcap encrusted with diamonds and sequins. As our mistress and the dressmaker came into the room, the cap's beaded fringe shivered, sending shards of white light ricocheting across the room. As Isobel approached me, I felt myself flush with embarrassment at the memory of seeing her naked body the night before; I was mortified by having touched her breasts.

She smiled broadly, put both her hands out to take mine. "Ellie, I am so pleased to meet you at last. Sheila has spoken of you so often." Her lips were an unnatural shade of red, a dark maroon that made her skin appear even paler than it was. She smelt of lilac—the scent of June, the month before I left home—and her skin was cool and dry like my mother's. Sheila was watching me nervously. She had forgotten to tell me how to act. I lowered my eyes and bobbed a curtsy. I felt ashamed of my instinctive servitude, but Isobel laughed, a light babble of charm, and behind her Sheila beamed like a proud parent. "I want my girls to look as pretty as pictures," Isobel said to the dour-looking woman behind her. "Fashion and comfort must be our top priorities!" The dressmaker lowered her eyes, well used to being bossed about by rich ladies; but as soon as Isobel left the room, her demeanor changed. She was clearly unimpressed by her commission of fitting out servants. She made us strip to our undergarments, then poked at us with her bony fingers and squeezed the tape measure around our sweating limbs, grunting instructions and prodding us this way and that. I felt she was not as French as her name suggested.

The very next day our new uniforms were delivered, on hangers, to the front door. They were very comfortable and extremely pretty—in a light, blue-and-white striped cotton with drop waists, large sailor collars and sleeves to the elbow. Isobel called us up to her dressing room to model them for her. She was sitting on the edge of her bed in the black robe; she told us she had designed our uniforms herself and feigned hilarious disappointment when Sheila told her that Mrs. Flannery had refused to be fitted for one. "Has Sheila told you, that ghastly old woman is a spy for my husband?" she said to me. She held my eye. I smiled nervously. Dramatically, she poked a fresh cigarette into an ornate ivory holder and indicated for Sheila to run over and light it for her. "She thinks I'm joking, Sheila."

"It's true," Sheila said to me. "Mr. Adams appointed Mrs. Flannery himself."

"To keep her eye on me and make sure I don't have an affair—isn't that right, Sheila? Did you ever hear anything so ridiculous?" She laughed, and Sheila laughed too.

I stood there dumbfounded, unsure where to put myself. I had never been in a situation like this before, but while Sheila's behavior seemed inappropriate to me, maybe this was how things were done in America?

"Oh, look—we've embarrassed the new girl," Isobel said. "Sheila, take Eileen around the place and show her the ropes before we shock her anymore." And she waved us away.

Later that afternoon, when Sheila was preparing her bath, Isobel called me into her drawing room. She was wearing a baby-pink satin robe that fell into a glossy puddle on the floor behind her chair; her hair was freshly ironed and, as she beckoned me over to the window, her nails shimmered like pearls. "I hope I didn't upset you earlier with all that silly talk," she said. "Here—I wanted to welcome you with a little gift." Across her lap lay the black, embroidered robe she had been wearing on the first night. She handed it to me. "I saw you looking at it earlier, and I thought you might like it."

"Oh no, Ma'am, I couldn't . . ."

"Call me Isobel," she said, and her smile seemed genuine and kind. "And take it, for goodness sake."

I took it from her. The smell of warm lilac wafted up from the heavy, velvety package. It was the softest, most beautiful thing I had ever held. I curtsied for the second time. "Thank you . . . Isobel." It was uncomfortable for me, using the name of this generous but strange woman.

"It's nothing—you deserve it . . ." As I was leaving the room, I heard her add, almost under her breath, ". . . after all you've been through." I realized that Sheila must have told her some ridiculous tale in order to secure my position, and guessed it was probably best not to ask.

My first week of employment passed in a whirlwind of instructions and lessons. As the parlor maid, it was my official job to fetch and carry for Isobel and her many guests, but in reality my duties spread into a good deal of cleaning and even some cooking as well. Everyone in the Adams household worked hard; our day started at seven and rarely ended before eleven at night—even later, if Isobel came home late from a party and wanted a snack or a nightcap in the middle of the night.

The ten-room apartment ran on a skeleton staff, because it was not the main family residence. That was in Boston. Yet Isobel preferred the Manhattan apartment, and so her Boston mansion with its twenty staff went largely unoccupied, and we had to accommodate her lavish, demanding lifestyle with just a maintenance staff of four.

Mr. Adams, a rich industrialist, was rarely in residence.

"That man's as close to a saint as you'll find," Mrs. Flannery said, when I asked about Isobel's husband as we were preparing the supper one evening. "Made his money in steel. A decent, hardworking and respectable man, from good English stock. A gentleman, a true gentleman." She had worked for James Adams and his first wife in Boston, but her employer had asked her to move to New York four years ago, to manage his recently acquired apartment. He had also arranged for Mr. Flannery to become chief doorman for the brand-new building, and had given the couple their own apartment on 64th Street, just a short walk away. Living off site was the ultimate accolade for a servant, and the Flannerys' independent lifestyle compensated them somewhat for the upheaval in this, the latter stage of their lives. However, at the time of her relocation, Mrs. Flannery had been unaware that her boss had fallen in love with the flighty New York socialite Isobel Fisk and was intending to make her his second wife. When Mrs. Flannery mentioned Isobel, she raised her eyes to heaven and shook her head to indicate her deep, unspoken disapproval.

"He's a cold bastard," Sheila interjected. "Leaves her here for months on end on her own. Isobel's lonely. That's why she drinks."

"And the rest of it," Mrs. Flannery said, with a derisive snort.

"If Isobel knew you were saying such things . . ."

Mrs. Flannery stopped chopping fruit and pointed the tip of her knife at Sheila; she narrowed her eyes and said, in a clipped Cork accent without a hint of an American twang, "You'd be the smart girl now to mind your tongue, Miss Connelly, or you'll be on the next boat back to whatever backwater bred you. You can be certain it's not your precious 'Isobel' signing the checks around here—you'll do yourself no favors cozying up to that one. Or to any of them, for that matter. As far as they, and I, are concerned you are an Irish peasant, and don't you forget it." Sheila tutted, but she was shaken and Mrs. Flannery resumed her chopping. "Know your place and carry out your duties with pride," she said to the audience in general, taking a handful of raisins off the table and stuffing them into her mouth. "Remember—there's many a fool goes hungry in the land of plenty."

Mrs. Flannery was a talented cook and taught me how to make yeast bread: fermenting the yeast, then adding it to the bread mix instead of soda and buttermilk, to make it rise. Its stretched, sinewy texture replaced my own, crumbly soda cake to become my new daily bread. I tasted things in her kitchen I had never tasted before—coffee, chocolate, oranges; I made her laugh at least once, when I took a mouthful of grapefruit and shuddered violently at its unexpected bitterness.

Every night, Sheila sat up in bed and read Isobel's discarded fashion magazines by the light of the electric lamp. She was thrilled to have me to share them with: we sat with our arms and legs crossed over each other's bodies to make more room, as she introduced me to drop-waist dresses and beaded bags, babbling on about the fashions of the day—"This is the Cuban heel, Ellie, it's a *must* for dancing, and a fringe . . . every dancing skirt must have a fringe . . . Josephine Baker made that popular. You've heard of Josephine Baker?"—until I nodded off on her shoulder. My arms loosening around her waist, I would hear her voice vaguely admonish me for my lack of interest, before she laid me gently on my side and spooned her body around me so that her soft breasts pressed into the arch of my back. "Good night, Ellie," she would whisper. "I am so glad you are here." And in the sweet fuzz of vagueness just before sleep came, I would forget where I was and imagine it was John beside me.

Chapter Twenty-Three

7th August 1920

Dear John,

    I have barely sat down this past week, but have now found a few minutes to tell you something of my new job. Mrs. Adams is very rich and very beautiful, and although I have not met Mr. Adams as yet, I am told he is kind. Mrs. Flannery is in charge and she is from Milltown in Cork, not so far from Queenstown where I got the boat. Sheila is changed, with short hair and all style, but I am glad to have a friend from home here. Our room is adequate. I am comfortable, although I miss you here beside me at night. I am cleaning and doing some cooking also. I have been given nothing I cannot do, so my job is safe for the present. I have to tell you about the inventions here! There are telephones everywhere. I've not used one yet, but you hold it to your ear and you can talk to people on the other side of the city (I don't know anyone on the other side of the city, so it's no use to me!). We have a machine that sucks dust up from the carpets—it makes such a racket you would not believe it! There are machines for everything, John. Machines to keep you hot, others to keep you cool, machines for spinning clothes and cooking food—anything you might want to do, there is a gadget for it.

*They have inventions for things you would have never have
imagined—like shaving the hairs off your chin or curling your
hair. Electricity is in every home here, as far as I can fathom,
and* CARS? *Goodness but you have never seen so many cars!
They are lined up along the roads here like giant, angry bee-
tles—black and noisy and belching smoke. I will never get
used to the noise. The simplest invention and the one I like
best is a "shower," where instead of washing in a bath, water
comes spraying out of the wall. It is most refreshing except
that I have to wear a rubber cap to keep my hair from getting
wet. Sheila thinks I should get it cut short like hers.*

*I get paid at the end of the month and will send money
then.*

*My love to Maidy and Paud and most of all you, my
dearest, darling John. I miss you more than words can say,*

Ellie

That August was hot. Isobel lay for hours on the chaise longue
in her drawing room, the tall windows at opposite ends of the
room standing open, fanning herself with copies of *Harper's
Bazaar* and complaining about the dreadful heat. She was un-
bearably crotchety, constantly calling for jugs of iced tea and
cold compresses. Sheila leaped like a hare every time the bell
rang, but it took two of us to wait on Isobel. Sheila would be
on her way downstairs with some fresh demand—for sorbet,
or to fetch the newest edition of *Vogue* from another room—
when Isobel would call me up with some tiny, needless request:
a change of water for some flowers, a fresh handkerchief. Sometimes I suspected she was just desperate for company. But although she spent her days lounging listlessly, she cheered up in
the late afternoon when the sun began to sink behind the high
treetops of Central Park and she could respectably have a cock-

tail before getting dressed for dinner. Prohibition was in effect, but we saw no real sign of it in Isobel's life.

After cocktails at five, if not dining in town, she might ask us to prepare a light supper for herself and one or two friends in her sitting room, before they went on to the theater or a club. Or, if dining alone, she would take her dinner on a tray in her sitting room. When not in the drawing room, Isobel lived in her bedroom and the smaller sitting room beside it. Our jobs were mainly carried out in these two rooms, and it was only when Isobel held her first big party at the end of that summer that the grand scale of the apartment was truly brought home to me.

It was also the first time I had seen my mistress show any real purpose.

She rose early, calling instructions: "Sheila, get François around here, I need my hair set by lunchtime . . . Ellie, tell Mr. Flannery I want two troughs of flowers left at the entrance to-night, and don't forget I want the silver polished by five and the table now set for twenty-six, not twenty-four . . ."

From eight o'clock in the morning there was a constant stream of deliveries as the apartment filled with extra staff—merchants, decorators, chefs, florists, hairdressers, waiters in fancy white suits, each bringing with them still more riches and the instant life of a party in waiting. Several magnificent ice sculptures in the shape of horses and fish were set in the dark, cold room next to the pantry, with buckets and buckets of ice, and Precious was left on guard, wide-eyed and terrified to look at them in case they would melt under her stare and she'd get the blame. Flower arrangements, dozens of them—many of them as tall as the men carrying them—were carefully placed all round the apartment, beautifying usually ignored corners, turning empty, austere rooms into lively, scented meadows. The ballroom was opened up, and men came with long wooden tables that they covered with enough starched white linen to sail a ship. They set up silver serving trays, like those I had seen on RMS *Celtic*, and a pyramid of glasses, from which they later made a fountain of champagne.

Downstairs Mrs. Flannery was faint with stress, not least because she was about to be invaded by Monsieur Jerome. One of the best chefs in New York, he swept through her kitchen with his team, filling her traditional domain with such monstrosities as quail and lobster, emptying cutlery cabinets in search of a single spoon, moving saucepans from their rightful places, complaining loudly about the shortage of jelly molds and sauté pans and generally casting aspersions on Mrs. Flannery's capabilities while taking over her kitchen. "Just go home to bed, woman," Mr. Flannery pleaded with her, when called up from the lobby to calm her mounting hysterics. But the Irish dame steadfastly refused to leave her post, guarding her kitchen from the Frenchman's chaos. Without the authority to admonish him, she simmered quietly, glowering in disapproval at his staff and putting things back in their places, only for him to move them again.

I stayed downstairs for most of the evening. However, once the event started, I found there was very little for me to do. Monsieur Jerome's dozen or so staff had completely taken over. Having prepared their lavish meal, they went about serving it with appropriate aplomb. "The show has begun, gentlemen," the chef called, and the kitchen became a whirl of action, dressed plates whizzing in and out of the dumbwaiter, waiters in immaculate white suits running up and down the service stairs, doors opening and closing simultaneously, dodging one another with hot dishes and trays teetering on the edge of raised fingertips. I sneaked out onto the service stairs to look for Sheila.

She had spent the afternoon dressing Isobel, and had refused my offer of help. I was hurt that she would not let me join in the business of Isobel's personal preparations, and felt certain Isobel would have been happy to have my assistance as well. But Sheila was possessive over her relationship with Isobel, and I could understand that she did not want me muscling in on her territory. She worshipped her socialite mistress and earlier that afternoon had come rushing into the kitchen, flushed with the glamour of it all, and started babbling excitedly, as if it were her own party, "Our mistress is wearing the red satin gown. She says tonight is a night for red *alone*. It's going to be the party of all parties, Ellie. She's booked 'Kid' Ory, who is coming all the way up from New Orleans with ten of his orchestra, and there are all sorts of wonderful people coming. The guest list is quite deliciously mixed. The guest of honor is a perfectly *brilliant* writer—Fitzgerald he's called—I wonder if he's Irish? Isobel has designs on him, I think, but it seems he is affianced. He wrote a book called something-something *Paradise* . . . anyhow, he's promising to be quite, quite famous!"

"Suffering Mother of Christ," Mrs. Flannery said, "will you quit out of that stupid talk before I 'quite, quite' tan your hide. It's bad enough having to listen to yer woman's flimsy wittering, without getting it from you too!"

"I don't think you should talk about our mistress like that, I don't think it's . . ."

"I don't care what you think, young woman. Our mistress is not 'Isobel,' she is Mrs. Adams—and she is *not* your friend, and this is *not* your party, and the quicker you get it into that stupid little of head of yours that you are a servant, a common-or-garden servant, no better nor worse than *that* poor creature over there"—and here she waved her tea towel in the direction of Precious, who looked over sideways from her washing-up post, her face impervious to insult, impossible to read—"the happier we will *all* be."

Sheila hated being compared to Precious. Although she would not see the scullery maid put out of her room on my behalf, I knew it irked her that the Negro girl had her own room while we shared a bed. ("That child is worth a thousand of you uppity Irish straps," I had once heard Mrs. Flannery say.) After Mrs. Flannery's tirade, Sheila stormed out of the kitchen and I hadn't seen her since.

The service stairs were full of waiters flitting, so I decided to take advantage of my virtual invisibility and go down to our bedroom and freshen up before going back upstairs to sneak a look at the party. The servants' corridor was empty of life, and as I came toward our room I felt a surge of relief to be on my own, away from the madness. I approached the door quickly, but, as I reached out for the handle, I heard something move inside the room. Nothing so definite as a voice, but enough to make me turn the handle with caution and open the door quietly.

There were two people making love on my bed. I recognized Sheila's knees and stockings; they were all I could see of her. By the cut of the shoes and trousers that lay on the floor by the bed, the man whose buttocks confronted me was a gentleman. They continued their grunting and grinding as, shocked, I closed the door. Hoping they hadn't heard me, I quickly walked straight back up the stairs into the service corridor to the guest quarters, where I correctly guessed there would be nobody around. There, I stood for a few moments trying to take in what I had seen. Sheila making love to a gentleman in our room. Was this somebody she knew? A lover? If so, had she just met him, or was she keeping the affair a secret from me? It made me panic to think Sheila had secrets from me. I was so far away from home, away from John and everything I loved. Sheila was my link with Ireland, and I needed to feel close to her. I hated the idea of her lying to me, or keeping things from me. Suddenly, I felt very alone, stranded in this strange place . . .

"Excuse me."

"Ah!" I nearly screamed. A man's head had appeared right in front of me, unconnected to a body, as if materialized out of thin air.

"I was looking for the bathroom and I . . ." As the whole of him emerged, wearing evening garb and squinting slightly as his eyes adjusted to the dim light of the service corridor, I realized he had simply stuck his head out from behind one of the bedroom doors. "So sorry—did I frighten you?"

"No, I . . ." I didn't know what to say.

"Oh—hello," he said. "It's you."

I bobbed slightly and turned to go.

"No," he said. "I really do know you . . ."

I pretended not to hear and kept walking away down the dingy corridor toward the service stairs. But I knew who he was, just as well as he knew me. It was Charles Irvington, the man I had met on the boat not one month before. It unsettled me that I remembered his name.

Chapter Twenty-Four

August 1920

Dear Ellie,

It is early in the morning and not a sinner awake, only me. The bog is pure mist at this time and the mountains a dark purple beyond it, and I wishing you were here beside me to see it, but you're not and that's as it is, but hopefully not for too much longer. I got the money you sent and won't say too much more about that, except to say that it was welcome. I enjoyed the news of your adventures on the boat and beyond, and read your letter aloud to Maidy and Paud after supper. They enjoyed it so greatly they made me read it again to them the following night. Doctor Bourke has made an appointment with the big surgeon in Dublin for three months' time and we will certainly have the money to pay him for this appointment, although I am still not happy about you being gone by any means, but I'll say no more about that at present. Everyone is caught up here in the excitement of Michael Collins signing a Home Rule treaty with the British, giving us rule of the South but not of the six counties up North. Thanks be to God the British have taken their vile henchmen out of our country, but Padraig and I fear there is

*worse yet ahead, with the man who agrees with Collins
set against those who wouldn't have had us compromise
and sign. I'm with De Valera that we should have held out
for the whole of our island and not sacrificed our brothers
in the North for our own gain, but I would not fight an
Irishman on any point—even were I able. I worry for our
friend Padraig. He's a fool for his principles, and we need
his like to rebuild the country and educate our children,
instead of picking up arms against those that used to be his
brothers. In any case the mood here is better than it was,
with the British finally gone. The birds are awake now,
Ellie, and singing with such a racket that I can barely hear
myself think. There is a miracle happening in the oak at the
back of the house with a song thrush nesting there. I'd give
anything to climb up and have a look, but must content
myself to sit and watch from here.*

> *With all my heart,*
> *Your husband John*

When I got my first monthly paycheck, Mr. Flannery had
accompanied me to the bank. It was his day off and he was
dressed in a brown suit and tie, with a smart trilby hat covering
his broad, balding head.

"You look like a proper gentleman, *Seamus*," Sheila teased as
he came into the kitchen to collect me.

"Are you ready, Ellie?" he asked, ignoring her. Nobody ever
called him or Mrs. Flannery by their first names, not even Isobel.
I felt slightly embarrassed when I saw how smart he looked. I had
brushed my hair back from my shoulders and was wearing Sheila's
Sunday jacket over my navy twill skirt. I had shortened it up to
where the hem had torn, and it looked quite fashionable.

"Don't go sending every penny home," Sheila said to me.

"Keep some aside for yourself so you don't have to go robbing all my clothes." Then she winked at Mr. Flannery. "We'll hit the town when they all go to Boston next week."

Mr. Flannery was not amused, and poked me gently in the small of my back to hurry me out of the door.

Although it was late August, there was no hint of autumn in the air. This was only the fifth time I had left the building since I had arrived here—the other four being for Sunday Mass at St. Patrick's Cathedral.

The first time I had walked in through the enormous arch of the cathedral's doors, my jaw had slackened and I had wept with the sheer scale of its grandeur. The marble interior, white and cold and endless; a dozen altars glittering gold in the distance; the complex piety of stained-glass windows that seemed to stretch upward forever. In Kilmoy, I had always sat with my family in the front pew, but here Sheila nudged me into a seat near the back and we sat and watched the congregation arrive and take their seats. Wealthy families, women in smart suits and hats, their children in starched shirts and dresses marching beside them, walked straight up to the front. The poorer souls gathered around us, shabby compared to the rich people, but nonetheless smarter than most folk back home. At the back of St. Patrick's you could not hear the priest at all, only the faint clatter of the city beyond the vast carved doors behind us and the mumbled prayers and coughing of the people nearby. Mrs. Flannery walked farther up and sat in a pew nearer the front. As we walked back to the apartment, she told us that St. Patrick's was "our" cathedral. "It was built with the dollars and the labor of Irish immigrants," she said. "The poorest of the poor built it for everyone to pray in, not just the rich, and don't you forget it!"

That day it was different, being out on my own business. I

felt important, with my check in my coat pocket, going to the bank. Mr. Flannery walked with purpose down 82nd Street, then left onto Second Avenue. He explained the layout of New York to me: "Streets go across, avenues down. Most of them are numbered, you just have to keep your wits about you and count to get where you are going. It's impossible to get lost." He kept pointing out landmarks and telling me historical anecdotes that did not interest me. I wanted to ask him questions about his life: How long had he been here? What had brought him to America? How had he fallen in with Mrs. Flannery? But I kept quiet. Men of that age were experts on everything, but did not like to talk about their own lives. The people they liked best were those who kept their own counsel and listened, and in any case it suited me to walk in silence alongside him. It felt, for a time, as if we were father and daughter, out for a stroll.

The bank was one of the tallest buildings I had ever seen and there was a uniformed man who opened the doors for us. He doffed his cap at Mr. Flannery, and my escort nodded at him importantly. I thought it an extraordinary exchange, given Mr. Flannery's job, and I blushed slightly at the thought that we might be masquerading as more than we were.

We entered a room not unlike a cathedral itself, with its tall, narrow windows and high ceilings. Desks were lined across the marble floors like pews, and antechambers were screened off by ornate banquettes. Voices were muted in hushed reverence. I followed Mr. Flannery over to a tall counter in dark wood and he spoke quietly to the stern woman in glasses behind it. As she picked up a large, black telephone receiver, he leaned down to me and said, "Let me talk on your behalf, Ellie. These matters of money can be very complicated."

Presently a small, thin man of indiscriminate age came over to us and greeted the doorman, shaking his hand and grabbing his arm with a hearty warmth that seemed at odds with his sharp, poky appearance and his almost funereal, formal black suit. He took us over to a leather-topped desk, moving my chair back for me to sit down as if I were a real lady, before taking his place opposite us. "Mr. Flannery," he said, "is one of our very best customers."

Mr. Flannery was bristling with delight at his warm welcome. He was barely able to contain a smile, and put the tips of his fingers just under the starched collar, stretching it out as if allowing room for his head to grow. "Well, we are very fortunate, Ellie, because Mr. Kaplan is one of the very best bankers in all of New York."

Mr. Kaplan's fingers scrabbled across the blotter with the thrill of the compliment. "Now, what can I do for you today, Mr. Flannery? Another new account?"

"Yes," he said, without even looking at me. "Ellie needs to open an ordinary checking account."

"And will you be paying the money into the account yourself each month, as with all the others?"

"Yes, that's right."

"Excellent. Well, if we can just have a few details. What is the young lady's name?" He tapped his finger, impatient for a quick answer, anxious to get his hands on my check. It was as if I wasn't there. I was furious. This was the whole reason I was in America. Money. I had earned my paycheck that month. I had cleaned out fire grates, peeled potatoes, been woken up in the early hours of the morning to help undress my drunken mistress. Me. Not Mr. Flannery. This was my money and I was not about to hand it over without the bank affording me due respect.

"Mrs.," I said, looking him straight in the eye, "Eileen Hogan."

"Ellie," Mr. Flannery corrected me.

But I ignored him and continued: "And I would like to inquire about stocks." I had no idea what stocks were, but there was a jolly-looking fat man sitting at a desk nearby with a sign in front of him that said: "STOCKS: INQUIRE HERE" and I thought I'd rather be over there talking to him than sitting with bossy Mr. Flannery and his wire-faced friend.

The two men exchanged a panicky glance. Mr. Kaplan smiled—an unconvincing bearing of small, broken teeth—and Mr. Flannery said, "Ellie, leave this to me, there's a good girl, stocks are too complicated a matter for—"

"Did I hear this young lady say 'stocks'?" The fat man had come over to our desk and was standing behind Mr. Kaplan, towering over us like a mountain of suit. "Why, Madam—I hate to contradict you, Sir—but stocks are not complicated *at all*!"

"This is Mr. Podmore," Mr. Kaplan said, with open disdain. "He is a stock*broker*," he added, dragging the last word out and opening his eyes wide as if it held some dark warning. I didn't care. Mr. Podmore was addressing me, and that was enough.

"Stocks are pieces you buy in a company," said Mr. Podmore.

"I'm afraid you'll have to explain," I said.

"You see?" Mr. Flannery said to me, all flustered. "You don't understand. Mr. Kaplan, I—"

"You're Irish, right?" Mr. Podmore asked me, speaking right across Mr. Flannery. "Your daddy got a farm?"

"No, but my husband has."

"Well now, Mrs. . . . . ?"

"Hogan."

"Mrs. Hogan. Supposing your husband had nine cows and that was his farm. He supplies most of the village with milk, but he knows if he makes it up to ten cows he's got enough cows to supply the whole darn village. Trouble is, he ain't got the money to pay for that tenth cow." Mr. Podmore was moving his hands this way and that as he told his story. Mr. Kaplan flinched as he sensed the fat fingers flying round the back of his head, but he said nothing. Mr. Flannery was still blushing, smarting from the humiliation of being sidelined. "So, a man comes along and offers to buy him a tenth cow. That man is called an investor."

"And the cow is his investment?"

"That's right. And in return for him buying the farmer the cow, the investor gets a ten percent share in the business."

"So the man owns ten percent of all the money from the milk?"

"Hey, she's got it!" he said, throwing his palms up on either side of his huge chest. "Young lady—you are after my job!" I couldn't help laughing. Mr. Flannery looked at his feet and Mr. Kaplan studied his fingernails. "Now, if the farm flourishes, Mr. Investor makes lots of money on his milk."

"But if the farm fails, his investment fails."

"That's true—but at any time while the farm is doing well, Mr. Investor can sell his share to another investor or the biggest shareholder, who in this case is . . . ?"

"The farmer with nine-tenths."

"Mrs. Hogan, you have a sharp mind. Poor old Kaplan here can barely keep up." He gave his colleague a warm pat on the shoulders that made the skinny banker flinch. "The trick, Mrs. Hogan, is to invest in things that won't fail, and I have to tell you we have a portfolio of businesses here that cannot fail. America is changing fast—why, we've got indoor plumbing in nearly every home in New York City, and it's only a matter of time before electricity is the same and—you'll barely believe it—but we'll all be talking into telephones before too long. Now is the time, Mrs. Hogan. Right here, right now: this is the time for investing in America."

I put ten dollars into an ordinary bank account, and bought five dollars' worth of shares. Mr. Podmore did not blink when he saw how little I was investing, and when I apologized he said, "Five dollars is tomorrow's million, Mrs. Hogan. Every one of them little bills is as precious as a lil' child—and they grow just as fast." The balance I took out in bills, the bulk of which to send home to John.

At the Western Union office, I made a great fuss of asking for Mr. Flannery's help in filling out the remittance forms, to soften the blow of embarrassing him in front of his banker friend. On our way back to the apartment we passed a small ice cream shop. I stopped in front of the glass cabinet filled with ice, and white bowls piled with delicious mounds of chunky, colored creams. I took a dollar bill out of my pocket and asked the man in the striped apron and straw boater hat for two strawberry ices. Mr. Flannery was still cross with me and objected when he looked back and saw what I had done, but I thrust the dribbling cone into his hand and he licked at it like a hungry schoolboy, gobbling it back while trying to hide the fact that he was thoroughly delighted.

"Good money after bad," he said, hanging over the cone, his chest concave to protect the bib of his suit shirt from the drips. "You shouldn't be wasting your money on fripperies like this, young woman—you'll never have a penny."

The ice cream man gave me back a handful of coins, which clattered in my pocket all the way home. It was the first dollar I had spent in America.

Chapter Twenty-Five

I could scarcely believe that Sheila and I were to be left on our own in the apartment while everyone else went to Boston.

Neither could Mrs. Flannery. Every time she tried to articulate her dismay, she ended up shutting her mouth again and simply shaking her head. Her only defense was to leave us a list of chores that would have taken an army of maids a full year to complete. Every piece of metal in the apartment, from brass fire surrounds to teaspoons, was to be polished; every drape was to be shaken outside to remove any dust, then hung back in its place; every tile on every floor had to be thrice-polished by hand until you could fix your hair by them.

The reason we were being left behind was that there was already a lady's maid in full-time employment in Boston. She was a surly young girl by all accounts, but Isobel had inherited her from the first Mrs. Adams and, for reasons best known to himself, Mr. Adams would not have the maid dismissed. So Isobel had to leave Sheila behind and have this other, strange girl attend to her on her duty trips to Boston, and I was left behind to police Sheila.

The morning everyone left, Sheila and I sat alone in the huge apartment and looked at each other across the kitchen table.

"Will we make a start on the drapes?" I asked.

Sheila looked at me out of the corner of her eye, then took a cigarette out of her apron pocket and put her feet up on Mrs. Flannery's scrubbed tabletop. She lit a match by striking it on the sole of her shoe, took a drag of the cigarette and, on the exhale, pointed it at me and said, "No. I've got a better idea."

Before I could blink she had run like a hare out of the kitchen and up the service stairs. I knew exactly where she was going.

By the time I got to Isobel's bedroom, she already had a beaded skullcap on her head and was spinning around the bed, twirling a fox fur by its tail and singing, "Let's have a party!"

"Sheila, I don't think that's a very good idea."

"Oh God, Ellie—don't be such a bore!" She threw herself backward on the bed and took another drag of her cigarette. "You are such a stick-in-the-mud!" She sat up again and rummaged around in the mirrored side table by the bed, and pulled out an ornate cigarette holder. Stuffing the lit cigarette into it, she added, "You used to be such fun at school—what happened to you?"

I had not told Sheila anything about John's war wound or any of the tragic circumstances that had led me to be in America. Every time I thought about telling her, I pictured the look of pity in her eyes at the thought of my being married to a cripple. I could not bear the thought of being pitied, even by my closest friend. In truth, it was my own shame that stopped me telling her. Poverty and hardship were never badges I was comfortable wearing. In any case, the subject never came up. Sheila never talked about Ireland or her own family. She preferred to live in the glimmering limbo of Isobel's shadow. She gathered up cast-off magazines, perfumed her wrists and curled her hair in imitation of our beautiful mistress. When I had first arrived, she talked of our years together and a little of her family, but as each day passed, she appeared to distance herself a little further from Ireland. Her clothes and hair were distinctly American and she spoke with an American twang, which receded only a little now when she was alone with Mrs. Flannery and me. She was still the mischievous, lovable girl I had been to school with, but when she spoke about our days in the convent to other people, she made them sound more privileged than they were: "Ellie and I were at a fee-paying boarding school run by a French order." I never contradicted her, in private or public. Sheila was estranged from her family, from the brothers I knew she adored. She was doing what she could to survive. Whatever her reasons, she needed to forget where she came from.

"Here . . ." She was back from Isobel's dressing room, and threw a garment at me. "Try this on."

It was pointless objecting, so I took off my uniform and pulled the soft bundle up over my body. I was surprised at how heavy it felt, and that it slid on so easily. I had lost weight since I had come to America. Although the best food was on offer, I was not so inclined toward eating as I was at home. I was becoming scrawny, but when I complained about it to Sheila, she told me it was a good thing.

"When Isobel throws her clothes out in spring, you'll be able to fit into them. Mrs. Flannery gets first look and she sends most of the good stuff home to her nieces, which is a shocking waste. That's why I don't feel bad about borrowing when she goes away."

The dress she had "borrowed" for me was salmon pink, in a heavy silk weighed down with intricate black beading at its hem and across the neckline. It was sleeveless and my arms hung like bleached twigs at my side. Normally I wore my hair in a tidy bun, but with the others getting ready to go that morning, Sheila had not had time to dress it for me, so it was tied back in a simple ponytail. Gathered at the top of my spine, it hung in loose pillows over my ears. Sheila stood behind and studied me in the dressing-room mirror.

"You look awful, Ellie," she said, tugging at the sides of the dress. "You'll never pass."

"Pass as what?" I asked.

"It's the hair gives you away . . ." Sheila had been hinting I should cut my hair from the first day I arrived. I always kept it a good few inches past my shoulders, but it had grown beyond that again, and I was loath to ask my friend to trim it back for me in case she cut it too short. Sheila's eyes were shining with excitement. I caught the flash of blue steel in them as she pulled a pair of dressmaking scissors out of her apron pocket and held them over my ponytail. "Go on, Ellie, let me. A bob would look great—you'll be all the rage."

I hesitated. Perhaps she was right, but I loved my long hair. At night, John would take the brush from me and pull it down gently from root to end, then run his fingers through it, languishing in the otherness of its softness and length. *Snap!* Taking advantage of my hesitation as a "yes," Sheila had sliced through my ponytail. I screamed as my hair sprang up, suddenly gathered in two blunt waves at my ears. "Oh no, Sheila, what have you done!" I reached to the space where my hair had been and felt the lightness around my neck. Instinctively, I reached down and picked the still-tied ponytail up from the floor. A part of me that had been touched and admired by John now lay in my lap, a lifeless lump of waste. I let out a shocked sob, but Sheila took no heed of me, only fluffing the sides down around my face and saying, "There now—that looks so much better already."

Sheila chattered away over the top of my silent shock for the next little while. She ironed my hair and powdered my face and rouged my cheeks. Reluctantly, I conceded to her prodding and bossing me into several changes of dress and stockings and pointed shoes. After a while, my anger became tempered by curiosity at the transformation that was taking place in the mirror.

A different woman was beginning to appear in front of me.

When she had finished, we stood side by side in front of the mirror; she pouted, "Curse and damn you, Ellie Flaherty, but you look more of a lady than I do."

My hair was short and straight, tapered into dark points that sliced across my cheekbones. Sheila had lined my eyes in black kohl and they looked larger and bluer—an exaggerated version of themselves. My skin, always freckled at home, was now pale from the months I had spent indoors and made me look sophisticated and older. Sheila had finally chosen me a dress in dark, dark navy, with a mannish, wide-collared jacket of the same shade that came as far down as my mid-thigh. I bent my head so that she could hang a long string of glittering glass baubles round my neck. They fell almost to my waist. She touched the bare nape of my neck and said, "You look—magnificent."

I could say I didn't recognize myself, but that wasn't true. The self-assured, elegant woman who faced me was somebody I had always known, but just never had cause to meet before.

"Come on—we're going out."

"Out?" I said, horrified. "Where?"

"Oh. Ellie!" She grabbed both my hands and pulled me down onto the narrow velvet chaise longue. She looked into my eyes. "It's a secret and I'm not supposed to tell, but, oh, I can't keep it in any longer, Ellie, I'm—I'm in love! His name is Alex Ward and he's a gentleman, Ellie—a real one, with money. And he loves me, can you believe it? It was love at first sight—we kissed at Isobel's last party. In secret, it was so romantic . . ."

I was horrified. There was a lot more than romantic kissing in the encounter I had witnessed in our room that night. I hadn't told Sheila I had seen her with a man the night of the party, and she had not volunteered anything—until now. Now she was bursting with joy, but I had a sense of doom. My friend was reckless and impulsive—what kind of an awful situation had she got herself into?

"We're to meet him in the Plaza Hotel at three this afternoon."

"Sheila—you can't possibly be serious."

"Oh, don't be such a nervous ninny, Ellie—we look great. Nobody will know that we're—"

"That's not what I mean."

She looked back at me, puzzled.

I had a duty to speak my mind. Rich men having their wicked way with serving girls was a ritual as old as time itself. I was widely enough read to know these things, but while I was absorbing *Tess of the d'Urbervilles*, Sheila was gossiping or playing camogie. "He's taking advantage of you, Sheila."

"You're wrong, he loves me!"

"He's using you, Sheila. He's a rich man, they stick to their own—"

"La, la, la—I'm not listening . . . I love him, I love him, I love him . . ." Then, she grabbed my hands and swung me around the dressing room, singing, "Come on, Ellie—come, come, come—it'll be fun, fun, fun . . ."

I pulled back from her and pleaded, "Sheila, please—you're making a big mistake."

Becoming petulant, she took up Isobel's stoles and said, "Oh, what do you know— I'll go alone."

Sheila was infuriating, but I loved her and didn't want her to come to any harm, so I went along.

We left by the front lobby. Sheila selected us two wide-brimmed hats with nets that we pulled down over our faces. "We're ladies now—we must protect our lily-white skin from the sun," she said, joking, although I could tell she half-believed it.

The residents' elevator was much nicer than the service one. It had smoky, mirrored walls, and as I admired my reflection I could see an army of women in navy suits lined up like soldiers behind me. Sheila was wearing a yellow chiffon confection, a light tunic over a silk dress, which I worried would draw attention to us, but she threw her head high in the air as we walked past the temporary doorman. "Good afternoon!" she cried, waving Isobel's yellow parasol slightly in his direction, in a parody of the way an important lady might behave.

My limbs were tingling with nerves and my stomach felt tight with excitement. If we got caught, we'd surely be fired, and I'd have nowhere to go and no money to travel home. The stakes were so high that once we were outside our own building, I nonetheless made Sheila walk a full block down Fifth Avenue before we finally collapsed onto each other giggling, relieved that we had got away with it. "'Good ofternoon'—you're quite the toff!" she said. "I thought I was going to explode!"

"I thought I was going to fall flat out on the ground in these wretched shoes!"

We decided to walk through the park. It was a hot day and the vague rustling of the treetops tempted us away from the noise and the cars. I had a yearning to visit the zoo. I didn't say anything to Sheila because it felt like a foolish, childish notion, and she was so intent on keeping this liaison with her lover.

"You are going to love the Plaza, Ellie. It is quite the most glamorous place—all the best people go there . . ." Sheila's affectations became more pronounced the farther we got into the park and the closer we came to the Plaza. The park was quiet, with only a few nurses pushing strollers and the occasional gentleman rambling by. I noticed we caught the eye of one or two of them. "Alex has said we shall have afternoon tea in the Palm Lounge and then . . ."

I stopped dead and reached for her hand. "Stop your wit-tering for a minute," I said, squeezing her fingers hard as she objected. "Just close your eyes." I tilted my head back to listen to the song thrush singing—phweet-phweet—so loudly, in the tree above our heads. I felt my heart fill like a balloon with the sweetness of his voice. With my eyes closed into the sunlight, the blackness turned a deep, glowing red and the bird's song carried me home to the back field and John.

"Come on," said Sheila, "I'll race you," tugging me back into her world.

We kicked off our shoes and carried them as we ran in our stockinged feet across the soft grass toward the Plaza Hotel.

As soon as we walked through the doors and into the lobby of the hotel, an elegant woman came up to us and tried to spray us with scent. "Chanel Number Five, ladies?" I shook my head, shy and also fearful we would be expected to pay. I realized suddenly that neither of us had a cent between us. What with parasols and hats, and purses full of powder and lipstick, we had neglected to bring any money. Not indeed that a cup of tea in this place would have cost us any less than a month's wages. I felt a sudden shot of anger at Sheila and her foolishness. This was not exciting, after all, this pretending to be rich. It was fake and frightening, and I would much, much rather have stayed in the park and gone to the zoo. Why had she not arranged to meet her boyfriend somewhere sensible like that? Or better again, not arranged to meet him at all? Sheila stuck out her wrist, and the woman sprayed it. Then the woman said to me, "Are you sure you wouldn't like some, Madam?"

I saw that Sheila had not been asked to pay, so I put out my hand and attempted a smile. But, looking round, I became even more afraid that we should not be here—that we would bump into somebody who knew us as Isobel's maids, a friend of hers who would recognize that we were wearing her clothes. This was, after all, her world, not ours.

The woman pumped the wide, gold air bag and the cold shock of syrupy water flooded out onto my wrist. It smelled like nothing I had ever smelt before by man or nature. No roses or lavender, like you might find in an ordinary perfume, but sweet in a decadent way, like chocolate or oranges, or the smell of a man's skin when you are hungry for love.

"Sheila, at last!"

By the time I turned in a panic to see who had spoken, Sheila was already standing next to him, grabbing his arm, grinning like she was fit to burst, barely able to push the words out for excitement. "Ellie, this is Alex."

Alex was wearing an impeccable dove-gray, three-piece suit. At once I decided that a man who was so impeccably turned out was surely suspicious. Everything about him—the starched white shirt and pink tie, the trimmed mustache and the gold cuff links—told me that here was a cur who was taking my innocent friend for a ride. Sheila was obviously blinded by love, but I couldn't be fooled by that kind of expensive charm.

Alex blanched slightly when we were introduced. He was clearly taken aback to see another woman with Sheila, which was further evidence of his bad intentions, surely. "Hello, Ellie, how delightful to meet you," he said, poking out his hand toward me quickly as if it might drop off in the effort of tearing it away from Sheila, then returning it immediately to her after one swift shake. "Will we go in for tea?"

"Let's!" she said, and I followed them both into the Palm Lounge as Ellie steadied herself on her lover's arm, all but legless with love. This was worse than I had feared.

Tables and chairs were arranged around a sunken dance floor, set with crisp white linen and silver for afternoon tea.

Couples danced to a slow waltz, muted by the sounds of polite conversation and clinking china. Alex guided us to a table at the edge of the dance floor. As the waiter removed the reserved sign, he said, "I hope this is to your satisfaction, Mr. Ward."

Alex said, "Thank you," and allowed the waiter to pull back the chair for me as he looked after Sheila. He sought our approval to order us a jug of iced mint tea and sandwiches. "Charge them to my account, please."

Despite myself, I felt a thrill at being in a place like this in the care of such a capable, and seemingly perfect, gentleman. But when I looked across at Sheila, my fear for her flooded back. I could see love so clearly in her face. It was in the open warmth of the smile that spread across her flat, made-up features, and the pools of childish wonder that her eyes had become—she no longer cared about the glamour, or the money, or the cuff links, or the fuss the staff were making; all she really cared about was him. Her pretensions had melted away the instant he arrived. She was looking at Alex Ward not as a rich man, but just as a man—as if he belonged to her; as if this was the real thing for her.

It was my duty to protect her. When Sheila announced, "I am going to powder my nose," I stayed behind and grabbed my opportunity. "So tell me about your family, Alex?"

"Well, Ellie, my father's business is manufacturing windows, which, as you can imagine in a city with so many windows, has turned into something of a successful—"

"He can't be very happy about you going about with a servant girl, then?" I didn't have time for niceties. I wanted to get the conversation over before Sheila came back.

A shadow of anger swept across his face. "I can see that you are concerned for your friend, Ellie . . ."

"I most certainly am."

". . . but I can assure you my intentions are honorable."

I tried to talk over him, but he continued on.

"It's true that my parents will be taken aback by Sheila's current lack of status, but mostly because they will see, as I do, that she was not reared to be a servant."

This infuriated me. "Neither of us were reared to be servants, Mr. Ward, but nevertheless . . ."

"Please," he urged, and his expression softened. "Let me explain, Ellie. My grandparents were Irish emigrants. They came during the famine. Half of the family died on the way over, but my Grandfather Pat survived. He was a carpenter, and he managed to get a job building tenements up around Harlem. He was lucky—he fell in with some other Irishmen and they started out working on their own. My grandmother had six kids, but she worked in bars down at the docks to make extra money. She was a tough cookie, broke up fights with her bare hands. Those were hard times, but by the time my father was born they had their own house, which was a big deal. My pop was one of the youngest, so he got an education and took over the family firm. Ellie, my family worked hard to make a life in America, and America rewarded them with wealth. They did pretty well for themselves, and we were always taught never to forget where we came from. It's true, my parents move in different circles now that they are wealthy, but I know they will be happy that I have found the woman I love. They will love her too, I am certain of that, but if it isn't the case—"

"If what isn't the case?" Sheila had appeared behind Alex. She said, "Come on, Alex—let's go up for a dance before the tea arrives. You don't mind, Ellie, do you?" She ran to the floor, but Alex held back, anxious to finish explaining himself. When Sheila returned instantly to grab his arm, he bowed slightly to me in apology.

I watched them slow dance, appearing and disappearing behind other elegant couples. Sheila's yellow chiffon train shimmered, as her hero in his dove-gray suit held her waist and whispered sweet nothings. I could not help but feel, watching him, that perhaps he was genuine—but somehow, to my shame, I didn't feel comfort in that, either. I only felt a bitter sadness that John was not there. There was self-pity in my heart at the thought that we had never danced together in such an assured, elegant way—and, in all likelihood, now never would. At one point, as the two of them came into my view again, Sheila had her arms about Alex's neck, and they were kissing so deeply and with such passion that I had to look away.

When the music stopped, Sheila ran up to me at the table, almost knocking back the waiter who had just arrived with the sandwiches. "Alex has asked me to marry him—and I said 'Yes'!"

"Oh, darling Sheila," I said, taking her hands. "I am so pleased for you."

Alex was beaming at us both. "We should have champagne, not tea!" he exclaimed.

"Ssh, keep your voice down," Sheila whispered anxiously.

"But champagne we must have," he insisted. "If you ladies would care to join me upstairs, I have a suite booked and a bottle of something special hidden away." Prohibition was one thing, but if you had money there was always a hotel manager willing to turn a blind eye, once you were out of public view.

Sheila said, "Say you'll stay, Ellie," but I knew she hoped I wouldn't.

"No, Sheila, I have to get back." This was Sheila's day—her victory, her engagement, her fairy-tale ending.

Sheila embraced me in the lobby, and Alex shook my hands warmly. "Are you sure you won't join us, Ellie? You are more than welcome." The expression was strangely Irish.

I shook my head and smiled, then walked through the revolving door and back into the real world.

I walked slowly back through Central Park. The day had lost its angry heat and it had turned into a temperate afternoon. I stopped under the tree we had passed on the way to the Plaza, and closed my eyes, and amazingly the song thrush sang for me again.

My friend had found her Prince Charming. It still seemed nearly impossible to me that her fairy tale could have a long-term happy ending—but then, I thought suddenly, why should she not take the risk? Let her enjoy the happiness she had found—all the trinkets and riches. Alex was a handsome, sweet-natured man with money, who seemed to love my friend for all that she was.

It was an unlikely scenario—as unlikely as a song thrush taking up residence in the center of New York City. In America, it seemed anything was possible after all.

Chapter Twenty-Six

Sheila left service and moved into an apartment on Third Avenue that Alex had rented for her. It had a little scullery kitchen, a bedroom and a boxroom, and was on the top floor of a narrow brownstone. It was small, but it was Sheila's palace and she wasted no time in spending the allowance Alex had given her on fripperies for it. Two days after she moved in, I made my first visit and found her sitting on the dusty tiled floor surrounded by packages and purchases.

"Look what I bought, Ellie—isn't it adorable!" she said, handing me a blue glass cat, which by the tag I could see had cost her five dollars—half a week's wages. I put the cat on a table by the window and the sun caught it, sending dainty sparkles across the wall. Sheila gasped. "See how pretty it is?" The sun went in and the cat instantly became plain again, but Sheila didn't notice, just carried on unwrapping her treasures: an embroidered tablecloth; a pottery vase; a set of butter knives; a delicate teacup and saucer, made from china as thin as butterfly wings. "Did you ever see anything more precious? I thought I would get one before deciding to buy the whole set," she cooed.

I was irritated by her showing off her new wealth. She had not even bothered to clean the apartment properly before filling it with showy trinkets. There was dust everywhere, and a squirt of anger shot through my veins as I imagined perhaps she thought I might clean it for her—being still a humble servant. Then I pushed my anger to one side and reminded myself that I was glad for my friend's luck, and just worried for her that she was spending Alex's money so easily and at such an early stage in their engagement.

Alex had struck me as a sensible man, who understood the restrictions of marrying beneath his station and was taking pragmatic steps in getting round any reservations his parents might have. He planned to introduce Sheila into his family slowly, while distancing her from her role as lady's maid and inventing a new identity for her as lady about town. The less charitable part of me feared that if my friend showed herself to be the grasping, lazy girl I knew she was capable of being, the engagement might falter—and I didn't want that for her. If, for any reason, the marriage didn't go ahead, Sheila would have nothing and nobody to fall back on.

"Have you thought about getting another job, Sheila?"

Sheila let out a derisive laugh.

"You could do a typing course," I continued. "A good typist can earn up to twenty dollars a week."

"Why would I do that? In case you hadn't noticed, I'm a lady of leisure now." And she waved the exquisite china teacup at me. It seemed that her intention was to make the transition from lady's maid to rich lady overnight, by simply leaving her job to lounge about and look pretty full time.

I was sufficiently annoyed to point out: "Alex hasn't still introduced you to his parents yet, and—"

"For your information, Ellie," she snapped back, "that's *my* choice." She put down the cup and pouted, then widened her eyes in her girlish, dramatic way. "Oh, Ellie—they're *so* rich. They're not going to want their son to marry a *servant*."

While her laziness infuriated me, I could see underneath the spoiled bravado that my friend was terrified her fairy tale might come to a premature end. "So why not do the typing course, Sheila? Then Alex can give you a job in his firm and introduce you to his family as a respectable working woman?"

"Well, maybe . . ."

I could see she wasn't enamored of taking a route that involved work and study, but I made her promise to discuss it with Alex. As I was leaving, Sheila ran to her purse and took out the gold, spherical compact she used for her rouge. It was one of her most treasured items.

"Here," she said. "You have this."

"Oh . . . Shelia," I faltered. I didn't want to deprive her of it.

"Go on, Ellie—I bought a new one today."

I took the castoff and put it in my pocket.

"Thank you for being such a good friend," she said, and kissed me.

As I walked away, my gloved hand wrapped around the gold egg, I wondered if I would ever be in the lucky position of giving charity rather than taking it.

As Sheila took up her new life, I fell into her old one.

It became my place to attend to Isobel as her personal maid. Isobel never rose before ten, and in the few early hours before she woke I completed the essential housework chores. Mrs. Flannery allowed Precious to help me, and together we cleared out grates, prepared the few rooms that would be occupied during the day, removing dead flowers and putting fresh water in the vases, straightening tablecloths and plumping cushions. Precious was easy company and delighted to be away from her corner of the kitchen and involved in the adventure of life "upstairs."

Isobel did not like to sleep late. "I hate to wake with wrinkles," she said about the folds that entrenched themselves in her cheeks if she had fallen into one of her frequent immovable drunken comas. So I would bring in her breakfast tray at ten, on the dot, every day, pulling back the elaborate silk curtains with a deliberate swish and arranging them into their heavy tasseled tiebacks while she stretched and gathered herself out of sleep. Then I would bring over the exquisite tortoiseshell tray, placing its legs at either side of her lap.

Isobel never ate the breakfast I brought her. Sometimes she complained that it was because the egg was too soft, or too hard, and the toast too generously, or too meagerly, buttered. More often she did not even remove the silver lid from the dish. The only thing I ever saw her consume with eagerness was the boiled, thick black coffee, which she poured from its tall silver pot into a cup the size of an eggcup and knocked back in one gulp, as if taking a dose of medicine.

I often wondered why Mrs. Flannery never seemed offended by the mistress's refusal to eat the breakfast that she had gone to such trouble to prepare, but I knew enough of both of them not to pass on Isobel's complaints to the kitchen. Then one morning, while running an unexpected errand after breakfast, I nearly tripped over Precious sitting on the back stairs, with the tray on her lap polishing off Isobel's untouched bacon and eggs. She had the starched napkin spread across her lap, and her thumb and forefinger precariously pinched the tiny triangular handle of a gold wafer-thin china teacup, which she nervously held to her lips as if it were so light that she was unsure it was really there at all.

She almost leapt to her feet when I caught her, and I quickly put my hands on her shoulders to save the priceless tray and china from tumbling down the narrow flight of stairs. "The missus gets upset if the plate comes back full—that's the only reason I . . ." The poor child was mortified, close to tears.

"Good for you, Precious," I said, "it would be a sin to let that good food go to waste." I grabbed a piece of toast to keep her company and carried on down the stairs.

A strange intimacy developed between Isobel and me. I was the person who woke her each morning and the one who bid her good night, often having to undress her as I had done that first night with Sheila. Within a few weeks I knew more about Isobel than any other person had the right to know about another. I knew every item in her expensive wardrobe, and I knew the color of her blood from the congealed rags she left for me to clean up in her toilet. I knew the brands of perfume she used and the acrid smell of her breath before, and after, she drank her morning coffee. While dressing and undressing her, I became more familiar with the juts and curves of her body than I was with my own. I came to know her completely and, while I may not have liked her so much as a person, I was exposed to her humanity—her physical and emotional needs. Isobel was lonely and she needed to be close to somebody. That person had been Sheila and now it was me; but where Sheila had idolized and flattered her, I took a stronger stance with my mistress, which placed me on a more equal footing with her.

It began one afternoon when Precious was helping me to clean Isobel's dressing room. The mistress was out having tea and I took the opportunity to spring-clean her wardrobe. I had decided to clear out a dressing-room shelf that had been bothering me for some time. It was a high shelf, containing hats that had been mysteriously separated from their boxes and were sitting in this ignored corner fading and gathering dust. I couldn't wait to get my hands on them and was excited at the idea of restoring them to their former glory. I was up on the ladder inside the cupboard and, as I handed each one down to Precious, she placed them on a white sheet, which we had spread out on the bedroom carpet so that we could clean them without disturbing the other clothes with dust. We were not expecting Isobel back for hours, and when Precious didn't come after my calling her, I struggled down from the ladder muttering my annoyance. When I came out to the bedroom, Precious was standing with her head right down on her chest and her hands clasped together tightly like she did when Mrs. Flannery was giving her a roasting. Isobel was standing opposite her, looking with astonishment at the white sheet and the scattered hats.

"What on earth is going on here?" Isobel asked me as soon as I came in.

"Precious and I were clearing out a top shelf and—"

Isobel interrupted. "Precious—would you leave us, please." There was a disapproving tone to her voice that at once made my hackles rise.

Precious shuffled out with a "Thank you, m'lady, sorry, m'lady."

"Ellie," she said, as soon as Precious was out of earshot, "I would really prefer it if you would not let the Negro girl touch my things."

"Why not, Ma'am?"

She put down her clutch bag and adjusted her collar. "Well, Ellie, it just isn't—isn't—*seemly*." Isobel often seemed to have a limited number of words available to her; on this occasion, delighted to have found the right one, she raised her eyebrows at me in triumphant conclusion.

"Oh, I see," I said. But I could not let it go. I was aware that Negroes were not considered equals to us pale-skinned Irish, and certainly nothing I had ever learned in school had suggested that they were anything but poor souls in need of the white man's support and guidance. But New York had opened my eyes. The kind stranger who had guided me when I fell had been a Negro; the jazz musicians and dancers Isobel readily employed as entertainment for her parties were all black skinned. On the one hand, Isobel was happy to dance in drunken abandon to jazz music, tripping over furniture and grinding her bony hips in a poor imitation of Josephine Baker; yet she considered the careful touch of an innocent Negro girl on her clothes to be "not seemly." I looked my employer square in the face. "If I am to attend to you properly, I need help around the apartment."

"That is fine, Ellie, but I simply would prefer it if Precious did not touch my personal things."

"It's a great shame you didn't tell me that earlier, Ma'am, as Precious has been responsible for washing and pressing your silks and undergarments for some time now." That was a lie, but it clearly worked, as Isobel's eyes widened. I continued, "And with respect, Ma'am, in my time here I have found that Precious is a dear and charming person, helpful to the core and meticulous in both her work and her personal habits."

"Really?" Isobel said, not entirely without amusement.

"Yes, Ma'am, and it is my opinion that she is more suited to the position of parlor maid than scullery maid—in her presentation as much as her capabilities. As far as I can see, Precious is a good, decent person and I cannot see, with the greatest of respect, Ma'am, why a person should be judged good or bad, dirty or clean, by the color of their skin."

Isobel studied my face and I felt my cheeks grow hot. Had I thrown away my livelihood, my future? Then I noticed that Isobel herself was reddening. As the red reached her eyes, they filled with water and I feared, dreadfully, that I had made my mistress cry. I would be dismissed surely! Except that she said, very gently, "Well, that is just fine, Ellie," then turned and walked out the door.

Chapter Twenty-Seven

Precious was not promoted to parlor maid—Mrs. Flannery would never have allowed it anyway—but she continued to help me as part of her duties and was given full access to Isobel's things. Although the incident was never mentioned again, Isobel's attitude to Precious changed. She was more respectful of her and went out of her way to praise Precious for the way she polished her side table or arranged her bangles by color. Yet it was Isobel's change in attitude toward me that was the more remarkable. My mistress began to seek my advice and approval.

At first it was just on what she wore. "Ellie—should I wear the feather hat with this or is it 'too much.'"

"I really couldn't say, Ma'am."

"Oh, come on, Ellie, I know you have an opinion—and stop calling me Ma'am. It makes me sound so old!"

"I think the red felt Lanvin would be better."

"You are right of course, Ellie," she would say, picking out one hat, or coat, or set of gloves over the other. "You are *always* right."

One day she said, "Can you read, Ellie?" I blushed in anger as she quickly redeemed herself: "No, no, of course you can read— What I meant to say is, do you *like* to read?"

The truth was that I had not had time to open a book since I arrived in America. "Oh yes, I love to read."

"Good," she said, "because I detest it, but I do like to know what is going on in the world. Perhaps you would read this to me now?" and she handed me a copy of *This Side of Paradise*. "F. Scott is such a sweetheart and he is *all* the rage, but the print hurts my eyes."

We sat in the drawing room, Isobel on the gold chaise, her stockinged feet tucked up to her tiny rump for comfort, and I on a hard chair opposite her. From the moment I began, the two of us were mesmerized by the charmed, privileged life of Princeton student Amory Blaine. After a while, seeing me shift uncomfortably, Isobel suggested I move into the large armchair by the window. It was so soft that I felt as if I was sitting on a cloud, and the seat was so wide and high that I struggled to keep my feet on the ground, my head resisting the temptation to fall back and disappear into its silk-covered duck-down cushions. At the end of each chapter I flicked my eyes across to Isobel, to see if she wanted me to continue. Although her eyes were closed, she had her fingers to her mouth, indicating that she was not asleep, but listening intently—perhaps drawing pictures of the handsome young protagonist in her mind, hoping some raffish suitor might barge into her own life and carry her off into a whirl of heady decadence without the restrictions of respectability that her husband's money demanded of her.

At lunchtime, she held up her hand for me to stop and called down to the kitchen for tea. Precious came up with a small plate of sandwiches and one cup. Isobel insisted that she go and fetch another cup for me. I was mortified and offered to go to the kitchen and eat my lunch there.

"Certainly not," she insisted, "you are engaged in very important work. I can't wait a moment longer to see what happens to our hero. Precious, tell Mrs. Flannery to make some sandwiches for Ellie, and I would like some coffee sent up also."

In protest Mrs. Flannery sent up a tin mug on an old wooden tray with two thrown-together crusts barely acquainted with a slither of cheese.

I read until the last line and, as I looked up from the gaudy yellow cover, I noticed that I had been reading virtually in the dark. The trees of Central Park were silhouetted against a steel gray sky, the streets empty as everyone sat down to dinner with their families. Isobel and I sat in the wake of our wasted day. Precious called up to tell Isobel her dinner was ready on a tray if she wanted it, and I sensed she was going to ask me join her for dinner so that we might sit and review Amory and his antics.

I knew that would be a bad idea, not least because of what Mrs. Flannery might send up to me a second time. I stood immediately and followed Precious out of the room before Isobel had time to ask. I turned as I reached the door, and noticed how her eyes had hollowed in the shadows of the gray dusk light. She looked more lonely than any person had a right to be. I flicked on the electric light switch as I was leaving, and she smiled and said, "Thank you." As the door closed behind me, I remembered I was lonely too, and with a brief, unexpected pang of bitterness I wondered who was there to turn on the light for me.

Isobel took a house by the Jersey Shore for the winter, where she hosted small weekend parties for her coterie of artistic and eccentric hangers-on. She always took me, and only me, away with her. This caused me the joint discomfort of fending off Mrs. Flannery's suspicions that Isobel was "up to something" and the backbreaking responsibility of being the sole servant in a houseful of demanding people.

While Isobel had adopted me as a confidante, gifting me with increasing numbers of her castoffs, and requiring that I waste afternoons reading to her or just sitting on the end of her bed discussing the fashions of the day, she still expected her stockings to be hung, her hats placed pristinely back in their boxes, her dresses pressed and her silks carefully wrapped in tissue paper. Drunk or sober, last thing at night Isobel would sit at her dressing table and slather her face in cold cream, wiping it off with a silk handkerchief that she carelessly threw after her. In the morning, when she checked herself again, the mirror had to be polished, any greasy smears removed first with soapy water, and a freshly laundered handkerchief left in place of the used one.

At the apartment in Fifth Avenue, Mrs. Flannery tended to all the servants' basic needs, as far as warmth and food were concerned, and I had Precious to help me with the smaller details. However, in Jersey I was expected to cook and prepare the meals, tidy up after everybody and tend to Isobel's insecurities and needs.

Isobel was lackadaisical in her habits and careless with her belongings. She would carry sandwiches into the bathroom with her and leave them on the sink, to be found by me hours later, in a dripping, swollen heap. She tossed her shoes off while walking up the stairs, the pair separating as one tumbled to the bottom and the other wedged itself treacherously in the carpet rail, to cause the person after her to trip. She had become so used to people cleaning up after her that she was entirely unaware of the mess she made and the work it meant for me. Rooms had to be aired and prepared for guests, food delivered, then menus agreed and meals cooked for up to ten houseguests. The first two weekends I was like a whirling dervish—running up and down the stairs, catering to the whims and demands of the noisy socialites, artists and hangers-on, while at the same time cooking their meals and running them baths, and doing everything but brushing their teeth for them.

On the other hand, these weekends gave me a break from the city, and the monotony of my daily routine. The best part was the car journey down, when there was nothing to do but sit and talk for two hours. We were collected at the front entrance of the apartment block by a uniformed chauffeur. In the emerald-green cape with matching hat and gloves that my mistress had given me, I looked more like her friend and companion than her servant as we walked out past Mr. Flannery and climbed into the big, black car.

Isobel confided nonsense to me about small flirtations and I inquired after acquaintances and socialite rivals, allowing her to babble on. On the journey for our second weekend, I asked after Charles Irvington.

"How do you know him?" she asked, astonished. "He's almost *never* in the society pages—although his family are *very* rich." She was thrilled to hear how I had met him on the boat, clapping her hands with delight. I felt so proud of my ability to entertain her that I even told her about commenting about his shiny white teeth, and she screamed with delight at my scandalous tongue.

"I saw him at one of your parties," I said. "The first one you gave after I got here."

"Oh, my God—that's right. He came with Dolly Vinewood, dreadful woman, looks like a horse. Where did you see him? What did he *say*? Did he remember you? Was there *romance* in the air, Ellie?"

"Of course not—I'm sure he didn't even remember me!" And I felt slightly giddy with the silliness of her suggestion.

"Oh, Ellie, how exciting. Maybe I'll invite him again—for your benefit!"

I blushed and she nudged me crudely, then her expression became serious, and she looked at me queerly as if thinking of confiding in me. I turned the conversation to some other frippery. I didn't want to carry any of Isobel's darker secrets. There had been times when I wondered if my mistress had a special lover. Up to now, she had made no move to confide in me—perhaps because she feared what I would say. I would have said nothing, of course. In truth I had no opinion on my mistress's behavior, one way or the other. I had married for love and had never experienced desires for anyone other that John. Isobel had married for money alone, and so she was alone in her marriage. For that reason it would not have surprised me if she sought comfort from other men.

We stopped at a gas station en route, and the boy who filled the tank doffed his cap at me. It reminded me of the boys in town back home, where I was considered a real lady on account of my father's job.

When we arrived, Isobel pleaded with me, "Don't start work right away, Ellie. I'll be too lonely here in the big house until my friends arrive. Sit and have tea." She was mindless of the fact that I had to leave her alone in order to go to the kitchen and make it.

Later, I heard her praise me to an unpleasant bearded young artist, as I was coming into the library with some cocktails. "Ellie is wonderful. She would do *anything* for you!"

"Having servants is *so* bourgeois," he rudely responded.

"Oh, Ellie's not really a maid, Franz, she's more a *friend*—isn't that right, darling?" Her hand reached out and touched the skirt of the castoff day dress she had encouraged me to wear instead of my uniform, the better to please her liberal friends. "We're all equal here, Ellie—isn't that right?" she pleaded with me.

"Absolutely, Ma'am," I said, adding meanly, "Please excuse me while I go and finish cleaning up the kitchen after lunch."

"You see," I heard Franz say as I was leaving, "it's people like you, Isobel, who are keeping our class structure alive. What we need is a revolution. For the Negroes and the working class to rise up . . ."

I felt like suggesting he might start the revolution by coming downstairs and helping me with the pots and pans. But I didn't. Despite the hard work, I enjoyed taking part in the delusion that I was more friend than servant.

Chapter Twenty-Eight

Mrs. Flannery disapproved of Isobel encouraging me to forget my place, yet she remained convinced that at heart I was a sensible type and not "a foolish flibbertigibbet" like Sheila, whose imminent marriage into money was a subject she derided with huge cynicism. Mrs. Flannery was part of a New York network of housekeepers who, between them, could trace the inside workings of every wealthy family along the east coast of America. "I know that family. That Alex lad is from self-made Irish stock. Hardworking. If Sheila doesn't bring something to the table, she'll never be let in. There's nothing in this life comes free. She'll have to earn her place one way or another."

When I returned exhausted after the second of Isobel's weekends, Mrs. Flannery decided that I was being exploited. "Expecting you to cater for ten people? What was that stupid woman thinking of! You're only a lady's maid, Ellie—you're not trained for that kind of work!" With her years of experience in such matters, Mrs. Flannery could organize a weekend house party without even being there, which is exactly what she proceeded to do.

She sat me down and planned menus for the whole weekend—simple food that I would be able to prepare and manage easily.

On the Friday night, a cold meat platter and potato salad because "people will be arriving at different times, so the food can be laid out in the dining room and they can help themselves." The same went for breakfast, with a selection of pastries—eggs and sausages an optional extra on the Sunday morning—to be prepared beforehand and left on a heated metal dish, a miraculous new invention in which she had recently invested, and released to me with severe warnings to neither break it nor blow up the house with it. For the Saturday she gave me the recipe for a minced meat and tomato-based sauce to be poured over spaghetti. "It's Italian," she said. "Put the whole lot in a big dish and let them help themselves. Trust me, these bohemians are well used to eating rough and ready." We practiced by cooking "spaghetti Bolognese" together for the staff supper that evening. It was tangy and sweet, hearty enough to eat every night. Mr. and Mrs. Flannery both passed it over for boiled bacon and potatoes, never conceding to like "foreign food," but as we were clearing it away, I saw the old woman dip a hunk of white bread into the burgundy sauce and stuff it back greedily while she thought nobody was looking.

When everything was set, the housekeeper then instructed me to give Isobel my drill for the weekend. Meals were to be eaten at set times only. Drinks and snacks could be found in the dining room during the day, but food was not to be carried up to the rooms and left there. There would be no laundry or mending services offered to guests, save what Isobel herself needed. No running upstairs and downstairs, willy-nilly, catering to every guest's whim. "Put your foot down now, Ellie, or those people will take advantage. You might be in Isobel's service, so you have to put up with her. But it is not your place to cater for that godless gang of fly-by-nights she has hanging about. Artists and writers, my eye—not a decent job between them! You are as good as any of them, Ellie Hogan, and don't you forget it."

Isobel had no problem ordering an extra car to carry all the food, much of it already prepared for me and packed with ice, for the weekend. Mrs. Flannery was a consummate professional and, despite her protestations about Isobel's guests, she had catered for every other detail. She packed away laundered napkins, bath- and hand-towels, fragranced soaps, bath salts, chocolates and lavender pillows for each bed, and had me write out ten times a welcoming letter to be left in each room explaining mealtimes and the availability of hot water. In addition, she sent a telegram to a cleaning service in Jersey and arranged for them to send me a girl on Saturday to stay over until Sunday to help me clean and work the kitchen. The bill was to be sent straight to Mrs. Flannery and the girl could sleep in the kitchen, so that Isobel, who never came downstairs, would not even know she was there.

As soon as we got to the house, the driver of the second car drove round to the tradesmen's entrance and helped me to unload the many bags and boxes into the large kitchen, side-scullery and larder. Once the last bag was in, I asked if he would like tea after his journey, but he declined politely and I gave him the dollar tip that Mr. Flannery had pressed into my hand for that purpose.

I briefly surveyed my boxes, rubbing my gloved hands together, both because of the cold and, I realized, with some excitement. In truth, I was relishing the prospect of the coming weekend, being in charge of proceedings. I knew what was in every box and bag, where it was to go, how and when each of its contents was to be stored and then dispatched. I briefly surveyed my field of battle, making last-minute decisions about where to put various items and then, full of energy, I ran up the stairs to check on Isobel. I was anxious to get her settled into her evening toilet and dressing routine so that I could come back downstairs and get on with my preparations.

Isobel was not in her room, but standing in the hallway. She was still in her furs and the door was open. Although I had heard our car drive away as the other was still unloading, there was another car at the end of the path, waiting with its engine running.

"Ellie," she grabbed both my hands. "I have the most thrilling thing to tell you. I am not spending the weekend here at all, but with . . . with a friend." Her eyes were already looking out the door. Her face was wild with excitement. "You understand nobody must know about this—only you, darling Ellie? I'll be back on Sunday."

So she did have a lover, and she was abandoning me for him. Her hands released mine, but I clutched at the soft, navy leather of her gloves. "What do you mean? What shall I do? What about all the guests?"

She was smiling, laughing almost, "I've canceled them all, Ellie . . . It was a trick!" And she giggled and drew back her lips in a naughty, child-like grin. "Goodness, Ellie, you must think I'm dreadfully wicked."

"But what about all the food—all the work that me and Mrs. Flannery put in? The expense of the extra car? How can I bring all that food back with me? What shall I do with it all?"

She snatched her hands away and her girlish expression darkened. "Oh, for God's sake, Ellie, you'll think of something. Frankly, I can't believe how selfish you are being! I thought you'd be pleased for me. Anyway, I don't have time for this," and she straightened her gloves as she walked out the door. "You have the whole house to yourself—do whatever you like."

I stood dumbfounded looking after her.

When she reached the bottom of the steps she stopped and, clearly remembering that I was her "friend," turned and called up, "Enjoy your weekend, Ellie, and remember, it's our secret!"

Chapter Twenty-Nine

I went back downstairs, furious. I started to work as a distraction from my rage, unpacking all of Mrs. Flannery's boxes haphazardly, unsure whether to bother placing the cheeses, cold meats and milk in a cool place or simply throw them out immediately. I could not take the food back, untouched. Even if I had not been told it was a "secret," I could not have offended the housekeeper in that way. As I worked I tried to imagine the lies I would have to tell about how much the food had been enjoyed, but I could not.

The more I unpacked, the more I became aware of the pointlessness of my task—until, in frustration, I emptied the linens in one hard shake onto the long kitchen table. They fell from their bag like white birds, wings unfolding onto the bleached wooden surface, landing lifeless, untouched, their meticulous, pressed beauty barely damaged. I grabbed at handfuls of them, scrunched them up in my hands to try and make them look as if they had been used. As I pulled and tugged at the starched fabric, my anger reached boiling point. I wiped the napkins across my face and mouth, until I felt my skin turn raw, and the more I rubbed and tugged, the angrier I got. Here I was putting on a show so as not to hurt Mrs. Flannery's feelings and to cover up for Isobel's sins. I had been looking forward to this weekend, to being in charge, meeting some more of Isobel's "eccentric" set and playing at being her friend. Now, here I was, alone. Everybody catered for except me.

I picked up a heavy towel and attempted to tear it apart to loosen some of my rage. It was too strong, so I tried to split the edge of it with my teeth. As I held it up to my mouth, I caught sight of myself in the base of a copper saucepan, my mouth contorted and my eyes wide with rage. I was struck by the absurdity of my anger and it deflated, leaving a terrible hollow feeling in its place. I took a deep breath and decided I would go upstairs and try to enjoy the house. Maybe set a fire, then sit and read a book or perhaps write John a long letter.

I walked from room to room, running my hands along the bookshelves of the study, locating paper and pens on the small lady's bureau, plumping cushions on the sofa and noting coal in the scuttle—but neither setting a fire nor sitting down to write. I could not settle. I was standing at the drawing-room windows, considering closing the drapes, when I noted there was only a little light left in the sky. It was a cold night. Soon it would be dark and the ice would begin to harden. Now would be the time to go for an evening stroll and let the cold evening air settle some sense into me.

Isobel had a second set of furs in a downstairs closet. Not the mink she was wearing, but a lesser fur—soft and black, rabbit perhaps. I put on the long coat, then the hat whose sides flopped down across my cheeks, then stuffed my ungloved hands into the huge muff. The black fur next to my skin felt deliciously soft and decadent, as if I was a blackbird flying through a cloud of soft, black soot.

A thin layer of snow had fallen since my arrival and it crunched satisfyingly under my feet as I trotted down the street. I breathed in, and the bite of cold air against my chest felt clean and refreshing. As each breath released itself with a visible white cloud, my earlier frustration disappeared into the night. I was alive and walking, undisturbed, through an expensive suburb of New Jersey in a beautiful fur ensemble. I felt happy and energized, and walked faster until it started to snow again and I decided to go back and finally set a fire.

As I reached the path to the house, I lost my footing on the hardening ice and fell. When I tried to get up, my right ankle flared with pain, and I collapsed back down to the ground. Gingerly inspecting the damage through my stocking, I thought it was not broken. Yet it was a bad sprain, and I would surely have to wait a while for it to settle before I tried to stand on it again. I packed some of the icy snow around my ankle to reduce the swelling and turn it numb, but my fingers went numb first. The street I was on was sparsely inhabited, and all of the neighboring houses were dark and empty. This was an area where the wealthy kept their weekend homes, and few of them were used during the winter. A veil of snow continued to fall like white feathers disappearing into the black soot of my fur coat. My hands were burning with the cold, but as I reached out for the fallen muff, my foot shot through with pain again and gave me permission to cry. So I lay down on the white ground, my hot tears of anger freezing on my cheeks, my heart pounding hard against my chest in self-pitying sobs. I knew I should call out for help, but the greater part of me just wanted to continue lying there, my glamorous costume reduced to a heap of fur, like a dying street dog. I felt completely alone. I was helpless and weak, the fight gone out of me. My anger softened to despair.

Then, just as I was closing my eyes, I heard the crunch of footsteps and a man's voice was saying, "Are you all right?"

I jolted up with surprise, and then cried out in pain.

"Ouch!" he said. "That doesn't sound good." He squatted down beside me and, touching the hem of my coat, asked, "May I?" I nodded. The light was all but gone and his hat shadowed his face, but something about him felt safe, almost familiar. He gently lifted the black fur where it flapped at my feet and looked at my leg. I didn't know why I was allowing him to diagnose me. I knew my foot wasn't broken, but I was just happy not to be alone. To have somebody—even a strange man—seem to care. "Yep," he said. "One—two legs. I'm no doctor, but they're still both attached."

I smiled, and as I did I cried a bit again, just at the fact that I was smiling. I felt such a fool, smiling and crying like that, but then he pushed at the rim of his felt hat, setting it back from his forehead, and smiled at me. In an instant twist of excitement, I recognized him as Charles Irvington.

"Look's kind of chilly down there. Let's see if we can get you up?" He slipped his hands under my arms and pulled me up onto my good leg in one strong move. "Now—let's get you into the house." Trying to keep the weight off my right foot, I leaned into his long cashmere coat, my head barely reaching his shoulders. How did he know where we were going? Why was he here? *"I'll invite him again—for your benefit!"* I felt a knot tighten in my stomach. I didn't know whether to be pleased he had been there to rescue me, or mortified at the idea that Isobel had invited him there for "my benefit."

"Looks kind of dark in here," he said, as we limped through the gate. "Where is everyone? I thought this was supposed to be a party? Oh, this is too awkward—here." And quite suddenly he scooped me up into his arms and started to carry me up the steps to the house. I laughed. And then I cried a bit more again, because now I was laughing. It was as if the catch I kept on my emotions had been released in my fall, and now all these messy, vulnerable feelings were spilling out of me. Through my semi-hysteria I suddenly realized that I had no key to the front door—only the large black key for the tradesmen's entrance that was in the apron I had on under my coat. "Sorry," I said. "You'll have to take me to the kitchen door." I added, "Around the back."

"Sure thing, Ma'am," he said, changing direction, and I felt disappointed for a second that he had showed no great surprise at my servant's familiarity with the kitchen door. When we reached it, he let me down on my good leg and I scrabbled around for the keyhole in the pitch dark. He took a lighter out of his pocket and held it to the door so that I could see what I was doing, but my hands were trembling. "Allow me," he said, and took the key off me and opened the door.

"Well, thank you for your help," I said, formally holding out my hand.

He took it firmly, and I felt the warmth flood back into my skin. "Is there anyone else at home? No party?"

"No," I said, avoiding his face as I pulled my hand away. "I'll be fine. Thank you again."

He did not move away and, in my anxiety, I stood on my bad ankle and collapsed, just inside the door. He rushed to pick me up and helped me over to a chair. "Would you like me to go and get a doctor?" he asked.

"No," I said. "I'm sure it's not serious."

"It seems pretty serious to me," he said. "Let's get you settled somewhere more comfortable."

"There's no need."

But he lifted me up in his arms again. "Nonsense. A lady can't be expected to travel up the stairs on one foot. By the way," he said, stopping for breath in the hallway. "I'm Charles—but you probably don't remember me."

He carried me all the way up two long flights of stairs to the small drawing room and laid me down on the chaise longue, pulling my damp coat away from my shoulders and throwing it carelessly onto a chair to dry. "Now, I'm going to light the fire." A fist of warmth opened in my stomach. Nobody had been this kind to me in a long time. He squatted at the grate. His woolen trousers were straining across his knees, shirtsleeves rolled up almost to his shoulders as he picked lumps of coal from the scuttle with his bare hands. His arms were thick, striped with veins and bulging with muscle, like a workingman's arms. He smiled at me over his shoulder. "We met on the *Celtic*? There was a party in the first-class dining room and we talked for a few minutes? About my teeth?"

I shrugged and smiled as if I wasn't sure.

"Then we met again at Isobel Adams's party? We bumped right into each other?"

He made it sound as if we had both been there as guests, as if I had been wearing a cocktail dress and then disappeared into the night like some modern-day Cinderella. He was still holding a coal, turning it in his fingers, dropping soot on the rug and making his hands so black I was afraid for the white shirt. He was domestically uninhibited. The kind of man who would drop things and make a mess without even knowing it; the kind of man who would make a tidy woman nervous to have about the place. "I guess you just don't remember me."

He sounded so forlorn that I asked, "How did the son of a tycoon get a workingman's arms?" I regretted it immediately. I had not meant to sound so flirtatious.

He grinned and his gleaming white teeth outshone his eyes in the growing flames of the fire. I could feel, more than see, that he was excited to know I remembered him. "Well, that's because I *am* a workingman. I work for my father's company, so I get to choose any job I like—and I like to work loading at the docks." I didn't know how to respond. It seemed unlikely, yet admirable, that a person of privilege should want to work alongside ordinary men, so I was relieved when he stood up and said, "Well, I'd better wash my hands."

"Go down to the kitchen," I said suddenly, surprising myself more than him. "I don't want you messing the upstairs bathrooms with that coal dust."

"Yes, Ma'am," he said, touching his blond forelock and covering it in soot.

When he came back, he was carrying a tray laden down with food. "I hope you don't mind me helping myself, but I'm starving with the walk here, and I was kind of expecting to be fed!" He had selected some cold meats and cheeses, bread, butter, a bottle of wine. There were two plates and a miscellaneous array of cutlery and crockery that confirmed he was not familiar with organizing his own supper. I hadn't the heart to send him away hungry, and the sight of food made me realize I hadn't eaten myself. I sent him back down for some glasses, a tablecloth, butter knives, napkins and various other sundries, so that we might eat, "if not like civilized people, then at least like human beings!"

As we ate, he told me that he knew Isobel Adams only slightly—he found her racy and a little foolish. It had surprised him when she had invited him to this weekend house party a few days ago, by telephone, and it surprised him even more that it had been canceled without warning. "But it's even better this way," he said. "We can have our own party." I should have asked him to leave then, after he had eaten. I was not afraid of Charles—although maybe I should have been—but I *was* afraid of what Isobel had done. It was quite clear she had managed things so that Charles would be alone with me, in her house, and I was shocked that she could be so careless of my safety and my virtue. I must have been looking at him queerly, as he quickly added, "Of course, our party shall be a far more respectable affair than one of Mrs. Adams's gatherings!"

Although I knew that was the sensible thing to do, the respectable thing to do, I didn't ask him to leave. Instead, I said, "I'm glad you came, because otherwise I might still be lying outside freezing in the snow."

We sat and talked. He told me he was staying in the neighborhood himself, preferring to winter away from his family. He talked of his life as a rich man's son. I told him nothing of myself in return, despite his asking. My life was in such contrast to his, I was certain he would not have understood. So I kept the conversation light, and we talked about everything and nothing in particular: traveling on ships, the making of cheese, the clarity of wine, the ludicrousness of ladies' fashion and the loosening effects of jazz. The curtains were closed, the electric lamps on, and the ashes built up in the grate until the coal embers glowed orange in the beige dust. He put on the gramophone and danced the Charleston with a mop for a partner. I sang him "My Lagan Love," then broke the spell by teaching him a rebel song—he feigned shock at its bloody, angry lyrics, until he confessed that he had known it all along from his navvy friends on the docks.

"John taught it to me," I said.

"John?"

"John. My husband." I knew immediately that I brought up John's name deliberately, to put a stop to this pleasant evening. It must have occurred to me that, in talking, Charles and I were making love of sorts.

Charles's face went from friendly and animated to blank. He stood up and walked toward the fire, his back to me. "I didn't know you were married."

I forced out a laugh. "I'm a good Catholic girl of over eighteen years of age, of course I'm married!" I hated the way my voice sounded, hard and shrill. "My husband is called John. Did I not say?" It felt wrong repeating "John" as if it was just a casual word in our conversation. John was my life. He was the reason I was here. "I love him, and he loves me. We've known each other since we were children." Now I wanted Charles to turn round and listen to me. I wanted to talk properly about John and my life. I wanted to make John real, and bring him into the room with us.

Eventually Charles did turn round, but all he said was, "Then where is he?"

"What do you mean?" I was shocked by his cold expression.

"Well, he's not here, is he? What kind of a man lets his wife travel to America without him?"

I cried, "My husband is a captain in the Irish Republican Army and he was badly injured. He has a medal! I came here of my own will to earn money for his treatment. He didn't want me to come. He tried to stop me!"

"If you were mine I would never let you go," he interrupted.

"But I'm not," I said, "yours."

In the moment's silence that followed I could not help but wonder what it would be like if that were not true. What would happen if I were to give Charles permission to love me? Would he take this thin veil of loneliness off my shoulders and replace it with a warm blanket of affection, allow me to feel the comfort of being held in somebody's arms again? John was not here, and love was love, from wherever it came. For an instant, I thought about reaching out and grabbing a moment, just one moment for myself. It had been so long. Except that I knew that one moment would stretch back into my past and wipe clean the canvas of my life. The days in the fields, picking hedgerow berries on the way home from school, starving myself for the love of John, our paupers' wedding day, the hard knocks of poverty and war—even the loneliness I was experiencing now was part of the fabric of my love for John. One moment of weakness would reach back over the years and pull it all away, like it had never happened.

I smiled at Charles. A blank smile, devoid of seduction. I tested my foot on the floor and stood, shakily. "My foot feels much better now. The swelling has gone down. Thank you."

"I'm sorry, Ellie—I shouldn't have said . . . It's just that—"

"I'm tired, Charles. I think I should go to bed."

He insisted on bringing me downstairs to my room, off the kitchen. I let him carry me, although there was no real need. I held my face slightly too close to his shoulder and breathed in the smell of wood smoke and sweat from his shirt, resisting the desire to let go and sink into him. In the maid's room, he laid me down on the hard, narrow bed, then turned his back quickly. At the door, he stopped and began, "If you ever need anything, Ellie . . ." but trailed off in the face of my silence.

I waited for the kitchen door to slam as he left the house, but it didn't. A few minutes later I heard a chair scrape across the kitchen floor. I lay awake for a short while, but fell asleep secure in the comfort of knowing I was being watched over.

I was woken by the maid arriving, soon after eleven the following day. I could not remember the last time I had slept so late, certainly not since my arrival in America.

Chapter Thirty

I didn't see Isobel for almost a week. She sent a car to bring me back to Manhattan alone. As the driver arrived, he handed me a note from her.

> *Darling Ellie,*
>
> *I hope you had fun with Charles. I couldn't resist the opportunity to make a romance—I'm longing to hear all! I can't bear to go home just yet—would you be a dear and tell everyone that I fell ill over the weekend and am staying on in Jersey for a few days? Just say I'm "with friends," and if that old spy Flannery interrogates you, you'll cover for me, won't you?*
>
> *Love, your friend, Isobel*

"What do you mean ill?" Mrs. Flannery asked as soon as I arrived back. "Is she in hospital— Did she take a fall?"

"I don't know," I said. "She just said she felt ill."

"Well, was she vomiting? Did she have a temperature?"

"I think it is just a bad cold . . ."

"And if you are here, who's looking after her?"

I hated all this lying. I invented wildly, "Her friends have lots of maids. And they have employed a nurse to look after her."

Mrs. Flannery became genuinely concerned. "A nurse? Who are these people she's staying with? Is it Dolores Wallander, or—"

It felt cruel, deceiving the anxious housekeeper. "Look," I said rudely, "I *don't know*. She just left the house in the car and told me to tell you she was sick and staying with friends. That's all. I am Mrs. Adams's maid, *not* her keeper . . ."

Mrs. Flannery was too astonished to admonish me.

I left and went up to my room. I lay down for a moment on the narrow bed and looked at the ballerinas on the wallpaper, dancing hopefully, torn off at the knees, their faded tutus disappearing into the cracked plaster of a servant's bedroom wall. This was not what I had left Ireland for—to be an accessory to some unstable socialite. I wanted to live my own dream, not be picking up the crumbs of somebody else's.

I took the note out of my coat pocket and read it again. "*Love, your friend, Isobel.*" She didn't love me and she was *not* my friend. Sending Charles to me like that was an act of irresponsible madness. More than that, it was an insult both to my virtue and to Charles's propriety—yet Isobel seemed to consider it as some sort of "gift" to us both, expecting me to lie for her as a favor in kind and cover her sins to Mrs. Flannery.

I decided to go and call on Sheila. It was Sunday, and with Isobel away there would be nothing much for me to do about the place. Sheila would doubtless think Isobel's actions charming, but at least it would keep me from following my instincts and confessing all to Mrs. Flannery.

It was late in the afternoon and Sheila and Alex were together in the apartment. They had finished lunch and, in Sheila's inimitable style, the kitchen was a complete mess, dishes piled up in the sink and a chicken carcass thrown to one side on the draining board. Alex didn't seem to notice or mind, and the two of them were sitting on the settee working their way through a bottle of hooch, still wearing its paper-bag disguise.

"How was the weekend?" Sheila wanted to know.

"Busy. How is the typing course?" I was keen to deflect any questions about my weekend in front of Alex.

"Ghastly," she said. "I'm going to give it up."

Alex looked over at me and raised his eyebrows. She saw, and gave his arm a poke. "Stop," she said, her eyes soft with the drink. "I hate it—it's too hard. Why can't I just stay home and cook and keep house for my darling?" and she pouted at him impossibly. Alex didn't look happy. I wasn't happy, either— except that I was more inclined to speak out.

"Well, firstly, Sheila," I said. "You are a terrible housekeeper . . ."

"It's true," Alex said, smiling amusedly.

"Then Alex will get me a maid," she said, pawing his arm. "Won't you, darling?"

". . . and secondly, you are a lazy, ungrateful, bone-idle strap! Alex is giving you the most wonderful opportunity to better yourself and you're throwing it back in his face."

"You're such a bore, Ellie," she said. Then she snuggled her face into her lover's neck. "Alex doesn't want me to be any better than I already am— It was *your* idea to do the course, Ellie."

"Actually," Alex said, "I've cleared a desk for you to start in a month, and I've already warned all the guys to keep their hands off my sassy new secretary!" Alex was joking, but I knew, from what Sheila had told me, that he was keen on the idea of her working at the firm and believed it would square things with his parents. It annoyed Sheila, both that she had to prove herself to his parents by working, and that Alex had thought my idea of a typing course to be a sensible one.

She pawed him again. "But it's so *difficult*, Alex—you've no idea—and I get so bored with all those other girls. Remember how much fun we had at school, Ellie? Why *hell*, it's not like that *at all*."

I felt that she was testing Alex by acting spoiled, and that annoyed me. She was lucky to have the man she loved on her doorstep—one who could give her everything she wanted.

"Hey, I've got an idea," Alex said, standing up and moving across the room to get his cigarettes from the low fire mantel. He took one out of the pack, lit it, turned to me and said, "Why don't you do the course with Sheila, Ellie? I'll be happy to pay for it, same as I pay for her." He winked. "That way you can keep an eye on her for me."

I could not believe what he had just said. I was still standing and could have sworn I felt the ground shift under me.

"Don't be stupid, Alex," Sheila said. "What would Ellie want to do that for? Leaving her good safe job with Isobel . . ."

"Well then, I can go one better and offer her a job. We've got girls in the typing pool moving on all the time— How long is the course?"

I was speechless to either accept or decline his offer. I didn't know where to put myself. "Eight weeks." I pushed the words out. I knew everything about the course, having gone along with Sheila to help book her into it. The hours, the duration and the (impossible) cost of it were embedded in my mind.

"Well, I can't guarantee you a job straightaway, but we have a dozen girls in our typing pool and there is always one or the other of them running off to get married. I can promise that as soon as one of the girls leaves, I'll bring you in. And in the meantime, you can live here with Sheila and help her around the place. Deal?"

"Deal," I said, keeping my voice as steady as I could. I wanted to scream with delight.

Alex threw his cigarette in the fire and politely took his

leave. On his way out of the door, he touched my arm and said, "Thanks for looking out for my girl" as if he had not just altered the course of my life with one act of cavalier generosity.

On my way back to work, I stopped and sat on a bench at the edge of the park. The sun was shining and rain from a recent shower sparkled on the damp paving stones. The bench was sheltered from the rain by the canopy of trees. I needed to sit alone and think things out. I needed to take in the consequences and possibilities of my new life. No more Isobel, no more servitude. Could my life really be about to change so much for the better? In school, the nuns had told me I was clever enough to be a teacher. They would have been disappointed to see me living the life of a servant. Now all that was about to change. Less than one year after arriving here, a whole new life was about to open up.

A couple about the same age as me passed by, and for the first time since coming to New York I allowed myself to think how it would be if John joined me here. With Alex's offer in place, suddenly it seemed a possibility. I indulged myself in a daydream. John and I, all dressed up and walking through Central Park. John was wearing a soft shirt and linen jacket over his tall, broad torso, and all the women looked after him as we passed. Together we named the birds and the trees and talked about how they reminded us of home. Near Fifth, we stopped at the fairground carousel and he bought me a ride. As I whirled around on the back of a gaudy gilded horse, a yellow chiffon scarf flying behind me, I saw him standing there waiting to wave to me as I passed and I knew that, even when he was out of my view, he was still there for me, within reach, waiting.

Chapter Thirty-One

Isobel was not happy at my resigning.

I told her the first morning after she got back when I was delivering her breakfast tray.

"I'm too nice, that's my problem," she said, circling her cigarette tip on the edge of her coffee saucer. "I show you girls my friendship, then you abuse it and leave me. I don't know what you think you're going to do that's better than the life you have here, Ellie."

"I'm going to become a qualified typist," I said, "in a respectable, well-paid profession."

Her eyes narrowed as she pointed her cigarette at me and said, "Let me tell you something, 'Irish'—it takes a lot more to become a lady than the brief attention of a rich man. Charles Irvington may have a fancy for you, but you're a fool to throw your life away for him."

The foolish woman had accused me of being stupid and immoral—her own two obvious failures. My revenge was silence in reply.

"You'll work a week's notice. You are dismissed."

They found a replacement for me within days. A dozen or more girls lined up along the staff stairs on the day Mrs. Flannery was interviewing. At the top of the line were the ones straight off the boat—their Sunday clothes made shabby with wear, the smell of carbolic soap disguising and yet announcing their poverty. One gaunt Irish girl caught my eye and said *"Dia ghuit"* to me in greeting. My stomach turned for the poor child. A native Irish speaker, she didn't stand a chance. *"Dia is muire ghuit,"* I replied. Her little face tore back in a huge smile, revealing her terrible teeth. I felt bad for the hope I had given her. Isobel would surely pick one of the pretty, neat agency applicants who arrived later. I had forgotten how lucky I had been to have a job waiting for me when I arrived in America, and seeing these poor souls made me feel grateful to Sheila.

It was that bit of gratitude that got me through the next few months living with my friend.

It should have been the happiest of times, moving in with Sheila and us learning our new skill together, as we had at school. Even though I was a few weeks late starting the course, I soon caught up. But Sheila had changed. The novelty of her new life as a girl about town had faded and she had become desperately anxious to get married and move into the big house in Boston. Sheila was frightened. I could see that as clearly as the ever-brightening rouge on her cheeks and the brittleness of her newly permed hair. She was frightened that Alex's parents would not approve of the marriage and that she would lose him. Frightened that she was not good enough, elegant enough, smart enough for this wonderful, rich man and that he would forsake her for some other girl. It was my belief that Alex was a man of integrity and would stand by Sheila against his family and all obstacles, if the need arose, although he was smart enough to guard against potential problems by biding his time. But Sheila had got herself wound up into a state of wanting, and I worried that her impatience was in danger of corroding their love.

Instead of confiding her worries in me, as her friend, Sheila kept the best of herself for Alex—remaining sweet and calm and untroubled in his company. She saved all her spitefulness for me. While the apartment had two small bedrooms, one of them was entirely given over to Sheila's growing collection of clothes. So she requested that I sleep on a sofa in the living room, which I gladly did. However, after a few days she complained that my belongings were "making a mess" and that if Alex called by unexpectedly and saw this, he would think her a poor housekeeper. I suggested that I make room in the smaller bedroom, but she snapped at me and said, in effect, that her clothes were more important than my comfort. So, I had to arise early every morning and pack all of my personal belongings back in my case, and store the case in a closet in the hallway.

Sheila was tardy about timekeeping, dillydallying about in the mornings trying on this outfit and that, concerning herself about what powder and lipstick to wear and dawdling over her breakfast. So I became responsible for getting both of us to college on time. A routine developed where I started to lay out her things, ensuring that her outfit was chosen the night before, her makeup and toilet things to hand, and a light breakfast prepared so that I could get us both out the door on time. It was not long before I became as intimately acquainted with her things as I had been with Isobel's.

In addition, Sheila showed neither the talent nor the inclination to cook. Soon I was preparing her meals for her with the same grudging disapproval as Mrs. Flannery. It infuriated me that she had started to treat me as her maid: "Ellie, would you be a darling and mend this hem for me?" "Oh, Ellie—you know how I hate rice pudding!" I was sure this was not what Alex had meant when he suggested that I "help her around the place."

But I could not say any of it out loud, for fear I would lose the roof over my head.

The more I bit my tongue, the worse she became. "Ellie, Alex is coming at seven—could you make sure the living room is perfectly clean, and please clear away the iron and sewing machine and all of your housekeeping things. I don't want him walking into a servants' quarters!" I felt like shouting at her that if breeding were to be the judge of us, I far outweighed her on that score. But I needed her as much as she needed Alex, and my old friend was so tightly strung that if I offended her, she might throw me out on the street and I would have nowhere to go. Fear and dishonesty poisoned our friendship as the threat of poverty hung over us both.

Money was as tight as ever. I took in some ironing and sewing to pay for my living expenses—small though they were, as my rent and the course was paid for, a fact of which Sheila reminded me daily. Also, I still had to send money home.

I wrote to John and told him of the course, and the splendid shiny typewriters, and of Alex's offer of a well-paid professional position.

He wrote back:

Curse the money. Ellie, I should never have let you go. Ellie, come home, come home to me, please.

When he begged like that, my heart no longer felt a tug for him or for home. Instead, it made me angry that John did not seem interested in news of how wonderful life was in America with all its modern devices, or impressed with the advancements I was making in my own life—advancements that, after all, I was making for the benefit of us both.

While the other girls, Sheila included, rushed out of the

building at break time to various coffee shops and drugstores, I stayed behind in the pool and worked up my speeds. I graduated after the eight weeks with over one hundred words per minute and ninety-eight percent in our written test—the highest mark anyone had ever achieved. Sheila scraped through and Alex gave her a job straightaway, and asked me to wait a month while one of his typists worked out the notice before her wedding.

In the meantime, the principal of our college had recommended me for a lucrative short-term job typing up a law book for a professor at Columbia University. I was paid per typed page and calculated that, if I worked day and night, I could get the job done in a month and earn enough money to pay entirely for John's operation.

Every day, I took the subway to Washington Heights where I sat in a cramped, airless room typing up a great pile of handwritten papers for a silent old man. Professor Liptka looked so old that I feared he might die before his enormous tome was published—an observation that speeded me up even more. He was not kindly, as one hopes older people will be, but had the air of a man who never liked talking much and took his great age as permission to dispense with it altogether. If I found a word unintelligible, I would underline it in red pen and pass it to the professor, who would fire me an impatient glance and re-write it in capital letters in the margin. We were united insofar as he wanted his manuscript typed as quickly as possible and I wanted my money. I brought breakfast, lunch and dinner with me as sandwiches, and for three weeks I sat from eight in the morning until nine o'clock at night and typed.

I typed until my nails weakened and split, and the ends of my fingers went numb with hard skin. I typed until I thought I would go blind from the endless black print on white and my head would fall off from the tension in my neck. I worked at a desk on the far side of the tiny room and the professor sat by the door. Every time I needed to go to the toilet or stretch my legs, he had to move his chair out of my way and it was such an arduous process for us both that I waited until he left the room before doing either. As a result, my limbs were often so stiff from sitting in the one position all day that I was almost constantly suffering from pins and needles or cramp.

After three weeks I had typed one thousand pages at ten cents per page. I had the money for John's operation in Dublin. In the meantime, I would continue to work and send money to the Hogans, until John had recovered and was well enough to work himself. Perhaps he could even work here in America. With my promised new job, I could save up the money for his fare.

Chapter Thirty-Two

I started work at Alex's family firm. Once I had my independence again and Sheila was on track to marry Alex, having been introduced to his parents as a respectable "working girl," the stress of uncertainty was lifted and our friendship returned to the easy familiarity we had enjoyed as carefree, privileged schoolgirls.

Every morning we gathered ourselves together in great style, planning and picking through our outfits so that we showed ourselves off to full advantage as the elegant, modern women-about-town that we were. I had acquired quite a wardrobe of clothes from Isobel's castoffs—including three suits, a printed day dress and the black silk kimono I had been so impressed with when I had first arrived. She had also given me a discarded vanity case, whose cream leather finish was no more than a little grubby and which, with some careful rubbing and a little baking soda, had come up as good as new. The lid opened to reveal a bevel-edged mirror under which was a warren of hidden compartments, whose lids could be opened by handles of pink ribbon just wide enough to accommodate the pinch of a lady's thumb and forefinger. With my urgent financial commitments met, I now felt able to indulge myself, and set about filling my pretty case with all manner of cosmetics and trinkets. My first lipstick was by Max Factor in a shade of rich plum. It was such a novelty, rolling up the gold tube and pressing the perfect angular wax edge to my cupid's bow—knowing mine was the first set of lips it had ever touched.

Sheila and I went to see *Down to the Sea in Ships* at the picture house. It was an epic drama with rousing music about the plight of the Quaker captain of a whaling ship, but we were primarily interested in the smoky, doe-eyed beauty of the hero's daughter and granddaughter. Afterward, Sheila persuaded me to have a permanent wave like the stars and Clara Bow. Every night I wet my hair with a damp comb, then held it in place with a metal clip. In the morning my hair sat flat to my forehead in a perfect wave, where it stayed all day. One of the tailors for whom I did small alterations gave me a gift of eight yards of heavy blue linen and I made myself a dress with long sleeves and a sailor collar, using a Vogue pattern, putting the rest of it aside to make a shirt for John.

With the hair and the lipstick and the fashionable clothes, I was "all the rage," and with the journey to work each morning I felt more and more as if I were truly a part of the growing city. I was at one with the women with waved hair in good coats, teeming down the broad streets, stopping only to release a high heel caught in a grate or to hail a taxi. Pouring down the subway steps in noisy, colorful gangs, as the subway trains stopped and started at such speed, like blood pumping through the veins of this city's heart. New York City never stopped moving, and I was thrilled to be caught up in its beating, energetic throng.

Ward Windows' sales offices were on 35th at Third, seven blocks south of Grand Central Station. The staff comprised five sales executives, and five women (or "girls" as they called us) who were there to serve the secretarial needs of each man. It was company policy that, with the exception of Alex, the secretaries were rotated among the executives, so that we never became "attached" to one another. On two occasions in the past five years, executives had been caught having "immoral relations" with their secretaries, and old Mrs. Ward looked very harshly on such behavior. (I assumed that, as her son, Alex was immune to her wrath.)

The building we were in was ten stories high, modest by the standards of the skyscrapers that were shooting up around us, and we were on the fifth floor. The office itself was extremely smart. Each sales executive had his own office, with all of us girls gathered on the floor outside in rows of generously proportioned desks, which contained a Remington typewriter and a large ledger in which we recorded our executive's sales by hand.

Alex himself had a large office, but he spent most of his time visiting the various sites, the majority of which were uptown from where we were. On the floor above us was a large conference room with a mahogany table as long as the tree it came from and twenty leather-bound chairs. Every week, all of the executives would gather there along with Alex and sometimes his father—a heavyset man with a big square head and a red face, who reminded me of some of the big farmers at home, except that his suit was a better fit and his hat more smoothly felted. We secretaries took it in turn to record the minutes of the meeting, while two others were on a rotation to serve refreshments.

I loved participating in these meetings. Just listening to the executives talk about targets and projections and quotas made me feel as if I was part of a new, important world of business. The role I was playing was small, often just serving coffee and passing around doughnuts, but it was still quite apart from what I was used to. While my farming life in Ireland was a world away from the rarefied wealth of Isobel's experience, it was still, essentially, domestic in nature. I had always been in the service of other people. As a daughter, wife, maid—even as old Professor Liptka's secretary, I was, essentially, a servant. Here I was in the service of a new master—"business." As part of a team that served a company, I understood that while I was pouring coffee at the weekly meetings, I was doing so not just for the executive's personal edification, but in the broader interest of Ward Windows, which, it seemed to me, was an entirely different and somehow more important proposition.

During one of these meetings at which I was taking the minutes, the senior sales manager made a complaint to Alex. "The problem is not in the selling, Mr. Ward, construction is booming—the problem now is that the demand for our product far outweighs our ability to service the customer."

"I agree," another butted in. "We're selling the windows, but there aren't enough men to fit them . . ."

Then all five men started bulleting in their complaints. "There's a bottleneck of panes at the warehouse and not enough men making the frames." "The builders are complaining about our designs, they say they take too long to fit." "The bottom line is they don't have enough men on-site, and some of them are using unskilled carpenters to handle our windows." "Then they fit them wrong and then we have to remake them."

Alex pressed the tips of his fingers together into a triangle and pouted in concentration as they talked. I thought how he looked like the Mother Superior when she was listening to a pupil recitation. When they were done he said, "Looks like we need more skilled labor at the construction end. But if the builders can't find it, darned if I know the answer. In the meantime, men, you'll just have to struggle on smiling at the customers and convincing them we can-do, until—well—we can 'can-do!'"

They all laughed and Alex smiled at them as if there wasn't a problem at all. He had confidence in other people and in himself, and I could see that made him a good leader. Watching him round up the meeting, patting the other men on the back while shaking their hands as if they were the greatest fellows in the world, I had a sudden flash of recognition. John had that ability to make himself loved by other men—in his IRA days, laughing and drinking through the night with his battalion, building them up for the next day. As with Alex, there was never dissent or disagreement when John was around. They were men whom other men trusted. They had authority.

I waited until all the men were gone, then caught Alex as he was on his way out the door. "Ellie," he said, "what is it?" and he instinctively checked his tie as if I were about to warn him of some untidiness or stain.

"I have an idea," I said, "for the business."

Alex raised his eyebrows in amused surprise. I knew it wasn't my place, but I did not care. There was too much at stake. I started to speak before he had the chance to make a joke of me.

"It seems to me that what you need is carpenters."

"Go on," he said.

"If Ward Windows had their own men going out on-site and fitting the windows, you could be sure that the job was being done quickly and efficiently, and . . ." I was making it up as I went along, but it sounded good, ". . . and as the only windows company providing this service, you'd be able to charge a premium that would certainly cover your costs, and possibly even increase profits."

"Interesting." I could tell that he was more taken aback by the forcefulness of my presentation than with the idea itself, but—remembering that Alex was not just my boss, but the beau of my oldest friend—I continued, "My husband John is an excellent carpenter and a man of great authority. We are currently looking at opportunities for him in America and he would certainly be able to—"

"Ellie," Alex interrupted me, putting his hand gently on my arm, "I would be happy to offer John a position in the company, in whatever capacity we can agree upon when he gets here."

My pride objected to the fact that, despite my good idea and my elevated position as a typist, John's fate and mine were still at the mercy of another man's charity. At the same time I felt regret for not having thought to ask for Alex's help before now. But as this small storm of conflicting emotion flurried inside my chest, it was almost immediately flooded out by an enormous wave of relief.

Now John had to come to America, as soon as he was well. Even for his principles, he could not turn down such an opportunity. At last, we were going to be together again.

Chapter Thirty-Three

My darling John,

It is such wonderful news that you are walking again, the timing of which makes what I have to tell you all the more an act of God.

John, I have a job waiting here for you as a carpenter, with one of the most reputable companies in all of New York. Ward Windows are in need of skilled men. With the building industry as busy as it is here, they are in desperate need of good carpenters and when I told Alex of your qualifications, he asked that I alert you right away and insisted that they sponsor your trip here. I know you will understand what an opportunity this is, John. Everything is set, and I enclose all the paperwork you will need to bring you here, along with your ticket and details of the ship you are booked onto three weeks hence. I am longing to see you, my darling, and will count the days until you come. I can barely write anymore, my heart is so full of longing and excitement.

> Love and cannot wait
> to see you again soon,
> Ellie

Everything had fallen into place.

Alex had called me into his office, to hand me a second-class ticket for three weeks' time and a month's money for John in advance. He would organize all of the paperwork, and John would pay him back his fare over his first six months on the job at a dollar a month. I did not quite know how to say "thank you," and it came out with a confident firmness that suggested this was no more than we deserved. Which, of course, it wasn't.

The same day, Sheila had told me that she and Alex were moving to Boston, where his father wished him to set up another office. The move would also mark the beginning of their formal engagement. The rent was paid to the end of the following month, and the apartment could be kept on by me and John. I had written to John immediately, enclosing the ticket and telling him the exciting news.

John had not written to me himself since his operation. Maidy had let me know how it went:

> *The operation was a great success, although John is not*
> *quite returned to his old self yet. Ellie, although he is*
> *mending well, Doctor Bourke says it will be a while before*
> *he's back on his feet good and proper.*

I was put out that he had not taken the trouble to write himself when he came home from hospital. Even before the operation, his letters had become shorter and less frequent. In truth, I was relieved that he had stopped his lengthy descriptions of life at home, and shortened his pleas for me to return. I knew that John was awkward on the subject of my sending money home and, indeed, about the fact of my being in America at all. These being the presiding facts of our lives, it was small wonder that communication had become stunted between us. I had grown tired, too, of detailing the small adventures I had so delighted in describing when I first arrived, and had got into the habit instead of enclosing short, cheerful notes with my dollars. I wasn't worried. John being the great love of my life, I felt we could easily afford times of silence. I imagined how overjoyed he would be to learn that we could soon be together again—and in a place where we would be free of all the problems that had plagued us in Ireland. "We will have money to spare," I wrote as a footnote to my letter, "and will be able to send enough home to keep Maidy and Paud in perpetual comfort. Unless, indeed, they wish to come and join us here!"

In the days that I spent turning the flat—now empty of Sheila—into our marital home, I composed yet another letter to John. I had found myself seeing things about New York that my husband would love at every turn. Hot dog and pretzel vendors on the street, the Italian coffee shop, picture houses, Central Park Zoo—now that he was coming, it was safe to write to him about these things again, and in detailing them I realized that I had not exactly grown tired of telling John about life in New York, but had in fact become increasingly sad at not being able to share the city with him in person.

I indulged myself by buying several decorative things for the house. Although Sheila had left me a great deal of her household things (including the glass cat of which she had been so determinedly fond), I wanted to make the place my own. I bought a lace tablecloth from a Polish woman who was selling them on the street near my office. I went to Macy's and bought linen napkins, which I embroidered myself with small shamrocks, and a tray cloth to match. I purchased new bed linens too, and washed them out several times so that they were worn and soft and ready for the first night we would share a bed in almost two years, and a new nightdress for that same occasion. Even though I already had a perfectly good nightgown, this was in a softer, more delicate cotton with a delectable lace trim that I felt convinced would excite him—not indeed that John needed such enticements, but I enjoyed the idea of pleasing him.

I cleaned and polished and dusted every corner of the apartment. I knew that John would not even notice, but the pleasure was in the doing of it, for him. I repainted the chairs in the kitchen with pale blue gloss, and I even bought a "toaster"—an electric machine for toasting sliced bread. It was a whimsical expense, but—oh my!—what an impressive gadget and, for some reason, it fed my domestic dream of him. I could see John, sitting on the sky-blue chair, a napkin tucked into his crisp white shirt, with a runny egg and a plate of toasted bread in front of him, breakfasting before work. That was the beginning of my American dream. Beyond breakfast together, there was a life of affluence and all of the promises that America held—but those dreams could be kept for when he got here.

The Manhattan ferry was quiet on the way out to Ellis Island. It was a crisp day, fresh, like autumn back home. I wore my moss-green tweed suit. John loved that shade on me. He said it made my skin paler and my hair darker. I touched my hair and wondered for a moment what he would make of my bob. I remembered the last time I had done this journey, and I thought how different it would be for John. To have someone he loved welcome him at the port, to be taken back to a home he could call his own and a well-paid, respectable job all set up for him. After what he had been through—what we had both been through since we were apart—it was no more than we both deserved. In a matter of hours we would be together again. I could barely contain my excitement and as we drew nearer the island, I could feel my toes wriggling inside my boots and it was all I could do to stop myself from throwing myself overboard and swimming the rest of the way. I must have been smiling because a young man who had been standing nearby came and stood next to me, as if I had been smiling at him. I should have put him off, but it made me smile even more. He was only a young man, not much more than twenty.

"You gonna meet somebody? A sister?" he said.

"Husband." I couldn't help grinning at him.

"One lucky guy," he said, crestfallen. His New York drawl was tainted with an Irish accent I vaguely recognized, and I asked him where he was from.

"Longford," he said. "Ballinalee."

I nodded and he said eagerly, "You know it?"

"No," I replied, and I was sorry then that I didn't know it, because he looked crestfallen again. He had an expressive, rubbery kind of face that made me feel like laughing—especially when he looked sad. I asked him all about himself to pass the time and distract me from my rising emotions. Desmond was eighteen and had been in New York for five years with his uncle and older brother. They had tried to get him into school, but he had insisted on earning his way and worked alongside the big men on the buildings from the age of fourteen. In the time they had been in New York the brothers had sent home for two of their sisters, and all five of them lived together in the one apartment in Hell's Kitchen. He was going to pick the third, and last, sister up now.

"She was ten when I left. She'll be fifteen—a woman now—we've got her work cleaning up in Murphy's restaurant. The other two girls are there already, but they've both been promoted to the kitchen." There was a pause, then he said, "They're hard workers, my sisters."

As he said it, his eyes briefly lost their humor and I remembered the privilege of my education and how, despite it, I had still ended up in service. *A hard worker.* It was such a loaded compliment to pay a young woman. A homage to hardship. "People only love you for your work," Mrs. Flannery was forever saying, and I had found it to be true. Even my best friend Sheila loved me especially for what I did for her. John was the only person who loved me besides what I could do for him. John hated to see me working. In the days before his injury, he would chide me gently for fussing around the house and often took over my chores, insisting that I sit and read. While we were children he had done all of the work while I did nothing, only amused him—and that was the way he liked it. When he lost the use of his legs he could barely cope with watching me work as he lay helpless. He hated that I had come to America to work.

"Only Mammy and Daddy now," Desmond said, "but they'll hardly come. They say they will, but sure, we'll send them back enough to manage, and why would they move now? They're happy where they are."

I looked up and saw the big ship in the bay and the ferries floating away from it like leaves on a breeze, each of them loaded with immigrants: each immigrant full of hope for the future, each one carrying promises to honor their past. I had created my new life, and now my past was going to become my present again.

As our ferry pulled into Ellis Island, my heart swelled with the succulent certainty that, now that my husband was joining me here, I could finally call this vibrant, glamorous, exciting, daunting, liberating place, which I had landed in two years ago, my home.

*

The terminal was busy, but not as crowded as the last time I had been here. People were milling about and, as I arrived, I noticed that Desmond was tagging along at my side. I realized, with some amusement, that the boy had not taken a fancy to me after all, but just wanted the kind company of an older woman. Like the mother he had left behind at thirteen perhaps, or the security of an older sister. If he had an uncle and five siblings living and working with him all the time, there was a fine chance he was not used to his own company.

I vaguely recognized the area I was in as the arrivals hall, and headed toward the bottom of the stairs that I must have come down myself—although they looked different from this angle.

"Will we go up above and look?" he said.

"At what?" I had a moment of anxiety at the idea that this boy might still be hanging around when John emerged from the registry room and would detract from our joyous reunion.

"There's a balcony upstairs—you can see them in the registry room before they are let through to where we can meet them. Follow me." Desmond led me up two flights of stairs and in through a door to a narrow balcony looking down on the registry room. I remembered the balcony now, remembered seeing one or two people looking down on me when I was a part of that heaving crowd the day I arrived. The registry room below our feet was only starting to fill up. It seemed almost empty from where we were, but as I searched for John I realized the room was so big there were more people than I'd thought, and they were arriving up the stairs all the time. Four or five times my heart was in my mouth as I thought I recognized his build and shape in a man. Every time it wasn't him, I felt my heart buckle briefly with the idea that I might have forgotten what John looked like. Or might he have changed to me beyond recognition—lost his hair, gained weight? I saw a man with a walking stick being led off by a couple of officials and felt panic until he looked up and I saw in his drunken, angry face that he wasn't my husband. That I had suspected it might be sickened me further. Frustration and anticipation built in me to such an extent that I wished I had stayed at the bottom of the stairs, where I could get a closer look as he came through from the registry and be absolutely certain. Yet I was in such a hurry to get my first sight of him that I stayed on the balcony. I walked round and round and strained my eyes to check the face of every man as he took up his seat for registration, watching each as he walked through the place of entry and down the final steps. I felt confident at least that I had not missed him going through.

The noise in the room was building, as the long benches running the length of it filled up. I heard Desmond cry out, "Noreen! Noreen! *Noreen Hegarty!*" A young girl stood up in the middle of the room below. "Noreen—up here, Noreen— *look up!*" She almost fell over with the strain of searching for him in the sky, and when she found Desmond, she called up to him, her arms outstretched, her face dazzled with happiness and relief. The woman sitting next to her made her sit down again, but she continued to turn her head toward us and point. Desmond ran up to me and said, quite unnecessarily, "That's my sister—Noreen." Then, "Any sign of your husband?" He was shuffling, unsure about whether to go down and wait at the bottom of the stairs or continue to stay where he was. He was in a hesitant, awkward place, where he could not greet his sister properly and yet had half greeted her already.

"You should go down," I said. "She could get called through any second, and you should be at the bottom of the stairs to greet her."

He seemed grateful to have somebody tell him what to do and put his hand to mine to shake it. "Good luck," he said.

I squeezed his hand and said, "Look after your sister."

"I will."

But my eyes were scanning the crowd beneath us before we had finished saying good-bye.

For a while there was still a steady stream of people filing into the benches, through the mesh gates and down the stairs. As people spotted their loved ones below, the balcony emptied. I told myself not to worry. John would be last off the boat. Let everybody else go before him. That was the way John was. Or perhaps his legs were not fully mended and he was slow to walk. I hurried to the far end of the balcony so that I could see the area where they did the medical exams just before people entered the Great Hall, but the area was now clear of passengers and one or two officials were walking away—their work done. Panic propelled me to run round and round the balcony, frantically checking each face below again—although I knew he wasn't there. I rushed downstairs into the arrivals area and grabbed a man in a uniform and asked him, urgently, if everybody from Queenstown was off. He said the ship had been emptied an hour ago. I ran back upstairs. John had to be down there somewhere. Leaning over the balcony, I called out his name. The two dozen or so people left to be processed looked up at me. I ran back down to the arrivals hall and waited at the bottom of the stairs until every last person was out—then I stood and looked at the closed doors, willing them to open and for my John to come through.

The official I had spoken to earlier came and put his hand gently on my arm. "Last ferry to Manhattan is about to leave, Miss," he said. He smiled at me—a sad, apologetic smile—and I realized he had seen this before. A girl left waiting for her love at the Kissing Point in Ellis Island.

The promise of a new life—broken.

Chapter Thirty-Four

I walked the length of Manhattan Island, as I had done the day I arrived, willing my legs to gather strength. I was weak with grief and knew that if I stopped and sat for one moment, I might never get up again. I did not want to travel by subway or bus because I could not bear the human contact of buying a ticket. I felt raw and rejected, as if my skin had been peeled back and my soul exposed for all to see.

When I got back to the apartment I crawled straight into bed, without even the energy or the wherewithal to get undressed, pulled the blanket up over my head and wept until I fell asleep. I was woken late the next morning by the postman knocking.

Dear Ellie,

I hope this letter reaches you in time, but I did not want to write until I had given your offer to come to America proper consideration. I have not been wholly myself, in truth since you left for America, but in more recent times for other reasons than that. I could get Maidy to write, but it would be the coward's way and this is something I must tell you myself.

The operation went well, according to the doctors, and although it was an ordeal in itself, it was not as much of an

*ordeal as having you away from me these past two years.
I can walk all right, but my legs are not back to the way they
were before I was shot, Ellie. I have a gammy gait, and am
afraid that a man with a limp would be put to poor use in a
smart place like America. That aside, I have to tell you now
that I am not inclined to leave Ireland. I fought for change
and was changed myself in the process. Now I want to stay
and enjoy the freedom we earned, building a home with my
wife by my side—and not beyond on the other side of the
world.*

*I can walk fine enough and have the house fixed up
grand. We have a few animals—the hens have bred and we
have enough eggs to feed the village—and the back field is
set with vegetables for the next two years. You have earned
the money to set us up, Ellie, and it is time for you to come
home. So I am returning the ticket you sent so that you can
use it to come back here to us where you belong.*

All my love, as always, your husband John

*PS: Maidy has the forty dollars you sent for my entry set
aside.*

My hands tightened around the letter and crushed it.

I must have passed a dozen Western Union offices on my
way back to the apartment yesterday, any one of which I might
have gone into to send a telegram home. An urgent telegram to
Maidy and Paud asking them to check that John had not been
waylaid or robbed on his way to Queenstown, or injured before
he got on the boat and wasn't lying, alone, in some shipyard
infirmary. But I hadn't, because buried deep down in a locked
grave at the bottom of my heart was the knowledge that John
was never going to come to America. Lying on that grave was

my heart's desire, my need to be with him, and surrounding it were the dreams and aspirations of how things would be if only he would join me there. Yet all along I'd known my John well enough to understand that he would never leave Ireland.

When I received his letter, the morning after a terrible night of grief, I was nonetheless enraged by it beyond the point of all reason. I had become entirely engulfed by my desire for a new life in America with him, and here he was rejecting it without any consideration. Without reason, without care—without, I told myself, any thought for what I wanted. Furthermore, he had been heartless enough to let me go to Ellis Island and endure the pain and humiliation of waiting for him when he must, surely, have known that his letter would not reach me on time. If he didn't, he was that much of an idiot, it was worse still.

He should have come—for a year at least. To try it out, to humor me. It was only cowardice and selfishness holding him back.

If he loved me, if he truly loved me, John would have known how important this was. He knew me well enough, surely, to realize that I had my heart set on his coming here, and that should have been enough to carry him to me. I had sacrificed so much to be with him—my education, my family—I had made the ultimate sacrifice in leaving Ireland, leaving him behind to come here, and this was the thanks I got.

I walked around "our" home—the painted chair, the shimmering glass cat sitting next to the sparkling window, the shiny new toaster all rendered meaningless now that he wasn't coming, and I reread the letter, over and over again—"*I am not inclined to leave Ireland*," "*. . . it is time for you to come home*"—each line making my blood boil more than the last. How dare he order me back in that way merely because he was "*not inclined*" to make the journey to join me? So his operation *"was not as much of an ordeal as having you away from me these past two years"?* How did he think it had been for me? Did he not think that my heart had bled for him and my body craved him every single day since I had been here? The very idea that he had been the only one suffering, the only one who had been through this "ordeal," and seemed to be blaming it all on me, when he—*he*—had been the idiot who had got his legs shot off and led me to be here in the first place.

My rage got the better of me and I picked up the glass cat and threw it to the ground. Miraculously, only the tip of its curled tail snapped off, so I decided to go out and get some air to clear my head.

With Alex and Sheila gone, I had no one to confide in, so I walked over to Fifth Avenue and called in to see Mrs. Flannery. I had called in a couple of times since I had moved out and, despite the comfort of my apartment, her kitchen still felt the closest thing I had to home here. I had John's letter in my pocket and threw it to her. It was a deliberate betrayal, sharing his personal correspondence in that flippant way, but I need not have worried on his account.

"The poor man," she said. "Go home to Ireland to your husband at once, Ellie Hogan, before your head is turned any more and you end up like that fool Sheila."

"She's moved to Boston," I said, then added, somewhat triumphantly, "they're getting married before Christmas."

"That won't last," the old woman said nastily. Then, thinking better of herself, her voice softened and she said, "Although God help me, I wouldn't wish bad on the girl, but these grand passions, they rarely work out. People running away with themselves 'falling in love.'" She paused and looked off as if she was thinking of something else before coming back to herself.

"Notions, Ellie, silly girls with silly notions—this place is full of them. You're too sensible for all that nonsense. Go on back to Ireland to your husband, and get on with your life, is the advice I'd give you."

It was not what I wanted to hear, though I should have expected little else from an old-fashioned woman like Mrs. Flannery. "But my life is here," I said.

"Aragh, '*life*,'" she said dismissively, although not without humor. "What kind of a 'life' would that be?"

"Well, I have my job and my apartment." I stopped, and touched my neck.

"Look, Ellie," she said, handing me back John's letter and picking up her tea towel, "there's a lot more to life than bobbed hair and pretty things, and all that nonsense you and Sheila and the 'Grande Dame' upstairs do be going along with . . ."

"Yes, but—" I tried to interject, but Mrs. Flannery was not in the mood for listening.

"Go on back home to Ireland, girl, it's where you belong, it's where we *all* belong. I'd go back in the morning if I had half the chance."

But I didn't believe her. Not for one second.

Chapter Thirty-Five

I did not reply to John's letter.

As the days passed my initial fury hardened into a selfish resolve. I was not going back. I was going to stay in New York for as long as it suited me, which would be, in all probability, forever! As I went through the humiliation of explaining to my work colleagues and boss that he was not coming, I softened the blow for myself by saying that my husband was still badly crippled and needed me to stay here and continue sending money home for his medical treatment. I said it with such sincerity that I almost came to believe it myself; and I kept sending money home to Maidy "until John was well."

Maidy wrote back to me—short, cheerful letters about how my money was being put to good use and detailing the improvements they were making about the place. She gave me news of John only in passing—*"John is extending the henhouse," "The two men are busy whitewashing the barn while the weather is dry"*—but her letters were free from the pleading and pressure with which John's were always laden. I received nothing more from my husband, which I guessed was Maidy's doing. I could almost hear her saying to him: "Leave her alone, John. She'll come home in her own good time." I was grateful to Maidy, but she could not possibly have known the depth of my resolve to stay.

To say I did not think of home for the next six months would not be true. Some mornings I rose early, opened the windows of my room to take the cool, damp air into my lungs and briefly longed for the silence of a dewy country morning instead of the yammering city sirens. I thought of John every day, until the anger and frustration and pain of his not being there with me became so repetitive that I trained myself to banish thoughts of him altogether. If I missed my husband, my people, the life I had known before, it was in flickering moments—small interruptions in the vast, busy seeing and doing and tasting and listening excitement of my New York life.

With Sheila gone, I became friendly with the other secretaries at work. One girl, Emilie Andruchewitz, and I became good friends. Emilie was a year older than me and lived at home in the Bronx with her Polish parents. When she heard I was looking for somebody to share my apartment, she offered to move in with me, and the two of us settled into the same routine of work and friendship that I had enjoyed with Sheila.

All of the girls were unmarried and most of them shared apartments, like Emilie and me. We went out together to coffee shops or ice-cream parlors and gathered in one another's homes on the weekends, playing music on one another's radios and phonograms. I didn't care for drink, but one of the men in work supplied hooch and some of the girls took it at these parties mixed with lemonade and went half mad dancing, flinging feather boas about the place and kicking their legs up in the air so that you could see their drawers, which was great fun to watch. Often, on weeknights, a couple of us would go to the picture house and wonder at the drama and style of Clara Bow, Mary Pickford and Louise Brooks, imitating them the next day at work with inappropriately smoky eyes and dark, defined cupid's bows drawn on our lips.

Emilie had no man, and was desperate to find one. She was unusual looking with nut-brown, almond-shaped eyes and small, bowed lips like a doll set in a round, pale face. I thought she was beautiful, but her looks weren't to everyone's taste. She was longing for love and was constantly complaining that all the men at work were already married.

"I'm *twenty-four,* Ellie," she used to say when I tried to placate her, "I don't want to die a *spinster.*"

Neither of us especially liked to cook and so we took the habit of eating once, sometimes twice a week, in a small café near work run by an Italian family. They always gave us the same red leatherette banquette facing the kitchen, and we sat like patient children as the Mama, built from the same cast as Maidy but with a sterner face, silently served us a mountain of spaghetti and meatballs in a rich tomato sauce, which we wiped greedily off the plate with slice after slice of the air-bubbled bread that she kept piling into a basket in the middle of the table.

Emilie also enjoyed Tullio's because of the number of good-looking, presumably single, young men who came to the restaurant. The trouble was, they usually walked straight through to the kitchen. However longingly she fixed her smoky Slavic eyes upon them, few of them paused to sit and eat before disappearing into the mysterious den behind the heavy swing of the kitchen doors. It was clear to me that Mama and her diminutive husband, Antonio, were running a speakeasy out the back. If it was anything like the ones at home, it was a men-only affair.

On one particular evening we were waiting for our food— Emilie staring in disappointment at the kitchen doors—when those very doors were flung open and, at great speed, three young men propelled themselves across the floor and pushed in beside us at our banquette. A couple of them grabbed our napkins, shoving them into the neck of their collars, while the others snatched up lumps of bread from the basket, deliberately scattering crumbs on the table. With great speed Mama threw each of us a plate and a fork, then disappeared into the kitchen just as two policemen marched into the restaurant, clearly casing the joint for illegal goings-on. The cross old woman came back out again seconds later, with a huge bowl of steaming pasta, which she thrust down onto the table between us. She glowered at the two uniformed officers, then shouted into the kitchen for her husband, who came out all exuberant charm and offered them dinner, which they, with some reluctance—given the seductive aroma of our garlicky spaghetti—declined. Meanwhile, the three men at our table quickly tucked in, curing the smell of alcohol on their breath. Emilie was smiling as if all of her prayers had been answered at once.

The whole thing had happened in such a whirl of hurried confusion that it was some moments before I realized that the man sitting next to me was Charles Irvington.

Chapter Thirty-Six

"Well, gentlemen, what do you think of my new girl?" Charles said.

He had obviously spotted me before he sat down and it had not knocked a feather off him. I was dumbfounded. I had not seen or heard anything from him since Isobel's ridiculous attempt at matchmaking. In all honesty, I had not thought about or considered Charles at all, but now that he was sitting here in front of me, I was speechless.

"Well, she's a cracker, Charlie—although I like this one too." His handsome, dark-haired friend nudged Emilie, who exploded in giggling delight. "How's your spaghetti, Charlie?"

"I've lost my appetite sitting next to this beautiful young lady. Anyway, Fat Pat has eaten everything," said Charles, pointing his chin at the large man sitting on the outside corner of the banquette, his mouth full of spaghetti and bread.

"How come you guys always get the girls? And me, Fat Pat, always gets left out in the cold?"

"We'll ask the ladies, shall we?"

I didn't like the way they were carrying on, teasing us, and the rude way they had sat down, making us part of their game. Also, I was angry that Charles had not bothered to acknowledge me properly—he was so caught up in his male bravado and seemed neither surprised nor especially pleased to see me. I felt like asking him what he was doing there, except that it was obvious—he'd been drinking, illegally, with his docker friends, playing at being "one of the boys." I wondered if they knew he was the boss's son. "So, Mr. *Irvington*," I said, "what brings a wealthy man like you into such humble company?"

Emilie's ears pricked up. Charles laughed heartily.

"Yeah, when you gonna fix our pay raise, Charlie?" Fat Pat mumbled through a mouthful of bread.

"He's useless," the dark-haired, handsome one told me. "Won't even pay his way in the barroom."

"Nothing humble about these guys, I'm afraid," said Charles. "And you never struck me as especially humble, either. If you don't mind me saying so, Ellie, humility never was your strong point."

I did mind him saying so, and told him as much, but not with too much conviction because he was right, and also because I was excited by the assumed intimacy that fizzed through our bantering.

"Do you know each other?" Emilie asked.

"Everyone knows Mr. Charles Irvington. One of the most renowned men-about-town in all of New York City—isn't that right, Pat?" I smiled at the fat one.

"Indubitably," he struggled to say, accidentally spraying a mouthful of bread onto the table. Everyone started laughing, and I pretended to be horrified at this uncouth display, forcing Pat into a blushing, apologetic wreck and making them all laugh even harder. I felt a pang of clever pride at my ability to amuse Charles, but when he turned to say something to me, his hilarity seemed to dissipate and his face melted into a soft warmth.

We stayed there into the early hours of the next morning. The police wouldn't come back to the same place twice in the same night—they were run off their feet checking every kitchen in the neighborhood. So Mama and Antonio pulled down the blinds, turned off the electric lights, hung a *Closed* sign at the door, and we stayed there in the restaurant until the early hours of the next morning. We drank syrupy amber wine by the light of candles stuck into wine bottles and the more we drank, the more we laughed. Emilie sang a Polish folk song, her small voice straining toward the high notes and her slanted eyes screwed shut as she got lost in the spirit of a country she had never visited, but loved as she loved her parents. I sang "Boulavogue," and Fat Pat joined in. After that everyone got quite drunk and, although I was scarcely aware of it, Charles brought Emilie and me home in a hire car.

The following morning I woke with a sore head. I had never drunk like that before. My mouth felt dry, there was a pounding behind my eyes, but worse still was that I could hardly remember going to bed, and I feared that I might have said or done something regrettable.

As we were getting ready for work, Emilie asked me how I knew Charles Irvington. I felt embarrassed and answered evasively, saying I knew him through my old job. She didn't push for any more information. People made friends and then moved on all the time in New York. Sheila had been a part of my life and now she wasn't. I would, despite the closeness she perceived between us, probably never see Isobel again. Girls at work lost old beaux and met new ones in a matter of months; became best friends with you, then got married and moved to the suburbs and lost touch completely. You could scarcely keep up with all the comings and goings of the people around you and, even as I was replying to her, I could already see that Emilie had no real interest in my business. I got a sudden revelation that my life was my own entirely. I could do exactly as I pleased and, in all likelihood, nobody would care less or be any the wiser.

Not indeed that I had been planning to do anything in particular—but nonetheless, I realized how much I had been enjoying the anonymity that New York afforded me. While I had been living my life free from the microscopic study of curious neighbors since I left Ireland, I only become aware of my freedom in that moment.

Emilie and I started to hang around with Charles and his friends and we became something of a gang. Emilie began dating all and yet none of the men, seemingly undecided about who she liked best—even though I suspected they were all good-humoredly more amused by than attracted to her. On our nights out, she moved between each of them with a skilled, almost choreographed flirtatiousness—pouting and throwing suggestive sideways glances at each of them in turn, lifting her chin with peals of pretty laughter at their utterances, stroking their hands, coquettishly resting her head on their shoulders in the booths of restaurants, and sitting on their knees in the seat-starved, smoke-filled speakeasies where we went to drink and dance off our dinners. She became more a romantic mascot to the group than a girlfriend to any individual—and served more as a visual deterrent to keep other girls from joining our circle.

I spent those evenings largely in the company of Charles. We watched the others flirt and banter with Emilie, as if they did so for our entertainment. We were apart from them in our closeness. We seemed to have an understanding of each other that ran beyond the short time we had known each other. We found the same things amusing, and while I admired his easy charm, the down-to-earth way he neither denied nor flaunted his great wealth and privilege, I was never in awe of him. Perhaps this was because I felt that his admiration of me was in equal measure. I cannot pretend that I did not notice or fail to be pleased by the fact that Charles considered me beautiful, and that, if the circumstances were different, he might have fallen in love with me. However, I never allowed myself to believe that passion played a part with Charles and me, choosing instead to define our relationship within the boundaries of intellect, humor and understanding. It seemed to me a solid, mutual friendship that I was confident did not interfere with my being married.

Three months after our friendship had been renewed, Charles invited me to a weekend house party in Westchester.

"It'll be a 'hoot'—as we toffs like to say."

"I don't know," I said, remembering how awkward I had felt about the last "weekend" house party that Isobel had set up, where there had just been the two of us.

"Oh, come on, Ellie—I've stayed with this crowd before, and they usually put on a pretty good show. It'll be great—get out of the city for the weekend. Live a little!"

Clearly there were a few of us going, so I agreed.

He told me to bring an overnight bag and to dress "smartly." I reproached him heartily: "Have you ever seen me any other way?" then briefly remembered that he had, and remembered too how my life had progressed in just three years from servant to typist. From scruffy, penniless emigrant to elegant, independent woman-about-town.

I decided to wear my green day suit for the journey, with a silk blouse in a shade of mustard yellow and a large paste cameo at my throat. A few days before we were due to go, I saw a pair of gloves and a clutch purse that were the exact match of the blouse in a leather shop near the office. While I was purchasing them, a travel trunk caught my eye. "Secondhand—make me an offer," the sign resting on it said. It was a good-quality piece and I was always attracted to a bargain. I went over and studied it, setting my face to vague curiosity—giving nothing away. In dark green leatherette with shiny brass buckles, it was obviously quite old, but of sound quality. A small gash in its side revealed an open wound of red wood. It was almost certainly too big to use for my weekend away, but it might be useful in the apartment for storing clothes . . .

"Are you interested in the trunk?" the shopkeeper asked. He had a foreign accent: European—Hungarian, perhaps? Polish? A tall, haughty-looking man, his angular face seemed designed to intimidate.

"There's a nasty tear on the side of it," I said, straightaway.

"If you are traveling, we have a very wide selection of beautifully crafted suitcases."

The suitcases were indeed beautiful and made of crocodile skin. But even the smallest was a full two months' wages—an indulgence I could not afford. "I'm not traveling," I said. "I merely want this thing for storage. I'll give you five dollars."

He smiled at my pitiful offer. I felt he was trying to shame me into upping it, so I stood my ground stubbornly and held his eyes until they narrowed. He glanced down at the counter, where lay the purse and gloves I had not yet paid for. Maybe he was wondering: would he lose this other sale, if he refused my offer? The shop was cramped and the trunk looked old and awkward and out of place. It was taking up valuable presentation space and this was his opportunity to get rid of it.

"I can have it collected from you by the end of the day," I said brusquely. "It makes no odds to me whether you wish to sell it or not."

Then, quite suddenly, the sour shopkeeper spread his palms and smiled broadly, his austere appearance instantly transformed into that of an affable old foreign man. "It was my trunk," he said. "The trunk with which I traveled here from Hungary. I made a pact with my wife that once that trunk was sold, we would never go back." His eyes misted over, but, while I felt sorry for him, I was late back to the office and did not have time to listen to an old man's anecdotes.

"Well, in that case, Sir, I am happy to leave it be."

"No, no," he said. "You misunderstand. Eva and I have been here for twenty years, we are never going back. She has never wanted . . . We have children here, you understand . . . It's the foolishness of an old man. I am a foolish old man, you see."

I tapped the counter impatiently. Was he going to sell me the trunk or not? "I have the money here with me now."

"If you can collect it today, young lady, you can have the trunk for nothing."

I was taken aback. "No, I—"

"Yes, yes, I insist!" He was smiling brightly as if a great weight had been lifted from him. "It is old and worth nothing and I wish to be rid of it."

"Well, thank you," I said. I paid for my purse and gloves and left, neither pleased nor displeased with my additional purchase—unsure about whether I had just been gifted an heirloom or been burdened with a worthless piece of junk.

Chapter Thirty-Seven

Charles collected me from the apartment in a silver Rolls-Royce. I did not ask whether it was bought or borrowed for the weekend. Charles's great wealth did not affect my friendship with him, and I observed that in all his friendships. Although I was aware of it, of course, Charles Irvington was a charming and affable man and money was neither a reason to like him or a particular bonus to knowing him. He was good-humored about us sometimes teasing him about being "the big shot" among us, because he was just one of us. Charles never flaunted his wealth in either the way he dressed or the way he behaved—so I was surprised by the showy car. And doubly surprised when he asked, "What do you think of the Rolls-Royce?" as I climbed in.

"How do you mean?" I replied, pretending not to notice that my neighbors were rushing to their windows to see me driving off in this magnificent silver vehicle. Children had already gathered to touch its glossy skin and make faces in its fat wing mirrors.

"It's English," he said. "The most expensive car on the market."

"In case you didn't know," I said haughtily, "English savages brought my country to its knees."

"Oh dear," he said laughing. "Will I get a different one?"

"Just drive," I said, "before you make a show of me in front of the entire neighborhood."

Although I was bound to pretend otherwise, I was secretly thrilled. Charles drove in his shirtsleeves and suspenders, his blazer slung casually on the backseat, his elbow resting on the open window. "You look nice," he said after a while. "Very smart."

"Why, thank you," I replied. "Who are we collecting first?"

"How do you mean?"

"Well—who else is coming?"

"Nobody else," he said breezily. "Just you and me."

For a moment, I felt panicked.

"Is that a problem?" he asked lightly, as if he couldn't see why it should be.

"No—no problem." I was calming down again.

"Good." And he smiled with a flash of his white teeth.

We sat in silence as Charles drove us through the city, carelessly humming some ragtime tune. I did feel somewhat tricked. Would I have agreed to drive with him if I had known it was just the two of us? The answer was probably not. Yet there was no romantic intent on his part, I told myself, and certainly none on mine. Charles knew I was a married woman, and we were just friends. The awkwardness between us gradually dissipated as we drove on. I decided that now that I was here, I was glad to be going on this adventure.

We swept past the apartment block on Fifth Avenue where I had arrived on my first day as a penniless emigrant; the Plaza Hotel where I had enjoyed my first taste of luxury; the typing school where I had trained; and the university where I had worked to earn the money for John's operation. As we passed each landmark, I remembered how far I had come. How much I had done and seen since I arrived here. In three years, it seemed a lifetime had passed.

As I looked out of the window I caught the white-eyed stares of black-skinned men sitting on the stoops of their redbrick tenements, the screams of children dancing in the rain of fire-hydrant fountains, the angry wave of a grocer as he chased some petty criminal out of his shop. New York City was in perpetual motion, a series of our small human happenings spilling into each other, rolling together until we had all become part of the city's rabble. Our lives were lived to its frenetic beat, both causing the tune and ruled by it—we belonged to the city, and it belonged to us. Living there was an adventure in constant change; each building strove to be taller than the next; each jazz song faster than the last; each new dance more exotic and suggestive. Not a day had gone by since my arrival here when I had not, at some point, felt the adventure of New York rip through me—in the shove of a stranger on the subway, the sight of a woman behind the wheel of a car—and awaken me with its thrilling slap. Just bearing witness to the city's lively throng made me feel alive, and driving through it with Charles, I felt more a part of it than I ever had before.

North of the city, the countryside, fresh air and simple green fields at first reminded me of where I had come from, and I felt the tug of home. But the landscape gradually changed. Along the wide roads were enormous trees, with trunks as wide as houses and thick branches spread out on either side of them like the arms of a shrugging God. All had leaves the color of fire, red and gold, nodding their huge, multicolored heads at us as we drove past. The trees parted at intervals, and beyond them appeared scenery on a grander scale than anything I had ever seen. I had never wondered what lay beyond the glamour and the bustle of the city, but now it seemed that America was unveiling herself to me—lying naked in all her glory before me. The countryside here was not like Ireland, with its small soggy fields bordered with tumbling shallow stone walls. The fields here were sweeping, rich with high golden crops and regal forests that ran on as far as the eye could see. It was as if God had designed America to His grand scale. The trees appeared taller, the mountains higher, the hills more sweeping, the landscape more spectacular than anywhere else could possibly be. The whole experience appeared unreal—as if we were traveling through a beautiful painting.

"Where are we going?" I finally asked.

"Do you care?" he said, laughing. We had already been driving for almost an hour.

"Of course I care," I insisted, although he was right—I did not. The sun was shining, I was away from work and the city, a happy-go-lucky friend at my side, and we were going to spend the evening with other friends, listening to jazz, drinking and dancing and having fun. I did not have a care in the world.

In that moment I felt nothing more than the warm, delicious wind whip through my hair and the speed of the car moving me toward my next adventure, and I felt free.

We turned off the main road and up a long drive lined with elegant silver birch until we came to a mansion so white and so large, it shimmered against the sky as if it formed part of it.

Four or five other cars were unloading in front of the house, and an assortment of wealthy, well-dressed people were variously greeting one another and wandering up the marble steps. I caught my breath and nervously stroked the breast of my tweed jacket as the car slowed down, crunching against the gravel.

Charles had not warned me how grand this place was, and I had stupidly not thought to ask. My day suit was utterly unsuitable—all the women I had seen were wearing shift dresses. The navy evening gown in my bag was almost certainly not elegant enough and all of my jewelery was paste. If I had been forewarned that Charles was breaking with habit and taking me somewhere so grand, I might have—what? Hired a dress for the occasion? Not bothered coming? Almost certainly the latter.

"Relax," Charles said, "you're not staying in the house. I've arranged for one of the cottages on the grounds." He drove round the side of the house and parked the Rolls-Royce on a courtyard of spotlessly clean cobbles.

As soon as the car stopped, two uniformed boys came rushing over to us.

"The lady is in the Laburnum cottage, Freddie," Charles said, winking at the first one. "We'll walk down."

"Will I bring both bags, Sir?" the other asked, as he opened the car door for me.

"Oh, I don't know," said Charles, laughing. "Better ask the lady!"

Although I hoped he was only joking around, I felt cheapened. Charles was on his own turf here, so at home with all this money and his fancy Rolls-Royce. He was bantering with these stupid, sniggering boys at my expense, playing with me, disrespecting me. I was here at his invitation, but also at his mercy. It had been a mistake to come here alone with him. Obviously I was sending out the wrong message. I said quietly, "I want to go home, Charles."

"Ellie, don't be silly." He raised his eyebrows at the two boys, disparagingly, as if I were some nagging, foolish woman.

His expression made me so mad that I got out of the car, slammed the door, then leaned into the backseat and lifted my bag out with such a swing that I nearly took the nose off the poor lad who was waiting on me. "If you won't drive me home, then I'll find somebody else to do it!" I started walking toward the front of the house.

Charles ran after me. "Give me the bag, Ellie—come on, don't be silly. I'm sorry—it's just us boys talking, you know?"

"No, Charles, I don't know. This was a mistake. Really, I want to go home."

He grabbed me by the elbow. "Stay, Ellie—don't run away just yet. Just wait until I tell you something important." I stared at him and his blond hair glowed in the hot sunlight, giving him something like an angel's halo. His eyes were squinting against the sun and I couldn't read them.

I handed him my bag, and he passed it on to Freddie. Then he walked me across the springy, perfect lawn until we reached the guest cottage. It was single-story white house, complete with porch and a swing. Cream and yellow roses grew up around the door from two varnished clay pots. A beautiful laburnum tree swept lazily back and forth in the slight breeze, its yellow petals scattering flirtatiously at our feet.

Inside, the cottage was as beautiful as it was outside. There was a small sofa, and on the polished table next to it was a crystal bowl of the fragrant yellow and cream roses, plumper and more luscious even than the ones outside. The floor was simple wood, laid with rugs. Through the doors off the living room, I could see a small kitchen, a bathroom and two bedrooms. One of the beds was covered with a white linen bedspread embroidered in white silk—the design no more than a glimmering suggestion.

"It's the best guest cottage on the estate," Charles said. He had been following my eyes, watching me look around.

"How do you know?" I asked. Then, unable to resist the temptation, I added, "Have you taken a different girl to every cottage? The owners must be *very* good friends of yours."

"Actually, it's my brother's estate and I normally stay in the house. Alone." Before I could recover from the surprise, he took a deep breath, closed his eyes and blurted out, "I love you, Ellie. I want to make you my wife." After a long silence, he opened his eyes with a hopeful smile. "Well, Ellie? What do you say?"

I thought he should have been able to tell from my face how shocked I was—and not one bit thrilled. I found my voice. It was shaking. "I'm already married, Charles."

He became even more eager. "We can get round that, Ellie—we can arrange an annulment. It's been done before. Even if we can't, my brother Edwin has promised us a home in this cottage. Married or unmarried, we can hide away here—Ellie, I love you, you know I do . . . And I'm sure, if you will only look into your heart, you will find that you feel the same way about me . . ."

"No, I love John!" I felt suddenly quite sick at the part I had played in this. I had made my husband disappear—otherwise why would Charles think it was acceptable for him to declare his love for me in this way?

"I would go to the ends of the Earth for you, damn it, Ellie—and you never even mention that wretched man's name—"

"His name is John! He's my husband and I love him!"

"Well, he obviously doesn't feel the same way about you. He has never come for you."

I could not answer him, out of pure despair.

Charles walked out, leaving the door open. I didn't follow him because I had nothing to say. So I stood, listening to the heaving of my heart in my chest—holding myself back from tears. I didn't want to waste any more time crying for John. Did I really love him still? I had not seen him for three years, not written to him for at least six months. Was I just defending my love for him out of misplaced loyalty? Or defending myself against my own fecklessness in allowing Charles to fall in love with me when I was already married? Perhaps Charles was right and I was simply afraid to admit my true feelings for him.

I should enjoy living in a place like this with John, I thought. Standing in a cottage on a warm day with the sun glimmering on an embroidered bedspread, thinking about our future. Living our life surrounded by manicured lawns and elegant flower arrangements and all the comforts of an easy life. I had offered it to him, and he had opted instead for the mud and the drudgery of Ireland. Even as I put these thoughts together, I was still watching Charles walk away across the lawn, square and solid in his beige trousers and white shirt—he had the spirit of a gentleman, but he walked like a navvy. As he reached the back of the house a couple appeared, arm in arm. When they saw Charles, they separated and rushed toward him. The man—his brother?—grabbed his hand and pulled him into a half hug and the woman embraced him fully, holding his face and smothering it in matronly kisses as if he were a child—how everyone adored him.

I spent the rest of the day alone. I could not leave without Charles to drive me. And after a while I found that, in any case, I did not want to leave. The cottage proved the perfect distraction from my problems. Every inch of that little house was a joy, from the scalloped edges of the cotton kerchiefs that lined the kitchen shelves, to the polished silverware and pretty painted china plates. I walked around opening drawers and cupboards, marveling and reveling in turn at every mannered detail.

There was a bowl of fruit on the table and, next to it, a single china plate with a folded napkin and knife and a glass bowl of water sprinkled with fresh rose petals. There was an electric icebox in the larder stocked with delicious food, cured meats and cheeses. There was a phonogram and a collection of records. In the bathroom, I found a small, antique cabinet stocked with soaps still wrapped in waxy paper and sealed with the stamp of their French perfumery. As the afternoon wore on, I made myself tea in a china pot and ate a dozen butter biscuits, which were as thin as paper. This was the life I wanted: one of simple beauty. Nothing too fancy or ornate, but surrounded by pretty, delicate things. With or without the company or the help of Charles or John, this was the life I needed to create for myself.

In the early evening there was a gentle knock on the cottage door and I opened it to find a young girl in full maid's uniform standing in front of me. "The lady of the house sent me down to see if you needed anything, Miss," she said, and curtsied.

I didn't know where to look or what to say in the face of this young girl's servitude. "No, thank you . . . er . . ."

"It's Mary, Miss."

"There's nothing, thank you, Mary."

She curtsied again and had turned to go when suddenly I called her back.

"But could you find Mr. Charles Irvington and ask him what time he is coming to collect me for the party?"

She smiled slyly, as if she knew something, and I realized it wasn't the lady of the house who had sent her down at all.

Charles arrived bearing a bottle of Chanel No. 5 perfume; it was the size of a whisky bottle, big enough to serve a whole funeral.

"I'm sorry," he said. Maybe he was sorry, but I suspected it was not for proposing to a married woman—I suspected he was only sorry that I hadn't gone along with him. "This is for you," he added, handing the perfume to me; then added inelegantly, "My sister-in-law said I should bring you this. She says I'm an awful ass with women."

I didn't like the way he said "women"—as if I were just one of a few mistakes he had made. "Case in point," I said, taking the bottle off him, and we both laughed.

"Do you like the cottage?" he asked.

"It's beautiful." I smiled at him.

"I knew you would . . ." He tried to add something else, but I put a finger to my mouth to shush him.

"You choose the music and pour us a drink," I said, "while I go and drench myself in this stuff."

It was the party to end all parties. Tables were laid out in banks along the wall of a ballroom that opened out onto the lawn, each groaning with food that would barely be eaten. Dozens of men in white suits wove among the crowds, their faces impervious, carrying still more trays of canapés and champagne, which the guests grabbed at without thanks as if the tray bearers were invisible. A band was set up on the lawn on an unlit podium, their black faces disappearing as the night drew in, the music eventually drowned out by the clamor and chatter; drunken clowns in shimmering dresses and expensive evening suits danced on anyway, spilling drinks as they moved and jerked, out of time, oblivious to their own inelegance. I had seen it all before and felt pleased that I was no longer the ingenue servant; I had gained enough knowledge of the way the rich lived to pass myself off as having a certain level of sophistication.

Perhaps my confidence that evening had been fueled by Charles's declaration, but I felt as if I had nothing to prove and that I stood as high as any of the other guests. It occurred to me, briefly, that it was not my position as guest at a grand party that was strange, but my earlier position of servant, which had been an aberration of both my fine education and my middle-class upbringing. I flinched briefly at the ugliness of my own snobbery, but nonetheless kept hold of it all evening to protect me from the judgment of this lofty company.

As it turned out, Charles's brother Edwin was a hilarious

buffoon. Despite being the elder of the two and the primary heir to the shipbuilding business, he was as down to earth as Charles. His wife, Gloria, welcomed me warmly and within minutes was confiding far more than she should. When I asked, somewhat nervously, if their parents were in attendance, she laughed coarsely and said, "No way! The Irvingtons are frightful snobs—real 'old-school.' They wouldn't be seen dead at a party like this. Besides they *loathe* me—if Edwin wasn't such a whizz in the business, they'd disown him for marrying a divorcée. But then, they only have one other son, and Charlie's a dropout, so . . . Oh my goodness, I've shocked you!"

I smiled and shook my head, but it didn't make any difference—she was going to tell me anyway.

"Yes, darling, I'm divorced—from a ghastly bum I married when I was eighteen. It can be done, you know." She dug her sharp painted fingernails into the white flesh of my upper arm. "Anything's possible when you have this much money, honey—*anything!*"

We danced and drank until the early hours of the morning, then, as the sun was pinking the edge of the night-gray horizon, Charles walked me back to the cottage. He made me wear his jacket and carried my shoes so they wouldn't get caught in the damp grass, and he slung one arm round my shoulders, protecting my neck from the chill.

At the porch he stopped and, knowing he couldn't come in, turned to face me. Then he stood there, his body not a foot away from mine, not touching me, but just looking down onto my face—his eyes slowly circling my features, nose, mouth, ears, hair and eyes. I had rejected him and yet he was still here, taking my friendship in place of my love. It seemed, in that moment, that my loyalty to John was misplaced; pity and proximity made me reach my hands up to Charles's face and pull it down toward me.

The kiss turned hard and hungry, traveling with the speed and heat of lightning down into our limbs. As our bodies moved in to lock, we pulled away from each other and stood on the quaint porch panting messily, unsure how to contain the pleading in our bodies. Charles ran his hand through his blond hair and grinned; his eyes were shining.

I said, "I think you'd better drive me back to the city."

We drove in silence. We had shared every joke, told every tale, said everything that needed to be said. What remained unsaid scarcely even mattered now, because even though I was still running away from him, we had moved into the realm of the inevitable. The kiss had set in motion a turn of events of which we were no longer entirely in control. Love had set in and, one way or another, seemed to be telling us that it would have its way. The unfinished kiss with Charles caught at the back of my throat like a song waiting to happen.

I could not think about what might or might not happen when we arrived back at my apartment in New York. I could not think about the future, or John, or anything beyond the sun rising up behind the copper trees and the two of us alone on the road before the rest of the world came awake.

Charles parked the Rolls-Royce on the street outside and walked ahead of me up the narrow stairs to my apartment door. Once there, he put the bag down and pulled from the door a letter that had been nailed up with a pin.

"It's a telegram," he said, handing it to me.

It was marked urgent. I pulled the flimsy envelope apart and read:

Ellie. Your father is very sick and close to dying. You need to come home. Sorry. Maidy.

Chapter Thirty-Eight

My father was dying and my conscience told me I had to go home, even though every other inch of me was screaming at me to stay in America and let my life unfold into the great adventure it was promising to be.

America had already given me so much: a career, friends, an elegant demeanor, a home full of beautiful things. Now my adopted country was offering me wealth and love and fulfilment—a lifetime without hardship or complaint. All I had to do was stay. I could ignore the telegram from Maidy, slice off the past, forget John, and pretend this was all there was. Pretend that the girl with the black bobbed hair and the independent life was who I really was now; pursue my burgeoning relationship with Charles; move on. My heart, which I had always been so certain of, was now confused and conflicted. There was duty, and home, and John. There was America. There was Charles. Whenever I stopped to ask myself what I wanted, I felt like a dog frantically scrabbling in the earth in search of a bone that wasn't even there.

My conscience won. Emilie arranged for her sister to move in and pay my half of the rent for the few months I was away. She was nineteen and her parents were happy to let her live in the city as long as she was with her sister. "Plus, she's fallen in love with a very bad man. My parents want her away from the Bronx until she gets over him. She's too young to be dating— they know I'll keep her safe."

I laughed and Emilie half smiled and half frowned back. "What?" she exclaimed. "I know it's hard to believe, but I am the sensible one in my family . . ."

"She must be pretty crazy then," I said. I would be missing out on all this madness. All the risky romance, the intrigues, the fashions, the easy come, easy go beautiful mayhem of our life in New York would be happening without me.

"Why are you taking so much stuff with you?" Emilie asked.

I was packing the trunk—everything I owned was spread out on the floor, as I methodically folded and rolled and wrapped everything, before placing it into one of the deep drawers.

"You'll only have to bring it all back with you again." She picked up the embroidered tablecloth and the set of matching napkins that were lying folded on the bed. "Table linens? Why on earth are you taking these?"

I looked down at some of the other items I had already packed—a small glass vase, a china dog, a crystal sugar bowl. "They're gifts," I said.

Emilie shrugged and, apparently satisfied with my explanation, left the room leaving the true answer in her wake: I was packing as if I were never coming back. Even though I was un-questionably going to return, I found I could not bear to leave anything behind.

"They're gifts for my mother and Maidy," I said again, firmly and out loud, although there was only myself in the room. "I have a return ticket," I continued, addressing the trunk. I could not help wonder if it was a fortuitous coincidence that I had stumbled across this cavernous case, or if this terrible turn of events was being driven by a Romany curse contained in it.

The small narrow trinket drawer at the top of the chest was stiff, and as I tugged it open I heard a faint rattle. A small, silver octagonal ball rolled across the green felt. It wobbled slightly before settling on one of its edges, inviting me to pick it up. It was a goat bell. I don't know how I knew that. I supposed I must have seen them tied around the necks of kids on fair days back home. I rolled it across the palm of my hand, but the tinkle was gone out of it. I thought about the man in the shop with his severe, pointed features and tried to imagine him as a goatherd. Immediately, then, I remembered my father and that he was sick. I tried to imagine him dying: how he would look, gaunt and white, clutching his large wooden rosary beads like the martyrs he so admired, his last words in devotion to the Blessed Virgin. A seam of dread loosened across my chest at the thought of him—at the knowledge that, alive or dead, my own father held no more pull on me than that of duty. The call of duty was not as loud or as tuneful as the call of love, but it was nonetheless as strong. Stronger perhaps—otherwise I would have returned home to John when he had asked me. I folded my fingers into a fist around the foreign trinket. It was clearly valueless, yet I did not want to throw it away. So I put the tarnished, silent bell back where I had found it, throwing a confused jumble of my own jewelery in on top of it before hurriedly closing the drawer.

Charles had arranged my passage with a first-class ticket—return. He called round to the apartment the day before I left and handed it to me without words or explanation. It was not given as an elaborate gift; such a thing was commonplace to Charles, valueless. "We can all meet in Tullio's and have lunch, then I and the gang can come with you down to the port and wave you off." His voice was forced in its jollity, but his eyes were dead. He had always had the happy, confident stance of a man who didn't stop until he got what he wanted—hoping for good things and, generally, getting them. I could not bear to look at him so sad, because of all he had come to mean to me—not just as a man, but as the embodiment of my dashed hopes and dreams.

"I'd rather go alone," I said, "if you don't mind."

He shrugged. "Whatever you want, Ellie."

I want to stay, ran through my head, yet as it did I realized I wasn't certain if that was true anymore. Now that I had the ticket in my hand it was as if a part of me had already left.

"I'll be back in two months," I said brightly—smiling.

One short year. John's words when I had left for Ellis Island rang back in my head. *Just one short year, Ellie.* How long had it been?

Charles and I embraced, and all the time he had his arms wrapped around me I was waiting for him to pull back and kiss me again. Fearful that another kiss would bring my propriety truly into question, but hopeful that perhaps that same propriety would be caught by the wind and sent flying across the sea, where it would be sucked into the depths of the Atlantic and leave me here, happy to live out my American dream without guilt or question. But Charles did not kiss me, nor I him.

When the door closed after him, I wrapped my arms across my stomach, leaned into them and pushed the anguish of my own selfish desires from me in a guttural sob.

The following morning I traveled to the port alone. The trunk had been collected by the shipping line the day before. It would be traveling first class, but I would not.

At the ticket office I made an almighty fuss until they agreed to cash in my first-class ticket for third-class, giving me a refund in cash. The woman behind the counter argued with me and asked if I was accompanied by a man. Clearly thinking I had lost my mind, to be both traveling with no man to protect me and trying to get myself downgraded to third class, she called out the manager. But the length of the line behind me persuaded him to concede, and he gave me my refunded dollars in cash.

It was an inauspicious end to my days in New York, but I knew I needed to return with all the money I could. I had no idea what hardship I would have to face when I got home. But I was certain of one thing—there would be hardship.

PART THREE

HOME
1924

Chapter Thirty-Nine

I was booked on the *Celtic* again, and I was glad of its familiar surroundings. The ship was more sparsely populated coming back from America than it had been in going there, so I managed to secure a cabin to myself. I barely spoke to a soul on the journey, as I had no desire for adventure and I had neither the energy nor the appetite for new friends; I was not in the humor to start explaining myself to anybody. Instead I read for company, because books can't ask questions.

There was a small library next to the dining room and after breakfast each day I would borrow two dog-eared paperbacks to take back to my cabin and devour, sitting up in the hard bed until lunchtime. When I started to get cabin fever, I went up and read in the smoking lounge or took a walk around the deck, my book in hand. Thinking about what lay ahead of me, or what I had left behind, was a torture. So every waking hour I immersed myself in penny-dreadful crimes and romances, existing solely in the imagined world of girls in dramatic costumes falling hopelessly in love with vagabonds, or troubled men catching out clever criminals in hotel rooms. In this way, I was able to place my own concerns aside and curl myself up in the cocoon of somebody else's imagination. My life was suspended—I was in neither one place nor the other. In that sense, I was sorry when the voyage came to an end.

I did not go up on deck when we were within sight of land, but stayed on the boat until the last minute. When I finally faced the cold, wet air of Queenstown, reality hit home. The quayside was packed with people arriving to take the boat the following day, the atmosphere noisy with expectation and emotion. My green winter suit, silk stockings and buckled shoes felt flimsy as I walked across to the station office to buy my ticket.

"Home for a funeral?" the dour-faced ticket attendant asked.

For a second I thought I must know him, but then remembered where I was and how even strangers presumed to know everything about you in Ireland. Sizing you up from the first second they saw you, so that they could strip you of any mystique. It wouldn't have taken much. He knew from my clothes and the size of the bag that I was off the boat, and he knew that people only returned from America for one reason—to bury their dead.

"My father is ill," I said. "I don't know that he's dead as yet. But thank you for your kind inquiry."

"Please God, he'll be all right," he said, not at all embarrassed.

On the train, I stared out of the window. I was home, but it didn't feel like home anymore. The landscape that had once been so beautiful to me was soaked in the dread I felt at being back, and at what would face me at my journey's end. The dread infected everything: the bare branches of the faraway trees spiked against the gray sky; the smaller branches blurring in the soft excuse of Irish daylight; the messy piles of twigs lacing along the limp hedgerows; the miles of bleak barren bog and the small grazing fields bordered with tumbling stone walls; the sad-looking cows, as they stood their patch of ground waiting for more rain to come, resigned to their dull fate of chewing the cud. Was my father alive or dead? I tried to draw my mother's pinched, worried face to mind and felt nothing but barren cold where love should have been. I thought about John. What would he make of me now? He was sure to be angry with me.

The platform at Ballymorris station was empty and I felt suddenly lonely at the lack of people there. I missed all the strangers in the city. I caught the vague hint of turf smoke in the air— a dusty, depressing smell that told me I was home. Back where I started, but not where I belonged. Not anymore.

Maidy and Paud were drawing up in front of the station as I walked out. The train had been a few minutes early and they had just arrived to collect me. Paud was anxious that they had not been on the platform to greet me, and ran to grab my bag, hauling it up onto the back of the horse and cart without saying a word. Maidy enveloped me as if I was still a child, and immediately I started sobbing with relief into the familiar warmth of her soft bosom.

"You're daddy's gone, Ellie. Your daddy's gone and we buried him five days ago," she said, rubbing my back and kissing the side of my head.

I didn't know if I was crying for him or for the relief of seeing my adopted mother again.

As Paud silently drove his aging horse along the muddy paths that passed for roads, Maidy told me she had thought about sending a telegram to the ship to inform me of my father's passing. "But what would be the point of spending money on bad news when you couldn't get here any quicker and you'd be alone on the boat, grieving? So we decided it was time enough to wait until you got here." I told her she had done the right thing, and she seemed relieved, then caught me up with all the news. My father had contracted TB and was taken to the county hospital. Maidy had insisted that my mother stay with them, so that Paud could drive her up and down to the hospital every other day in the horse and cart. It seemed unlikely to me that my mother—or my father, no matter how ill he was— would agree that she travel any way but in a hire car. When I wouldn't let the point drop, Maidy finally spat it out that my parents' "hire car" days were over. My father had lost his good British government job when the Free State was legally formed. He was offered another position, which he had refused out of loyalty to the Crown.

"Why did nobody write and tell me?" I said.

"Sure, you were in America, Ellie—what could you do from there, only worry?"

I was shocked that this drama had happened without my knowing and didn't know whether to be angry or grateful for the conspiracy not to tell me.

She continued, "They tried to put him out of the house, Ellie—the IRA. John had a word with a few of them and they let him be, but there were arguments in our house over it, I can tell you. It was a disgrace the way they treated him. They should have had more respect for a man like your father—with all his experience and a God-fearing man too, God rest his soul. He's with the Blessed Virgin and all her angels now."

I thought about what a trial it must have been for the Hogans, dealing with all of this. My parents were not easy people and I had not thought about how my father's pro-British politics would have gone down with the new order. I sat there taking it in—as if it were relevant, as if he weren't dead. Something strange was happening to time. Talking to Maidy felt so familiar that it seemed as if I had only been away for a day or two. Yet huge things had happened—the birth of the Free State, Civil War, the death of my father. It was as if I was reading about it all in a book. It seemed implausible that these dramatic events had taken place in my life and I knew nothing about them. All I had thought about was John, or rather his injuries and his operation—and that had seemed like enough.

"Where is my mother now?" I asked.

"She's still staying with us, Ellie. She won't go back to the house now that your father is gone." Her face tightened and I got a glimpse of how difficult a houseguest my mother had been. When Maidy saw my worry, she opened her face into a deliberate smile that in a split second had reached her eyes. Maidy could change her mood simply by smiling. "Oh, she has been so looking forward to seeing you, Ellie. She has missed you so much."

I doubted that was true, although I did not doubt that she bitterly resented all that had happened to her in the past few years and would have a clear opinion of the part my elopement and emigration had played in it.

I took a small woven blanket out of my bag and wrapped it round both of our legs. Maidy made a tremendous fuss about how beautiful it was, saying, "Oh no, Ellie—it's too good, it'll get ruined!" and made me put it back into my case while she tugged out an old sheepskin from under the bench.

The flatulence of Paud's aging horse, the rancid smell of the sheepskin and the rough tugging of the cart wheels on the stony ground made me nauseous. I leaned into Maidy and, closing my eyes, buried my face into her neck and took in the familiar smell of her kitchen that always seemed to resonate from her skin and clothes. I was a grown woman, but I would never be too old to revel in Maidy's motherly warmth.

"My wee girleen Ellie," she said. "But it's good to have you home."

Loved as I felt in that moment, I knew it was temporary. I was out of place here, chugging along in a cart. This wasn't who

I was anymore. I felt the contrast of my shoes on the stained wood, the suit fabric against the sheepskin, and I felt sad that I had moved beyond all of this. But I had, and I could not go back now.

On the one-hour journey I did not ask about John, and Maidy did not offer.

There would be time enough for him to tell me himself, and the longer I could put it off, the better.

Darkness descended in the last mile of our journey, so I was barely aware of where we were when we arrived. As we drove up the lane, the exhausted horse trotting the last few yards in a final push for home, my stomach tightened. I did not want to go in.

The house was in total blackness, and Paud muttered to Maidy about my mother not lighting the lamp or preparing the house for our arrival, and she hushed him up. I followed them in. My mother was sitting by the dying fire in a hardbacked chair, gazing at the pathetic puffs as wind from the chimney blew them back into the room. Maidy ran about immediately, putting on the lamp, rushing to throw a few dry sticks on the fire to breathe some life back into it, filling the cottage with friendly chatter: "Now, we'll have some stew heated shortly— and there's a few spuds hidden in those embers, so no need to worry about them. Look who's back, Attracta, and wait till you see the cut of her, she's like a movie star . . ."

My mother did not even turn her head.

I walked across and stood in front of her chair. "Hello, Mam."

"Welcome back," she said coldly. Her eyes crawled across my face briefly, then settled back on the fire.

My stomach tightened, the painful clench of reality taking hold. Paud was bringing turf in and loading it up to the hearth, saying nothing. I could see frustration and anger in his eyes. Maidy passed by my mother's back and nodded at me to stay where I was.

I knelt down at my mother's feet and said, "I'm sorry, Mam. I'm sorry I went away and I'm sorry I wasn't here when Father died."

She didn't look at me, but said, quick and sudden before I had my last words out, "He asked for you, Eileen. He asked for you at the last to say his final rosary."

And as suddenly as she said it, I realized he was dead. The loveless slab of life they offered to me as a childhood, their rejection of me for refusing to join the convent, then disowning me for marrying John—none of that mattered now. Death had taken all the bad things with it. All that was left behind of my father for us was the endless, meaningless hours he had spent in devoted prayer.

"I'll say it now, Mam," I said. "I'll say his rosary now."

She shrugged, but I picked up the beads that were hanging on the arm of her chair and placed them round her frozen hands.

"I believe in God, the Father Almighty . . ." Kneeling at her feet, I said the words to the crackling of the growing fire. Presently, my mother's voice was added to mine. Maidy and Paud continued to potter about their tasks as they also joined in, *"Holy Mary, Mother of God, pray for us sinners now and at the hour of our death . . . Amen."* The old couple's actions—piling up sods of turf, stirring a pot of stew, sweeping the floor— played out in a kind of methodical dance, making the rhythm of the words seem almost melodic. This would have been considered an appalling irreverence by my father, and I looked up at my mother for her disapproval, but there was only the blank resignation she always displayed in prayer. Then, as the decades of the rosary mounted up, something unusual happened. Her

voice and mine became stronger and more in unison. During the third decade, my mother leaned over and poked some more life into the fire, and during the fourth I stood up and pulled over a chair to sit opposite her, in preference to kneeling. It was as if the prayer itself was sending us a message, or we were sending each other a message through the prayer. He was gone and we were to grieve him in a way that suited us. My father's death had given us both some of the freedom he was unable to give us in life.

At the very last prayer, "Hail, Holy Queen," I got a shock as a fifth voice joined our chorus. For an instant I thought it was my dead father, but, in the spirit of our enlivened, sacrilegious rosary, I turned round and saw that it was John.

Chapter Forty

Without thought or hesitation, I ran across the room and threw myself at him with such force that he staggered against the table, toppling a chair. He laughed, and grabbed me round the waist and kissed my face. The memories of him, as he was, came flooding through me with his familiar smell, the confidence of his touch. Despite our parents being there and the circumstances of our loss, my limbs were straining to wrap themselves around him.

"Be careful, John!"

I knew Maidy's reprimand was meant for me.

"Stop fussing, woman!" John said, angry with the public reminder of his failings. He gently pulled away from me and walked across the room. His limp was pronounced, his hips circling as he moved, his trousers airy—suggesting that his legs were thin and wasted. I was shocked. Maidy had warned me that his recovery was not complete, but in some sense I had not truly believed it, or indeed prepared myself for what he might look like, or that his injuries might have changed him forever, not just for a short while.

"There look, our boy is walking again, Ellie. And it's thanks to you." Maidy's voice was full of gratitude and I tried to see the miracle of John being on his feet, but all I could see was his disjointed gait, the imperfection.

He picked up a lamp and said, "Right, people, you've had enough of her now—it's time for me to take my wife home."

"You're not going back to the cottage at this time of night, John?" Maidy said.

"Ah now," Paud said, "it'll be time enough to travel in the morning." He had one eye on my mother, who was setting the table for dinner.

"I'm taking Ellie home to our house, and that's that," John said. "I've the cart all laid out with blankets and everything, we'll be grand."

My heart sank at the word "cart." I would not have expected John to own a car, but I could not help the image of Charles in his Rolls-Royce flying across my mind.

"Will I get changed out of my travel clothes?" I asked, then immediately regretted how foolish it sounded.

John shrugged, but my mother suddenly burst in, "It would be a disgrace to ruin those good shoes, Eileen. I have a pair of boots in the back, I'll bring them in for you." When she disappeared into the scullery, Paud looked after her, astonished, and Maidy whispered to me, "That's as much as your mother has said since your father died, Ellie. She is so happy to have you back."

"She can move in with us as soon as you're settled back home," said John. "Then Maidy and Paud can get their bed back."

All these decisions being made about and around me. The curve of my life had been taken out of my hands and was being drawn into a crude circle made of old-fashioned assumptions. A life where I traveled in carts on dirt roads, wore borrowed boots and martyred my married life to my mother.

A flint of anger sparked inside me and lit a flame of resolve in my heart. My family meant well, but they didn't understand who I was anymore.

John drove the horse as far as the road, then stopped, pulling in among the hedgerows. I looked up at him, finding his face in the dark. The moon came out from behind gray, painted clouds and cast blue shadows across the contours of his face. His features had matured, become sharper, their scoops and hollows carved by the realities of war and physical pain. I saw the last dredge of loneliness drain out of his eyes as they became soft, and he was looking at me with that curious mixture of pride and amusement that was John's version of love. Nobody else had ever looked at me in that way because nobody knew me the way John knew me. For all we had both changed, for all I had feared seeing him again, the bond between us remained intact.

By the time we got to our house it was dark. John lit an oil lamp and I followed behind him up the path, my mother's old boots sliding on the muck, the acrid smell of burnt oil catching in the back of my throat.

"Here now," he said, as he lifted the latch.

As I went inside my hand instinctively scraped the wall next to the door for an electric light switch. Of course, there was none.

John turned and his face cast ghostly shadows on itself. He laid the lamp down on the table and I took it all in. The cold stone floor, the rough walls, the open fireplace for cooking and the meager scraps of wood that passed for furniture.

"Home," John said, smiling. "You're home at last."

That night in bed, I kept my clothes on to try and protect my skin from the rough wool blankets that John had on the bed instead of cotton sheets. At dawn, I woke with cold as John had pulled the blankets off me in his sleep. At first, I did not know where I was. In my half-wakened state I thought I was still in my New York apartment, and had merely dreamed I had fallen down some freezing black hole. Then I noticed the breath in front of my face and the spikes of branches tapping against the bedroom window, witches' fingers against the growing dawn, and I remembered.

I turned toward John. The low, dozing sun shone a pink light on his back and, as I reached my hand out to touch him, I felt the same thrill of his being there as I had the first time we had kissed. It was really John. He was really mine. His back was a wall of muscle, harder and more defined than I remembered it, and as I drew my fingers in a feathered stroke down his spine, he rolled over and crushed me against the mattress in an immediate and desperate kiss. We made love as the sun yawned in a new day, then fell back into an easy sleep, our limbs locked into each other like branches woven together by time.

I woke late. I was alone in the bed and the house. The blankets itched me horribly. My skin felt raw where I had scratched at my arms in my sleep, and when I finally hauled my legs from under the rough blankets, I saw I had clawed my good silk stockings into tatters. I threw on an old woolen sweater of John's that I found hanging on a chair and walked out to the kitchen to review my domain. In the daylight I could see that John had made a good attempt to prepare the house for me. There was turf stacked to the side of the hearth and a fire set with twigs and folded paper sticks ready for me to set a match to. The floor was swept, and the walls whitewashed. Above the fire, John had put up a wide rough-edged shelf, which held a number of books and a picture of the Sacred Heart, which I recognized as Maidy's—kind gifts for my return. In pride of place at the front of the shelf were two framed photographs. One was the "Hands Across the Sea" postcard I had sent him from the boat, the other was of me posing in a photographer's studio. My back was straight and I had one leg crossed over the other, so that my smart T-bar shoes were pointed one to the side and the other straight ahead. The coat was crushed velvet with a dropped waist and a wide fur collar, and I was wearing a tight-fitting cloche hat; my eyes were heavily made up and burned out at the camera from under the tight brim. Both the hat and coat belonged to Sheila; it was she who had made me get my photograph taken, to send to John with the ticket for his journey across. "Let him see what he's missing," she had said.

The old anger made me flinch and my hand shook as I reached up for the frame. It was heavier than it looked, and was good quality with a mirrored finish and delicate shamrocks etched into the beveled glass. Even though he had sent the ticket back, John had gone to some trouble to display my picture properly. I swallowed the anger and replaced it with a little hope. Perhaps this was a sign.

There was little else to impress me. No ornaments and the skimpiest of practical implements: a battered brush, its handle worn with use; a few tortured-looking dishcloths. The dresser was well stocked with simple crockery and basic food, but there was so much that needed doing to make this place into any kind of a home. The day was dull and the room darkened with rain clouds. I looked absentmindedly around the white walls for a light switch, and with growing horror absorbed the magnitude of what I did not have. No electricity. No electric lights; no electric cooker; no electric iron. I had become as reliant on electricity as I was on my own breath. I wanted to cry.

No sink; no toilet; no shower; no soft towels or nice soaps or scented tinctures. The list went on and on those first few days. The primitive living conditions were not a surprise to me, and the absence of many of the smaller household items could have been remedied. Nonetheless I could not stop my mind becoming a litany of what was missing. My resolve hardened with each new lack. I would not live in this poverty for any longer than I had to. In time, my mother would recover her strength and settle back into her own house. After that I would insist that John come with me to America. Till then, I would have to make do as best I could.

The trunk was delivered to the post office in Kilmoy, from where we had to go and collect it. When we got word it had arrived, I wondered why I had bothered bringing it at all. It would have made better sense leaving it in New York. However, it would be our first outing into town since I had arrived back and, as it was also fair day, John and I got dressed up for the occasion.

I washed in tepid water in a shallow tin basin at the kitchen table, using a slither of soap I had kept from the boat. I consoled myself that my trunk contained a few luxuries from home that would tide me over for the few months I'd be here. John had insisted I keep the water from the kettle for my own toilet, while he bathed in cold water outside. I watched him through the kitchen window as he stripped naked, balancing the large tin bucket on a milking stool. It was a cold day to be washing outside, but I knew John. I knew he would relish the sharp air on his skin and the smell of morning and the feeling of being naked against nature.

It was the first time I had seen his body fully unclothed since the operation. When we made love it was in the camouflage of night or under covers. Once, I had felt the deep ridge of the scar along his hip. The tips of my fingers had curled unexpectedly into the hole and my hand leapt back in horror. Neither of us said anything, but I knew John had felt my shock.

Now, watching him, I could see that his arms were stronger than they had ever been, from doing the work of his legs while he was in the wheelchair; but the defined muscular broadness of his torso threw a bad light on his legs, which were thin and saggy—the limbs of a much older man. Across one hip, two deep ridges were carved out of the skin, shockingly deep; one of them ran in a bending road, almost down to his knee. I recalled the day of the shooting, carrying him back to this house, staunching the blood, trying to press together the shattered flesh. I felt the miracle of him still being alive, and pride in the fact that he was standing there in front of me—war torn, but standing nonetheless.

Unaware he was being watched, John lathered himself with carbolic soap and then, turning his hands into wide bowls, scooped the freezing water across his hair and face, letting out an amused shout with the shock of cold before picking up the whole bucket and throwing the contents over himself, shaking and laughing and rubbing himself with a rough towel until he emerged pink and smiling. I felt such a surge of love that I knew I could never again leave him behind.

Chapter Forty-One

Later that morning, John packed up two boxes of recently born chicks, put them in the back of the cart to sell at the fair and drove us in. He was all dressed up in a white shirt and tie and a tweed jacket; I had parted and combed his hair over to one side, vowing to purchase a sharp pair of scissors in the town haberdashery store so that I could cut his hair properly. I was wearing a simple woolen day dress and a coat that I had come to consider rather ordinary. I did not want to draw attention to myself on my first public outing, but was surprised at how nervous I was all the same, as we came toward the main street.

The town was alive with people and animals. The old and poor women were in shawls and woolen skirts as they had always been, and the better-off ladies wore hats and gloves. I saw a young woman pass by in a beautiful red felt hat with matching gloves and regretted, for a moment, my ordinary coat. Then I noticed that she was a girl from the class below me in national school. I was about to lift my hand when, instead of greeting me, she turned to the old woman next to her and whispered. I was convinced she was talking about me and color drew up to my cheeks. I felt the same cruel rejection I had experienced as a child and had a sudden craving for the anonymity of New York.

We came to a halt halfway down the hill as scores of farmers unloaded their prized cattle into the market square, abandoning their carts without regard for who was before or behind them. It was chaos. John pulled up behind an old farmer struggling to control an angry-looking bullock; greeting him, he swung himself down to help. My heart pinched as I noticed the stern set of his chin as he handled the bullock by the nose ring, staggering slightly and then quickly straightening up, proving himself a man in front of his farming peers. I felt for a moment that it was not just the lack of things that made me want to go back to New York, but rather the monotonous sadness in this rural life where men had to prove themselves by being physically strong and women by being virtuous and long-suffering. I wanted to be back in a world where a man could define himself by looking smart and reciting verse and a woman by her wit and how fast she could type.

Once the bull was calmed, John made a deal with the farmer that he would sell our chicks for us. The toothless ancient proffered me a grin that would have frightened Satan back to hell in an instant. I smiled back as cheerily as I could, then John lifted me down from the cart and we walked through the town together.

The ground was wet with dung and the air thick with the sickly sweet stench of animal breath. The shops were the same as when I left. Wherever possible, businesses doubled or even tripled up. The undertaker was also a publican and a grocer. The butcher was a blacksmith, and the baker had a barber out the back. The chemist shop was tiny, and sold every type of medicine for man and horse, but if you wanted a lipstick or a bottle of scent you had to travel to Galway. Moran's the drapery shop was the only place in town that sold clothes, but practicality took precedence over fashion. In its window, tweed hats were piled next to ladies' nightdresses and cotton towels, against a backdrop of filthy, flocked wallpaper that had not changed since I was a child.

A few doors down from there was Regan's, the haberdashery. They sold household items—buckets, brooms, mops, saucepans, cooking pots and ovens, along with "gift and luxury" items, such as crockery and glassware. Their small window was always filled with the latest in popular religious paraphernalia. Before going into the shop, I stopped for a second to look at a statuette of St. Francis of Assisi standing on a grassy knoll with a collection of birds on his shoulder and rabbits at his feet seeming to nibble on his bare toes. Although some attempt had been made to give the patron saint of animals a face, his vestments were simply daubed in dull brown paint, the grass a lump of flat green. No gold leaf, or detail or varnish to liven him up. A duller and more miserable-looking saint I had never seen.

"Do you like it?" John asked.

I let out a derisive puff, then, regretting the small cruelty, quickly said, "We have better things to spend our money on, John." In the shop, I let him engage Mrs. Regan in polite conversation while I walked round and picked out my purchases: a sweeping brush with firm bristles; a mop—I checked for firmness by pulling at the soft string head until I found one that did not shed; two good flannel cloths for cleaning and dusting; a tin of beeswax; starch and blue; a box of powdered bleach; a small scrubbing brush. As John chatted, Mrs. Regan's eyes followed me round the shop. I didn't like Mrs. Regan. As a child I had once been in here with my father and witnessed her loudly refusing credit to a woman in front of her children and in full view of the other customers. She was also in the habit of looking down her nose on country people. Town people often considered themselves infinitely more sophisticated than those who lived a rural life. "Tuppence ha'penny looking down on tuppence," Maidy used to describe it as, and Clare Regan epitomized that backward attitude. If America had done one thing to me, it was to reduce my tolerance for meanness—fiscal or otherwise. I had no reason to fear the likes of a small-town snob like Mrs. Regan anymore.

"Do you have any scissors?" I asked, without offering her a cursory greeting. She raised an eyebrow at my rudeness, then reached under the counter and placed a pair of small, shiny scissors in front of me. They were perfect. I picked them up and gently felt along the blade with the tip of my finger, being careful not to slice through my skin, as it was razor sharp. "I'll take them," I was saying when I heard a voice behind me.

"Ellie Hogan—I had heard you were home."

It was Kathleen Condon, standing so close she was breathing practically down my neck. She had gained some weight, or was perhaps pregnant. She still had the thick glasses, and she gave me a sideways smile as she added, "And look at John walking around . . ."

"Good morning, Kathleen," he said, tipping his hat, all smiles as he packed our purchases into a box.

"It must have been wonderful to come home and find your husband all well again for you, Ellie?"

"Some small comfort after the death of your poor father," Mrs. Regan added, before crossing herself and saying, "He was *such* a gentleman. We all miss him terribly, you know . . ."

I felt sickened. America may have armed me with some attitude, but I had forgotten what a weapon knowledge was here. These women had surely seen my father laid out in his coffin, said the sorrowful mysteries of the rosary at his grave, perhaps embraced my mother at the church. They knew about John's injuries, and my parents' brush with poverty—in this place, they knew more about my life here than I did. To them, I was not an enlightened woman returned from the sophistications of New York, but a local girl who had abandoned my husband in his hour of need and neglected my daughterly duties in not even making it back in time for my father's funeral. I would have felt less hurt if I had not feared there was some shred of truth in what they had said.

"Thank you for your kind concern, ladies," I said, my hands shaking slightly as I held my purse over to John. "Would you settle our account please, John, while I get some air?"

When I got outside I tried to calm myself down. Breathing deeply, I turned and looked at Mrs. Regan's tatty window and suddenly I was filled with anger. Who did these women think they were, judging me? *"You watch your step, Ellie Hogan,"* they had been telling me, *"you're back on our turf now."* But I wasn't going to be chased out of a shop by the likes of Kathleen Condon. I was better than that!

As I turned to go back in, I saw John nodding at the window and asking, "How much is the St. Francis, Mrs. Regan?"

Chapter Forty-Two

All the way home, I fumed in silence at John for buying that horrible statue of St. Francis. As soon as we were back at the house, I hopped out of the cart without him helping me down and went straight into the kitchen, where I immediately set about lighting the fire and clattering about generally.

It was not the statue in itself, although I hated giving the Regan woman money—it was the whole thing of being back here in Ireland. The cattle, the clothes, the cart, the way that everyone knew my business, the frustration of stepping into a life I had hoped I had left behind. Except that I had not even hoped it—I *had* left it behind. This wasn't who I was anymore. I had shopped in fancy boutiques, eaten in restaurants as if such a thing were commonplace, traveled the ocean twice, mixed with people of all colors and creeds, and socialized in mansions with people of great wealth and culture. Now, here I was, quibbling over a pair of scissors, my shoes dirtied with dung and the hem of my skirts splattered. It felt as if I had been grabbed by the ankles and dragged facedown in the mud backward into a world where I no longer belonged.

"I want to go back to America."

It just came out. I had planned how I would approach the subject with John and knew I had to wait for the right time and place. But John loved me, I knew that now. He loved me more than ever, I had known it from the first moment I saw him again, and I knew he always would. He had not meant to let me down, he had not come to America because he had not realized how important it was. Once he saw how much I loved it there, how miserable I would be if I had to stay in Ireland, he would concede and come with me. "As soon as my mother is settled," I repeated, "I want us to go back to America."

John went pale and sat down on the edge of the trunk, rubbing his hands across his chin and mouth.

"We'll miss the family, but, you know, we can send for them, John. We will have enough money within weeks to bring Maidy and Paud across. My mother might even join us."

John did not lift his eyes from his feet and continued rubbing his face.

"In fact," I said, riding the wave of his silence, "we could bring them with us now. My job is open, and a place for you as well. We could get a loan from my boss . . ." Or Charles would send me as many tickets as I wanted—he was, after all, still a good friend; Emilie would move back in with her parents once she knew how important this was, or perhaps we could find a suitable house to rent in Brooklyn. My mind was racing. "We will find the money easily enough, John—nothing is a problem, anything is possible . . ."

"I'm not going to America, Ellie," he said firmly, his head still down.

"You say that, John, but—"

"I'm not going, Ellie," he said again, quietly. "Don't think I haven't thought seriously about it, because I have. I've thought about it every night you were away, and me longing to feel your soft limbs wrapped around me—"

I wasn't in the mood for this romantic nonsense and burst

in, "Listen, John, I can't live here anymore. Not now I know
how much better things are over there." I listed them off on my
fingers: "There's electricity, there's telephones, cars are commonplace . . ."

"Those things aren't important, Ellie."

"No, John—not when you live in a backwater like this
where nobody knows any better. When they've never been to
proper department stores, or taken frequent trips to the picture
houses or restaurants. Where everybody is used to making do
on boiled bacon and cabbage, living every day with muck on
their boots like paupers. But I have *been* there, John. I have
seen what is possible—the luxury and the freedom—where you
can say and do as you please and everything is freely available:
everything. I won't stay here, John, where there is nothing for
me, *nothing!*"

He looked at me bitterly. "So that's how it is," he said quietly. "There's nothing here for you, is that it? What about me,
Ellie? What about your family? Am I not the man enough for
you, now that I'm crippled? Is that why you went, maybe, to get
away from me?"

"No. No!" I shouted. "I love you! That's why I'm back—to
bring you back with me. I want us all to go."

"Why can't you just be happy with what we've got, Ellie.
Why?"

"I just can't, John. I want more than this. I want to go back
to America. I *hate* it here—it's backward, it's poor, it's filthy
backwater . . ."

John's lips curled, his eyes became flinty with anger and I
knew before he spoke out that I had gone too far. "How *dare*
you speak about our country like that. This is the country I
fought for! If you hate it so much, what did all of it mean?"
He banged his leg with his walking stick, then broke off and,

breathing hard, dropped his head into his hands, calming himself down.

"I'm sorry, John," I said, though it was in words only, and we both knew it. "I just believe we could make a good life in New York, and I want that. For both of us."

"Well, Ellie, I . . ." He faltered and for one glorious moment I thought he was conceding.

"Just for a year, John—see how you like it?"

For a year he might agree, then once we got there . . .

He said, "I love you, Ellie, but I can't leave here. I won't leave Ireland." His voice became so soft that it was barely audible as he added: "My roots are here. It's where I'm from. I can't explain it any more than that."

I stood and looked at him; his face was a mixture of sadness and fear. As each second passed I hoped that he would change his mind, but I knew deep in my heart that he would not. John had fought for this country. He had given Ireland his loyalty and he had martyred to it his strong, young body. He loved me, but he *belonged* to his country. John's dream was for the two of us to live out the loving rural idyll of his parents—in the house they had built. His dream was nothing without me, and yet he was prepared to sacrifice his marriage for his love of Ireland.

I dreamed of New York and I wanted to return there, but I knew that my future would be meaningless without John. I was trapped in Ireland by my love for him. So America was not my destiny after all, but the wet, boggy soil of home. In my mind, I took my dream and threw it at my husband's feet—dashed it on the cold, bare flags of our kitchen floor.

John was staring down at his feet now. He was terrified, yet ready for me to say I was returning to America without him. I had never loved and hated him more than in that moment.

I turned to poke the fire and slowly lifted the kettle onto the grate, living out my last few moments of power—wondering if I should leave him overnight, believing I was going to abandon him all over again.

After a while I said, "I want you to put boards down on these floors, John. There's no comfort in the stone."

Forty-Three

John wasted no time in doing my bidding, and over the coming days he put down soft oak floorboards throughout the cottage. He worked discreetly, moving aside the furniture as he needed to, sawing and sanding outside, then carrying in the planks as he needed them and fitting them with the minimum of hammering or fuss. He knew that my disappointment had not yet settled and that, if he hammered too hard, he might shatter my thin veil of tight-lipped decorum.

During that time we danced around each other, carefully avoiding conversation and therefore conflict. As he fixed the floor, I tackled the menial tasks of a country wife. With little pride and no joy, I scraped and scrubbed the black crust from our cast-iron oven, I swept out the hearth—cursing John for not having cleared out the chimney more thoroughly, as clumps of black soot fell down into my hair. As John was putting down the floor in our kitchen, I worked outside. I dug out planting beds around the house—throwing stones up behind me into scattered piles. I didn't give any thought to what pretty flowers I might plant, but just worked my body as hard as I could, scooping deep trenches out of the ground, trying to redefine my surroundings by digging holes into it. When the anger was worked out of my arms, I would kneel then on the cold, damp ground and crumble the earth in my fingers until the brown muck lodged between my nails. When I felt the punishment of my inelegant predicament overwhelm me, I would stand up and dig with my anger again.

Once the floor was complete, John seemed content that his duty in persuading me to stay was done. I had asked for a wooden floor, and he had given me a wooden floor—as if that were the only obstacle to my complete satisfaction with life in Ireland. He carried on about his business as if there was never any question of my having sacrificed everything for him. After all, I felt he had reasoned, what other comfort could a woman possibly want in her house aside from a bit of wood under her feet?

I placed the small embroidered rug I had brought with me from Manhattan to my side of our bed, and each morning I slid my bare feet into a pair of Isobel's satin slippers and went about setting the fire and preparing the breakfast without needing to put on woolen stockings or boots to keep me warm. However, as soon as I caught myself aware of the comfort in my new floor, I would start thinking about all that was missing—hot water from the tap, electricity, a future, and my freedom. I distracted myself as best I could with my daily work and kept my anger bottled, because there was no sense in indulging it. The situation was set as it was, and there was nothing I could do or say that would change things. But still, as the weeks passed, I was not only miserable at all I had lost, but inwardly raging with John for making me stay and seeming so blasé about it.

In truth, although I could see that my husband was trying his very best to appease me, he could not do anything right.

As the weather grew warmer, John hoped that my humor would warm alongside it.

"I'll finish early today and you and I can take a stroll down to the river, Ellie? I saw mayfly hatching down there yesterday, I'll surely catch us a trout for the tea."

"It's too wet," I'd say, "the fields are muddy yet, and I don't want to ruin my skirts."

In truth I didn't give a damn about my skirts. I just could not bear to be around John's relentless optimism and childish awe of nature.

"There's a great draw in the days, Ellie—spring is here." "Look, the moon is full to bursting, Ellie." "Can you hear that beautiful singing—it's a skylark, Ellie." *"Everything's grand— isn't this better than New York, Ellie?"* Although he never said it out loud, it was implied in the way he tried to cajole compliments out of me. As if a jam jar of bluebells and buttercups was a match for a career, wealth, refinement, a future full of excitement and opportunity, the litany of conveniences that I had left behind.

"You can wear a pair of my breeches, Ellie—I won't tell," he said, pleading with me to join him and make things as they had been. Reminding me of a past when I was a different person, with different needs and different desires. When I was a carefree child with plaits and ruddy skin and scraped knees, before I learned about life, and love—and all both could offer, and take away. I had changed and John refused to see it.

I smiled at him with weak sarcasm and he walked off. I didn't want to hurt John, but I found that I could not resign myself to my fate.

At the same time I knew that I could not continue to be this angry forever. I was becoming pale and pinched, and I could feel an ugliness hardening inside me.

Nonetheless I clung to my grievances. It seemed that if I let go of my anger, I did not know what would be left of me. Or perhaps I hoped that if I continued to punish John with my quiet, withdrawing resentment, he would change his mind and come with me to America.

Despite my inner anguish, the farm flourished and the house improved with the distraction of my labor. The spring scallions came early, and each morning I scrambled them through our eggs and served them with soda cake spread thickly with my own, salted butter. I lit fires and polished my new floor and made the cottage as clean and pristine as it could have been. However, aside from a few essentials, I did not unpack my trunk. Instead I placed it under our high iron bed and sometimes, just as I was dropping off to sleep, I felt as if I were elevated, sleeping in a Manhattan apartment at the top of some high skyscraper block. In a place where my feet need not touch the ground for weeks on end.

One of our cows was pregnant and when John came in for his breakfast that morning he looked worried.

"Her bag is flagging, she could go today," he said. "I don't like the look of her, though—I'm going to get Paud."

She was an old cow, and John was nervous about the birth, but I had no interest.

I heard the cow braying in the shed and craved the distraction of a radio to drown out her distressed hee-haw. I missed the radio more than anything else—the frivolity of everyday music was gone to me completely now, another acute source of resentment. John and Paud came back an hour later and went straight into the shed. "She's coming," Paud said as he rushed in onto my spotless floor in his dirty boots—"have ye some soap and water and I'll wash my hands?"

I brought out a basin and soap and left it on a stool in the front porch for both men to wash by—then left them to it, loudly singing my favorite Fanny Brice song ("It's cost me a lot, but there's one thing that I've got—it's my man. Cold and wet, tired, you bet, but all that I soon forget—with my man"), to drown out the cries from the shed.

I had just put the buttermilk to the flour to make bread when John stuck his head in the door. He was wild-eyed and panting. "We need you, Ellie." As I was shaking my head and pointing at the unmade bread, he shouted, "Now, Ellie—we need another body—there's no time—the calf is breach!"

I had no choice but to follow him. If a cow ran into problems birthing, it was all hands on deck. That much I knew. I had, after all, been around the Hogan farm through most of my youth, although I had never been present at an actual birth before.

I wiped my hands on my long apron, grateful that I was wearing it for protection. As I followed John into the shed I almost fell on my back as my feet skidded across the inch-deep puddle on the floor. The air was thick with the salty, mossy smell of this large farm animal, and her agitation mingled with the men's obvious fear. She was penned in at each side, and Paud was at her head, holding her to the wall with a rope and making soothing noises. By the twitching of her legs, and her pained braying, it wasn't working. A white bag hung from her back end and dripped with fluid, and above it two small hooves, crossed at the ankles.

"John," I said, "I'm no good with . . ."

John tied a rope around each hoof and passed one to me so that both ropes crossed over each other, then handed me the end of it and placed the two of us diagonally across from each other about four feet away from the back end of the cow. Then he looked across at me and said, "Now pull like hell."

As John started to tug, I stood holding the rope in horror until he shouted, "PULL, ELLIE, PULL!"

So I pulled. My shoes struggled to get a grip on the wet ground and I pulled and pulled, but the calf wasn't moving.

The cow was getting more and more distressed and Paud was struggling to hold her steady. John was wild-eyed and sweating.

"She's not coming," John said. I heard panic in his voice.

"Stretch her," Paud said, "she won't like it, but it might help."

"Here," John said, handing me his rope, "let's give it a try."

He stood to the side of the animal and, putting his hands inside her, pulled back the tight, steaming flesh that flanked the calf's tiny feet.

"Pull," he said barely able to get the words out with his physical exertion, "come in closer, Ellie, hold the weight even on either side and pull."

I could barely believe what he was expecting me to do, but at the same time I could see we had no choice. I wrapped the rope round my forearms and wrists and leaned back with my full weight against the calf's hooves. Almost immediately I felt some loosening on the rope, but before I knew it the back end of the animal had showered me with the contents of its bowels, covering me from head to toe in fetid brown muck. I screamed so loudly that some went into my mouth and I screamed again. The men could barely hide their amusement and when John said, "I think we're getting somewhere, Ellie, keep pulling," his voice sounded high-pitched as if he might laugh at any moment, and that made me so mad that I pulled even harder than before.

I pulled on the contents of that wretched cow's womb until she hollered and struggled against Paud. I pulled until my shoulders felt they were going to tear apart from each other, and until my shoes were so full of muck that my toes were scrabbling around inside them.

"Here she comes," John said.

As he did, the calf suddenly slithered out onto the wet floor, easily, as if it had just been waiting for its time.

It fell at my feet—a slime covered oblong of flesh—then immediately started to unfurl itself into a calf. As I watched the infant animal flick out its limbs and engage in its feeble struggle to become what it was, something stirred inside me.

I squatted down next to it and looked into the confused slits of its eyes and smelt the sweet, warm fog of its first breath. John came over and handed me some straw.

"Clean her off and rub some warmth into her there, Ellie, she'll be in shock. I'll go and get cleaned up."

I sat with the struggling calf in my lap and cleaned her off, rubbing her silky black and white coat into rough peaks, until Paud came and took her away from me, leading her up to her mother's teat.

When I got outside it was raining hard, but instead of rushing back into the house, I turned my face upward and let the shower rinse me down. I felt the cool water trickle down my scalp and the back of my dress, dripping from the tip of my eyelashes down onto my cheeks, drumming down the front of my clothes until they were stuck to me.

With my eyes closed, I could hear the thrash of the raindrops on the trees and the continuous splat of water hitting the muddy ground. I opened my eyes and turned my face toward the house. Two small birds were feeding from crumbs I had left on the windowsill and John was standing in the doorway, barefoot, stripped to the waist and holding a towel.

"Come in before you get your death of cold," he said, smiling. I remembered that I loved him, and in that moment the part of me that I had left in Ireland with John when I went to America came back and greeted me. As much as I yearned for the sophistication of New York, for all the muck and the rain in the wake of the savagery and miracle of the animal's birth, I felt I was home again.

Chapter Forty-Four

I wrote to Emilie and Sheila, telling them I wouldn't be coming back to America. Sheila's letter back contained mostly news of her moneyed life in Boston. I smiled as I read, knowing that my foolish Sheila was so caught up in her own life that she had barely noticed I had gone. Once she and Alex were married, she had given up work and I could see that she was turning herself into Isobel, complaining about getting staff she could trust and spending huge amounts of money on haute couture and lavish furnishings. She ended:

> *Alex has promised me that we can take some time off to tour Europe next year and of course he wants to visit the "homeland." We'll probably stay in Dublin (The Shelbourne looks tolerable), but we'll call in and surprise you. I'll write and let you know when we're coming.*

Emilie seemed to care more that I wasn't coming back.

> *I miss you, Ellie—it's not the same without you here. My sister is so caught up in her romances that she doesn't make the time to come out and play with me. Things will never be the way they were when you were here.*

She reminisced and gave me news of speakeasies we had frequented and gossip about disgraced acquaintances. At the end of her letter she added the postscript: *"I bumped into Charles in Tullio's and, although he didn't ask me outright, he looked sad and I know he is wondering when you are coming back."*

The sight of his name on the page in Emilie's round, looped handwriting made me flinch.

I had not been able to think about Charles. The thought of what might have happened between us, had I stayed in America for just a few more days, had been kept at bay by my love for my husband. There was no place in my mind for might-have-beens with another man because there was no room in my conscience for regrets. There was no need for John ever to know about Charles and, with an ocean between New York and my old life, it was easy for me to pretend that my burgeoning American romance had never happened. As I read Emilie's postscript, conflicting feelings came flooding into my heart. There was guilt at having betrayed John, but also I remembered that Charles had been more than that. He had meant something to me as a person and his friendship had offered me comfort as well as confusion. I knew that, in all conscience, I had to write and tell him I was not coming back.

I waited until the following morning, when John had left for work, and sat down at the kitchen table with my paper and pen. I would have two, maybe three hours before John came back home. I decided to send Charles's letter in a sealed envelope to Emilie and get her to forward it to him from New York. Better again, I said in my covering note to her, she could deliver it to him in person, as I was unsure of his exact address. Perhaps he had moved. She knew where he hung out and would find him easily enough, I said. Emilie would enjoy the adventure of a mission, and I imagined her trawling the docks in some frivolous confection, shrilly calling his name among all the bare-armed, muscled men.

My letter was brief and to the point.

Dear Charles,

I hope you are keeping well. Emilie wrote and said that she met you in Tullio's.

I am writing to tell you that I have decided to stay in Ireland. My husband, John, has made a full recovery, we are back in our family home and settled, so there is no cause for me to return to Manhattan.

I missed my father's funeral, which was a sad state of affairs, but I have been here to help look after my mother, which is a blessing in itself.

Thank you for your generosity and friendship and I sincerely hope that we shall stay in touch.

> *Warmest wishes,*
> *Ellie*

As I reread the letter, I realized that each line of it was a lie, and no greater lie than the brevity and formal tone with which it was written. The truth would have been an impassioned pleading:

Emilie said that I left you distraught; my husband John refuses to return to America, so I must stay here and abide by his wishes; my father was dead anyway, so I might have stayed there with you and who knows what might have happened if I had. I miss you, and my life in New York and the person I was when I was with you. I wish there was some way I could be there and here at the same time. I will never forget you.

> *Love, Ellie*

At the same time I knew that I could not tell Charles what was in my heart, as I could barely admit it to myself yet. I was firmly, happily back in my marriage and I would not risk my love for John being confounded by recalling old romances.

I hooked up the horse and cart and drove into Kilmoy myself, leaving bread, ham and a note on the table for John saying that I had taken a trip into town. The postmistress turned the letter in her hand, studying it before stamping it, as she always did, then looking at me over her glasses and smiling coldly as if she had intuited what was in it. I blushed slightly, even though I knew she did the same with every letter that passed through her hands. As she dropped it into the bag I felt a moment of panic, as if once that letter was gone there really was no going back. But as soon as the feeling came, it passed again, and I felt lighter.

It was still morning as I drove back home and the sun was just beginning to filter through, spreading watery pink and orange hues between the dusty gray clouds. Cool air pinched at my nostrils, filling them with the scent of hedgerows—elderflower, honeysuckle—masked then by the mossy smoke from my neighbors' turf fires as they prepared their meals and warmed their water and went about their day in much the same fashion I did. We all shared the simple struggles of tending cattle and building fires, feeding ourselves from the land, and I felt the comfort of all our lives being the same.

Having let go of New York, my life fell into a routine. I helped John a little with the farming work, milking on the odd occasion, tending the small vegetable patch outside our back door, but it took every hour of the day to keep the house clean and running in an orderly fashion. Household work was trebled when ashes had to be cleared from the grate, and then turf carried from the shed before the fires could even be lit for cooking and warming water. All clothes had to be washed by hand, and meals cooked from scratch. No corner shop in which one could buy sliced bread or baloney. There were no pretzel stands or hot-dog carts—each meal had to be planned in advance so that a chicken could be killed or a cabbage pulled. When the basic chores were complete, there was plenty besides for me to do in making the place more habitable. Between planting flowerbeds, keeping the walls whitewashed against the battle of soot from the fire, sewing curtains and fashioning decorative touches, the house kept me busy.

As time passed I began to accept the lack of conveniences and was less anxious for the luxuries I had left behind—but nonetheless a nagging restlessness was tugging at me, holding me back from contentment. One sunny morning I stood at our back door and watched John as he headed off to work. Walking across our back field, his confident stride belying his uneven gait, he gradually disappeared into the landscape, became swallowed into the hues of green and gold—the emerald fuzz of a distant forest, the sun sending mirrored shards of light flying from the surface of the lake. Stretched across the sweeping scene God had laid out for me that morning, I saw my life. John owned much of the land I could see and he would continue to work it to feed us. Soon we would have a child, or two—and they would play in the fields we played in and climb the trees we climbed. I would cook them hearty dinners and teach them to read. John would sit by the fire in the evenings and watch over us, chiding the children on my instruction, but more often playing the fool alongside them.

I drew my eyes in around the house: the hay-strewn floor of the red barn, the crumbling stone wall to the side of it that I was always nagging John to fix, the mound of our turf stack—like

the rounded cave of some mysterious dweller, fallen chunks of
the brown mud-like fuel scattered at its rim—the circular bed
of earth and stones I had started the day before as part of my
continued attempts to turn our ordinary patch of ground into a
garden, this was my life now. I would cook and clean and mend
and soothe and love my way through the rest of my life. I was
wife and, when the time came, mother. For all that I loved John,
for all that my heart knew my life was to be played out in this
place with him, it wasn't enough. The nuns had told me I could
have been a teacher and, but for my marriage to John, it would
have happened. In New York I had been a typist, but now that
I was home all my education and training were being wasted. It
was no longer that my life did not feel grand enough, but rather
that the part I was playing in it was too small. It was not that I
wanted for anything in itself—but that I knew I was capable of
more than simply being in the service of those I loved. There was
a nugget of life inside me that was hungry: growling and unsatis-
fied. A part of me that wanted more.

Every Wednesday as we went to town for market day, to sell
our surplus produce and collect our groceries, I grew less impressed with the meager sundries on sale in the Kilmoy shops.
Occasionally I found something I wanted to buy—a passable
ream of tweed in Moran's or a new hat for John to wear to
Sunday Mass—but I resented paying the inflated prices. I was
used to bargaining, a custom that was frowned on here because
it was considered an admission of poverty. It seemed to me that
the shopkeepers were growing rich on our good manners, and it
infuriated me that I had no choice but to give them my custom
on those terms.

As we walked through the town, women stood around in
small groups talking and catching up on the week's news. Because I had been away at boarding school, the short time I had

spent here as an adult before going to America had been so fraught with drama and poverty that I had never truly connected with my peers in any significant way. While most of them were friendly and greeted me by name whenever I passed, I remained wary of them and secretly believed that, collectively, they bore the same petty, jealous grudges they had against me in national school: that I had airs and graces, that my mother was a snob, that I thought I was better than them. When I reasoned it out, I knew that my fears were probably, in most cases, unfounded, but nonetheless I balked at making friends with them. I missed Sheila and Emilie, the glamour and sophistication of our lives together in Manhattan—meeting in coffee shops and restaurants, sharing lipstick and hooch, borrowing one another's clothes and sharing the intimate secrets of our lives. Friendship in America was about fun and adventure, and it felt as if it would be some admission to the death of those qualities in me were I to replace them.

However, it fell upon me to be polite and on this particular day I ran into Maidy talking with one of her neighbors outside the solicitor's office in Kilmoy. As I stood, half listening to their tittle-tattle, I saw a notice in the window behind them. "SECRETARY WANTED. Typing skills essential. Apply to Mr. Padraig O'Nuallian."

I could barely believe it. Immediately my head started to spin with possibility. This could be the answer to everything. Working in town every day in an office, putting my skills to proper use. It was perfect!

I excused myself from Maidy and her friend and ran toward John, who was already approaching us.

"John, John—there's a job for a typist going in the solicitor's office, will I apply?"

John seemed reluctant.

"It will mean more money for us, John—and I can cycle in each morning myself."

"No, no, it's not that," he said. I felt crushed by his seeming ambivalence.

"Well, if you're worried about the housework, John," I said sarcastically, "I can assure you I managed to work and feed myself perfectly well in New—"

"No," he said, touching my arm, "you apply, Ellie, I think it's a great idea. It's just that—"

"What, John?" I was irritated by his hemming and hawing. "What is it you want to say?" Perhaps John wanted me there in the house always at his beck and call and didn't want to see me better myself?

"It's just that I don't want to see you disappointed, that's all."

I smiled.

"There's not much chance of that, John. I doubt there's a faster, more proficient typist than me in the whole county, never mind Kilmoy."

"I don't doubt it," he said, putting his arms round my shoulder. "I don't doubt that for one second, Ellie Hogan."

Mr. O'Nuallian was a stocky man with a rather ebullient head of gray hair that refused to be tamed into a tidy side-parting and instead had formed into messy mounds at intervals across his square head. He wore small gold-rimmed spectacles, and had a round, friendly face. I liked him instantly.

The room was not as large or as grand as I had imagined it would be. There was red linoleum on the floor and Mr. O'Nuallian sat behind a desk that, although large, had thin metal legs and was not in the least bit as impressive as a solicitor's desk should be. There were law books and papers piled up on the ground, others on the verge of tumbling from a pitifully inadequate set of shelves, and I immediately thought how I would enjoy the challenge of organizing this man and licking his paperwork and library into shape.

"So, Mrs. Hogan . . ."

"You can call me Ellie, Sir."

"Right so, Ellie," he said fingering the application letter I had posted through his letterbox just the day before.

"Now, I see you have had some experience of secretarial work in America?"

"Yes, Sir, I worked for some time in a company that manufactured windows, and also was engaged in work for a professor of—"

He started to move papers around his desk, then found a handwritten letter, handed it to me and said, "Good, good— well, let's see how you get on with typing this up."

I sat at a typewriter on a small table in the corner of the room as he excused himself to get a glass of water.

By the time he got back, I had the typed letter placed on his desk and was sitting with my hands on my lap, waiting for him to return.

"Oh," he said, surprised, "is there a problem?"

"No problem," I said brightly, "I've finished."

He let out a small laugh and picked up the letter.

"It's perfect," he said, his eyes scanning up and down the page from behind his spectacles. "I'm most impressed." Except that he didn't look impressed, he looked somewhat baffled and a little nervous. He was an eccentric type, I noted, like the university professor.

Our meeting ended somewhat abruptly. "I hope you don't feel I'm rushing you, Mrs. Hogan, but I have another appointment."

"No, no," I said smiling, then I shook his hand firmly, all business, and said, "I look forward to hearing from you soon,

Mr. O'Nuallian—and thank you for the opportunity to interview for the post."

I was certain I had got the job. Over the next few days I even prepared some of my "work" clothes, rinsing out my silk stockings, pressing a suit and mending the button on a smart blouse.

Four days passed and I was just beginning to get anxious about not having heard when John came home from Maidy and Paud's with a gloomy head on him. He sat down at the table and sucked in air through his teeth.

"Ellie—you didn't get the job." I didn't say anything, just pursed my lips together. "Maidy said he gave it to the young Connelly girl, she's his third cousin."

"I know that," I said and turned my face to the dresser, pretending to set the table for tea.

That wretch hasn't even been to school, I wanted to say. *She probably can't even read properly, never mind type.*

"They're poor," John said. "Padraig has the reputation of being a kind man—that's why he gave her the work, surely. You were the better candidate, you can be certain of that."

"Oh, don't you worry, I *am* certain of that," I said, trying to keep the bitterness and disappointment out of my voice. I didn't want John to see me begrudge a poor girl a chance in life, or know how much I had come to depend on things outside of him for my happiness.

Chapter Forty-Five

"You'll get another job," John said, but we both knew that wasn't true.

Jobs for people with my qualifications rarely came up in Kilmoy, and when they did they were almost always going to be given to either relatives or neighbors who had fallen on hard times.

Having come close to the possibility of earning my own money, then losing it, made me more miserable than I had been before the job had been mooted. There really was no escape from this small, rural life I was leading. I really was simply Ellie Hogan, farmer's wife, for the rest of my life, forever and ever, amen.

Meanwhile my mother had announced that she was ready to go back to her own house. It had been two months since my father had died, and Maidy agreed that my mother seemed to be through the worst of the grief and appeared "happier in herself." In truth, she seemed more content to me than she ever had, living there with Maidy and Paud, fitting in with their easy manner of living and casual eating customs, but it was a situation that could not go on forever. John and I had offered her a place with us, but she had said, "You have your own life to lead, Ellie. I have my house, and I have no need of a daughter's charity."

I planned to stay a few nights with my mother. Although it

was not exactly a holiday, it was a break from my everyday life, a change of scene that, importantly, encouraged me to think of somebody aside from myself.

I picked her up from the Hogans' in the horse and cart. The day was dry and the journey quick. It was a beautiful morning, with the lazy clopping of the horse's hooves against the mud road, and the clouds stretched in long clusters across the sky, the pink of an early-morning sun behind them. We chatted, idle gossip, and my mother even pointed out a huge white rabbit scurrying across a nearby field, but as we drew closer, and the house itself finally came into sight, she fell into a dour silence.

I had not been back since running away from school, and had long since ceased to think of my parents' house as my "family home." The stark gray house I grew up in was just that—a house. I had never "lived" there, in the sense that I had come to understand through the adventure of life; it didn't hold any joyful or happy memories for me. As I turned our horse into the driveway I remembered how truly unhappy I had been there, and yet I had no sense of fear or dread. Instead a kind of defiance took me over. I had been right to run away, from the house, from my parents and their miserable life—into the warm arms of John and his family. There was nothing for me, good or bad, in this place.

My mother opened the door and the two of us stepped into the cold, dusty hallway. The curtains were drawn throughout the house and it was as dark and silent as a tomb.

"I'll get the bags," I said, anxious to break the stillness, but when I came back holding my mother's two small suitcases she was still standing where I had left her, her face pasty and blank like a statue, stiff and frozen in her navy coat as if she had had a spell cast over her.

I considered putting down the bags and embracing her, but decided against it. I occasionally showed affection to my mother, but usually during times of mutual contentment: a smile across the churchyard after Mass, an exchanged glance when Paud or John made a joke, the touch of an arm as one or the other went to clear the table. It felt wrong to intrude on her grief, so I simply walked past her into the kitchen, nudging her out of her torpor by touching her leg with the edge of one of the bags. She immediately followed me into the kitchen, lifted her apron from the hook on the back door as if she had never been away, then forgetting to tie it as she picked up an old dry cloth from the mantelpiece and began to fuss halfheartedly about the room. She was listless in all her movements, barely holding the duster, dabbing hopelessly at the abandoned surfaces in the near dark.

I realized, with a mix of horror and sadness, that my mother was not fit to take charge of the house. The dark fact of my father's death appeared to have gripped her as soon as she walked in the door and put her back into the shocked trance I had found her in when I returned from America.

"Come on, Mam," I said, taking her by the arm and leading her up the stairs. "You lie down."

She lay on top of the bed and curled her legs up to her chest like a frightened infant, barely noticing as I took off her shoes.

The walk back down the stairs seemed interminable as the confused chill of my childhood crept after me, then leaped on my back and chewed at my conscience. Why did I not feel more grief at the loss of my father, or realize how much my mother must have loved him to be put into this state? Why had I brought her back here and not insisted that she come and live with John and me—and was it wrong of me not to want that? Not to love her more than I did?

I stopped and stood for a moment in the drawing room. The dreary, dark furniture crowded in on me; damp crinkled the corners of the painted walls like a creeping demon. There was no ornament or picture aside from the Sacred Heart and the cross above the fireplace. I remembered the endless rosaries we had said night after night, the turgid, miserable meals—my discomfort at my parents' awkwardness with each other, their indifference toward me, the stuffy closed-off atmosphere—the three of us locked together in the convent-like surroundings of my father's making. No flowers or frivolities allowed. No silly adornments—the air always heavy with the suffocating aura of solemn respectability. I remembered how unhappy I had been. How my childhood had been devoid of beauty and humor because of his authoritarian standards. Standing in my father's house, I reached down into my heart and searched for the core of sadness that I knew must be there, the sense of loss, but couldn't find it.

Instead, I felt myself propelled across to the windows. I pulled back the heavy curtains and tugged at the sash until they fell open in a relieved gape, miraculously loosening down like butter as if they had been waiting for this moment all their lives. I ran to the back door and opened it, filling the house with air. Without even removing my coat, I set about the place like a dervish. I opened every drawer and cupboard and rummaged about for decoration. I was amazed at how much there was: piles of embroidered linens; beautiful lace antimacassars; at least half a dozen vases of all shapes and sizes; the exquisite silver cutlery my father allowed us to use on Christmas Day; two dainty tea sets; a brass-handled coffeepot; china dog ornaments that I remembered discovering as a curious child and nervously rewrapping in the cloth that protected them and returning them to their hiding place. There was more, far more than I had accumulated in America, or could have collected if I had stayed another twenty years. I was surprised by how many things my family owned, yet there was nothing that I did not recognize. All these beautiful things had been in my life, but it was forbidden treasure. We had cake, but we weren't allowed to eat it. The nice napkins and crockery were locked away in a cabinet in the parlor and used on high days and holidays when my father liked to pretend he was a priest.

In a matter of hours, I completely transformed the house.

I covered surfaces in embroidered cloths and placed on them vases heaving with foliage from the garden. I arranged ornaments on the mantelpiece and filled the kitchen with crockery—placing eggs in a beautiful glass bowl, and setting the table for supper with the silver cutlery and good china. I took down the heavy, velvet curtains from the windows and flooded the house with light and air. I lit a fire, baked a cake and called up to my mother to come down for tea.

As I waited for her I looked around. This was, after all, an elegant and affluent house—and now it was warm and alive. Pretty colored glassware twinkled in the light from the bare windows; brass candlesticks glowed from the reflections of the fire.

I had assumed my mother would be pleased with what I had done, so I was surprised when she walked into the room and her mouth instantly tightened in anger. She walked over to the vase on the dining-room table, grabbed it, then threw the water and flowers into the fire in one swift movement and put it back, damp, into the cupboard.

"How dare you touch my things," she said, not looking at me. "How dare you interfere with the things in this house," and she began to gather up everything I had taken out and to put it back where I had found it.

The truth flashed before me. It wasn't my father who had kept these things hidden—in fact, the good china and cutlery were only used during our mealtimes with him. The penny dropped. It was my mother who had created our austere lifestyle. These accoutrements of fine living were not things that my mother loved and to which my father had denied us access. They were the vestiges of her shamed history.

The spoils of her shopkeeper grandparents' greed, belongings that should have been given up to feed their neighbors during the famine, but were kept, instead, for future generations to hoard. Each vase, each china dog was an heirloom shrouded in guilt. My mother could not bear to look at them because they reminded her of where she had come from. She could not give them away or sell them for the same reason.

As I watched her frantically fold an embroidered napkin around a glass sweet dish and try and stuff it back into a drawer, I realized I could not let my mother go back. How could I live free of my own childhood, when my flesh and blood was still living out the miserable legacy of her ancestors? For all the love that had not been evident between us, she was still my mother and I could not, in all conscience, let her continue to live like this.

Quite out of turn, I picked up a china dog off the mantelpiece and said to her, "Look, Mother—they're only *things*" and deliberately dropped it. She ran toward me to catch it, but then stopped herself short and allowed it to fall. The two of us stood as the pretty ornament smashed into little pieces on the floor. "Is that what you want?" I asked. "Because that's what you might as well do, having all your things locked away in cupboards. What's the use of having things if they are not going to be used?"

"That dog was very precious," she said, in quiet astonishment. "You clearly don't appreciate how valuable my things are."

As she said it, I realized that my love of fine things was not something that I had learned in America; it was inherited from my mother. From her delicate polishing and handling of our silver cutlery, the way she pressed and folded our napkins on our side plates on special occasions, the delicate way she held her teacups. My predication for mannered living came from her.

My love of beautiful things was not a reaction to poverty, but a craving for my mother.

I walked across and put my hand on her arm.

"Leave them be for the time being, Mam, and if you want to, we can put everything back away tomorrow."

Her clench on the glass dish loosened and I caught it and placed it carefully on the polished mahogany surface.

"This house is your home," I said, "you've no one to please now—only yourself."

"And you."

She said it so quietly and so suddenly that I almost missed it.

In those two words were all the apology for the past that I needed, and a seed of hope for the future.

The following morning she was up preparing breakfast when I rose. All of the things I had brought out the day before were still in place, but she had moved an ornate pen on an ebony stand that I had given pride of place on the mantel. It was sitting half wrapped in a cloth ready to be put away. I picked it up and she shook her head sadly and said, "That was the pen that my grandmother used to record each one of her debtors. It sat on the counter next to her ledger, and she would leave the list of those who owed her money hanging behind the counter for all to see—to shame them into paying her quicker. She was a cruel woman."

My mother had never spoken to me about her family before. What I knew of them had been jigsawed together from overheard comments and gossip. She came from a long tradition of shopkeepers in a neighboring town. When her grandparents had inherited a shop from their parents, they had refused to give charity or credit to the thousands of starving families in the area and watched their neighbors perish while they prospered. As a result, when their own children inherited the shop, the locals kept their custom away until the business was lost. The past was never forgotten in this small place, the sins of the father were meted down generation after generation so that, four generations later, I was still being punished by my classmates for my great-grandparents' greed.

I looked at my mother's pale eyes, expecting to see the usual resigned sadness, and was surprised to see them flicker with defiance.

"It was a beautiful shop, though, Ellie," she said, "elegantly laid out and full of anything you might care for. Not just everyday groceries—oh no, you could buy linens and crockery; it was criminal it was lost in the way it was, my parents didn't deserve that." She tapered off and became wistful again, "Although it's true that my grandparents were very wicked people."

"Just because your family are one way, that doesn't mean you are the same," I said.

She smiled and I realized she knew I was talking about myself.

"Here," she said picking up the ebony trinket, "you have the pen."

"No, Mam, I can't take that, it's too valuable."

"Nonsense," she said, "it has no bad memories for you and I can see how you appreciate nice things, Ellie." I took it, closing my hand around the glossy surface of the polished wood stand.

"You must have got the knack for good quality in New York," she said, and then, as she went back into the kitchen, she added, almost out of earshot, "or perhaps you've a bit of the shopkeeper's blood in you after all."

Chapter Forty-Six

The moment those words left my mother's mouth it was like a revelation. This was what I wanted—a shop.

The next day I went home, and before I had even taken my coat off at the door I said to John, "I want you to build me a shop."

He didn't know what to make of it at first, he thought I was joking—but the idea had set in my head overnight and had already grown into an absolute.

There were certainly enough people living in the hinterland of Kilmoy to need the service of a country shop. Not everyone had horses or carts, or indeed the wherewithal or time to go into the town every week. A local shop could provide those people with the basics they needed—sugar, tea, flour, starch and blue—within a half-hour walk or short bicycle ride. From an advertisement in *Sketch* magazine, I wrote to the Dublin food wholesaler Findlater's, and they sent me a catalog by return of post. Flicking through its pages, my enthusiasm rose to boiling point. Alongside the everyday basic shop-bought foods, such as baking soda and currants, were exoticisms that I had not expected to find in Ireland. Chocolate, coffee and spaghetti! And almost any food in a tin: tomatoes, apricots, beans, corned beef! Foods I'd thought I would never eat again could all be had from Findlater's—at a price, of course, but I did not care. I would be able to eat like an American again!

One room would certainly not be enough for this shop. I would have to have two—one as the shop itself, and a smaller one to store the stock. From our farm, John was already selling on as much produce as the shops in Kilmoy would take from him, and still there was more left over than we could use. I decided we could sell that too. In which case we would need a cold room as well, with no windows and walls thicker than the rest, and a dugout chamber for burying our apples to keep them fresh through the year, and hooks along the ceiling for hanging meat and draining chickens.

John and I had both become frugal savers, determined never to repeat the earlier failures that had plunged us into poverty. John had money saved in a small bag stuffed into the side of our horsehair mattress, in addition to the forty dollars that he had given to Maidy to keep for me. That gave us enough for the materials to build the shop. And I had money saved from my American salary, and more from cashing in my first-class ticket—plenty to cover the initial stock. I decided I would write to my bank in New York for my savings, although—suddenly reluctant to sever all ties—I also made the quiet decision to retain my American stocks.

At first John assumed that all I wanted was a simple room added to the side of our house. This was how most country shops were laid out and, with Paud's help, he would have it finished in a matter of weeks. But our house was too far back from the road, I protested. I wanted people to be able to pull up their bicycles and come straight in—and out—again. I wanted a shop that would thrive and grow, not just make me a little pocket money. A shop on the roadside at the edge of our front field was the only option. I drew out the design

I wanted on a piece of paper, and measured it out on the ground in stones.

John seemed daunted by the prospect. "Are you sure this is the best place to have it, Ellie?" he said as the two of us stood at the roadside. "It seems very—big?" It started to rain and John hunched his shoulders against the flimsy collar of his shirt. He had a worried look on his face that was unlike him. He seemed tired and vulnerable, and part of me wanted to make it easy for him and forget the whole thing.

"It'll be fine," I said. "I'll manage the farm while you build it. I've managed the farm before. We'll get Vinny Moran in to build the walls. Paud will help. You can oversee the work and do all the carpentry. Together, you men will get it up in no time."

"I don't know about that," he said, sighing heavily. But he walked all round the boundaries I had made, taking long steps, his lips moving as he made a mental note of the measurements. And the next day Paud was there, walking the boundaries himself, also shaking his head.

I hadn't meant John to build the walls with Vinny—it was strong man's labor and he still could not lift. But John, as well as being determined and hardworking, was also vain. He would not have me see him as weak. He struggled to break stones and lift them into place, his legs buckling and giving way beneath him, until I had to take Paud aside and implore him to find a way of dividing the labor between them so that John would not kill himself or hinder his own recovery. At last, between the three of them, they got a system going where each man was doing the work suited to him—Vinny, the heavy lifting; John and Paud, the smaller stone and mortar work. Still, even by working from dawn to dusk each day, after four hard weeks the walls were barely halfway up.

Maidy, anxious to get her husband back, came out to survey

the fruits of their labor and immediately announced, "Pssssht. You'll be dead before this is finished. We'll have to call a mehil." The mehil was the system whereby all the neighbors gathered together to help one farmer complete a big task, such as haymaking or building. Up to thirty men would work for one or two days for no fee, and the women would prepare their meals and pour their porter while the work was being done.

The idea of a mehil horrified me. Every nosy neighbor for miles around would be getting a look round my house—dozens of women clattering around my kitchen, gossiping and bringing back news to the surrounding parishes of my crockery and my clothes and my "airs and graces." *"She was bad enough before she went to America, but now she's pure stuck up altogether." "Running off to America after she brought poor John Hogan to his knees in poverty . . ." ". . . And him crippled, and her swanning about the town as if she's somebody."* I knew what they all thought about me and I didn't mind as long as I could avoid them all. Now Maidy was bringing them down on top of us.

John was against the idea too. He felt humiliated by the idea of asking for help. He was a giver—he liked to be generous, but he was not comfortable receiving.

"Can we not just pay some more men to come and help?" I said.

"I think that's an excellent idea," John backed me up. "The Moran boys are all strong, and none of them are working at present."

"That's not the way things work around here," Paud said. "The Moran boys will come anyway, for all you've helped young Vincent over the past few months. The men like to help each other out—that's the way it is."

"And the women like to get into your house and rummage around looking for news," I said crossly.

"John has helped every farmer in this townland take in the hay since he was a boy," Paud asserted. "Time enough they paid him back."

Maidy persuaded me into it. She assured me that she would keep the numbers of the women down. One woman was enough to cater for the needs of half a dozen men, she said, and she promised to keep the worst of the gossips at bay. "In any case, Ellie," she said, "you have nothing to be worried about. These people are your neighbors and they want you to succeed."

I gave her a look that left her in no doubt that I did not believe her.

"And they'll be your customers too," she reminded me sagely. "So you had better get used to them."

With a sudden shock, I realized she was right. Kathleen Condon and her cronies were my potential market. The mehil, although it was not a prospect I relished, was one that I realized I would have to throw myself at with some effort if my business was to succeed.

My parents being the kind they were, I had never attended a mehil myself. I consulted Maidy and over the coming days I planned as thoroughly as I had with Mrs. Flannery for Isobel's weekend party.

Each of the women would bring food—gifts of bread, butter and sweet things—and it was important that whatever I prepared complemented their efforts rather than competed with them, so that they could flatter one another's talent for baking without fear of the hostess upstaging them. With this in mind, I would simply provide the meat, two large hunks of bacon and several roasted chickens for the table—there was no showing off in the presentation of it, but it was an expensive commodity and people would appreciate the sustenance. John bought in a box of cigarettes, a barrel of porter and two bottles of whisky.

The men arrived at first light, more than thirty of them walking up from the road. Some of them were carrying tools over their shoulders, and with the red sky behind them they looked like an army marching toward us. Following behind them were a scattering of women, many of them older, lifting their long skirts clear of the damp grass. It was clear that our invitations had been taken up by all the men of the townland, but by far fewer of the women.

Maidy greeted each woman at the door, taking their cakes and tarts and placing them on the kitchen table. All of the women knew who I was, but I struggled to place many of them, which set me at a disadvantage at once. While I recognized some faces, I could not then remember their names, which created an awkwardness in me.

The first hour passed in a flurry of business as the men had to be fed before their day's work began. Maidy acted the hostess, running around shouting instructions at all of us, looking for more tea, another hunk of bacon and faster slicing of the soda cake. When the men had left to do the work, the women were able to settle then with our tea and sweet things. There were around ten of us in all. It was the discreet handful that Maidy had promised me, but I could see by her face she was disappointed that more women had not turned up. Accustomed to how crowded these gatherings could become, several of the older women had brought their own stools and chairs to sit on, but there were so few of us that one or two of them were still empty. I put a plate of cake down on one milking stool to take the bare look off it, but the old crow who had brought the cake gave me such a look that I removed the plate straightaway.

Maidy was wonderful. While the women clearly felt awkward in my house, she kept the conversation flowing between church news and general parish gossip. After a while, however, she saw that Paud had forgotten his jacket and she excused herself to take it down to him. After she left the room a terrible awkward silence descended, and I was at a complete loss as to how to break it. We smiled weakly at one another, and I thought one of us might faint with tension. Then I noticed the oldest woman, Brid Donnelly, a religious matriarch whom all the younger women respected and feared in turn, shift uncomfortably in her seat. Relieved at having an excuse to break the silence, I said, "Do you need a cushion there, Brid?"

"No, I'm fine, really I—"

I leapt out of my seat anyway. "You do, you do—wait there a minute . . ."

I all but ran into the bedroom and sighed deeply in relief for a few seconds, before grabbing a small cushion from the bed. It was a small hand-embroidered one that Emilie's mother had given me to use for comfort on my journey home. I did not want to go back in, and wondered how long it would be before Maidy returned to rescue me. But I forced myself back through the door.

"There," I said, smiling and handing the cushion to Brid.

"Thank you," she said.

Then, before she put it behind her back, she held it up to her face and exclaimed, "What a *beautiful* piece of embroidery."

"Thank you," I said—but Brid ignored me and handed it over to a woman sitting over at the table.

"Carmel," she said, "take a look and tell me what you think of that."

Carmel took the cushion and, as soon as her hand touched it, said, "Mother of God, it's as *soft,* what class of a fabric is that?"

"It's velvet," I replied.

"Well, my word," she said. "And I never knew velvet could be embroidered." She rummaged in the pocket of her apron and took out a tiny pair of glasses. She hooked them around her eyes and began to examine the cushion like a diamond dealer. "Oh, that is magnificent," she said. "Truly now—and the *colors* . . ."

"Now did you ever see the like of that, Carmel Flaherty?"

"Never in my life—where would you get thread that color, I wonder? Nuala—take a look at this . . ." Carmel handed on Mrs. Andruchewitz's cushion to Nuala as if it were made of gold leaf, and every woman gathered about to look at the intricate embroidery work and feel the soft brush of the velvet. It was clear from the close way they were studying the workmanship that these women were keen craftswomen themselves, and I felt a surge of pride that my little black cushion was getting such attention and praise.

"Who embroidered this?" Nuala asked. "Was it yourself?" She looked at me directly, her voice full of amazement.

"No," I replied, "it was my friend's mother, in America. A Polish lady."

"Polish," several of them said together, nodding.

"And is she living around here?" a younger woman whom I didn't recognize asked.

"You silly fool!" Brid reprimanded her. "Eileen was in America—isn't that it? Isn't that where she got it?"

"Have you anything else like it?" Carmel piped up.

"I have some more of her work, I think . . ."

Emilie's mother had given me several things she had embroidered, but I had never placed any particular value on them before—in truth, finding them a little bright and gaudy for my tastes. But seeing her work through the eyes of these discerning crafts-women I could see the beauty in it.

I went into the bedroom and dragged the trunk out from under the bed and into the kitchen. The women dispersed from around the embroidered cushion on Nuala's lap and gathered in a circle about me. I felt like Ali Baba, as I lifted the trunk onto its side and began to open the drawers.

"Here," I said, finding a set of embroidered cotton napkins in a garish purple, and passing them around.

The women cooed over them for ages until Brid said, "I declare, Ellie, well, thank you for showing us all this. It's the most delicate bit of work ever I've seen." She folded it and held it up to return it to me. "You can keep it," I said. Then, seeing her confused look back at me, I said, "As a gift—please have them."

"Oh, no I couldn't possibly . . ."

She bristled and I became worried that I had offended the older woman.

"Certainly you can." Maidy had come back and was stand-ing at the door. "I declare you women have given away crochet work to cover half the fields of Kilmoy, you can surely afford to take something back."

Brid puffed, but put the piece on her lap.

"Besides, Ellie has no use for them here, have you, Ellie?"

I followed her lead. "No, indeed," I said, adding, "and Carmel, please—you take the cushion."

Both women put their heads down and waved their hands around in violent objection, saying firmly, "No, no, no—Ellie . . ." But with Maidy's encouragement I kept going.

I opened another drawer and pulled out the glass cat Sheila had given me. It was wrapped in tissue paper. "Here, Nuala,"

I said, passing it across to the astonished redhead, "you take this."

She unwrapped it and gasped. "Oh no, no, no, Ellie," she said, "there is no way I could take this off you. There is no way on God's earth I could . . ."

I looked at Nuala holding the mended glass cat—the incongruous frivolity of it against the plain fabric of her navy woolen skirt, the delicate poise of its marbled arched neck in her worn, working hands—and I realized that this was what all of us women were craving: a bit of beauty. Something pretty for us to look at, and touch, and wonder at, to break through the monotony of our hardship. I had come back from America with a trunkload of beautiful things and that was all that separated me from my neighbors. I wanted to give each of them a piece of the beauty I had hidden away in this trunk.

I stuck my hand in and pulled out Isobel's black silk gown with the embroidered peonies. It was the first beautiful thing I had seen when I arrived in America, the garment that for me had most epitomized the glamour and wealth of New York. I handed it across to a plain, round-faced girl who had pushed herself to the front of the circle, and she yelped with delight as she grabbed it.

"Dervla!" a woman who was probably her mother said. "Give that back!"

Dervla's eyes widened as she closed her eyes and held the soft fabric to her cheek. I realized that was the moment of beauty. The fleeting joy of acquisition—and then it was gone. I was glad to be giving these things away with the same ease that they had been given to me.

"No," I said, "you keep that, Dervla. All of you—please, I brought these things home from America to give as gifts. And you've all come here today, and brought your men with you to help us. Well, I really appreciate that, and you're all going home with something and that's that."

Nuala and Carmel put up a good fight for the rest of that day, objecting and calling me crazy and saying they were having none of it, and asking Maidy what kind of a daughter-in-law I was at all to be giving away my precious things like that, and claiming I was surely mad. Maidy shook her head and said I was a stubborn strap, and always had been, and objecting to the gifts was a pointless exercise and that, in her experience, they were as well off to take them.

"That child sent home every penny she earned from America to pay for John's operation," I heard her quietly say to Brid in a corner. And the old woman shook her head in amazement and admiration.

The following morning there were double the number of men marching across our field and behind them every woman in the townland. "Oh God," I thought, running to put the kettle on, "they'll all be looking for gifts from the trunk." But that turned out to be far from the case.

Unlike the day before, the wives had taken care that each of their men had brought their own breakfast of tea and bread with them, so they were dispatched without ritual to get on with their work, allowing the women to get on with the business of chat. I had the kettle boiled by the time they arrived and there was a tin plate piled with potato cakes keeping warm on the fire stoop, while others sizzled away in the pan. The women settled themselves immediately, pouring themselves tea into the cups that they had carried with them. Someone had brought honey, and we drizzled it over the warm potato cakes, overloading the fire to meet the demand for more.

As soon as we were settled and fed, Brid presented me with

a piece of her own work, a knitted tea cozy with a beautiful crocheted flower on its top. I promised I would treasure it and placed it straight over the china pot on my dresser.

"Now tell me, Ellie," she said, having gathered around her a small audience of her cronies, "this shop of yours will have windows, I take it?"

"Well, yes," I said, amused.

"Well then, you will be needing curtains," she said, and pulled a length of cotton from under her apron. As she did so, a half-dozen other women did the same until they had built a pile of patchwork fabric on the floor in front of them.

"No," I insisted, "it's too much trouble," and they were as thrilled with my objections as I had been with theirs the day before.

For that day, my house belonged entirely to the women of our townland. The weather was dry and we all gathered round in circles outside on stools and stones. When we ran out of those, men were dispatched for bales of hay to use as makeshift tables and chairs. "Ladies of leisure," the new curate joked as he called by to offer moral support, "sitting around enjoying yourselves when the men are hard at work. I declare—is this a spraoi or a mehil?"

"Don't we deserve a day off, Father," said Carmel, "to welcome back one of our own?"

I had never felt like "one of our own," but, to my surprise, I was glad to be viewed as such. I worked hard that day, lavishing each of the women with praise for their gifts of food and with thanks for their help—stepping aside to let the strident take control of my fire and graciously serving the lazy with tea where they sat. I seduced them with chocolate and coffee, melted into warm, creamy milk and sweetened with sugar, and when the men came in for their tea when their day's work was done I let them see that, while John Hogan's wife had been absent this long while, she was back now and happy to make ready with porter and cigarettes. I allowed my house to become home for everyone that day and by the end of it, I was the toast of the village.

Chapter Forty-Seven

My shop was beautiful. The counter was of a dark polished wood and John had given every shelf five coats of gloss paint— a beautiful sunny yellow, which we had bought in from Dublin and had had delivered with my first Findlater's order. Behind the counter I placed chunky glass jars filled with sweets the color of jewels; the tinned fruit and vegetables were stacked in pyramids; the chocolate bars, coffee and spices for baking were arranged in decorative piles. I had also bought in some satin ribbon, colored buttons and a small selection of silks that I kept in glass drawers underneath the counter, so that they were visible, but not immediately available to grubby hands.

I believed there would not be as much call for the expensive items, but none of them were perishable and they gave the shop an air of something special, adding to my own sense of pride in the place. "It's important," I said to Maidy, when she pointed out to me that there was scant need for luxuries such as tinned pears and satin ribbon in our vicinity, "that my customers know we are as well stocked as any shop in town."

If they all thought I had come back from America with "airs and graces," I figured it made sense to build on that. Let me pass my airs and graces on to them so that they might feel we country folk were as good as the snooty townspeople, with our very own shop selling fancy goods and frivolous items, and with a shopkeeper more delicate and obliging than any you might find in the town of Kilmoy!

In addition, of course, I had taken great trouble to have stock that would meet all of their everyday needs. Flour, baking soda, blue—these things were available for a small price when bought in bulk, and I believed I would be able to sell them on at a good profit while still maintaining lower prices than the greedy shop-keepers in town.

On the first day of business I was so nervous that I went down to the shop at half past seven and started to fluster about the place, moving things around, polishing the countertop. I had taken in a small amount of hardware—buckets, mops, sweep-ing brushes—and I put these outside the front door to serve as an advertisement that I was open.

By eight I was very worried, having told myself that I would doubtless be alone in there all day, demented with fear that I had wasted all of my money and time on this vain venture. To settle myself I went into the small back room to make tea and, as I did so, I heard the door rattle and the counter bell let off a loud *phwriiing.*

It was Maidy, and she had persuaded my mother to come with her. "We'll not stay more than a few minutes," Maidy said. My mother held her bag to her chest and looked around ner-vously. I knew it would be strange for her, me opening a shop, given our family history. This was not what she had intended to happen when she made her throwaway comment, but before I had time to consider this, a half dozen or so of the local women came flooding through the door in a gaggle of enthusiasm and started poking around, "oohing" and "aahing" and firing ques-tions at me. "How much are those bars of chocolate—are they the same ones we had at the mehil?" "Will the handle on that bucket hold? If it doesn't, can I bring it back and buy the handle alone?" "Can I buy that ribbon by the half yard?"

More neighbors followed, and Maidy and my mother had no choice but to help me fetch and carry from the shelves and count out the money as the women filled their baskets and emptied their pockets in a constant stream of custom. Maidy took it all in her stride, but my mother was flustered and kept disappearing into the small stockroom. At one point I walked in to collect some tinned peaches and found her sitting alone, as still as a statue—as pale she had been while grieving for my father.

"Mam?" I said. "Won't you come outside?"

"Too many people," she said. "I want to go home."

"Ah, stay for another while, Mam," I said.

Then she suddenly snapped, "All this fuss—you're not the first person to open a shop around here, Eileen!"

I didn't know what to say to her, but just knelt down and put my arms round her in a half embrace. "It's all right, Mam," I said. "Everything is different now."

For the longest time she refused to come back into the shop, until at last Maidy insisted on my mother keeping Brid Donnelly company. The old woman had arrived mid-morning for a quarter of currants and had been so delighted with the place that she had taken up residence on a stool by the stove, surveying the comings and goings as if she were at a Broadway show. Maidy persuaded my mother to sit with Brid—"As a charity to me, Attracta, to stop her asking so many questions of me"—and although my mother was very stiff at first, before long she and Brid were discussing methods of embroidery and were in danger of becoming great friends.

Two or three other women were standing at the counter gabbling away, and I was just coming back from the stockroom

with more raisins when the room suddenly went quiet. A young
girl stood framed in the front door. I wiped my hands on my
apron and, as I went to greet the newcomer, an unpleasant
feeling clenched my stomach. It was Mary Kelly's daughter,
Veronica.

Mary was our nearest neighbor, shunned because she had
become pregnant out of wedlock and given birth to an illegiti-
mate daughter before anyone had realized what was going on.
Nobody had the faintest idea who the father was, and that, I
had always believed, added to people's mistrust of her. It could
have been any one of their husbands, or sons, or fathers. John
and I seldom saw her out, though John had been down and
fixed Mary's thatched roof once or twice, and I had delivered
messages to her door.

Veronica had the unkempt appearance of a troubled waif.
She had been a small child when I left; now she was a young
woman of thirteen, but I recognized her by the sadness in her
eyes and the proud set of her mouth. "Veronica," I said, "how
lovely to see you." I walked across and led her by the shoulders in among us. "Where is your mother, Veronica—is she not
coming up herself, today?"

"No," the child answered, barely audible even in the silence.
"She just wanted to say she wishes you and the Mister the
Lord's luck with the shop, and for me to buy some starch." She
held out her fist and dropped two warm pennies into my hand.

The women of the village stood and stared. I looked past
them to my mother. She was sitting, her back as straight as a
post, and her eyes were wide and full of a fire that was fear or
pride, or both. She gave me an encouraging nod that was so
small as to be imperceptible.

"You tell your mother to keep her money for now, Veronica,"
I said. Then, still looking at my own mother, I added, "In any

case, I have a proposal for her. I'll need an extra pair of hands about the place, so perhaps she will allow you to work for me?" At this, my mother gave me a slight smile. I looked at the girl again. "If that's suitable with you, Veronica?"

My new employee nodded wildly. Brid Donnelly let out a scandalized "Humpf" and was drawing breath on some sharp comment when Maidy stepped up and put one hand on the old woman's shoulder to silence her. Signaling to the child, she said, "Never mind all this talk. As long as you're here, Veronica Kelly, you can start work and get Mrs. Donnelly a cup of tea—she is half parched. The teapot is out in the stockroom, and for the love of God, Ellie, find a clean apron for the child." Then she clapped the shocked girl into action. "Come on, come on—out back, girl, and smarten yourself up, or there'll be no job here for you. Now, Ellie, have you forgotten you promised Brid and me a taste of those new Garibaldi biscuits?"

I sent Vinny Moran down to tell Mary we would be keeping her daughter in the shop to help out for the day, then had the lad walk her home when the shop was cleared out, long after darkness had come. Veronica had a full stomach and a happy heart that day, and it was, I knew, the first day for a long time that she had experienced any luck.

My own luck had been plentiful that day and, on reflection, I realized, for many days before it.

Chapter Forty-Eight

I put in my second order the very next day and it was all sold in advance of it arriving a week later. So then I put in an order twice as large, using the very last of my American dollars. This time I included yarns, knitting needles and some inexpensive but brightly colored cotton fabric and threads. All this, too, sold out within days.

As the months passed, the business flourished. It seemed I had been right in believing there was a need for a shop in the area, but in addition I had the knack of choosing well what my neighbors would and would not buy.

As for John's surplus farm produce—eggs, milk, turnips, spuds and the like—we sold very little of it, as most of our customers were farmers themselves. So I took the habit of giving some of his fresh produce away as an incentive for the customers who bought our meat. For every chicken sold, I threw in a few turnips alongside it. For a hunk of bacon, there was a half dozen eggs free. The leftover produce was only going to feed the pigs otherwise, and it worked a treat. Within a few weeks we were as busy as the butcher in Kilmoy, and John was buying in pigs for slaughter and trading chickens with the very neighbors who were buying our bacon.

Veronica had come to work for me, but as the shop became

busier I found I needed help with the house as well. So I took on her mother, Mary, to help me with my domestic chores. They were good workers, the pair of them, and the shop became a great success in no small part because of the freedom their labor gave me to concentrate on the business side of things.

John kept Vinny Moran on to help him build an additional room to the side of our house, the nursery I wanted before starting a family. With all these employees there were many mouths to feed, and I was so busy that I barely had time to think.

When the shop and nursery were built, my husband was able to return to his true passion—the land. John grew stronger and stronger as every month wore on. He was a hard worker and a talented farmer. He rose with the crow and was happiest with his feet in the clay and his hands covered in muck or wrapped round the warm udder of a cow.

When we were children, John's propensity toward the land had fascinated and impressed me, but on my return from America, it took a while to get used to the simplicity of his days. At times it irritated me to see how satisfied my husband was with the plain tasks of plowing and milking, when I knew a man with his mind was capable of so much more. How could he happily spend an entire day in the open air, only coming home to perform the basic human tasks of eating and sleeping or making love? Nonetheless, I was pleased by what he produced for our table: creamy milk, fat eggs with orange yolks as thick as butter, an abundance of floury spuds and huge heads of cabbage so solid you could play ball with them. We roasted a chicken every Sunday and there were always two pigs curing in salted barrels at our back door.

For all that I disapproved of my husband farming, I never

balked at the smell of the land from him. Often when he came in dirty from the fields I would take him, unwashed, into the bedroom to taste the earth on his bare skin.

Wednesday, as it was market day in Kilmoy, was our quietest day and many of our regular customers would be in town selling their wares, rather than in our shop buying them. By this time my customers knew me well enough that they would price what they needed in town, then come in to me and I would better the price for them. It was on the third Wednesday of every month that I took my delivery from Findlater's. I looked forward to those days like no other—the sealed boxes delivered in a shiny black wagon to my door, the excitement of unloading crisp packages of brand-new things. Even the everyday, like mop heads and carbolic soap, were elevated by the privilege of never having been used before.

Because my house was so off the beaten track, I got into the habit of providing the deliveryman, Joseph, with a meal. A generous pot of sweet tea, bread and ham and two eggs was his usual preference. If he had been driving by night, he would refuse proper food lest his satisfaction made him fall asleep on the way home, in which case I would give him strong black coffee, cigarettes and cake instead. In return, he did me the favor of collecting parcels for me, from the post office on Harcourt Street, in Dublin.

Sheila regularly sent me her cast-off clothes and other delectable trinkets, such as *Vanity Fair* magazine and chewing gum, and I'd found the post office in Kilmoy far too interested in my American packages. Once or twice I had sensed an air of informed anticipation, a whispering as I walked up the aisle in Mass. While I found it vaguely amusing that my American wardrobe was the source of such entertainment, I preferred to maintain some air of mystery and found that it was just as easy to have Sheila forward my packages to Harcourt Street, where Joseph could pick them up and bring them straight to the shop.

On this day, Joseph did not stop for long and I allowed Veronica to unpack the boxes and put the stock away as I took a rare break. I was feeling unnaturally tired and had slept poorly the night before. I had not bled for almost seven weeks, but was pushing the obvious thought to the back of my mind until more definite signs were upon me. I had been bleeding irregularly since my return to Ireland. Sometimes the blood would come every two weeks, at other times I would wait almost three months before it flooded through me in an angry outpouring, crippling me with pain for days on end. My body seemed to be acting against us starting a family and I did not want to raise anybody's hopes—not even my own.

I put a blanket at my back and sat in front of the fire, with my feet on a milking stool, and peeled back the brown paper at the top of the parcel where Sheila always slid in newspapers and magazines as extra protection for the clothes beneath.

My fingers drew out a copy of the *New York Times*, and I decided to flick through it quickly, just to delay the sweet treat of *Vanity Fair* magazine, whose social pages I devoured—my efforts sometimes rewarded with a face or a name that I fancied I recognized from one of Isobel's parties. As my eyes wandered casually down the announcements column, they fell upon something that almost ripped them from their sockets.

> *Mr. and Mrs. R.M. Irvington of Westchester County would like to announce the engagement of their son Charles Irvington to Miss Dolores Vinewood of Houston, Texas.*

I must have let out an involuntary noise, because Veronica stopped unpacking the boxes and looked across at me.

"I'm going into the house for a rest, Veronica—call me if anybody needs me." Still holding the paper, I ran out the door, dropping most of it as fluttering debris in my rush, but still gripping the page with the news of Charles's engagement. I slammed the cottage door as if there were an angry mob behind me, then went into our bedroom and sat on our bed. Slowly I unfurled the page again. *"Mr. and Mrs. R.M. Irvington of Westchester County would like to announce the engagement of their son Charles Irvington . . ."*

It was still there. And it was certainly Charles. Dolores Vinewood was the girl Isobel had joked about looking like a horse. Charles had even mentioned her to me himself once. He had pointed her out in a society magazine, saying she was some silly rich girl his parents wanted him to marry. We had laughed about it together.

The small printed announcement stripped me of my reason. Even though I was on the other side of the world—even though I had said my good-byes and was married to John, whom I loved—I still felt as if something that belonged to me had been snatched away.

Instinctively, I reached under the bed and pulled out my trunk. Most of my belongings had been unpacked and were in everyday use, but there was one drawer that remained unopened. It was my secret place and contained my most private things. Within the dusky-smelling, felt-lined drawer was my American dream. My typing and shares certificates, a box of matches from a speakeasy we used to frequent, a napkin from Tullio's, the invitation to Sheila and Alex's wedding, a corsage from a dinner dance I once attended with workmates—scraps from another life. Evidence to remind me, only me, of how I had lived. Of who I once was and of who I might have been.

I reached in for the largest item—the bottle of Chanel No. 5 that

Charles had given me. The stopper was stiff and I had to tug at it, noticing how worn and rough my hands had become. As it came free, the heady scent leaked out of the wide neck and filled the room. I was transported back to that day at the Plaza, when the woman had sprayed it on Sheila's wrist, then mine; then I thought of the party with Charles. My head became dizzy in a swirl of lost glamour, chiffon capes, dancing in beaded hems, high-heeled shoes, and parties and fun and freedom.

Freedom. As quickly as I allowed myself to be carried back into my other life, my other world—I knew it was gone. Quite suddenly it seemed as if I had capsized and, as I fell back onto my marital bed, the expensive perfume emptied itself in three or four greedy glugs all over the counterpane. I grabbed at the bottle, but only managed to rescue a smear of gold dew in the corners. Holding the ordinary clear glass, the pristine label stained and skewed to one side by my clumsy thumb, I felt as if somebody had died.

"Ellie?" John had come in from his morning's work and was calling to me from the other room. "Is there any food ready?"

I didn't gather myself up as I usually would have done. I didn't want to pretend I was content. I didn't want to pretend this life was enough for me, not anymore. John was sure to ask about the spilled perfume, and if he did I would tell him its provenance. That it was given to me, as a gift of love, by one of the wealthiest men in all America. That I had been offered every luxury, every benefit of body and spirit, but that I had turned it all down to come back and be with him. I wanted him to know the sacrifices I had made. I wanted him to understand how close he had come to losing me, and to admit he had been wrong to stay at home. I wanted him to know the truth of who I was, even though I knew it would hurt him. If he asked about the perfume, I would tell him how I had kissed Charles and would have—*should* have—stayed in America with him, and that if he, John, wanted to thank somebody for my return it was my dead father—for it was his death alone that had brought me back.

"Ellie?" John was standing at the bedroom door. "Are you all right?"

Every inch of me wanted to scream and my hands tightened around the large glass bottle, willing me to throw it across the room and smash it against the wall. I wanted to break something—something outside of myself.

"What's that in your hand, and what's that smell?"

I looked at John's face, and into his eyes, one last time before I told him. One last time before I showed him the bitterness and regret that had plagued me every day since he had left me standing alone, waiting for him on Ellis Island. His face was full of concern, the tired lines of everyday husbandry. He looked older than his years.

I opened my mouth to berate him, but I lost the words. Snatched from me by the girl who loved him, who couldn't hurt him.

"What's the matter, Ellie? You don't look like yourself at all."

I gripped the perfume bottle, willing myself to tell him the truth, but instead I said, "Who am I then—when I'm myself?"

John smiled and his face opened, suddenly shedding time and worry like sunshine flooding a gray day.

"Why, you're my Ellie," he said. "You're my only one."

Epilogue

My mother was recovering from a bad attack of flu and had been staying with us for a few weeks. It was a crisp day, and I had moved her into our bedroom and lit the fire.

A short while before I had said good-bye to Father Mac, who had come back after Sunday Mass to minister communion to my mother. Spring was early that year, and as he left the priest commented cheerily on the banks of daffodils and tulips that I had planted along the edge of our drive, and on the budding roses that were already creeping up the terrace at the side of our front door. Now John was driving the priest back to Kilmoy in our new vehicle—a covered trap, drawn by two lively horses. The shop was doing so well that there was even serious talk of buying a car, but John was anxious not to draw too much attention to our growing wealth and, in any case, the roads were still too rough to chance it.

I was sitting by the small bureau at the end of the double bed, which almost filled the small room. The laburnum directly outside the window was blooming and golden. Blue tits flitted pointlessly from branch to branch, shuddering the delicate yellow petals off their stalks so that they rained down onto the rich, damp grass. A robin came and sat on a twig regarding me directly, his fat breast swelled and red. I touched my stomach and allowed myself to hope that this time the pregnancy would last. It had been ten weeks since I had last bled, the longest time so far. Although we wanted a child to complete our marriage, we were both still young and full of love and hope for the future.

On the desk was the silver pen I had bought on my last trip to Dublin, and some expensive marbled writing paper held down by a crystal paperweight gifted to me by Findlater's for my loyal custom over the past two years.

By my mother's elbow, on the bedside cabinet, was a china cup and saucer full of tea, and a small matching plate with two of the imported English biscuits she was so fond of, and a folded napkin to catch the crumbs.

I was reading a copy of *Sketch* magazine, giving some consideration to purchasing a new hat on my next trip up to the city. John had promised we would book into the Shelbourne Hotel for a few days once my mother was better, and had agreed that we might repeat the delights of our last holiday, with an afternoon tea dance in the Gresham Hotel followed by a trip to the cinema. John was a terrible dancer, but it had come to the point that it didn't matter as long as he indulged my desire to get dressed up and go walking and dancing in the capital city at least twice a year. So, as often as I could persuade him, John would walk me down Grafton Street in a serge suit and trilby hat, carrying an ivory-topped cane, and parade me in my carefully chosen finery; we would both pretend to be the rich lady and gentleman that my land-loving husband feared we were becoming. For all that, he basked in my happiness because he knew that, as long I invited him to walk with me, he could not lose me entirely to my foolish affectations.

"I love that smell," my mother said.

"What smell?"

"Of scent," she said, closing her eyes and pushing her head back to drink it in. "It's coming off the bed."

I sniffed the air, but couldn't get it. "There is no smell, Mam."

"There *is*," she said firmly. "Perfume. I can smell it quite clearly. It's always been here, but with the fire lit, it's stronger. You must have dropped perfume on the bed—then forgotten about it."

I had forgotten. At once I closed my own eyes and tilted my head back, but the scent of Chanel was gone from me. In that moment, as much as I had regretted dropping the perfume on the bed, I regretted even more that the smell of it had become so commonplace to me that I no longer noticed it was there.

My mother shook her head in wonder and said, "It's so beautiful."

In the weeks after the spillage, I had lain awake in bed every night with my head full of memories—my senses tainted with the perfume of my dreams, my head filled with mansions and glamour and all that might have been. Over time the scent had faded into the background, and my shallow disappointment and bitterness had ground itself out of my mind and freed me to create a new life as a country shopkeeper and farmer's wife— my new life, which belonged to me.

I realized then that America had given me so much more than a trunk full of beautiful things. It had introduced me to a life that was deeper than the fashions and gadgets I was so in thrall to. It had given me hope for a better future and, despite all that I believed differently at the time, I had carried that hope back home with me and used it to build a business and a marriage and new friendships.

My time in New York had given me a new confidence and taught me how to create opportunities for myself, instead of allowing circumstance to shape my life. It had encouraged a fresh demeanor and shaped my ideas, and showed me a way of living that was better and brighter and easier than the one I knew. Yet, ultimately, in its acceptance of me and in what it had offered me, America had challenged me to see who I truly was. I had needed the bobbed hair and the trinkets and the fancy manners so that I could see beyond them. I had needed to experience progress so that I could step back into who I was and appreciate the love that I had found with John and understand that was where my wealth truly lay.

I had come to accept that Ireland was where John belonged, and that I belonged with him in a way that I might never have known had I not been away from him for those three years.

Deep in my heart I still held my dream to return to New York and have a life there with John, but, more important, I came to see beauty in the life we already had.

America had planted the seed of freedom in my heart, but it was the rich soil of home that had enabled it to grow.

Acknowledgments

Many thanks to the following for editing, research, advice, practical help and support and encouragement: Johnny Ferguson, Marita Conlon McKenna, Eileen Grogan, Frances McCann, Helena Moran, Dr. Joe Gilvary, Alison Walsh, Imogen Taylor, Marianne Gunn O'Connor, Theresa Gilroy, Vicki Satlow, Steve Dunford, the Murray family, New York, Sheila and Bobby Smyth, Holy Hill Hermitage, Sligo, Gillian Marsh and Eammon Connor, and my husband, Niall Kerrigan.

A special thanks to my mother Moira and to the brilliant Helen Falconer, whose advice and support were invaluable.

READING GROUP GUIDE

1. Ellie and John find a connection from the moment they meet and become childhood sweethearts. Do you think it is possible to sustain that relationship into adulthood? Are they truly soul mates?

2. What is Ellie's relationship like with her parents? Is it understandable why she prefers spending time with John's parents, Maidy and Paud? What do they provide that Ellie's own parents can't?

3. How is early married life difficult for Ellie and John? When Ellie decides to go to America, John says that she's running away. Do you think there is some truth to this statement? Why or why not?

4. Isobel Adams treats Ellie not only as a maid, but sometimes as a confidante. Do you think this kind of behavior is appropriate? Is Isobel a good mistress and employer?

5. Seeing how happy her friend Sheila is with her fiancé, Ellie makes the observation that anything is possible in America.

How is this true compared to what life was like in Ireland? Do you think this is true today?

6. Why does Ellie find Charles Irvington attractive? What can he offer her? If you were Ellie, who would you have chosen to be with, Charles or John, and why?

7. Why doesn't John want to move to America? Are you sympathetic with his views, or do you think he should have seriously considered Ellie's plan for him to join her in New York?

8. Do you think Ellie made the right decision in going back to Ireland? Why or why not? What would her life have been like if she had stayed in America?

9. What difficulties does Ellie encounter when she returns home? How does she use what she's learned in America to improve her situation there?

10. Ellie's story, which takes place in the 1920s, is a classic immigrant story. What are the similarities and differences with the immigrant stories of today? How about the immigrant stories in your own family?